The Alanyo Heir

Mind Games: Volume One

by

Lee F. Patrick

Javari Press
Calgary, Alberta
2018

The Alanyo Heir
Mind Games

Javari Press,
Calgary, Alberta, Canada.
http://www.javaripress.ca/

ISBN: 978-1-895487-19-0 (pbk)
ISBN: 978-1-895487-20-6 (ebook)

First trade paperback edition, October 2018.

Tags:
Crime thriller, Science Fiction, Mind control, Conspiracy

Set in Gentium Book Basic
Printed in the United States of America

Author's Commentary and Thanks

Thank you. Yes, you. I hope you enjoy reading this book as much as I enjoyed writing it. Please consider letting others know what you think of it by leaving an online review, or raving to your friends how good it is. And books always make good birthday or holiday presents.

Many thanks to my Beta Readers (Amurlee Stobbs and Mike Thompson) Helpful suggestions and 'is this what you meant to say?' always makes the ms much more readable. And to my Gary, who makes the computer things happen easier. Also to Javari Press, for another book for my shelf!

What would happen if...

This is the start of many, if not of every story, this one included. One of the reasons I enjoy reading (and writing) science fiction and fantasy is the ability to explore new and different cultures and the myriad ways a world might work (or doesn't).

Jaren's world started with the idea of mind control for those in the prison system so they become useful workers and never have the capacity to re-offend. The story expanded and mutated from there. What if someone wanted to lose bad habits such as addictive drug use, or even phobias, or nervous tics? Go to a therapist and have them erased.

As with all ideas, the possibilities exploded and it took a little while to focus on what might work well for this story and which characters would tell it. Some other ideas and characters are waiting for a chance to tell their own tales on this world. Soon. I hope. There's a big backlog on my hard drive.

In an early critique, it was suggested that I play up the Romeo and Juliet angle of this story and make their respective clans much more powerful than they are currently. While an interesting idea, that wasn't the book I wanted to write. Both clans are, at this point, mid-sized and have worries about larger ones taking advantage of any mistake. The four function calculator and its development is going to unite them and jump start more powerful computers. Many people do not remember a time before calculators and cell phones, but this is where this world's development has reached. Eventually, they will reach the stars and begin to colonize other worlds. But right now, they are at the start of that long journey.

Any device or idea has a light side and a dark side to its use. While the light side of mind alteration can be beneficial for many people, the dark side can destroy lives and trap the people affected into an eternity of endless suffering before their deaths.

The underlying cultural idea is that clan-led mega-corporations in this world decided that war and conflict were eroding their profits and disrupting their supply chains. And killing thousands, if not millions, of consumers. They essentially bought out the governments of competing nations to ensure that peace. The populace might think they are in charge thanks to elections, but in reality, the clans are.

That idea melded with the mind control scenario above. The corporations like keeping consumers alive and with enough money to keep buying the products made by them. Innovation has been slower than would happen if the press of conflict forced armies to constantly seek new ways to kill people and destroy infrastructure.

There are always occasional leaps in technology, which can shift a smaller corporation into a higher level if they are able to position themselves to properly exploit it. We have many examples of these developments, both good and bad, on our world. Remember trolls and pet rocks? Microsoft and Amazon?

This economic model can create a world with a steep divide between the haves and the have-nots as this one is. There is a middle class here, which at this time is growing, as people have more money to spend and there are more opportunities to advance personally and professionally.

The poorest groups provide base level workers for the many farms and factories. Many people work at the same job, for the same corporation, for their entire working life, but can have a satisfying life and advance if they have the drive to do so. Crime rates tend to be relatively low in this world, since serious crimes result in offenders being mindwiped and reprogrammed into drones for the most tedious and dangerous jobs available.

On the other hand, the corporations also have a vested interest in keeping their workers happy and content. Don't rock the boat and you'll do fine is the message the workers get year in and year out. Troublemakers end up mind-wiped and working at drudge jobs. Forever. Or feeding the roses. Literally.

Life can be very much stranger than fiction can ever dream of. I 'invented' a method of memory manipulation for this series. Well. A beta reader (Mike Thompson) happened to see an episode of Nova called Memory Hackers. It describes how to interfere with the storage of actual memories and how to implant false ones. All relatively simple and easy. The drugs involved are available and, well. This resulted in revision to several sections.

The method used in the book is far beyond what can be done today, but the genie is out of the bottle and scientists are making great strides to better understand how memory works and how to manipulate it.

Lee F. Patrick
Calgary, Alberta
October 2018

Works by Lee F. Patrick

Stand-Alone Books:

Alter Egos

Anthologies and Collections:

Return
The Okal Rel Anthology 2 (Fandom Press, 2007)

The Fire Mage
Enigma Front: Burnt (Analemma Press, 2016)

Shadows in the Mist
Polar Borealis #4, 2107 (Prix Aurora Award Finalist)

Exports to the Stars
In Places Between, 2017

Dark Reflections
Wild, Wicked and Sparkling (Starlight Press, 2017)

It was a Dark and Stormy Night
Polar Borealis #5, 2017

The Beginning and the End

From the Journal of Jaren Alanyo

I know that today, probably this evening, I'm going to die. Don't worry, I've had some time to get used to the idea and I can't think of any other way for everything to come out the way it should. I know that you'll blame yourself when you read this journal, but there was no other option that could give you back the life you deserve. There never was. We're so sorry we couldn't do better.

Chapter 1

We still have plenty of time," Jaren Alanyo said to his bodyguard without looking at him. Feneir Caldon responded with a sigh and rolled eyes. Again. "We *do*. It's only an hour or so back to the estate. I won't be late for dinner with Father."

Serit Jaren Alanyo, only child and heir to the Alanyo clan holdings looked up from the girl beside him. Twenty-one, tall with light brown hair. Good looking but still growing into himself. Not usually an idiot. But he had help in this madness and the two would-be lovers had dragged all six of their bodyguards into conspiracy with them.

"And neither will I," said the young seris beside him. Sanil Kendef, the youngest child of ser Paknol Kendef, head of the Kendef clan. Their fathers were mortal enemies.

She was slightly shorter than Jaren, with slightly darker hair and blue eyes. Thankfully she did not have the anger management issues that her father did. She had, however, inherited his stubbornness in full measure. He felt bad for her bodyguard Casteron at times. She turned to the other man who had been ignoring the beautiful mountain scenery with him and smiled at him. Casteron sighed. Loudly.

Feneir checked the drivers, in position near the cars. They weren't watching the young couple either. Any determined assault was unlikely here, but his job was to keep the serit safe and out of trouble. This place was neither. It was however, popular with them for various reasons. Not being observed by their fathers was the main one. Finding love anywhere was generally regarded as a blessing. However, this match was not one that anyone who knew the pair would find amusing. A train wreck to be horrified about, definitely. The guards all knew the besotted pair were the ones in control. Not them.

"Can we come back this weekend?" Sanil asked her bodyguard. She must be smiling at him, Feneir guessed. Feminine wiles. Jaren occasionally tried for sad puppy eyes. It seldom worked. Except in regard to his love for Sanil. Still, he and Casteron had managed to keep the few truly insane suggestions from being implemented. So far.

"No, seris," Casteron said with his jaw clenched. "We are *not* coming here this weekend or any other. There are herds of people all over the mountains every weekend during the summer. We discussed this, seris. Several times, as I recall. Some members of the populace might recognise one or the other of you. One of them might decide to contact a society reporter. With pictures. Or to blackmail one or both of you."

"Or one might hold a grudge against either of your families and pull out a gun. We will, of course, shoot him or her, but then we'd have to deal with the police. And your secret would be revealed." Feneir checked the pistol riding in his shoulder holster by reflex.

"That is why we are here today. During the week. And leaving *very soon* now. The hordes of tourists are currently hard at work. There are two more months of summer. You will be studying in the fall, seris. Not spending your time together in the library staring at each other. And it is time to go." Casteron checked his pistol as well. A minute shrug.

"That is going to be a problem," Jaren said to Sanil. He shifted on the blanket but made no effort to move further. "I'll have to come up with some excuses to go back there for a visit or three. Or you can come home for all the weekends you can."

"That would make my parents suspicious," Sanil opined. "And we don't want them or your father to know we've been seeing each other."

"And are serious about our future," Jaren said. They stared at each other again, ignoring their surroundings. Two brains, completely shut down as they focused on each other. Both were very smart people, except in regard to each other. On the other hand, it was now a known condition for the guards so they knew how to adjust for it. Mostly.

Feneir sighed, then rotated in a slow circle, looking and listening for anything out of the ordinary. Twice. He noted that the sun was considerably lower than the last time he'd looked at it. He checked his watch. The timing was getting tighter. Any delays and...

"It *is* past the time to be heading back, serit and seris," Casteron said. The two men exchanged glances. Picking their charges up and stuffing them into the cars was possible, but would slow down the process of packing up the picnic supplies. Of course, those could be abandoned with fewer problems than either of them arriving home late.

"If we don't leave soon you could be questioned by your fathers," Feneir echoed. "Jaren, you might recall that your father said he would be home early this evening to discuss something with you. Do you want *him* to ask what you've been up to this afternoon to make you late? He could change out me and my team in an instant. Then what would you do for these meetings?"

"I told him at breakfast that I was meeting a friend from university this afternoon. That should cover our timing issues if he gets home first. He usually doesn't really care what I do unless it makes a mess." Jaren grimaced slightly but Sanil took his hand. A smile returned.

"I told my mom the same thing," chimed in seris Sanil. "Neither of us are going to be in trouble if we're late for supper."

Feneir glanced at Casteron, who shrugged. Their charges might not get into trouble over these meetings, but if their fathers discovered and objected to the romance, as they were all too likely to do, all of their guards would be. Getting fired was the minimal response they could hope for. There were other possibilities that were very deadly.

"But they're right," Jaren said with a sigh that everyone could hear. Feneir signalled one of the drivers to move in to start packing the picnic gear. "It's not like we won't see each other forever. There's Dayil's birthday party next week. It's not going to be a big crowd, he said."

"But we won't really be able to talk," Sanil objected. "You know we'll only be able to chat a bit, maybe one or two dances. We *don't* want our names linked on the clan gossip pages. Not yet, anyway."

"Once you reach twenty-two we'll be able to do more," Jaren said.

"It feels like that will be forever, not just two more years." Sanil stood and brushed her skirt down. "I wish our dads actually liked each other. We'd be able to tell them now and not have to wait or skulk around."

"I thought you liked the skulking?" Jaren said as he stood and took her hands. "Although it *is* hard to skulk with each of us being followed by at least a pair of bodyguards armed to the teeth."

"And it'll be harder to get together now that you're home instead of still with me at the university. I'm not sure we'll be able to meet much. We'll just have to be creative." That simple comment sent a chill down all the bodyguards' spines.

The seris' driver reached the young couple and started putting away the picnic gear. Feneir didn't let his smile reach his lips as the two moved off the blanket and headed slowly toward the cars, hand in hand. At least they *were* moving now.

They did take the time it took for the seris's driver to pack up the picnic supplies to have a last kiss before they got into the cars. Seris Sanil's car left first, the back windows opaqued and the Ident plate flipped to a different sequence than the one it normally used. This one would swap to the usual one after it reached the main highway halfway to the city.

Neither of them were really aware of how much effort their guards put into making their secret meetings secret. The false Ident plates were just the beginning. A second set of Alanyo and Kendef cars were parked in the middle of the city of Hantil near a popular meeting place for the scions of the clans. It had its proper Ident plate showing and the drivers could tell the relevant clan security, only if they asked of course, via the radio that Jaren and Sanil were there, not here in the mountains nearly fifty klicks away. In an emergency, Feneir could activate their own radio in a second if he was next to it. More commonly, their next radio message would merely inform the other driver on their schedule so that it would reach them in time to rendezvous and arrive together at the compound. Arriving separately would be Noticed. In a very bad way.

"Any idea what Father has in mind for his surprise?" Jaren asked as he got into the car, also now equipped with a false Ident plate. They would wait a few more minutes for the other car to reach to the forestry trunk road so it would be unlikely that they'd be associated with each other. At least all of these roads were paved, so they didn't have to worry about the car picking up dirt or debris that the mechanics would notice.

"Chief Steffent didn't give me any particulars when he called." Feneir said as he settled into the front passenger door after sealing the rear door Jaren used. "Just that when he arrived at the office your father mentioned he wanted to chat with you tonight. He wanted to warn me so you wouldn't be late."

"Wow. A real surprise." Jaren looked out the window at the scenery. No enthusiasm echoed in his voice. "Great."

Feneir didn't bother to make conversation as their car sped along the highway toward the Alanyo compound on the west side of the city. He'd become Jaren's primary bodyguard six years ago when Jaren was fifteen. It still bothered him that there wasn't more overt affection between father and son. A boy needed affection from his parents, not just from his bodyguards. But Darit Alanyo was seventy-three, an old man who had buried most of his relatives decades before and his second wife when Jaren was ten. He'd almost lost Jaren then as well.

No one was sure why that car had crashed. Mechanical failure was posited but the wreckage left little evidence intact. Three guards had died at the scene along with Jaren's mother. Jaren had been thrown from the car by a defective door that had opened moments before the car compacted into the cliff. That was the only reason that he was still alive. Five weeks in a discrete hospital followed by another five months in physical therapy before he'd been allowed to return home had been hard on the boy. His father seldom went to see him and those visits weren't long ones. Busy running the clan holdings, no doubt.

Feneir had heard stories of the old man's withdrawal from his son, probably blaming the boy for surviving when his mother hadn't. None of those stories made it out of the compound. Loyalty to the clan that employed and cared for them was paramount in the guards, and truth to tell, everyone else who worked for them. Those who thought disloyalty might pay better soon found out that it wasn't an option. They became fertilizer for the garden or were conditioned and sent to the mines or various factories that the clan owned. It depended on how upset the ser was at the moment. Either way, they had no chance to repeat their error in judgement.

***

Jaren watched the countryside change to suburbs as they skirted the city, then back to farms and finally the Alanyo clan compound, nestled in a wide valley. The other car met up with them as they passed a large shopping area. The guards at the gates checked the cars in, then they cruised sedately down the main drive but pulled in at the side entrance Jaren preferred rather than the ornate frontage his father always used.

"Thanks, Feneir, Pagil. See you later." Three *twenty-five notes lay on his seat, as if forgotten. That was one thing he had learned early in life – you take care of your people. He couldn't do much while he was still underage but at least his allowance was good enough to provide some monetary rewards for their hard work at arranging his dates with Sanil without going through official channels or his bank account.

"Serit Jaren," said the butler with a slight bow as he approached the door. "Your esteemed father will be home in twenty minutes according to his driver. Dinner will be in the smaller dining room in one hour."

"Thanks, Marin," Jaren replied. "Formal or family?"

"Certainly more formal than your current attire," the butler replied with a slight smile at his very casual open shirt and jacket. "However, no other guests are expected at this time. I will send someone to inform you if there is a change in your esteemed father's plans."

Jaren smiled as Marin expected, then checked his watch. Time enough for a quick shower, though he hadn't gotten sweated up. Not much, anyway. He did need to peel off the tight exercise shorts that hid his very serious interest in doing intimate things with Sanil that went far beyond the few kisses they exchanged up on the mountain. Then he would find out what impossible task his father had for him now.

He beat his father into the dining room by a few minutes and waited next to his chair until the old man entered and sat down. His father was still in his office formals so Jaren was glad he'd changed.

"You'll be coming in to the office tomorrow and for the foreseeable future," Father said without preamble as Marin and the footmen withdrew after serving the meal and pouring wine for his father. Jaren nodded, sipping from his juice. At least he wasn't still getting milk. University had been the thankful cause of that changeover. Maybe once he was of age, he'd get a wine glass. He didn't think it would happen, but he could always hope.

"Of course, Father," he replied. "The purpose?"

"It is time for you to start getting some practical experience to go along with your business degree. You need to also start meeting with the various subsidiary officers. Preparing yourself for more responsibilities."

"My professors did say that the practical was more important than the theory they taught. That life is much more complex than the limited examples we had to illustrate specific points of concern."

"Hmph. They're more than right. Which company of ours did you do that project on for your last semester? Bayside Chemicals, wasn't it?"

"Yes, Father." *He'd remembered!* Jaren had thought his father hadn't been aware of that paper. He'd asked ser Ofelan, the clan's head analyst, if he could use that company for his course. A box of files had been the response, along with a travel itinerary and plane tickets for himself and Feneir for a site visit.

"Bring a copy of the report with you, if you still have one. It was a decent start on the analysis but ser Ofelan will be going over it with you to show you how to expand it into a document that will actually be of use to anyone in terms of acquisition."

"I did get an honours mention on that project," Jaren said. "My professor was very happy with the result." He'd spent two weeks visiting the company, going over its financials, seeing the physical plants and systems. The next two weeks had been spent surrounded by charts and graphs, trying to incorporate everything he'd learned into that report. Sanil had been glad when it was finally done. So was he.

"For a school project, it was adequate," his father replied. "To invest millions in a company, there were missing elements that would be crucial to the decision making process."

Jaren cut into the tender steak on his plate and ate slowly. The same old thing. Nothing he ever did was really good enough for his father.

Chapter 2

Adnil Calyno and his son Gred were in their mansion on the outskirts of Hantil, finishing their dinner after another long day working for their cousin Darit. Adnil was the son of Darit's older sister Calitha and Gred was his only child but Darit regarded them as minions who would do anything he said and be happy to have the honour to serve him. Neither man liked that attitude of their cousin's. At least he had the grace to pay them fairly well and with adequate stock bonuses.

Some clans followed the path of the eldest child inheritance of the chairman's position. Others didn't. Alanyo held to the eldest *son* and had for seven generations. Only if there was no direct male descendant would the clan leadership pass through the female line. To them. Finally. They had been waiting for years, but everything they'd tried so far had gone wrong. Sometimes horribly so.

"Jaren will be coming into the office from now on," Gred said as he lifted his wine glass slightly. "Heard from office gossip. Idiot expected me to be thrilled, so that's what I gave him. All hail the heir." He didn't sip any of the red wine, but forcefully set the glass back onto the table, almost spilling the contents on the snowy white tablecloth.

"Of course," his father replied with a grimace. "What else can we expect given the situation? Jaren finished university this spring, is twenty-one now and will be of age next year. Darit *has* to bring him in and start training him to take over to keep all the subsidiaries happy. They're already nervous about Darit's health and the possibility of being led by a boy with no experience. We're not big enough to survive many missteps, you know. The real players have been eyeing some of our subsidiaries for years. We need strong and reasoned leadership to survive, not a boy's fancies that he has any idea how to run anything larger than a roadside fruit stand. If that."

"Haven't the presidents been suggesting that you'd make a great interim clan head? Who else is there, really?" This time he did sip at his wine after saluting his father.

"Several of them made comments to that effect at the last general meetings," Adnil admitted. "I have a good base of support, both overt and covert. Those comments are what led to Darit bringing the boy in. He's not really against having me as interim chairman if needed but wants the boy to show his strengths. I think if he makes it another five or six years, he'll retire and let Jaren take over, but be available as a resource. Realistically, I'm the only option he has for an interim head if he wants to keep the subsidiaries satisfied. If he tried to bring in anyone else there would be a lot of questions asked about his choice."

"As we expected." Gred snarled. Both men were silent for several minutes, eating the delicious meal but paying no attention to the movements of the servants out in the main part of the mansion or the guards making their rounds of the gardens.

"Any word on our investment?" Gred asked as he pushed his empty plate away. "You said there was a message at lunch?" His father smiled broadly. They couldn't talk about some things in the office dining rooms. Too many people who couldn't know anything of their other plans to regain the wealth and prestige that should be theirs. Even if they were kept out of the chairman's office for much longer.

"The prototype calculator works. The four main functions are solid with two digits per input and they're hopeful on three or even four on the next model. They've also managed to miniaturize the components even further than they'd hoped in the beginning. Soon we'll have hand-held computing power that rivals those behemoths we've been using for so long. It seems like such a simple device but it will change everything."

"Twenty percent of that will make us wealthier than the rest of the clan," Gred said with a smile. "The clan holdings will be pocket money at that point. So we won't care about changing Alanyo Holdings to Calyno."

"I'd still like to be in our proper places, no matter how well the calculator does. Darit needs to die before the boy is ready to take over so we'll have a better chance to arrange an accident for Jaren before he can ruin everything." Adnil scowled. "I thought that the flu last year would have eliminated the old man. Can't any biological keep its potency for more than an hour? That sample killed how many workers?"

"Four in the immediate family, with another five or so secondary contacts. I'm glad we found out about it in time to get the sample. Putting it onto his handkerchiefs was the best vector possible at the time. He *was* very ill. To bad Jaren was at university and was told to stay there. We could have tried for both of them."

"Random mutation, the medics said." Both were silent as they sipped at their wine.

"I've been thinking about a new idea, Dad," Gred said after a few minutes, now toying with his wine glass. "What if we don't care when Darit dies? And have the permanent succession guaranteed to you?"

"What are you talking about? If the boy is alive and breathing when the old man dies, he'll inherit with no questions asked. I'll get the interim position if it happens in the next couple of years, but once he's over twenty-seven or so and hasn't screwed up visibly, all the power will go straight to him. If he dies too soon after the old man, even in a real accident, red flags go up all over and the big players will start looking for any irregularity. Much too risky."

"What if he really *isn't* Jaren?"

"I don't follow, Gred. Of course that's who he is. We've known him all his life." His father lifted his wine glass but didn't drink this time. Just tilted it from side to side, watching the ruby liquid swirl around.

"What if the real Jaren died during that accident when he was ten? And the old man replaced him?"

"With whom?" His father set his wine glass onto the table and stared at him, starting to anticipate his next words.

"An indentured orphan taught or conditioned to *be* Jaren. There were new tutors, new guards, and several months when no one except Darit saw him at all after the accident. You know how fuzzy he was when you were finally allowed to visit. And they rushed you out after a half hour."

"The doctors said it was due to the pain medications and the rehab he had to go through because of the broken bones. And boys change a lot at that age." Adnil paused. "He also grew at least three inches during that time, I recall. It's true that the only people who saw him on a regular basis were the medical staff at the hospital, then the rehab centre and the old man. The only other people who could know the truth were his guards. The ones really close to him were dead and the others could have been well paid to pretend, then were promoted to cushy job within the clan holdings. Any other physical records could have been altered within that time span to correspond with the new Jaren. It would be very easy to do with that much time available. Blood type is pretty easy to match up, if you've got a few months to look for the right boy. A quiet funeral, probably a cremation, and no one would be the wiser."

"And what if that poor badly conditioned boy collapses when the old man dies because he can't continue with the lies he's been forced to live with for the past however many years? The board would hand everything to you, Dad. We'd finally be where our family should have been all along."

"It sounds like an interesting idea, son. How could we arrange it? Conditioning takes time and I doubt this is going to be a simple job like a non-disclosure arrangement. And if we wait until the old man dies, we couldn't arrange for Jaren to spend that much time out of sight or someone would notice. Again, not good for us."

"I've actually gotten a man in as a backup guard for Jaren's detail to pass information to us. Nothing important so far, but he hasn't spent much time with Jaren yet. The regulars take most of the shifts when he leaves the compound, no matter what time of day it is or what else they've been doing with him during their other shifts. We may have to wait for a good opportunity, but I was chatting with an acquaintance about his recovery from drug addiction at a party last week. He's one of the Trebethan younger cousins. It's a fairly minor conditioning: takes a couple of days and the therapist he went to is quite popular. His parents and Trebethan himself insisted he do it or he'd be disinherited. No allowance, no job in the clan's holdings, and warnings so no one from any other clan would hire him. He decided that money and power was better than the buzz he got from the drug."

Adnil snorted in amusement. "I hadn't heard of that use. Mostly we've just done security conditioning or hired mind-wiped criminals for our nastier jobs."

"It's gaining popularity in some circles as people realise that they'll never advance with the habit. You never start up again with that or any other drug. You physically can't. You get sick and pass out if you keep trying to take something on the list. That got me thinking about a possible scenario." His father sipped his wine, now with a slight smile on his face. Gred echoed it.

"I managed to do a very discrete check on Jaren's finances thanks to a clerk down in accounting who likes the occasional finer things in life. Jaren's spending near the limit on his allowance and I can't understand how he's doing it. My man is keeping an eye on Jaren but hasn't seen anything odd. Jaren doesn't have a lot of things that we know of so he's not buying clothes or toys that we've seen or heard of. He doesn't visibly spend. He's using cash for something, not simply paying for things through his account as most of us do. There isn't much that he'd want to hide from the old man. Drugs are a strong possibility with the amount of cash that's not accounted for. It also goes back three years that the clerk was able to document. So this isn't something new since he graduated. Only the three usual guards were with him there. I know drugs are a problem from my days there. And they're fairly easy to buy. Not cheap, but the amount missing is reasonable for occasional use."

"And this helps us how?"

"There's a fellow we may want to consult. Rader Kessem suggested him. I mentioned the subject when I dropped off our last payment on the loan. Events can be taken out of someone's mind, he said, but they can also be put in place. With no one the wiser. I hadn't realised that was possible, but really, it's a variation of the personalities downloaded into the menial workers. I didn't really start to consider the idea as a viable one until I talked to Vanis."

"Perhaps we should open negotiations on that matter." They smiled and the wine glasses clinked. "Get his contact information after dinner."

Falg Hantel met Gred at a small office in a small town just outside Hantil two weeks later. The man was shorter than average and totally bald. His clothing was suited to a man of the lower classes, but one who had aspirations to move upward.

"Please sit, ser Calyno. Glad to meet you. How is your little problem?"

"He's not that little," Gred snapped. "Sorry, but this isn't trivial. We do wish to avail ourselves of your expertise if we can come to an agreement. And if you can do what we want."

"What do you want the young serit to believe about himself? Curing a drug problem, I understand? Kessem spoke of your conversation when he told me you wanted to meet. That would be relatively simple but I fail to see how it would advance your ultimate goals."

"That's actually the least part of it. He doesn't currently have a drug problem that we can discover. The whole plan is quite complex. We need a separate personality installed who thinks he's an orphan bought by our cousin Darit to replace his dead heir. A short time after the old man dies, that boy has a breakdown, admits the deception, then my father and I take control of the clan holdings and pension him off it a fit of looking good for the subsidiaries. Later he can commit suicide or have a completely accidental accident." Hantel sipped his coffee and motioned Gred to continue.

"The drug problem becomes the interim reason he voluntarily asked for conditioning in the first place. So we have an excellent reason for the original to believe that *he* asked for conditioning. That nothing was done to him without his consent. He won't be suspicious and neither will anyone else. And he should become somewhat dependent on me because I helped arrange it and didn't tell his father what happened and how. That way I can continue to monitor him."

"A good cover for my other work. And for myself?" Hantel asked.

"Will be very well compensated for your work and under our protection, now and in the future. I understand that you do work for Kessem and they will also be working with us more closely once my father and I have control of the holdings. There are several advantages for us to work with you both that do not need to be discussed at this time and place."

"How long will it be until you need the impostor activated?"

"That's the tricky bit," Gred said. "Not until the old man dies. And he's survived some illnesses that we were sure would kill him. He's seventy-three but still in fairly good shape. We don't want to chance anything that looks like we had anything to do with his death. The police and company security would be very suspicious and we don't want that."

"Biologicals can be unreliable. My work is guaranteed." Hantel glanced at a mandala on the wall, obviously thinking. His right forefinger tapped a complex pattern on the tabletop. "It is possible to construct such an alternate personality. I have some procedures that can be used. The implementation has given good results so far. This is an expensive procedure as several weeks are needed for preparation of the tapes and at least two to three weeks for implementation and testing phase."

"How does your process work? Compared to normal conditioning? We have a number of factories who use conditioned felons or the indentured. My cousin insists on free workers for many tasks but there are simply too many good economic and security advantages to using the indentured or the fully conditioned for routine and menial tasks."

"Conditioning is more of an art than the prisons and public know. Most felons, of course, are simple wipes of the basic personality and replacing it with a semi-aware idiot who can do basic tasks with training, as well as feed and take care of itself. They are thus useful to society rather than sitting at ease in the prison system or let loose to re-offend. The more advanced drones are still wiped of the original personality but the process copies a more detailed constructed personality into their brains." A slight snort of laughter.

"It can be quite amusing to see a crowd of them at a factory, all with the same mannerisms. Once the conditioning is installed, you realise, the personalities change and develop based on the experiences that a particular one has. No one can guarantee what a long term conditioned will become without updating their programmed responses on a regular basis." Gred nodded. "Those in prison or other workforces are monitored regularly and any major deviance results in a reset, and sending that worker to another facility."

"The merely indentured have a loyalty conditioning added that keeps them obedient and hard at work until their debt is repaid. It is removed as part of the out-processing procedures, although some choose to keep that drive for their own gain. Shutting it down or modifying the focus is easy enough as the necessary triggers are installed as part of the original conditioning." Gred nodded again. Old news to him but there might be nuances that he wasn't familiar with.

"You might also be aware of the phobia treatments available now. A good therapist can eliminate those fears with only a few visits. Frankly, it usually takes longer to get a person to agree to the treatment than it does for the actual visits and for the patients to be amazed that they ever feared anything so much."

"I hadn't heard of that, but then I don't have any phobias." He had other triggers for pleasure and those he wanted to keep.

"Well, it removes the inciting incident of the phobia. Fascinating work is being done, ser. I keep very up to date on the advances that are being made in the field." Hantel sipped the coffee.

"As for your needs, part of what I do for Kessem and some others is much more subtle. Adding or subtracting a particular event from a subject's mind, or reinforcing loyalty to a superior leaves the original personality in place, but they totally believe what their new memories tell them. Much like the drug cure your acquaintance told you of. My version of that cure is in considerable demand in my more public practice. I have two well trained associates who run those sessions in my absences. They are completely loyal and devoted to me." From Hantel's smile, he'd ensured his people would never betray him. Another possibility for the future. Especially for bodyguards.

"Are there fail safes?"

"Of course. The people I treat as you desire will never identify me or my employers as someone they know was involved in the alteration of their memories. They will suicide if someone gets too close to the secrets that they have been told to keep. I have created very stable personalities, ser Gred. Ones that can and have lasted for decades. For a number of clients, many of whom you might know socially. An *unstable* one will take some thought, since it must also be stable enough to pass as the original for a time. I will need the subject's medical records, any vid recordings of past events, pictures, so on. The more information you give me the faster it is to build your impostor."

"We have some, and can access more."

"There will actually be two personalities added: the unstable impostor and a controller based on the complete conditioning model. The controller will be able to update both complete personalities with events the other has experienced as directed. That should take care of your time delay to activation. I would suggest that you activate the impostor and the controller on a regular basis just to ensure that the system is working well. Perhaps once a month or so."

"There aren't any opportunities we know of to have him disappear for three or four weeks at this point," Gred said. "He's just starting to work at the holdings, so you have time in hand for your research. There's no immediate rush, but we would like to have the conditioning completely finished within a half year or so."

"Then it should be possible to implement. I should inform you that this has been recorded," Hantel said. "My apologies, but some of my employers have had changes of heart that required me to protect myself and my work."

"I've also recorded our conversation," Greb replied showing a voice transmitter the size of his hand in his coat pocket. "Not stored on my person, you understand. Precautions like this are simply good business."

"It is good to work with those who understand proper procedures. I will contact you when my research is complete."

Gred handed him a slim envelope. "Here is the first instalment of your fee. I'll send what information we have at the house in a day or so with one of my trusted guards and more as we assemble it. I look forward to hearing of your success."

Chapter 3

Jaren looked at the stacks of file folders on the desk and side table of the medium sized office, then at the man beside him. Seven of them. "Do I want to know what's in all of these?"

"Absolutely, serit." Kenfen Ofelan gave a wry grin. A tall man with the darker skin and hair of the Handaral people and corrective lenses, his family had been with the Alanyo clan for three generations now and he was promoted to chief of the analysis division last year. He and his family were often at social functions held at the compound and elsewhere. His oldest son was working somewhere in the bowels of this building as an auditor. His other three children were at various subsidiaries in lower moving up to middle management.

"This will be your office for the next few months. Ser Darit wanted you one floor up but we weren't able to free up a space. The papers in those folders are everything we currently have on Bayside Chemicals. Ser Darit gave me a copy of your paper to read when you finished the project and I went back and reread it when he mentioned that you'd be coming in for me to get you started on your first real analysis."

"And that's what I didn't know for my school report?" Jaren indicated the papers with dismay. He'd missed a *huge* amount of data. It was no wonder that his father hadn't been impressed with his report. His stomach tightened. After years at university, he obviously still didn't know anything about business.

"Not really, Jaren. Given the constraints of the assignment you had, the paper was quite good. You'll recognize a great deal of the material in these piles so it's not all new, just updated from what you had before. I just gave you the basics for your course. Now, there are extras that are important. You do need to have it all for a complete analysis. Have a seat, and I'll explain a process that works well." Ofelan moved to the small seating area and took the visitor chair and smiled. "Let's get started. I'm sure you'll find this fascinating."

An hour later Jaren's head was spinning. This was far beyond what he'd learned in university. He wished he'd taken notes. Or recorded it.

"It is a lot to take in at one time," Ofelan said with a small smile. "There's a cheat sheet on your desk and the piles are already separated into those categories. Just make sure you don't get the piles mixed up until you know what's in them and why."

"How long would it take a trained analyst to make sense of all of this?" Jaren hated to ask, but he needed some sort of timeline.

"About a month once all this had been brought together," Ofelan said. "Several months from an order to 'investigate this company and is it worth our trouble?': collecting the facts in those piles, doing site visits and so on. Don't worry and *don't* spend all your life on this as if you were cramming for a term paper or an exam. Ser Darit won't be happy about that. Getting it right is much better than getting it fast. In the general scheme of acquisition, it can take over a year to go from the investigation through analysis to making an offer. Or deciding not to bother. Since we already own Bayside, Ser Darit is looking for a fresh eye to see what you come up with."

"So, no pressure," Jaren said. Like he actually believed that.

"It isn't the same as for a new prospect, at any rate. Any suggestions for improvements in how they run the company should go into the final report. Don't limit your thinking: one of the best suggestions I had as a young analyst was to change the location of the dining hall at one of our isolated chemical plants. We moved it far enough away from the production line so the noise and smells, which were loud and pungent, didn't continue to ruin everyone's appetite. It did cost a tidy sum to build the new section but having that one simple change raised morale through the roof and productivity hit an all time high and stayed there. Paid back the construction costs in less than a year. You never know what effect a minor change like that has sometimes."

"I'd better start reading your list," Jaren said.

"The main reason ser Darit has for you to review this and other subsidiaries is to give you a look at our people, especially the top management and have them get to know you during your site visits and meetings. To understand what they do and how they do it. I don't know if he intends for you to go through all of them, but I'd count on keeping busy at least until you reach your majority next spring. I haven't seen the entire list of the subsidiaries he wants you to look at. On the plus side, you're now on salary as a beginning analyst. Same pay rate as any other new hire in that position but better than just your allowance, I'd imagine." Jaren hadn't thought of that aspect and repressed a smile.

"Tomorrow there will be someone at the desk outside if you need additional files or other help. Talfer Brannet is his name. It would have been today but he's finishing off another project. He'll get you set up on the computer network as well. You've used them at university, haven't you? We bought one of the newest ones last year. Amazing how much more it can do than the one we replaced. Very cost effective. We did have to put in cooling units to keep it from overheating. But during the winter we use the heat for the rest of the building and that cuts other costs. Synergy can be very important in a production facility. Waste heat should never be wasted."

"I hadn't realised they were such heat generators. The techs never let us anywhere near the actual systems. But the computers at school had the latest analysis and graphing software and I used them a lot, especially in my last semester. Thanks for the advice. Really." Jaren tried to smile. Nine or ten months of this? Or longer? Maybe it would get easier once he'd done a few and became used to ser Ofelan's cheat sheet.

Ofelan started toward the door but stopped just before opening it. "Ser Darit won't expect interim reports. He might ask you in general how you're coping, but he never bothers an analyst until the final report is ready. If you have any questions, come talk to me. Anytime."

Near the close of the business day, Feneir knocked softly at the office door. "Your father will be leaving in an hour. Do you want to wait and go home with him or leave now?"

"I'd better go with him." Jaren said. "I'm part way through this report on their distribution system and if I stop now I'll have to start all over again with it tomorrow. Plus, we don't have a car with us. I suppose we could use Father's and send them back for him."

"That's another issue. Coffee?"

"Yes, please." He handed the large cup across the desk.

His father was silent most of the way home. Jaren hadn't been able to finish the distribution report and had tucked it into the book bag he'd used at university so that he could finish reading or, more likely rereading it tonight. With notes. He'd put his original report in the bag this morning. It was full now.

"You need a proper case for those papers," Father observed. He looked toward the front section of the car. "Caldon, arrange that tomorrow. And for the tailor to come out on the weekend. Jaren, you need several more sets of formal business wear now. Image is very important. Especially when you're going to a new location. Wear an outdated suit and they think you're not important, despite the context of the meeting. On the other hand, having a competitor discount your ability and brains can give you an excellent advantage in negotiations. But one should treat any visitor with respect. Some of our competitors use that tactic to fluster an opponent at the start of a meeting."

"I'll see to the tailor and a case, ser." Feneir nodded.

"Thank you, ser." Jaren paused. "It was a most instructive morning with ser Ofelan. I see now why you were not satisfied with my original report. There is a lot of information that I didn't find."

"It was what your teachers wanted to hear," his father said with a dismissive wave of his hand. "To invest millions means an analyst takes a serious look at all aspects of the company."

Jaren looked out the window. About halfway home. Maybe he *should* travel by himself from now on.

"Hmph. Your cousin Adnil found a company a few years ago that he was very passionate that the clan invest in," his father said after several minutes of silence.

"KRT Electronics was the name, I believe. But I said no in the end. He was quite upset about it. Like several other small firms, they're trying to miniaturize electronic components. The idea man is quite brilliant and he might be able to succeed, but their management team was the weak point. They'll never manage with that team running the company. None of them had the necessary business background to take any company from start up to full production. I told them that I would agree to a minority stake of forty percent if they went with a complete restructuring with someone I trusted as president and our engineers to build the devices. They said no. So I walked away. Adnil was quite upset at first, but calmed down quickly. I told him what I'd told their president."

"Has anyone else bought their shares that you know of?" Father had never been like this before. Just chatting with him about business as an equal, not interrogating him on what he'd been doing or how late he'd stayed out. It felt strange. Very strange.

"No. Not that I've heard. Our interest was noted by several other clans, but when we passed, the others didn't even bother to look at them. I believe there's been some private investment since then, and their shares are available to the public at present, but the investment is nowhere near the amounts they need to complete the research and testing. I did consider just hiring the idea idiot for our research facility and letting the company collapse under their incompetence. We'd have at least one good product out the door by now if that had worked out."

"Why didn't it happen?"

He shrugged. "The existing patents on the device are held by the company. The idea idiot, Karthgat, I think his name was, assigned them as his investment in the company while others put up cash and thought they could become management, sit in fancy offices and take big salaries from all the other investors. It would have been more efficient and much more likely to succeed if they'd all kept their old jobs and just funded the research until they had something to bring to the market." Father looked at him. Jaren forced himself not to look away and put an attentive smile on his face. This *was* actually interesting. And important for the future.

"Always look at the corporate offices of a company you're considering buying. Then compare their cost to the production facility. There should be at least eighty and better ninety times more money in production. If the offices of a start up look like they were brought from home or from a salvage yard, they have a better chance of being worthwhile." Father shrugged and looked out his window, then chuckled. "Sometimes I have an art appraiser visit corporate offices with me if I wasn't sure on their decor. They pretended to be a flunky, left to wander around the office, carry my case and fetch coffee. Saved us several times from paying full price for three, no, four different companies. If this company goes down, Karthgat might have a chance at getting back his own ideas from the rubble. I'd look at him again if that happens. Assuming someone else hasn't succeeded, of course. Being first to market can be an advantage that is very hard to overcome, even if you have a better product that does more and is cheaper."

As the weeks passed, Jaren found that ser Ofelan had been right. His father never pestered him about his progress. He did answer questions in the car, but it was all general information and the occasional anecdote. Those were making sense for a change. He'd just been confused by the myriad details in the past. He must have learned more than he thought at university.

Jaren kept coming back to the Bayside employee report in writing up the report. Several things in there just didn't make sense.

"Ser Ofelan, I have a question." Jaren had asked his secretary Talfer to make the appointment for just after lunch.

"Only one?" Ofelan smiled as he directed Jaren to the seating area near the windows of his opulent corner office. The sun was muted by sheer curtains so he didn't have to worry about glare.

"At the moment. The employee situation at Bayside really bothers me. I don't know why it didn't show up when I did that other report or maybe that was the biggest thing I missed."

"Is it the numbers? Or the type?"

"Honestly, it's both, ser," Jaren said. "They shouldn't need that big a workforce. Most of their processes are large volume and they've started to use computers to track their inventory. They don't have an on-site re-search facility and their delivery system is geared to trailer-sized bulk orders to other manufacturing plants, not packaging products for indi-vidual consumers or even small plants to modify further."

"Good job. They *are* over populated, but it's from one specific depart-ment, which *is* in another location and not obviously part of their opera-tion. You weren't told about that one when you originally visited the main plants and offices."

"Why? What's going on there that's so secret?"

"One of Bayside's main products is glycerin, correct?"

"Yes. They make twenty percent of the world total. Good stable in-come source from what I can see. Not fancy or exciting, but always in de-mand. Probably forever."

"This information is *not* in the reports you have or had for the other report." Ofelan cautioned. "They produce nitric-variants of glycerin as well as other explosive chemicals for the army and for our own mining applications. Along with a few of our allies. The army is also doing solid rocket fuel research. That's where the extra workers and supervisors are needed. Deada is the section name. No one remembers what it actually stands for."

Jaren leaned back in the chair and snorted. "*Dead* in the department name? And that's why they can't use conditioned drones from the pris-ons like some other sections," he mused. "For that sort of work you need very capable workers. And their salaries cost money."

"All the line workers for that section as well as the research staff have had a partial conditioning. They're paid extra because of that. It would skew the bottom line except that other mining companies and the army pay extremely well for the other products coming out of that factory. The conditioning is quite limited: they are always paying attention to what they're doing while at work. Once they get in the factory door they could have had a catastrophe at home and they don't think about it until they leave. Although, if something terrible did happen at home they have administrative leave with full pay. There's being cautious and being a concerned and caring employer."

"That also explains the larger security force," Jaren said slowly, thinking about the other anomalies in the reports. "That kind of delivery can't go on a regular shipping container or cargo truck. Some trucks on the major equipment list didn't seem big enough to hold a worthwhile shipment of their usual products."

"Gold star." Ofelan smiled. "Those are special armoured trucks kept at the Deada production site and have internal shock absorbing tech for uneven roads. President Cahtharan was a little nervous that you'd chosen Bayside for your project. Ser Darit overrode him. Said it would be simpler for them to hide the evidence of Deada's existence than for someone to come up with a reasonable explanation for you why you couldn't use that subsidiary for your project."

"Ser Ofelan said you'd found the discrepancy in the personnel at Bayside," his father said as they headed home that night. "Good."

"I should have the report ready in three days, ser. The employee matter was the last issue I had."

"Present it to Kenfen and me then. First thing in the morning. Steffent, arrange that with my secretary." The security chief simply nodded.

"Thank you, ser." Jaren was quiet the rest of the way home.

Jaren finished the last page of his presentation and went to his father's door to turn the lights up. The overhead projector whirred to silence. He returned to stand by the front of the table and waited for the verdict. His stomach clenched and he tried to relax.

"Your thoughts on the proposed changes," his father turned to ser Ofelan and sipped his coffee.

"They will save several percent on expenses. Not a great deal, but Bayside has been a well run company for many years and there isn't much slack. The bonus pool for suggestions and accident prevention will raise morale and that's always a good incentive. We should have put that in place years ago. The transport change is quite ingenious. The army doesn't want anyone to know about their solid fuel research and high security trucks showing up every month is noticeable. Making it look like a convoy of provisions instead will certainly confuse any watchers. Same thing for the miners. The solid nitroglycerin gives them a big advantage in clearing rock from their quarries. It will cost little beyond the new paint jobs for the existing vehicles. The increase in security will be welcomed by all of those clients and I think that we'll pay off the costs in a month or three."

"I agree. Send them the changes and ask for implementation." Father turned back to Jaren. "Go down to the beach house this weekend if you like. Take some friends with you. We'll have another company for you to start analyzing early next week. This time you'll need to go on a site visit once you've read through their files. We didn't bother this time since you'd already seen the main facility. Caldon will make the arrangements once you're ready."

"Thank you, sers." Jaren took the transparent sheets and slid them into the folder already holding the written report and set it in front of his father. Then he left the office. The door closed and he felt like he was finally able to take a full breath for the first time today. He bypassed the elevator and ran down the stairs to get rid of the rest of his tension.

Feneir waited in his outer office, reading a magazine. Talfer looked up and smiled. "How did it go, serit?"

"They approved the changes I suggested." He managed a smile. "I even have the rest of the day off. Thanks for all your help. Once you get all the other files back to storage, then you should leave early as well. They're going to come up with another set early next week. No idea which company it will be, but I will go visit them."

"That's what they say is the result of successful completion of a task: another task. Have a good weekend, serit."

"Where to now, serit?" Feneir asked as they waited for the elevator. Jaren checked the hallway and no one was in sight.

"I really want to see Sanil before she heads back to university. Father said I could use the beach house for the weekend and bring some friends. I just need her. Can you call Casteron and see if she's free?" He still spoke a quietly as he could.

Caldon smiled. "I think we can manage to set that up. I'll alert the house that you and a guest will be arriving when we get home. Separately, of course." He reached for the phone next to the elevator doors and dialled the security office to alert Pagil they were leaving.

"Of course," Jaren said. Seeing Sanil would be wonderful. And not having to worry about getting home in time for dinner would give them so much time together. His account now had enough for thank yous for the staff for their implied silence. Having a job certainly made many things easier to arrange. Even if he did have to pay for the new five suits hanging in his closet.

"Is Pagil in the break room?" A pause. "Feneir here. We're heading out now. See you downstairs by the car. Home first. A trip to the beach house later once we can pack our gear. With a guest for the weekend." Another pause and Jaren saw a smile which vanished as soon as Feneir realised he was watching. "You guessed right. I'll contact him once we leave here. Random phone booth is best as usual."

Chapter 4

Sanil stared at the sprawling beach house. She'd heard about it from Jaren before this, but the reality was impressive. Two stories for the most part, with a third story tower where one could go to watch the ocean. A single story section to one side for guards and staff. The buildings had recently been painted, she assumed. Off white with slate blue accents. Slate grey roofing with a pair of sea birds perched on the peak. One ruffled its wings and cried out. Not a very melodious song.

Several cars were to one side of the smallish garage. Only a dozen or so guards and staff would be here, Julin had said. Just for her and Jaren. He came out of the house trailed by Caldon. She waited impatiently until Casteron opened her door.

"Welcome, seris," Caldon said. "We'll get everyone settled and your luggage into one of the upstairs bedrooms." Then Jaren took her hand and brought her into the house.

The first floor of this section was one large room, discreetly separated by the furnishings into lounging and dining areas. A large vid unit to one side faced couches with plenty of pillows. The seaward side of the house was mostly glass. She caught sight of the small beach below them. This late in the summer it might be fun to swim in the ocean. Her father hated swimming and water sports in general so they'd never gone to anywhere by the sea or a lake for family holidays. She'd just had whatever swimming pools were at the resort they stayed at.

"It's marvellous!" she said. He smiled back at her.

"The view is better without the windows in the way." He led her toward the sea, through one of the sets of sliding doors. There was enough of a breeze to toss her hair around. Tucking the errant strands behind her ears, she gazed outward and knew that Jaren had moved behind her, holding her around the waist. She snuggled against his chest.

"I've missed you so much. And it will be worse soon."

"I know. Dratted school. I can't come home very often or the parents will suspect something is up." She half turned. "When you're doing site visits, maybe we can schedule a day or so either side?"

"We can try. I have a new company to start reviewing next week. Once I know where it is, we can make some plans. It should be easier staying stealthy without all our relatives in the same city as we are."

Dinner was facing the ocean. Fresh fish from not far away and a chowder from the mussels growing on the rocks below the deck.

"That was amazing," Sanil said, putting her fork down. The server came to take their plates. "Please, tell the cook that was truly excellent."

She smiled. "I'll tell her, seris. I will bring coffee in a moment."

After the server left, Sanil put her hand on Jaren's. "Thank you, love. This was a great idea."

"It was Father's, to tell you the whole truth. He suggested I have a bunch of friends come out. That might have been nice, but I just wanted to spend some time with you. By... well, just us, our bodyguards and the house full of servants." He managed a smile.

"As alone as we're ever going to get, even after we get married," she replied. "After coffee, what shall we do until bedtime?"

"There should be enough light for a short walk on the beach, but it gets quite chilly out there even at this time of year, especially once the sun goes down. We can bundle up on the deck and chat if you want. Go for a walk tomorrow when you can see everything. It'll be warm enough in the afternoon for us to go swimming."

The server came back with the coffee service. "Thank you," Jaren said. She cleared a few more oddments from the table and left. The door to the kitchens was now closed. Jaren poured the coffee and they moved to the deck, wrapping themselves in the blankets on the double lounger. The breeze was gentle and somewhere out in the growing darkness, the chime of a channel buoy echoed, lonely. Further out, a sad noise from something. Another buoy?

"We're actually -- alone," Sanil whispered. "It feels so..."

"Different. I know we've wanted to be alone, but now that we are, I'm not sure what to talk about."

"There's work, or school, which is coming up soon. Yuck."

"But what do we want, Sanil? When we're both of age."

"I want to be your wife, Jaren. Help you manage the clan holdings when your father passes. Have your children, and bring joy to your soul. You've gone through so much. I don't know how you survived, from what you've said. I've been very lucky."

"At least my father doesn't scream at me all the time," Jaren said, trying to lighten the mood.

"It's not that often. You'll find out what that feels like eventually," Sanil replied. "My usual distraction is giving him a hug and kiss mid-rant. That might not work for you, though."

He snorted in amusement. "Who knows? It might distract him enough to disrupt his rant. Then a change of topic to complete the process." He kissed her hand. "I feel so much, Sanil. I want to be your husband and see you at the desk beside mine until we're both old and wrinkled. Bring joy to your soul. We just need to get through the next two years."

"And once I'm done with school it will be easier for us to meet," Sanil observed. "Any sign of your father sending you to one of the subsidiaries for an extended stint? That would be okay to arrange times together."

"I don't think that's his plan. He wants me to meet with the presidents of our most influential and prosperous subsidiaries. That's what is actually behind the analyses I'm doing, according to ser Ofelan. I get to know more about the businesses the clan owns and the senior executives get to know me. Uncle Adnil will be named interim CEO if Father dies in the next few years, I think. After that, we'll be in charge. It's... a daunting task. I'm so glad that I'll have you beside me."

Sanil smiled. "To keep you on track, you mean."

"There is that." The wind ruffled their hair.

"I suppose we should head in," Sanil said some time later.

"I guess." Jaren paused. "But I'd like to snuggle more. A lot more. Where our noses will stay warmer."

"In bed?" She shifted a little from lying on his shoulder to look at him. "Together?"

"Yes. I know we can't..."

"A child would reveal our secret," Sanil said. "It's going to be very lonely without you at university. I would like some good memories to keep me warm. But how can we evade the guards?"

He smiled. "That's the easiest part. There are strips on the doors that send a signal to the guard room in the basement when one is opened. I have a solution. Two of them actually. One for each of us."

They went upstairs hand in hand, passing two guards to do so. None were in the upper hallway at the moment. Jaren handed her a length of thin wire with the copper showing on both ends. "This jumps the connectors," he said quietly. "I've used it a couple of times here, just for practice. I made the second one as soon as I got home from the office."

"Where were they?" she asked. "I didn't feel anything in your pockets while we cuddled."

"In my belt, with some lock picks and such. I did some Escape and Evasion training and sometimes Feneir and I practice. I'll tell you more about that tomorrow."

"All right." Sanil grinned and her eyes were bright with mischief.

Jaren opened her door and pulled the backing off a small bandage. A small knife let him cut it in half. Then he places the leads on the inner corner of the door and tucked the middle part of the wire to the inside of the door. She looked, seeing the contacts for the alarm system now covered by the bandage. She grinned again.

"Just close the door normally," he said. "We should give the guards a little while to do a sweep, now that we're inside. I'll come to you as soon as it's clear. Okay?"

"Definitely." she gave him a quick kiss. The door clicked shut.

He went to his own room, two down on the other side of the house and almost forgot to set his own wire. Climbing out the window and over the roof would be more hazardous than he wanted tonight.

It seemed to take forever until the house was quiet. Several times he heard footsteps near the stairs. He should have expected that they'd check more often this time. Just to be sure nothing was going on.

He slipped from his room, wearing tight exercise shorts, pyjamas, and his robe, then tapped at Sanil's door. She'd been standing next to it, because the knob turned as he reached for it. Seconds later he was inside, easing the door closed as silently as he could.

And the sound of footsteps on the stairs froze them into immobility. Halfway up, he guessed. Then went away. They both started to breathe.

There was a little light from the full moons so they could see the furniture and each other. "I'm nervous," she said.

"So am I," he replied. "Can we start with snuggling? Honestly, Sanil. It doesn't have to go further. I just want to hold you."

There was a faint hint of dawn in the sky when he slipped back into his room, wearing the pyjamas and robe again. Sanil's room shared a bathroom with the one next to it so they could clean up a little with a damp towel. Each of them had explored the other's body. And ... more.

Jaren pulled the wire loose when he officially left his room about an hour later. Showered, shaved and dressed.

He knocked on Sanil's door. "Hey, sleepyhead. Breakfast will be on the table soon." Footsteps on the stairway was one of the maids, not a guard this time.

"Just coming up for the fifteen minute warning," she said with a smile. "I see the good salt air didn't make you sleep in this time, serit."

"Not this morning, anyway." He smiled and the maid headed back down the stairs. Sanil's door opened a crack.

"I'll be down in time," she said. "Just need to get dressed." She handed him the wire and he tucked it into his pocket. They both grinned, looking forward to another night together.

Chapter 5

Gred sat at the corner table of the busy restaurant and tried not to look at his watch too often. The conditioner was late, again. He saw Hantel finally enter and ground his teeth together rather than shouting at him. Attracting any attention was bad. His driver had paid attention to the weather reports and left the mansion early to ensure he'd get here on time. Snow this early in fall was unusual, but always possible.

"Traffic," Hantel said with a wave of his hand as he sat and accepted the coffee the waitress stood ready to pour. He smiled in thanks. As soon as she left, he set the cup to one side and his smile faded.

"I've had the implementation ready for the last two months. When do you think we might begin? I have other clients who have major work for me to accomplish. With continued updates from you, it is possible to incorporate any new information that comes up while I am otherwise occupied."

"Excellent. We do have an opportunity coming up in a month, more or less. I'll know the exact timing within the week."

Hantel raised an eyebrow. "Where?"

"I've been supervising some major developments in a subsidiary out in Balgarath province. It's a think tank, so the entire style of the company management is different. My dear cousin is going to accompany me there early next month and spend some time seeing it in action. After that, he's supposed to take some holiday time. He's expected to be away about three weeks, he was told by his father. Balgarath is several hours south by plane so staying near there would be sensible given the time of year. Quite a popular destination for people escaping winter."

"That will work quite well. I shall ask Kessem to source a place where we may work undisturbed and would be a reasonable place for a vacation. Do you have enough guards to provide adequate security?"

Gred shook his head. "Half. I don't trust most of my guards with this sort of operation. One I do trust is the bodyguard I have in Jaren's team. He'll be with us as you suggested, to provide context for the impostor during testing. I'll suggest to Jaren that he leave his regular guards at home – let them have a holiday as well - and that company security will cover both of us since we're working. I'll have my two men with me, but I'll have to go back to work during the weekdays. I only have a week free, and that's mostly to keep my little cousin company. We just need a day to get everything started."

"Your name will be on the lease as part of the scenario. Would the serit be able to cover some costs afterwards?"

"He's getting a salary now, so I can get some cash from him once the conditioning is finished and he knows just how much he owes me."

"I'll be sure to include that detail in the tapes."

"Are you packed for tomorrow?" Gred asked Jaren. They were just outside Jaren's office near the end of a busy day.

"Two cases are already packed and waiting in my suite back home. One for work and one for vacation."

"Good. You might not need so much business wear at this place," Gred cautioned. "Very different corporate culture than most places, as your dad said. I've seen several of the senior scientists wandering around in sleepwear and a robe because they hadn't bothered to change on their way in or because they'd had an idea during the night."

"Or because they don't go to their quarters and camp out in the labs?" Jaren gave a wry smile. "How did we get involved with them? I just finished my last analysis and haven't had a chance to look at any of their files yet. That's a large stack on my desk and I know I don't have everything."

"It was ages back," Gred replied. "Our grandfather actually started it about sixty years ago. He grabbed all the odd ball idea guys he could find in all the subsidiaries and built this place, which *they* refer to as the playpen, by the way, and told them to have fun and invent lots of stuff we can make money on. Then he brought in good, fairly sane engineers and told them to make those screwball ideas work. The science guys have decent bonuses based on how well previous work keeps selling. Very good incentive to do more."

"It did pay off." Jaren said. "Feneir isn't too happy that I'm leaving him behind but when I pointed out that *he* hadn't had an actual holiday in two years, he shut up and agreed. I think he's gone over all the protocols with Sarnd at least twice. Maybe more."

"We'll meet at the airport at seven am. It's a five hour flight, including the interim stop, so don't forget something to keep you busy."

Jaren lifted his case slightly "That's already in here. I have some of their files to read up on what sort of things they've invented so far. Talfer found their last two year end reports for me. That should keep me awake for the entire time."

"Or put you right to sleep." They grinned at each other.

***

"So it begins," Adnil said as they sat in the living room of their mansion, whiskey glasses in hand. "Any difficulties with the arrangements?"

"None. He's eager to get away from the old man. Sarnd will be his only guard as we had planned. The rest will be from AR&D while we're on site there. He thinks the other guards for his vacation are from the general pool of the holdings based near there."

"In the strictest sense of the term, they are our men," his father pointed out. "We've hired them. Tell me again about the estate you're using."

"Twenty acres almost entirely surrounded by a nature preserve. Swimming pool, enough room to land a helicopter if we need it, but it's only an hour away from Balgarath the city by car. Enough space for everything we need to do. There's an isolated room in the basement that Hantel can use as the conditioning chamber." His father nodded.

"Hantel will head straight there in four days to set up his equipment. He has a truck and needs a day or so to set up and make sure nothing was damaged. He'll have the other three guards with him and I've arranged for Patnar to pick up the keys and so on. He'll stay there as lead guard."

"Jaren thinks you're staying there with him the whole time?"

"Only for the first week. He knows I have to go back and oversee the prototyping being done on the new rotary engine design. I told him if it was successful I'd make sure he'll come back with me and try it out on the track." Both men smiled coldly. "He thinks we've only got the place for a week. Wants to go to Sacarnil and catch up with some old friends at university after that. Sarnd will call his contact to cancel that trip."

"Keep me updated on Hantel's progress as you can. No real calls through the company switchboard unless it's an emergency."

"Of course, Dad."

***

Jaren smiled at Gred as they boarded the corporate plane. The triple propeller design was one from the playpen, one of the stewards told him. Most mid-sized corporate planes had them, which translated into a steady stream of royalties and income from the ongoing maintenance parts and supplies.

"I am glad you're with me," Gred said as he sank into a well stuffed chair. "Otherwise I might be in for a long car ride or squished on a commercial flight. Hard to get sensitive work done either way."

"It does make things easier," Jaren agreed. "Having the entire plane to ourselves does seem inefficient, though." He gestured at the empty seats around them.

"It isn't just us on board, you know. There's more people than just our guards up front, and I understand from my man there are some things in the cargo section that neither of us have clearance to know about. So you might say that we, or to be accurate, *you* are the cover story for the secret whatevers."

"Misdirection." Jaren thought, flipping mentally through a list of aphorisms. "Let the other see what you want him to, not what is real."

"Was that a quote?" Gred's eyebrow went up a little.

"Yes. Way before the unification, Suntz was a general on Grathil. Someone rooted around in all the archives they could and collected the bits he wrote on how to wage war and published it last year. The authors think military theory works the same way in business as it did in war."

"I remember him now. Another idiot fad." Gred rolled his eyes. "I've seen some very bizarre things applied to business theory in the past few years. The worst one was the 'which character are you?' from that silly children's book. I'm just thankful that your dad said no to any of their management seminars."

"As you say. One of my professors was a real fan of Suntz and he made us practically memorize the thing. Every one of his exams had something from his writings as an essay question. I'm very happy that they just found fragments of his books, not the whole things."

Jaren shook hands with the company president and smiled. "Thanks for letting me come visit, ser. I know these trips can be very disruptive for productivity."

"Not a problem, serit Alanyo," Ser Tilnar replied. "Attention from head office is always welcome here. We have some amazing developments on the go." He indicated an individual in a dark semi-formal suit. "Ralth Calthor will show you around, introduce you to the inmates and provide whatever you need. There's an office down the hall for your use, next to ser Calyno's. Your guard will have your personal things arranged in one of the spare bachelor quarters in the next building. Your meals will be with me and the rest of the executives in the small dining hall. Calthor will let you know the times." He smiled and gathered the other managers then shooed them away. Back to work, or to gossip about what his presence here actually meant. Well, he'd find out soon.

"I did wonder why this place is so far away from everything when I learned I was coming here," Jaren said as his guide showed him to the office. The man had picked up his briefcase before Jaren could do it himself. "It's an hour to the city of Balgarath, isn't it?" Having the same name for the city *and* the province made references odd at times.

"Just about, serit. Management decided when this place was established that keeping temptations away from the inmates was a good idea. They're distracted enough on their own. The company owns a sizable percentage of the land between the city and here as a buffer zone. It is currently leased to three local ranchers, mostly to offset the tax expense of owning it. Most of Balgarath's growth has been to the east instead of north, so we're safe for the foreseeable future."

"Sensible. Do the researchers really refer to themselves as inmates?" Having the company president using the term might be a symptom of a serious personnel issue. Calthor sighed.

"They do, with great glee at times. They petition for a major redecorating every couple of years. Nursery themes or something equally appalling. Ser Tilnar keeps saying no, but they always get some other concession that they do want. Or think they want. Several years back they wanted only certain brands of soft drinks allowed on site. Two years later they changed their minds and wanted their rivals. Just *after* we'd renewed the supply contract with the first lot. Cost quite a lot to break the contract." He shook his head. "An incredible waste of time and money. Half of them ask the regular staff to bring the other brands back with them when we go anywhere there's a store that carries it. The transport drivers usually have a case or three in the cab of their truck for resale. So it works out. Mostly. Another year to go on this one, so we'll have to wait and see what the inmates decide to do next."

"How do the rest of the staff feel about the situation?"

"We're the adults and they're the idiot children. Some inmates have egos the size of Yithra, so sometimes we just want to spank them silly, especially when they're on a redecorating fit." Calthor opened a door. "Here's your office, serit. Not very fancy but at least you have a view of the hills instead of the residence tower."

"Leave the case here, and let's see what the children are playing at this week." Calthor grinned at him.

Jaren wrote up his notes before turning out the small desk light that night. The suite was tiny compared to his own back home, but it would do for a week. It wasn't as if he had much gear with him. Calthor's attitude bothered him a lot. This place was amazing but there was a serious undercurrent of tension, not just from him. Each rank in the hierarchy seemed to have a different section of the cafeteria, which seemed odd. Wouldn't people who worked together want to eat together? Or was it their opportunity to vent with people at their own pay grade? He'd try to ask Calthor a few questions. Being confused was a great way to get people talking about things they probably shouldn't.

Right after his breakfast with ser Tilnar and the now introduced senior managers, his tour resumed. Every one of the inmates left whatever they were doing to show him around their workspace. Several times their assistants had to shut down experiments. They didn't look very happy about it.

"You do have access to our computer system," Calthor said after his lunch with the senior administrators instead of the project managers. "The log-in is pretty simple. You're Guest and the password is..."

"Guest?" He hoped not.

"Close but not quite. Visitor. Sometimes it's swapped the other way. Not that it really matters."

"That doesn't seem very secure," Jaren said mildly.

"That's what the inmates wanted. And they pouted until management caves. Everything comes to a screeching halt until they get their way. Two weeks that time. Since President Tilner doesn't want head office to know anything's wrong, he gives in to whatever they want. Eventually."

"Why are you telling me this?"

Calthor shrugged. "It's the first time we've had anyone from top management here and not all snooty about talking to the lower staff. And the people like me never get real access to head office. That's part of the restricted area of the computers. You have to have a real password and log-in. Which I don't."

"Wait-- *everyone here* logs in as a guest?" His jaw dropped slightly.

"Everyone but the lead scientists and upper management. It limits what access their assistants have to the data and so on. I really don't understand their reasoning. Maybe it's just petty power stepping. No one at my level is sure." He shrugged. "We learn to deal with it. Or try to get a transfer to somewhere else. I'm very close to requesting one."

"Doesn't make sense to me either." So was the administrative control name root and the password control? Or the other way around. A late night ramble through the computer's file directory might be useful. And fun. He'd have to tell Feneir once they got back together. His Escape and Evasion training might be more useful than either of them had thought. He smiled, but not enough to make Calthor wonder why.

"There's a few more things for you to see officially, then you can wander around as you need to. I think they're doing some motor testing tomorrow morning. Your cousin's involved in that project."

"Sounds good. Let's go derail some other experiments before supper." Calthor smiled. A real one this time.

The engineer's tiny office was filled with models of various projects he hadn't been shown yet and the desk was almost overflowing with files despite three four-drawer cabinets against the wall, one blocking the only window. Several pieces of paper were stuck to the cabinet next to the desk with cryptic notes on them. He didn't see any adhesive tape or magnets to hold them in place.

"I can't get access to half the data I need," Marthon snarled. "And that's slowing me down. Then the inmates blame me because they aren't ready to demonstrate their latest flight of fancy on their idiotic schedule! Mostly to prevent someone from having the resources for *their* demo."

"I think that's one of the major problems here," Jaren said. "Any idea when the log-in system changed?"

"Three, maybe four years back?" Marthon shrugged. "Upstairs signed off on it. Like they've caved on every idiotic demand the inmates have made." He glared at Calthor, as if he was personally responsible.

"Ser Tilner did manage to derail the last redecorating binge."

"Yeah, but what did the inmates get instead? That horrible soft drink. I don't think anyone really drinks it."

"True," Calthor said. "But the transport people are making money by smuggling the other brands in. I have the weekend free. Want to make your co-workers happy? We could do a run to Balgarath and stock up. That might help calm them down at least."

Jaren took a step back and pretended to read a report as they quietly planned the supply run. No money changed hands. Yet. But the small piece of paper on the cabinet intrigued him. Maybe he'd come back here late at night and look at it more closely.

He'd managed to pack dark grey exercise pants and a dark green sweater with a hood so he could keep up his exercise routine. His soft shoes had to be wrapped in waste liners since they were white and very visible in the dark. Tonight was a trial run. To see if he could get to his little office without being spotted by security. He opened the suite's outer door and headed for the main stairs in the housing wing.

It took longer than he liked, but he made it to his office without being seen. He hoped the outer security was better than the men inside. Four guards passed by him at one time or another. None of them were paying attention or looked around. One had a small radio playing. He frankly didn't think his skills were that good but maybe they were. Another thing to ask Feneir about later.

The monitor in his office flickered as he turned it on. The drapes were already drawn so he didn't have to worry about someone outside seeing him. His sweatshirt now lay on the floor to block any light from escaping and warning one of the guards. If they bothered to come down this secondary corridor, that is.

He had a good idea how the system stored data from the computer classes he'd taken. What he needed was a listing of *all* the projects, not just the ones that were in active development. Root *was* the admin name, but the password was inmate. It took him two tries. He shook his head. Maybe he should let that engineer know what it was before he left here. Generate some good will. Maybe he'd be a resource for other problems he could bring to Father's attention. There had to be some major changes made here before the entire system collapsed under the inmates' egos.

Four days later, he was sure of his conclusions. The inmates needed a smack down of epic proportions. They thought only *they* could have an idea that worked. There were numerous projects stalled completely because they wouldn't listen to the engineers or anyone else for that matter. He smiled. Millions could ride on their development. Father would be very pleased with him and the other top people would be impressed. He did wonder why Tilner hadn't tried to control who he talked to. Maybe he hadn't realised Jaren wasn't like others from head office.

Two days later he stared at his notes of the latest fruit of his late night rambling. The legal department had a lot of files, but a trio of attentive secretaries kept everything properly filed. Patents had an entire four drawer cabinet to itself. Sorted by year. That made his trip there much easier and quicker.

He discovered there was a serious decline in the number of new patents over the past ten years. Most of the patents that were filed were only incremental improvements of their existing patents. Few really new ideas were being developed to a useful stage, possibly because of the inmates' attitudes. That would have to change, and soon. If someone else managed to replicate this research, all their efforts would be worthless.

The gathering the following night was another symptom of the problems with the patents, he realised. The inmates paid a lot of attention to him because they saw him as a conduit to his father. And power.

"We have some terrific new ideas coming up," said a senior inmate. "My team is poised to increase revenue by thousands. I was wondering if you'd heard anything about the CSO position? Any word on who is being considered for it?" His posture said *'I'm the best scientist here and why haven't you given the position to me the moment you arrived?'*

"I haven't heard anything," Jaren said. Again. "My father didn't mention that the position was empty before I left. I can imagine it's difficult to arrange priorities without someone in that position." Chief Science Officer: the one who doled out research funds, minions to do the actual work, arranged special (and very expensive) equipment, and the size of the workspace the inmates were given to play in.

The inmates wanted him to get them more toys and higher salaries, sometimes in reverse order. Many, like this one, wanted the vacant chief science officer position. He was reminded of a terrible management team Father had referred to a few weeks ago. A development team had to play with all its members, not just a few favoured ones and ignore the rest. That split in cohesion had led to the collapse of the company and the clan took the opportunity to pick it up for pocket change. The entire upper level management had been sacked once the ink was dry on the contract and the payment cleared. Their replacements brought the company to profitability in less than a year.

"Ser Tilnar is trying, of course, but he doesn't have the knowledge and experience that I do. His training is all in business, not science. I've offered to help out, but he just keeps saying that the new CSO will be appointed soon."

"Then I'm sure one will be," Jaren held up his empty soft drink can to explain his departure. And escaped. For about three strides. Another senior inmate moved into his path. Jaren glanced at the ornate wall clock. Another three hours of this before he could leave and not cause any hurt feelings. Although, if this kept up he might have to be rude to stop the politicking. And backstabbing.

"Why hasn't Gred done anything about this situation?" he mused to himself when he finally closed the door to his suite. "He has the seniority to push this, or at least make sure Ser Ofelan knows about the conflicts. Why hasn't he? Did someone tell him what was going on and he just ignored it as petty attempts to undermine the managers?"

He wouldn't comment on it right now. He might ask Gred when they reached the back country estate where they'd spend next week. Then he'd be off to Sacarnil and Sanil. Feneir had arranged to rent a holiday cabin near a resort that was less than popular with anyone who might recognise them. With a little luck and planning, they'd have a few nights to themselves, like at the beach house. He didn't want to have to tell Tossem about her but Feneir had agreed to come back early from his holiday and take over. He didn't want to add to the people who knew about Sanil but did want Feneir to have a decent holiday.

The estate's main building appeared briefly between the trees. Jaren craned his neck to try to see more. "Wow. How did you find this place?"

"Connections from school," Gred replied. "I like the idea of quiet, especially after any amount of time at the playpen. It always takes me a couple of days to come back to normal after being there. I also never spend the weekend on site if I can help it. Usually go into Balgarath the city and enjoy the beaches and the nightlife there. We could go there later this week if you want. Still warm enough to swim, I've heard."

"Let's see how relaxed we get after a day or two. I think every one of the senior inmates wants me to support their attempt to become chief science officer. They didn't let up so I was considering asking Tossem to stuff a couple into the nearest waste truck so the rest would get the idea. If we'd been there any longer, I think I would have had him do it."

"They really *do* need a new CSO to help manage developments and reassign the teams based on their progress. Is there anyone there that you think would be good at it? You met most of the senior people."

He shook his head. "I wouldn't give it to any of the current inmates. An outsider would have an easier time getting them under some sort of control. An insider would have everyone cranky that he'd made it and they didn't and the infighting would stall everything worse than it already is. At least your engine prototype is working out well."

"It should be into production in another year, just in time for the new models. Only in a few of them at first. We'll also have to help train the mechanics at those dealerships on how to repair and maintain them."

"Hadn't thought about that aspect. Will that take much time?"

"Not really. The car plants will send around several demo engine models early in production with mechanics in tow. And limited availability will drive up interest in them."

The sprawling tan two-story house appeared along the drive, a guard coming out of the front door to greet them. "At least it's not our problem this weekend. And we're here!" Gred said. "Time for some fun!"

Dinner was excellent for coming out of the caterers' packaging and Jaren was pleased that the guard serving their meal gave him wine to match Gred's. He did limit himself to one glass, not the half bottle that Gred drank. Jaren stumbled slightly as they headed into the salon to watch the vid. He didn't remember hitting the floor.

Chapter 6

Gred smiled as Jaren came into the dining room. All was in preparation. Tossem indicated which chair he should take. It was fairly obvious since only two sets of dishes and such were in place and Gred was already seated. The guards would eat in the kitchen. The same thing they were eating. A bonus to keep them happy.

Hantel was still in the basement, with his own dinner and a book. The room he would use was quite soundproof. Nothing was going to go astray with this project. Jaren sat down and Tossem poured him some wine. Another of the guards brought out the meal.

"The pool's warm enough for swimming," Gred said. "And the park has hiking trails and horses for rent. Some beautiful scenery that you might want to record."

"That sounds like a good idea. I've ridden a few times, but I'd guess the rental horses are chosen for being suitable for novices."

"I'd agree. I did lessons during my summers from university. Enjoyed it but I don't have enough free time now to make keeping a horse practical. I'd like to go out here at least once. Maybe twice, so we can see different areas. Lots of wildlife here as well. You should bring a camera with you if you brought one."

Jaren shrugged. "Didn't bother with one, but I suppose the resort has them for sale." He sipped the wine with a happy expression.

Gred smiled and raised his own glass. "To freedom and happiness!" The glasses clinked together.

Gred called his father. "We're in business," he said as soon as he heard his father's voice. The phone line here wasn't the greatest but he had to let his father know that the first part of their plan was now happening. The few crackles and pops didn't bother him. They were usual for any long distance call.

"No suspicious activity from him before the sedative took effect?"

"All good. Seemed to be happy that he was offered wine without having to ask for it. Like he's a grownup. One of the guards dried the sedative into the bottom of his glass so the rest of the wine was fine. Falg Hantel has him downstairs now, starting to put the drug use and recovery scenario into his brain. Once that's done and tested, the controller, then the impostor. Final testing and we head home."

"What about his trip to Sacarnil? Won't they miss him?"

"Sarnd has the contact number for the person he was going to stay with. One of his friends who is due to graduate next spring, Jaren said during our trip here. Sarnd will phone him at the end of the week to let the friend know that Jaren was called back to work. That's also being factored into the tapes. Hantel is very good at what he does. Lots of detail that keeps the person from ever questioning what happened."

"Good. It's costing us enough. After this is all over, we might need to adjust a few of the upper management. Simpler than this is, I hope."

"I'll mention the idea during the week. What they might need could be similar to the loyalty conditioning, which is pretty simple, from what he's said. Talk to you in a few days."

Gred went down into the basement room after saying farewell to his father. Hantel sat at the control interface with a glass of wine. The monitor showed eight different spiky patterns of brain waves. The computer itself was the size of a wide four drawer filing cabinet. It didn't have to calculate anything, or do much other than control the devices playing the audio tapes and the drugs going into his cousin's body. Some drugs to inhibit memory storage and others that accelerated the process. Several spools of memory tapes sat to one side on a small table. One tape rotated slowly on the separate data transfer box.

Jaren lay on a recliner brought down from the main living room. Straps around his chest and hips fastened out of his reach. Padded wrist and ankle restraints completed his immobility. An intravenous drip fed into his left hand and an automated syringe full of something clear was slowly moving. Another, smaller syringe was full but immobile. Ready to go when the signal came, he guessed. Jaren's head wasn't visible under the helmet and its muffling headphones.

Gred knew the procedure worked by drugs, voice activation and reading brain waves but really didn't care about the minutia, though he'd pretended to be for Hantel. As long as Jaren was made to believe what they wanted by the time they left here, anything that was done to his cousin was fine with him.

"I just told my father you'd started," Gred said. "Anything I can do to help down here?"

"Not at the moment. I'm just making sure that all is well," Hantel replied. "The tape will finish, then automatically start a second run to fix the changes in his brain. By late tomorrow afternoon he'll believe he came here to get cured of his drug addiction with the help of his own very trustworthy cousin."

"Why did you pick poppers as his drug of choice? I thought something more addictive, like the ecstatic drugs that many young men near his age are using would be more effective. Those were the ones that gave me the idea originally."

"Poppers are currently the most common drug among students. Trying to stay awake and alert to finish an assignment is endemic, especially near the end of term. Since he finished university recently and has been under stress to finish the re-analysis of your subsidiaries to prove he is capable and trained properly, it fits better with his personality. He really does have issues with his father, you know. Wants nothing more than to have the old man be proud of him. He will do almost anything to get that attention. Ecstatic drugs would never attract him due to the low regard the older population has for them." Hantel raised an eyebrow. "You didn't suspect the extent of his attachment?"

"I knew he idolized the old man," Gred said slowly. "But I think that I've spent more time with him in the last week than I have in the past ten years. I really don't know him that well."

"Pity. Personal details would have given an extra layer to the tapes, but the controller will be able to access what's needed once that personality is installed. The desire to please his father is also good cover for our impostor. Of course for him it is based on the fear of being punished and sent to one of the worst mines the clan owns without the proper conditioning to ignore the harshness of the situation. I needed to take care in the implementation as that need is overtly similar. The change could be something that would be noticed by a close associate."

Gred laughed softly. "He doesn't have any close friends. That I am very sure of."

"I do hate to keep correcting you but he does have one person who knows him extremely well: Caldon, his main bodyguard. Perhaps not a friend in the usual sense, but still the most dangerous for this enterprise. He's the one who is your greatest danger when the impostor is active. He has been with the serit for six years, day in and day out. Believe me, he knows the boy and would be the most likely person to notice any irregularities. The one who usually drives him might also notice any differences. Discounting servants is the most obvious way to have any plan discovered. If Jaren had a valet, then that individual should also be conditioned to accept any changes without comment."

"Should I arrange to have his other guards removed?" Dead, in simpler terms. "Radem knows people who could do so. A traffic accident would work to keep the reasons hidden."

"It isn't necessary at the moment. It would be a difficult assignment given Caldon's expertise and training, even in traffic. There will be time for that later if it proves necessary. A failed attempt on the serit, with his loyal man taking the bullet for him would be completely in character for them both. Jaren would mourn him as a true father figure. It would also make managing him easier in the long run. Perhaps in a year or so, it should be arranged."

Gred smiled at the thought. "Sarnd would be his next choice as his major bodyguard and he's already my man. An elegant solution to several issues in the future."

Abbreviated movement from the recliner drew their attention. Jaren moaned in pain. Gred looked at the prone figure, then back at Hantel with a raised eyebrow.

"Withdrawal symptoms. Poppers are relatively benign at low levels. With what he was allegedly taking, tapering off slowly rather than the sudden cessation *he* insisted on would have been much more sensible. Fortunately the larger syringe contains a nice little drug that gives much the same symptoms as the withdrawal does. It is necessary, if you're wondering. Physical symptoms must match remembered ones to keep the mind from noticing discrepancies. He'll be going through withdrawal off and on all night if you'd care to watch him suffer. Once the conditioning is done, he'll also have some episodes when he is awake and aware to reinforce the tape's message. You and Sarnd will be involved then. One of the reasons I arrange them is to integrate the implanted memories with new ones with outside witnesses who can refer to it later."

"I hadn't realised you would have him experience physical symptoms, but I'm tired. Didn't have much time to myself since there were events just about every evening at the playpen since the heir apparent was there. I'm here for the rest of the week. I'm sure you'll let me know when he's more aware that he's in dreadful pain." He smiled in anticipation.

"Of course. Sleep well." Hantel returned his smile and returned his gaze to the monitoring equipment. "I'll be heading up to bed myself in a few minutes."

A day and a half later, Gred watched from beside the door to Jaren's room and smiled: Jaren was half awake and in considerable pain from withdrawal thanks to the drug. He'd been there for two hours already, arms curled around his stomach. Sarnd had been in earlier with sympathy and an offer of a popper to take the edge off. All done so the addiction scenario was more believable. He shrugged: More fun for him. He didn't mind seeing his cousin in pain but Jaren had been sweating and that, combined with several days of not bathing offended his nose. He tried to remember to breath through his mouth. Hantel came up beside him with a glass of juice spiked with a sedative. It was time to end this exercise and get ready to install the controller. *Oh well,* Gred thought, *there will be other times in the next few years I can have fun with him.* He nodded, took the glass and went in.

"Jaren," Gred said, shaking his shoulder slightly. It was late in the afternoon but the drapes were pulled to limit the light in the room. A small lit lamp was near the bed. Jaren's pupils were dilated but he did seem able to focus on Gred's face after several blinks. "How are you doing? The doctor says you're almost out of the withdrawal. Hang on. It'll be getting easier now."

"Gred?" breathed Jaren. "Can't believe I was so stupid to keep using the damn pills. Glad you're here to help. Thanks."

Gred picked up the glass of juice but waited to help Jaren drink until the next several sets of spasms eased. This was good. This was very good.

Jaren relaxed as the sedative in the juice took effect.

"Excellent," Hantel said as Gred left the room and shut the door. "We'll leave him here for a little while to get him in the proper state of relaxation, then the guards will take him back downstairs."

"Two runs with the controller implementation?"

"Yes. He's actually an excellent subject for conditioning, you know. Our timeline may be shorter than anticipated. I thought you might like to know that while I use controller as a term to inform my more squeamish clients, you might want to think of that personality as the slave."

Gred smiled. The future was looking very good.

Two afternoons later Bergrant and Sarnd brought the controller to Gred's room. The controller wore only a pair of shorts and kept his head lowered. The padded cuffs still circled his wrists and ankles. His hair was still damp from the shower. Good. He only wanted to smell the new fear from the slave, not stale sweat or piss. "We've got it, ser."

"Good." Gred said from his chair. "Put it there." He used Hantel's neuronal whip to point to a spot on the floor about a meter away from his shoes. The two guards brought their victim over and Bergrant kicked the controller's knee from behind, dropping him immediately. The guards let his arms go as he fell, so the controller sprawled on the floor.

"You kneel before the master," Bergrant growled. "Always." The controller got his legs and arms under him and didn't raise his head very far from the carpet. "Understand?" Sarnd poked him in the side with a boot.

"Yes." came a faint response. Sarnd leaned down and slapped the back of the controller's head hard enough to almost make him fall over.

"Yes, what?" Bergrant said.

"Yes, master." the controller said, his voice fainter. Another slap to his head but he was braced for this blow so he just rocked to one side.

"Louder. The master didn't hear you."

"Yes, master." The voice was louder, but Gred smiled as he heard the fear in it. It was too bad that he had to go back to AR&D for another week of tedium in less than three days. Oh well. He'd make good use of the time he did have.

"You didn't get the work done that you were told to," Gred said. "You were told the price of failure. Now you'll learn it." He stood up and the two guards moved away from the kneeling figure. The whip's thong was now fully extended and it was set to the lowest level. Hantel wanted the slave to take a lot of punishment before he passed out. They had to train the controller that he had no option but to obey their orders immediately and completely. If this wasn't done properly, the controller could do unfortunate things to cause problems later. Hantel had mentioned an early failure to emphasize how badly it could turn out for the people he'd worked for on that occasion. And was why he'd built his own neuronal whip for the training. Gred decided to ask Hantel to build one for him.

"Let's see how many times it takes for you to learn your lesson." He flicked the thong so that it lay across the controller's back. Activated it and watched as the body of his hated cousin jerk in pain. Life was very good. And he would have a lot of fun with the slave once they left here.

Chapter 7

Sanil looked over her cluttered desk at her bodyguard in shock. "What do you mean, Jaren just cancelled our vacation? Did he say why?" Had he found someone else? What about his... She took a deep breath to calm herself. She knew that Jaren loved her. There must be a real problem for him to cancel with so little notice.

Julin Casteron nodded. "Just received a call from his new man, Tossem Sarnd. He said that the serit had been summoned home. His vacation was cancelled by his father. He was sorry but would try to make it here in a month or so for a long weekend."

"That's way weird. Why wouldn't he call you himself? Or call Caldon and have him do it?"

"Maybe he couldn't arrange to be alone long enough to call, and Sarnd isn't in on your secret so he couldn't send a more personal message. And he might not be able to reach Caldon for the same reasons. Jaren *is* supposed to be on holiday but he has no real confidant with him. I'd be happier if even one of his regular people was with him, even the second driver." Julin shook his head, obviously in agreement with her that something was going on.

"It's winter break next week. Let's go home and we can try to get together there. It won't be the same, but I miss him." And he'd better have a very good explanation for his absence.

"I'll make the arrangements, seris."

She was more confused after she reached home. Mom was home but Dad was away terrorizing some hapless subsidiary manager, Julin told her.

"Just needed to get away from the dorm," Sanil told her mom at the dinner table. "Too loud and too many parties to get any work done."

"Are you thinking of finishing early?" Mom asked. "Or do you have a problem that I need to know about?" An eyebrow went up.

"No, Mom, I'm completely fine. But I *was* thinking to finish off early. That's why I took an extra course this fall. I've got good grades in everything. There's a couple of projects that I need to finish off and I can't think straight at the dorm Even the library isn't quiet enough. I can barricade myself in my room here. Not have to brave the elements to eat, for one."

"There are a number of parties," Mom said. "If people know you are in the city, they will expect to see you. Is that a problem?"

"I'll go to a few of them," she said. "Clear my head between projects and get some exercise, which has been spotty the last few months. There's one tonight, in fact."

"Are you hunting for a spouse?" Mom toyed with her wine glass.

"Not really, Mom. Dad scared off most of the boys I know, and the others aren't worth my time. Maybe in the summer, once I've settled into a work routine somewhere." And she would be twenty-two. Mom looked mollified. Sanil hoped her fears were for nothing.

Jaren wasn't at the party. No one had seen him for several weeks.

"Tried to invite him for this," Dayil said after she'd asked after several other missing acquaintances. "Phoned the holding and was told he's still on holiday out in Balgarath, I think. Much warmer than here, I guess. He's supposed to be back in a week or so, the butler said. Wasn't expecting you to be here, though. Glad you could make it."

"Had to get away from school for a few days. The neighbours in my dorm party too much during the break and I have a project I need to finish up. It was either get a hotel room or come home, so I decided to see the parentals, bring home some stuff I don't need any more at school and come celebrate with you."

"A win-win-win, as they say," Dayil said with a smile. The musicians started to play. "Let's celebrate with a dance."

"Of course."

"He's not actually at home," she said to Julin as he handed her into the car for the ride home. She hadn't wanted to stay until the party started winding down but to leave early and looking worried would cause comments. That would be Bad. "Still in Balgarath, according to Dayil. I'm sure something is wrong. This isn't like him at all."

"This is getting stranger and stranger," Julin replied. "I'm in favour of calling Caldon ourselves. He gave me a contact number before he headed out. He's our best bet to find out what's going on. He can access their records or talk to other guards to check up on where the serit actually is. It's totally in character for him."

"Do it tonight." Sanil said forcefully. "I want to know what's happening with Jaren. This is not like him."

Julin came to her the next morning as she worked on her most recalcitrant project. "Shall you go out for brunch, seris?" he asked looking at her sternly. "To clear your head, of course." He knew what she planned to tell her parents as excuses for going out. And had some good suggestions on wording.

"Of course." She put down the file she'd been working on, her stomach tightening.

Caldon met them at an unfashionable eatery near the industrial district. The food was surprisingly decent but the news wasn't.

"I expected the serit to call me to take over once he headed for Sacarnil to replace Tossem Sarnd. He didn't want to add another person to your secret if he didn't have to. I've heard nothing since he left to visit AR&D two and a half weeks ago. I checked, very quietly, with our other driver and the serit was *not* summoned back here. Everyone in Security believe he is still at the vacation estate, having a great time. I asked him to watch for any other mention of Jaren's proposed travel arrangements. He'll tell anyone who asked that I obviously need a longer holiday since I've gotten paranoid. That should divert suspicion if anyone mentions my call since I had to go through the main switchboard at the estate."

"And we were sent an impersonal message by Sarnd that he was heading back here," Julin said. "Can you find him?"

"I am still technically on holiday, so I can head out to Balgarath and see if he's still there. I might have to find Gred and encourage him to tell me where the serit has gotten to if he isn't there." Caldon's teeth ground.

"I think you should check out that vacation estate very quietly," Julin suggested. "Is there anyone you can take for backup? One of my men could go with you if he can't get away. If the seris goes back to university no one would know where he is. Or where I am, in fact."

Caldon shifted his shoulders to look more relaxed and not frighten the other customers in the restaurant. She was sure he wasn't relaxed at all with their news.

"I can contact my usual alternate, Pagil Semant. He's usually our driver. He's also on holiday right now, visiting family. We can catch a flight later today and check out the estate tomorrow or the next day. I did get an overview of the place from the initial briefings so I'm fairly familiar with the terrain. I'll call you once we know anything."

"I'll get us some more help," Sanil said. Both men looked at her quizzically. "I need to tell Dad. And Mom. If there's something wrong, we'll need his help to sort everything out. I don't want Jaren's father involved if we don't have to. The three of us can't deal with a major incident on our own. And I think there is something very, very wrong."

Julin snorted and she slapped at his arm. Nothing happened, but she hadn't expected any other reaction.

"You both have gone to extraordinary lengths to keep this from your families. Why tell them now?" Caldon looked at her and she tried not to squirm on the hard bench seat.

"Because I don't have a good feeling about this and I haven't been able to sleep well since we got the call. That's why."

Her dad's reaction was about what she'd expected since he'd come back from his trip at the worst possible time. Mom would have been easier to deal with alone. Dad, well, there was lots of sound and fury and stomping back and forth, waving his arms.

His home office had been designed with plenty of space for him to stomp and the best available noise suppression technology, upgraded each time new methods were invented. Julin stood impassively but she wasn't fooled. He was worried. Very worried. Her dad's temper tantrums were the stuff of legend in the clan. People had gone into this office and come out broken in more ways than one.

She shifted on the chair she'd been pointed to when they came into the office. Dad had been calm. At least until the door was firmly closed.

"What did you think you were doing, girl? Allying yourself to another clan while you're under age? And with an Alanyo of all things! You know how I feel about Darit and his policies!" His face hadn't gone bright red yet so he was still in control. That could change in an instant.

"And now you know how I feel about Jaren, Dad." She wondered if using Daddy might defuse his anger more. Maybe not. It might make everything worse just now. Baby girl was an endearment he still used for her. Not at the moment, of course.

Paknol Kendef wasn't a particularly tall man but he'd learned early to tower over opponents in person or in the boardroom. He turned back to Julin, eyes flashing in anger. "And you and how many others in my guard know about this? Covered up for her sneaking around behind my back with that whelp of an Alanyo?"

"Don't attack Julin, Dad," Sanil replied to distract him. "I told him what to do and it's not *his* fault you told him and the others on my detail to obey my orders."

"Do not go there, girl," Paknol growled. Her mother rose from her chair at the side of the desk.

"Paknol, now is not the time for that discussion," Barith said calmly. "What matters now is where the young serit is. If he *is* in trouble as a result of his own cousin's actions, then having Darit Alanyo indebted you for helping his son from a difficult situation is not a bad thing. An alliance with Alanyo could have other positive aspects. His father will not live forever, after all. He is over seventy, after all. More a grandparent than a father in age."

Paknol suddenly relaxed and took a deep breath, turning to stare at his wife. Sanil bit her lip trying not to smile at her dad's sudden change of posture. Mom's calming influence on the tantrums was also well known in the clan. Many considered her the only safety valve that Dad had. They might be right.

"As I recall, your father was none too pleased when we started to see each other," her mom continued. "And what was your reaction? To yell at him that you were going to marry me and dare him to do his worst." She smiled at the memory. "Why not eliminate all that shouting and carrying on this time? It makes for a more restful day for all of us. Your doctor did suggest that keeping your blood pressure down was a good idea."

Her dad glowered at them all for several breaths, then turned to Julin. "Casteron, find some of our people near Balgarath and let them know we may have a situation. Tell the whelp's man that he'll have backup if it's needed." Her dad turned back to her. "We'll talk more about any alliance you think you want, girl. Later, much later."

"That went well," Sanil said as she and her mom went back to her suite. "I should have recruited you a long time ago."

"I am not entirely in favour of this alliance, Sanil," Mom replied with a slight frown. "You also lied to me on your arrival. That you were not seeking a partner."

"Well, technically, I'm not, Mom. I've already found the one I want."

"Semantics." Mom Looked at her. "There have been several incidents between your father and ser Alanyo that you and your paramour know nothing about. They have reasons, very good ones even to my mind, for their acrimony. Your actions will not help diffuse that tension. "

"We knew from the start that they didn't get along, Mom. That's a big part of why we hadn't mentioned anything yet. We didn't plan to fall in love. It just happened."

"Who among the Alanyo holdings *does* know what's been going on? His bodyguards, I assume?"

"All but one of them. Caldon and his other guards still haven't told the one who is with Jaren at the moment. Caldon and Semant, his usual driver, both took holidays for the duration of this trip. Jaren just has the new man with him. That's all. No one else. Same for me. All four of my guards have helped cover for us."

"How have you been communicating? I imagine it has been quite dis-crete?" An eyebrow arched up. "I have seen and heard nothing unto-ward, nor has your father."

"Mostly we sent messages through Caldon and Julin. They use pay phones to contact each other to arrange security for our meetings and we send letters via them when we're too far away to get together. It was easy at university, since the library has a lot of odd places to study and they each took an exit. They had to get more creative while we were here during the summers. We did meet at various parties but didn't do much to draw attention to the fact that we like one another."

"And how far has this relationship developed?"

"Not *that* far, Mom." Sanil flushed. "We haven't slept together if that's what you're asking. The past summers we mostly met up at the lookout at Mount Yupin. During the week. With four bodyguards watching us like hawks, there wasn't any chance we could do anything. Mostly we talked. With some kissing." No need to tell Mom just now about that weekend at the seaside. It might distract her in ways Sanil wasn't prepared for right now. Once this was over. Maybe.

"No opportunities for physical intimacy or actual restraint?"

"Both. We were going to wait til I turned twenty-two to let you, Dad and his father know we planned to get married." Well, there had only been one weekend's opportunity for the physical side of things. Those nights had been wonderful but they hadn't taken any chances she could start a child. Still, it had only made them want each other more. She'd really been looking forward to this holiday. For another chance to touch each other. To talk without looking at the clock to tear them apart again.

"At your ages, the height of restraint." Her mom hugged her as they reached her room. "Get some sleep, dear. We'll know more soon."

Chapter 8

The slave cringed as master Gred came near him as he lay on the recliner, completely immobilized. It was going to hurt, he knew.
Whenever master Gred came near him, there was pain, no matter how
well he had obeyed. Master Gred had the whip with him, held lightly in
his hand, slapping gently against his thigh.

"How far have you gotten with the transfers?" master Gred asked the
other master who currently stood on the slave's other side. The other
master's name was never mentioned. The slave just addressed him as
master whenever he was called on to speak. That wasn't unless he was
reporting on a memory transfer. Questions were never allowed. They
told him what to do and if he did it properly, there was real food, and
sometimes he was allowed to swim in the pool to exercise the body and
be tanned for the impostor's return. If he hadn't understood or the masters didn't like how much he'd been able to do, there was pain.

"As you can see, the slave is active right now and the impostor is almost done. I'm double checking the transfer of his teenage years right
now and it is going quite well. The child years I took from a previous
commission. The need for love and approval was quite marked in that
personality. Direct transfer made it go quickly and it makes a good base
for simulating Jaren's need to please his father."

There would be much pain if they knew the slave hadn't transferred
all the primary's memories of his life. What had he gotten for his fourth
birthday? They or anyone, wouldn't care. His romance with the girl, they
would. He didn't really understand why he hadn't transferred the information or simply told them about the relationship. He just knew he
couldn't do that to the primary. She was so precious to him. The slave
liked to go through the primary's memories and see them together
whenever he had a bit of time to himself. Their joy was so pure. Maybe

that was why he couldn't betray the primary's lover.

"Send him up to my room later," master Gred told the other master. "I'll do some checking of my own."

"Nothing permanent, remember," the other master cautioned. "I can't hide physical evidence. He's going back home soon. Everything has to be healed by then. *Not* like last weekend."

"He'll be fine when we send the impostor home," master Gred said with a smile that didn't reach his eyes. He looked down at the slave and the whip's thong trailed across his chest. "Won't you?"

Several hours later the slave was taken to the primary's room and told to shower and shave. Two guards waited outside the door and he knew that others were on watch outside the building. There was no way he could escape. *Hide your goals until opportunities arise* was something the primary had read for school. It made sense here and now.

A meal of soup and crackers waited for him when he emerged wearing a pair of swim shorts. They never let *him* wear the primary's real clothes. He ate quickly, in case the summons to master Gred came before he finished. Hot meals were rare enough that he didn't want to miss any of it. Usually he had lukewarm liquid meals from a can while he remained immobilized in the downstairs room, remembering what the primary knew and moving those memories, slanted to what the masters ordered, of course, to their impostor.

He could also transfer new information to either personality and change their understanding of the event so that it suited the masters' wishes. Master Gred had told him to be sure that the impostor was all that he wanted. The slave ignored anything that they didn't have on the tapes. If they didn't know that information already, he would do his best not to give it to them.

Master Gred waited in his room. The slave went to his knees as soon as the door closed behind him. He'd learned that quickly. The whip he saw in the master's hand was something else he'd learned about quickly.

"I think you should not refer to yourself in the first person, slave. Use the third person whenever you're with me. Only with me, understand? No one else."

"Yes, master Gred. This one understands." The slave looked down and swallowed. Was that sufficient? What should he have said?

"Not quite good enough." The whip had the thong extended so Gred could hit him without leaving his chair. He felt the thong land on his back but it didn't activate. He couldn't repress a shudder as it trailed across his skin, finally dropping off his shoulder.

"Yes, master Gred, your slave understands." The thong snaked across his bare back again, still without activating.

"I'm sure you do. This should reinforce your understanding." The slave felt the thong again. This time pain jolted through him. And again and again until the darkness came.

Sometime later he felt arms around his chest and knees as they carried him down the stairs. "At least he's lost some weight," one of the guards muttered. It was Tossem Sarnd, he knew. He had betrayed the primary, serving the masters instead. If only the loyal bodyguards had come on this trip, he wailed in the depths of his mind. But that would have meant their deaths in defence of the primary, the slave knew. The masters would do anything necessary to create an impostor who would destroy the father master's dreams of an unbroken line of succession from father to son for eight generations of the clan.

* * *

Feneir parked their rental car several kilometres from the estate in a thick stand of pines not visible from the road very early in the morning. The dark sky was starting to lighten in the east and he wanted to be in place before most of the inhabitants woke.

"I packed everything in these," Pagil said quietly, pulling the two packs from the trunk. "Food, water, thermal blankets and cameras with three rolls of film each. What bearing do we need?"

"Three ten degrees," Feneir replied, handing one of the compasses over. "Let's go." The two men picked a tall tree on the line to their destination and set off at a ground-eating lope, their camouflage blending in with the dried grasses and trees. At least there wasn't any snow at this elevation, but higher up, the peaks showed white instead of grey and green. They both wore cold weather clothing since they'd be sitting still for long periods during the night. Easier to remove clothing if they were too warm than to deal with frostbite.

The scattered trees surrounding the house let them approach with ease. There was no sign of an outer guard perimeter. The grasses of the outer field were beaten down by wind and weather, hiding any tracks they made on their entrance.

"Over there," Pagil said quietly, looking toward a line of trees that started along the driveway. "Up in that middle tree. There's a ladder of sorts so we can get up easy."

Feneir glanced at the tree. It had a tree house: in bad shape, it was true, but there was enough of it left to screen someone as they observed the estate. "You go and set up there for now. I'll circle the house, see if I can spot another hide or two. I'll take my pack with me, in case I find a good hide or can make one quickly."

Feneir saw one guard by the back entrance to the house and another on a second floor balcony. He took pictures of each with the telephoto camera but didn't recognize either of them. The light wasn't really good enough for a decent picture but he could try again later during the day.

There was a good vantage point on that side of the house courtesy of a large but now mostly leafless tree. It was a little further away than he liked but that would make their presence less noticeable. With the telephoto lens they'd be able to see everything. The hardest part for that one would be building something to stay warm in during the night. He'd have to climb up to see what could be arranged. A glance at the ground showed several downed branches. There would be others closer to the tree. A small saw wouldn't make much noise, not like an axe or hatchet.

A third hide was needed to cover the other side of the building, where the pool and lounging areas were. He moved further around the house and went into a stand of young fir trees, most of them double his height or a bit more. Each one was too small to support a man by itself, but they were close enough to each other that he could construct a blind of the bits and branches that littered the area. Most guards would dismiss such thin trees as possible hiding places. He almost grinned. The trees would also be a good windbreak and some could be bent over to provide overhead shelter.

He left most of his gear below those trees and continued to circle around until he reached the broken down tree house.

"Any sign of Jaren or Tossem Sarnd?" he asked on reaching the floor of the structure.

"No one showing on this side," Semant replied. "Don't put your foot over there," pointing past his backpack at the wooden floor. "It's rotten. Any luck on your end?"

"Spotted two guards at the back and found two other locations to keep the windows in view. This side isn't very good. Few windows on the house. But it can do to sleep in. I doubt they'd go anywhere or have visitors once they go to bed. One could keep watch here while the other sleeps or go meet up with our contacts. Days in the other hides."

"Any cars visible back there?"

"There's a three car garage in the back. An older four-door sedan and a panel van are parked outside. No idea what might be in the garage. I didn't want to take the chance on the first pass around. Someone might be up early."

"No sign of it from here. Why don't we go around together and you can show me where the other hides are." He glanced at a watch. Five-thirty. Sunrise was in twenty minutes. "They'll be getting up in an hour or so, I figure. Maybe two."

"Agreed. We'll do random radio checks with at least a one hour spacing. One click for okay, two for bug out. We'll compare notes in person here once it's full dark."

"Sounds like a plan." They slithered down the tree and moved into the grass.

The day passed quickly. Five different guards he didn't know were visible, only one actually doing a sweep around the entire house. However, he behaved like he would have to trip over an intruder in order to detect him. An older, short, bald civilian came out and sunbathed for an hour near noon. Feneir took pictures of them all. Later in the day two other guards came out to wander around the property in a properly random pattern. Feneir ground his teeth. He knew these men. One was Sarnd and he didn't know the other's name offhand, just that he worked for the Calnyo branch of the clan and was usually with Gred.

He waited for Semant at the base of the tree house once it was full dark. He'd already rewound his film and had it in a storage canister for transport.

"Saw Sarnd a couple of times," Semant said. "Might have spotted the serit, but the drapes were mostly closed on that room and I couldn't be sure. I managed to drag some decent branches up that tree and made a floor to lie on. Used some pine branches to cushion it and a small tarp to give a roof. Not great to sleep on, but it's better than perching on a bare branch."

"Didn't see him on my side," Feneir replied. "There was a civilian sunbathing by the pool for an hour or so. Took several good shots of him. I want you to take the films in and meet up with our Kendef contacts. We need to know who these guys are. I'll try your hide and see if I can spot the serit or this civilian again once it gets dark. They might leave the drapes open and it isn't that cold here. I'll take up more pine branches to give more of a cushion. Maybe take a nap once everything's dark inside."

"Okay. The third set of windows east of the stairway is the one I think the serit was in. I'll be back well before daybreak and put the car in the same place."

Feneir ghosted back to the large tree and worked his way up into the hide, then pulled up the climbing rope with a bundle of pine branches tied to the end. Lights were on in several of the windows but the third set from the stairway remained dark. He managed some sleep, but kept waking from the noises of trees rubbing against one another or some animal calling for another. Or having branches poke him as he shifted position. He really hated the wilderness.

Semant appeared as Feneir was moving toward the tree house in the last of the starlight.

"Any news?" he asked quietly.

"The Kendef guards set up a relay point in that abandoned motel we passed on the way in here. When I phoned the contact number Casteron gave us from the park visitor's centre, they said to go there instead of driving all the way into the city and back out here. Made life a lot easier. Passed on the film. They had a guy with a motorcycle take it in for processing and analysis." He handed over a closed container.

"Had some hot food. And brought some supplies with me. Mostly bars, but decent ones. Plus two jugs of water with me and another two in the car. Just before I left to come back here, they got a call on the radio. Three of the guards are Calnyo, assigned to Gred, according to the Kendef files. The skinny guy sunbathing? Doctor Sumon. Came up clean at first, but one of the Kendef men at their headquarters recognized him from another operation. He's a conditioner. That led to a lot more information from various contacts. Sometimes works with a gang criminal named Rader Kessem, does other commissions for various operations. They think the other guards might be some of Kessem's people but they weren't positive. They're getting a police contact to check records in the general system. As soon as we get back, can you check in our databases? Varget doesn't have high enough clearance. No idea how they were hired, unless it was the sers Calyno who've orchestrated this whole thing. Though Gred being here is a major tip that they're involved."

Feneir nodded. "Of course. What do they think is going on? What could they be doing to Jaren?"

"Nobody's sure as of four am. If they get a clue, they're going to send someone out here to let us know the plan. And they're looking to see if ser Gred is anywhere we can lay hands on him."

"And his father?"

"Last reported as where he should be, shuttling between home and in the office. Ser Gred's the one in the wind this weekend. Current guess is that he's in that house."

"Didn't see him or his usual guard. Did you get some sleep?" Feneir asked. "I took some cat naps after the house went to sleep and I did a circuit. Everything was quiet."

"Sacked out for a couple of hours while I waited at the motel. Damned lumpy mattresses: no wonder the place is vacant. What's going on here?"

"Not much. There's only two guards on at night outside. One roaming out on the edge of the mowed grass, the other nearer the house. Hourly circuits, going opposite directions. Neither is very attentive. Didn't looked around much that I saw. There are two cars in the garage, one an Alanyo plate, I think." He handed over a sheet of paper. "Copies of the Ident plates on all the vehicles."

"Plan for today the same as yesterday?"

"You got it. I'll go check in at the motel tonight if things don't change in the interim."

"I have two sniper rifles in the trunk now. Sweet bolt actions with silencers. Just in case, they said. We can put one in each of the other hides so we'll have them if we need to take the guards out quickly." Feneir smiled.

It was slightly after dusk when Feneir pulled into the driveway then up the slight hill to the abandoned motel. A sign pointed to more parking in the back so he headed around the side of the main building so no one would see this vehicle and come to see if he needed help. Two guards were on either side of the car three seconds later, weapons at the ready.

"Caldon." Feneir recognized one of them. He'd seen him with seris Sanil for outer security several times. "Any change up at the estate?"

"A car brought someone out this afternoon. My best guess is that it was Gred, but I didn't actually get a visual on him. He must have come out the front door and we were on the sides, since there's a better chance to see everyone that way. Did you catch a glimpse of the occupant to confirm who it was?"

"Not from here, but we did get the plate Ident and sent the information to our command. They have someone closer to your facility to keep watch for it. Come on in. We have food and news."

The dim light in the dining room was easy on his eyes after the drive. He inhaled a plate of stew and two hunks of bread; shook his head at the coffee. He didn't want *anything* to interfere with getting some sleep once he learned whatever he needed to.

"So, do we have a plan?" He asked.

"We're still waiting on a call from ser Kendef. He's going to be contacting your boss tonight. There's a lot of shit happening and he doesn't want any to drop on him. Given their history I'm not surprised. Orders are to get one of you headed back there as soon as possible in case ser Alanyo needs information on any of the bits you can verify. After you eat, I'll have someone drive you to the airfield. There's a late night flight you should be able to make. I have someone getting the ticket and they'll meet you at the check-in desk."

"We still don't have confirmation that the serit is there," Feneir said. "Semant is going to keep the window we think is his under observation, but if there is a conditioner there, he'd have set up somewhere else in the house and the serit is probably there, getting who knows what stuffed into his brain." His teeth ground. "Several weeks here mean that it could be anything."

"We managed to get a copy of the house plans from the county development office late last night. They need a security upgrade. There's a storage room in the basement that they might use for the conditioning set up to keep the ambient noise level down. One door, thick walls and ceiling. Against a corner of the house. Might have been built for wine storage originally. It's the most isolated part of the house." He pulled a set of floor plans onto the table and flipped to the basement level.

"I'll send in two other men while you're gone," one of the other Kendef guards said. "I'm Nargil, clan Kendef's local commander."

"Works for me," Feneir said. "We set up three hides for maximum coverage. Pagil can show you where they are. One doesn't have a good view of anything but the front door. We didn't bother using it once we got the third set up in a cluster of smallish pines. If you have three guys, you can alternate having someone up there to catch a decent nap."

At least he was able to sleep on the way to the airport and during the flight once they turned the lights down. He hated late night flights but knew he needed to be at his best for the interview with ser Darit.

Chapter 9

Sanil watched the crowd swirling around on the dance floor at the Consule's town mansion. The party's guest list included all the local clan heads and their scions to celebrate the Consule's second son's betrothal. Darit Alanyo would be present, if only to be seen and see who else was in attendance. If Jaren was home, he would be here.

It was also their best chance to contact his father without drawing attention to the interaction. She spotted Jaren's older cousin Adnil dancing with one of their female clan dependents. Then she saw ser Darit, standing just a few feet from her. Her mom also noticed and made her way over to him just as the next dance began. Sanil couldn't tell what was said, but the two were soon circling on the dance floor.

After that dance, ser Darit had bowed his thanks for the dance but his eyes were cold. He glanced around and spotted her as Vanis brought her a cool drink. She looked past her escort and stared until he dropped his gaze. Good. He'd better learn he couldn't intimidate her.

In the car on the way home, she couldn't contain herself any longer. "Well, is he going to meet us? What did he say? What did you tell him, Mom?" She made herself shut up by biting her lower lip.

Her dad snorted. "In order: yes, humph and our children are in love but your son seems to be in a great deal of trouble that you know nothing about but we do." He smirked. She rolled her eyes.

"A little more detail than that, dear," Mom said, patting Dad's hand. "I've set up a meeting with him at the hotel Korolian tomorrow morning. He has a meeting at nine with one of his politicos and we'll meet in that same room at ten. Are you sure you want to come with me, Sanil?"

"If I don't, I'd just pester you when you returned home until you told me everything," she replied. "This way I hear all the details first hand and don't have to annoy you later. Plus, I'm an information source."

Her parents looked at one another. Dad waved a hand at Mom, who dimpled. It was the '*She's your daughter, you deal with her,*' wave.

"All right. Ser Darit might be upset at you." That was a given.

"I've been yelled at before by a *real* expert." Dad looked very smug at that compliment. "I'm sure I'll survive. Is Caldon on his way back?"

"Yes, seris," Julin said from the front section of the car, just behind the driver with the other bodyguards. "He's current on a plane and we have someone standing by to pick him up early in the morning. They may have seen serit Jaren at the estate, but couldn't make a positive identification. Sarnd is there so it is most likely that the serit is as well."

Sanil wasn't sure what to wear to the meeting. Five outfits were strewn across her bed when her mother came into her room. An eyebrow raised slightly to question the need for the mess.

"What *does* one wear to an initial meeting with the father of the man you're going to marry and for planning his rescue at the same time?" she asked. This wasn't covered in any etiquette book she'd ever heard of. Then again, she hoped most couples didn't have their problems.

"I'd concentrate on impressing your potential father-in-law at this point," Mom said. "Worry about the rescue aspect later." She pointed to a conservative grey suit. "That one and the pearls from your grandmother. We're leaving in ten minutes."

Sanil grabbed the suit as her mom left.

The hotel Korolian was used for discrete meetings between clan heads and the politicians they influenced and in some cases, owned outright. Or anyone else who wanted to meet with no witnesses and had money. There were five entrances besides the main one and security forces were everywhere, armed with pistols and neuronal whips. *No one* wandered around unescorted and if the staff didn't know someone in one of their uniforms they were likely to shoot or stun first and apologize if needed.

They provided banquet facilities and musicians for any sort of party one could think of. Many weddings were now held under their roofs as the neutral venue allowed for guests who were not quite welcome at a clan's headquarters but had to be invited anyway.

They weren't part of any clan but many regarded them as a nascent clan. They held a strict neutrality in their dealings with *all* the clans. They had branches in all the major cities now, which was a testament to their success and the need by the ruling clans to have their services as a neutral and well-protected meeting place.

"I will take the sera and seris to a most private chamber near your appointment," their guide said. He sounded and looked like a useless flunky but he was also heavily armed and wore a protective vest and radio.

"Come this way, please. The route has been cleared for your convenience." A quick elevator ride using a key to unlock the floor and shortly thereafter they were ensconced in a small sitting room, a gently steaming coffee service and a glass covered plate of pastries already in place. "One of our men is outside to ensure your privacy. Your own men will be in here with you. To use the phone to consult with the outside world, just dial your number. These do not go through the hotel switchboard, sera."

"We are expecting another arrival," her mom said. "Please show him up as soon as he arrives."

"Of course, sera. I will see to it personally." He bowed and left the room. They saw the hotel guard take up his position as the door closed.

Ten minutes later Caldon entered the room, an envelope in one hand. "Sera, seris," he said with a head nod. "We still cannot prove the serit is within the house. His bodyguard is, but this cannot be definitive proof. It is however, our current and only assumption."

"I know, Caldon." Sanil replied. "But where else could Jaren be?"

Ser Darit's eyes narrowed as he recognized Caldon in their party then he turned his gaze to her mom. She ignored his lack of invitation to be seated and took a seat on the other side of the low table between the two sets of chairs. This coffee service sat untouched on the table. Sanil took the other empty chair beside her mother. Caldon moved to stand partway between the two sets of guards. A neutral observer and witness?

"Well, sera? You suggested that my son was missing last night. I called Gred last night when I reached home and left a message for him to have the boy call me today at the office."

Sanil gasped. "Why did you call Gred? We *were* trying to keep everything quiet! Jaren could be in real trouble and Gred has to know and be involved with it! Some of his people are at the estate."

"Hmph." was his reply.

"Let me explain what we know as fact, ser Alanyo," Mom said in her best '*calm Dad down before he explodes*' voice. "Caldon and my daughter can verify other things for you." Her voice became the '*you have pushed me too far and get ready to grovel*' version. "Or we shall leave now, rescue your son ourselves and not bother you further? *Which* would you prefer?" Sanil locked her lips together to keep from grinning.

"Hmph." Ser Darit waved a hand at them. "I'll listen. I may not agree with what you say, but I'll listen. Realized after I'd phoned Gred that I over-reacted." He glanced at the oldest of his guards, a stocky man of nearly fifty, with hints of silver in his hair, then back at Mom. "So. What do you know about my son's whereabouts? And how?" A hint of a glare.

"My daughter expected your son to meet with her two weeks ago up at Sacarnil University or nearby. They, with connivance from their body-guards, have been seeing each other seriously for well over a year." Ser Darit looked at his guards. They all shook their heads or shrugged their lack of knowledge. Then he stared at Caldon and almost spoke.

"That is true, ser Alanyo," Caldon said. "Only three of the serit's guards, including myself, are privy to the details of their relationship. No others in your employ had any knowledge of those meetings." Sanil was relieved that Caldon hadn't mentioned their weekend at the seaside. The staff there certainly knew Jaren had a female visitor. But had they known exactly *who* she was? Maybe not. She concentrated on not looking guilty or embarrassed.

"The news was a significant shock to us as well," Mom continued. "Sanil received a message via Jaren's new bodyguard Tossem Sarnd that you had summoned the serit home and there could be no meeting at that time. My daughter decided to come home for winter break and hoped to meet with your son in town at various parties and whatever else they could arrange. Through various sources, she discovered that her lover wasn't here either. In a welcome, though belated return to clarity, she sensibly told her father and me what had been going on and about their efforts to discover what was really happening at this point. We called your man Caldon to assist in discovering the serit's whereabouts."

Darit's glare focused on Caldon next. "We determined that the estate leased by ser Gred for a week for their mutual holiday was in fact leased for a month, ser." Caldon didn't look ruffled at the glare.

Another glance at the older guard. "Ser Gred has been at AR&D during the work week," the guard said. "But not on weekends and he was not seen in Balgarath, nor has he rented any other rooms under his own name or that of his guards. No one at AR&D knows where he has spent that time thanks to a discrete contact of mine among the guards there. Ser Gred signed out a company vehicle, which he has done in past visits. He does not tend to stay at the facility during the weekends but goes to hotels in or near Balgarath in the past. He is often seen in various bars and other entertainment establishments. But not the past weekends."

"Semant and I went to the estate two days ago and determined that there were still someone in residence." Caldon opened the envelope and brought out a stack of photographs and started to hand them to ser Alanyo. "The identities are written on the back, ser. Several are Calyno men, this is Sarnd, who accompanied serit Jaren to AR&D and this man is Falg Hantel, a conditioner for hire. He had a legitimate practice as Dr. Sumon. He has been linked to Rader Kessem, a businessman who runs several entertainment venues in the past, and is known to work for other groups who do not care about the legal niceties of his profession. We think, but cannot prove, that the other guards work for Kessem, not for the Alanyo holdings as I was led to believe when the vacation was planned. I called the security office before I came here this morning and found that their names were added to the database as new hires the week before the serit left for his site visit. Ser Adnil authorized their employment and waived the background check. He stated he had personal knowledge of their character and background. An enquiry to our police contacts with photographs and fingerprints might provide their true names and who they really work for."

Ser Darit took the photographs and glanced at each one, then handed them on to the older guard. "Banak Steffent, my chief of security," he said by way of introduction. "Is there any reason that Jaren would seek such a person to work with? *Any* reason *at all* to subject himself to conditioning of *any* sort?" Ser Darit stared at them.

"No, ser," sounded their slightly ragged chorus.

"He doesn't do *anything* that would warrant such measures," Caldon said. "No drinking, drugs or other issues. He would never give you cause to be ashamed of his actions, ser."

Ser Darit looked at the security chief. "Call my office. If and when Jaren calls, have my secretary tell him that I am waiting for his report on AR&D. I expected it a week ago. Have him record the conversation. Trace the call's origin, if possible. Let's see if it originates from where Caldon thinks he is. That will eliminate other possibilities."

"Ser." the security chief went over to the phone and dialled.

"That takes care of that loose end." He turned his gaze to Caldon. "If he is in that place, can you get him out safely or should we wait until he reappears on his own?"

"I have been thinking a great deal of what we can do while watching for him, ser Alanyo," Caldon replied. "I propose that we kidnap him as soon as possible. All the guards at the house will either die or be taken with us for questioning. As for Hantel, we should try to keep him alive for now to help undo what he has done already."

They all looked at Caldon in various stages of incredulity. Sanil blinked. "Why?" she asked, her voice shaking. "What do we gain?"

"We get the serit out of their hands hopefully before whatever is being done is completed. Partial conditioning is always easier to undo. More important, we get copies of the tapes and related data and we get *time* to understand what they've done to him before he is free to implement their programming. As well, depending on how involved ser Gred and likely his father are, we get conformation on who else is involved and why. It is, I believe, our best way to control the situation without our enemies being aware that we know anything of their plans."

The security chief put down the phone and came to stand by ser Darit. "I will have their financials examined, ser. *Very* quietly. That would be the most likely motive to do something to serit Jaren, although I am unsure at their tactics. Why condition serit Jaren? What could they do to him that would change anything or not be detected once Caldon was back with him. How or what can they gain if ser Alanyo is still alive?"

"If they started the process when he first arrived at the estate, they've had over two weeks to re-arrange his memories." Mom said. "As such, Jaren should not be allowed to wander *anywhere* unsupervised until we know more about what truths he believes. Your murder followed by suicide would be very tidy from their point of view. That would leave Gred and his father in complete control of your clan and all its assets. Even if the suicide was not completed, Jaren would still be in prison or mind wiped as a murderer and patricide. Your health might be affected if he failed to kill you, so they would normally take on some of your duties until you recovered. That could turn into more control of various parts of your holdings than they currently have." She turned to Sanil. "This means no secret meetings. I want your word on this, dear."

"Definitely." she replied instantly. "No secret meetings unless all of you know about it and have someone watching us." She tried not to grin at the incongruity of the idea. Then again, all of their other secret meetings had at least two other people present for each of them. Four guardians ensuring nothing happened between them. Except at the seaside house. She repressed a smile. This was very serious.

"Hmph. I think the kidnapping might be best at this time. It keeps our awareness of the plan from them and everyone else who might be watching. Do you have enough men to arrange it and a secure location?" Ser Darit asked Mom. "Jaren knows many of my compound guards and this must seem to be the act of a third party. We can construct a narrative later to account for any inconsistencies."

"We'll manage. Caldon and Semant would be useful in determining the extent of any changes in Jaren's behaviour. They can also be outer security thus limiting the number of guards to be let into the mission." Mom looked at Julin. "The men we have stationed near the estate should be more than enough, I believe. Will you lead them for us, Casteron?"

He nodded then turned to ser Darit. "Do you want any of the serit's captors to remain alive, ser?"

"No," ser Darit replied. "They should all die for their actions. If you are able to keep the conditioner alive until he can confess what he has done and tell us how to undo it, that would be acceptable."

Julin glanced at Caldon. "We shall begin our preparations, seran and seris. We will bring the serit home."

Chapter 10

Gred looked at the message slip in the middle of his desk when he walked into his office that morning. It had come in late Sunday night, according to the time stamp. From Darit, telling him to tell Jaren to call in, right away. Damn! He wasn't Jaren's secretary! He took a deep breath. Hantel had said the conditioning was almost done anyway. It should be possible to activate the impostor for a few minutes to make the call and deflect the old man's attention. He took another deep breath and reached for his desk phone.

"It is possible," Hantel said to his proposal. "Everything has been loaded, it's simply been cross checking for the last two days. Thank you for not causing any noticeable damage. The slave was slightly stiff and in pain from your coaching yesterday but nothing serious. You will also need to be careful when you check in with the slave not to let anyone suspect what is going on. Just remembering the pain will be enough to keep the controller in line."

"I will. Here's the old man's number at the office." He recited the numbers and listened as Hantel read them back to him. "Get him to call in as soon as you can arrange it. Let me know what happens. I'll be in this office most of the afternoon. Remember there's an hour time difference. Do not call between noon and one-thirty Hantil time. The old man's always at lunch then and Jaren knows better than to disrupt that ritual."

"It will take me an hour or so to tidy up from what I was doing when you phoned. Don't worry. It will all be fine."

Gred kept an eye on the clock and couldn't concentrate on the stack of requisitions he was supposed to be checking. Finally, the phone rang.

"All done," Hantel said happily. "The impostor behaved exactly as predicted. Anxious that he might have done something to make Darit angry but cool and calm as he spoke." A satisfied sigh came clearly through the line. Good that he had pride in his work.

"Did you record the call?"

"Of course. You can hear it later if you want. Best of all the old man didn't even bother to take the call himself. He wasn't in the office, it seems. Left word with his secretary to remind Jaren about a report on the playpen that was overdue. The secretary asked when he'd be back at work and suggested that he'd better have the report done and ready to hand in when he showed up. I think I'll leave the imposter active for the afternoon to see how well his cognition is coping. Might as well have him begin writing up the dratted report, eh? That way the primary won't have any hints that his life's been changed for the worse."

"Good idea. Tell the guards to bring him in the morning of the sixteenth, before noon, directly to the airport. One of the holding's planes coming in early that afternoon and I've booked us onto it. I'll phone to confirm the time either late night on the fifteenth or early the next morning. There are people from other subsidiaries aboard, so we won't be as alone as I'd like but he can also work on the report then."

"He *will* be the primary when you meet him," Hantel reminded him. "Don't forget or all of this will be wasted effort."

"No, I won't." He would find plenty of other times in the next few months to be alone with the slave. He smiled.

* * *

Feneir checked his pistol again. He, Semant and Casteron would be in the outer ring tonight, just in case Jaren was awake and could recognize them. Pagil managed to spot the boy in the third room during the afternoon. He was dressed casually, looking thinner than before, but clearly visible. He seemed to be working at a desk until someone appeared to summon him to dinner. He went downstairs but never came back up.

"Ready," echoed through seven men. Each man had a silenced pistol as well as a neuronal whip. If they could use the whips, their victim would be completely incapable of resistance for at least three hours as they were using the highest setting possible. They could be quietly shot at leisure with no chance to warn the others. Once Jaren was free, or rather, safely kidnapped.

Each man knew his target. Feneir followed his man for a minute to be sure of his spacing. Then the whip's thong snaked forward and wrapped around the guard's throat instead of his chest and he fell instantly as the charge jolted through him. Feneir unwound the thong and retracted it, then checked for a pulse. Nothing. Oh well, he thought. He pulled his silenced weapon from its holster, put it against the guard's temple and pulled the trigger. It sounded like a cough. If they waited until the raid was over, the autopsy might show the delay. And the lack of blood around the body would also be obvious. This all had to hold up under serious scrutiny by personnel who would have no knowledge of the truth. The police might also become involved at some point but the cleanup team would dispose of all the inconvenient evidence. With luck, the owner of the property wouldn't know that anything had gone wrong. He took a calming breath.

One of the Kendef guards came out of the side door ten minutes later and waved. "All's clear in here," he called loudly. "All the targets are neutralized."

"Where's serit Jaren?" Feneir asked as he joined the other man.

"He's in the basement room we figured was being used for the conditioning. On the machine, so we can't move him yet. The doc we consulted said just stopping a tape could really mess up his mind. Markine just started photographing the data books. There's about fifty or sixty pages worth. Hantel fell against the fireplace when the whip hit him and he's dead. Sarnd was in bed and is unconscious for now. I thought you might want to shoot him yourself. One of my men is watching to make sure he stays put. Just in case he wakes early."

"I appreciate your consideration. That will be my first stop." It might make him feel better, but he doubted it. Still, he'd promised ser Darit that all of these men would die.

Feneir stood just outside the door to the small room in the basement and peeked around the corner. Jaren was only wearing a set of underwear and his head was obscured by the helmet. The clothes Jaren had been wearing earlier lay neatly folded on a side table. A guard was just draping a blanket over the unmoving form.

"How much longer does the run have?" Feneir spoke softly, in case.

"Nearly done, from what I can tell," replied Markine. "We're replacing the tapes on all the spools here with blanks. That's the second addiction one." A second data transfer device was running at high speed to remove the tape from the original spool for Gred to tidy up once he found out what had just happened. A stack of spools labelled 'blank' lay on the floor.

"He was *not* an addict!" Feneir tried to keep his voice down.

"I know, I know, Feneir. But they made him think he was." Markine spread his hands in a placating gesture. "You have to admit it makes a heck of a good reason why they were here so long. We found this thing as well." He picked up a neuronal whip from behind the data transfer device. "It's not a standard model. Don't know which of them brought it, but it means we let them all die too easily."

Feneir held out a hand but it was hard to unclench his fist. "May you spend eternity in torment, Gred." Markine waited until he was back in control before handing it over.

"The control knob has a lot more settings than usual. Haven't tried it since everyone's already unconscious or dead."

Feneir rotated the knob, hearing far more than the usual ten clicks. He should have waited until Tossem Sarnd had woken up to shoot him. Starting somewhere non-lethal and painful. And doing it again, and again. "What's on the tapes beside the addiction cure?"

"Those are labelled early life, addiction and controller. The worst is that one." He pointed at the slowly spinning tape on the actual data transfer device. "Go look at the label."

Feneir did, his breath hissing in anticipation. It took several tries to read it as the tape spun on. He finally puzzled it out: *Impostor*. He turned to see another guard enter and beckoned him to follow. When they reached the main floor, they stopped next to one of the dead guards. Blood pooled under the corpse's head and Feneir smiled.

"Do you want to take anything from the serit's room?" the other guard asked. "Clothes, personal items and so on? I'm sure he'll want all that back."

"Not for now. We'll leave all his personal items for the response teams to send back to the compound. He should wear what was down there with him when he wakes up. And make sure his belt has the lock-picking tools so he can escape in a few days. He's all we need. And kidnappers wouldn't really care what he's wearing."

"True. We'll get an instant photo of the serit with today's paper for our first ransom demand when we get him off the machine and dressed," the guard said. "Maybe one of Sarnd for effect, showing we knew who his primary bodyguard was. We'll set the downstairs room up so it looks like we didn't bother looking in there. After all, why would we search the whole place when we'd gotten our quarry upstairs?" Feneir nodded.

"As soon as that tape finishes, we'll swap it out and get the serit loaded into the back of the van. We added a couple of blankets and pillows from the closet upstairs for padding. One of our guys is almost a doctor. He'll make sure the serit stays unconscious for as long as we need. How far is the clinic from here?"

"About three hours drive, your commander said. We'll stay there until the mind doctor can figure out what those bastards did to him. We have people looking for a good place for him to escape from once it's safe to let him do so." Feneir took a deep breath. "I'm going to head back to the motel and call in. Let everyone know that we have him back and the basics of what we found here. They're not going to like it." That might be an understatement. Another deep breath. Maybe once Jaren was at the clinic, he'd get drunk. He already knew it wouldn't help how he felt, but at least he'd have a couple of hours free from thinking about what he should have done to prevent all of Jaren's suffering. Including going on a holiday by himself. Having fun. His teeth ground together and he growled in anger. Then he kicked the body nearest him in the face.

The trip back to the motel took less time than usual since two of the guards were now ferrying vehicles forward to the front door now that the estate was theirs. Casteron returned with them.

"I'll call Ser Darit first, then the seris," Feneir said as he opened the car door.

"If he's up," Casteron said.

"I doubt he went to sleep. Not tonight."

The ser's private number at the house went to his bedroom and his office in the house, nowhere else. It was answered on the first ring.

"He is safe, ser Alanyo," Feneir said. "There was a conditioning tape running. As soon as it's complete, we'll be on our way to ser Kendef's medical facility. Is there anything we need to know?"

"Gred made a call through the AR&D switchboard just after he arrived at work this morning. Jaren phoned in at eleven-fifteen. My secretary took the call, as we agreed. I listened to the tape when I returned from lunch and there was something *odd* about how Jaren spoke. It was him, and yet it didn't sound quite right. I can't explain it. Sanil also said there was something different about him when she heard the tape. The trace wasn't conclusive because the call wasn't long enough, but it was near your location so that's sorted."

"There was a tape labelled impostor in the conditioning room, ser. The conditioned personality might have been the one who called in as a test, not the original Jaren. We'll need a copy of that conversation for the doctor. Ser."

A heavy sigh was followed by the click, then a dial tone. Feneir handed the phone to Casteron so he could call Sanil and her parents.

Feneir looked around the living room of the small house they'd rented just outside the medical facility. There was plenty of room for the six of them here since the facility wasn't really set up for patients with guards. It catered to mid level employees who needed or wanted conditioning for work or personal reasons. Jaren was currently in an isolation room with two guards outside at all times. For their shifts, Feneir and Pagil would be paired with Kendef men, who would be the only ones to go into the room in case Jaren woke up unexpectedly.

He was sedated and had tubes running in and out to feed and keep him hydrated. He was also handcuffed to the bed by his wrists and ankles and still wearing the same outfit he'd been taken away in. The facility staff had *not* been pleased by their orders. Casteron had suggested it before he'd left to return to seris Sanil and Feneir had agreed. In theory, that is. Then he found out the team had carried Jaren up to the base of the stairs where they'd decided that he would be surprised and subdued, dropped him to the floor from several steps up, put the cuffs on him, then dragged him out by his feet to the waiting van. A number of scrapes and cuts had resulted. His teeth ground together as he remembered the admission. He'd nearly gone after those men but Casteron and Pagil had grabbed his arms.

"Handcuffs leave marks, Feneir. The serit could be examined by outside doctors once we get him back home," Casteron had said. "Same with the clothes. Kidnappers wouldn't take a change of clothes for him. They might strip him, but he needs his belt since that's where the lock-picks are so he can escape once you're at the other site. All the physical evidence has to fit the scenario, Caldon. Even though he's not moving much, there's going to be some chafing on his wrists."

"Let's *not* tell the seran about that part yet." Feneir said slowly. "And that also means we'll have to use a whip on him, to explain why he went down without a fight. Or we'd have to keep him sedated for a week to let all the damage heal. I'd rather get him back to the compound as soon as possible. He would have fought. Maybe not well enough to get away but he knew enough to try to break free at the start of an attack. We spent some time on what to do when he was younger."

"Should we do it now or wait until you're ready to wake him up for the escape?"

"I'd rather wait. Disabling one arm is probably best. If he was hit in the chest, he wouldn't be able to do anything toward escaping for a couple of days after the hit. Using his arm actually limits the total damage and the time to recovery. At setting four, the residual pain should be in line with the total time line."

Wednesday evening he sat in on a conference call with the senior conditioner that the head of the Kendef clinic had on staff, the seran, and their security chiefs were listening in.

"I've studied the notes and skimmed the tapes, seran," Doctor Hallent said. "It's well done work and I'll let certain of my colleagues quietly know that there may be others out there who've had something similar done to them. It's going to take time to understand what they've done to the serit. Even more time to understand how it all works. What I *can* do at the moment is to add the kidnapping scenario to all the personalities. I'll use the same protocols and inductions that Hantel used to minimize any discontinuity. Then you can arrange his escape and get him home. We'll try to unravel everything while your other matters are settled.

"It will take time to transcribe all those tapes and understand what their plan was. I do need to warn you all now that it may not be possible to undo all or even most of the damage. We may need to do a complete personality wipe and use what information we have to reconstruct him. Which will include some data from these tapes." The silence was only broken by line noise from the phone.

"How long will it take you to add the kidnapping scenario to all of his personalities?" Ser Alanyo said finally.

"Another day at most, seran. It's a small addition but I'm checking the layout of the estate with the guards that escorted him here to ensure I get the details correct."

"His papers for the playpen report were still on his desk, seran," Semant said. "For the scenario we've developed, he was working on the AR&D report most of the day and into the evening. He'll have gone downstairs for a snack and run into at least one of the kidnappers at the bottom of the stairs."

"We have arranged a place for the serit's escape," Feneir said. "It's near Bayside Chemicals. It's actually closer to the estate than Balgarath the city is. Serit Jaren knows a handful of the guards at Bayside and the weather is fairly clement for this time of year. There is an abandoned ranch that we'll be using as our hideout. It's about five kilometres away from the intersection of two major highways. There is an unmanned rest stop that few people use at this time of year. It also has a phone that works. Transit time from Bayside's facility is an hour or so."

"How obvious is the rest stop?" Sanil asked. "We don't want him heading in the wrong direction or just getting lost in the woods."

"It is well lit intersection and the lights are visible from the ranch, seris," Feneir said. "There is also good cover near the roads that he can use to hide while he waits for the team to pick him up. The danger would be if he thinks that the kidnappers are aware of his escape and are hunting him. He might try to catch a ride to get out of the area quickly or double back into the woods to head for the city lights which are also visible once you get near the highway."

"We plan to have cars stationed on both roads just in case, seran. Driven by either a young couple or two women," Senmat said. "We have

the first set of pictures and a ransom note on its way to you. It will be delivered to the main offices the day after you're officially notified that
he's missing. Does anyone know when ser Gred is supposed to pick up
the serit from the estate?"

"They are leaving for Hantil at the end of the week, but Gred has
probably arranged to have the guards bring Jaren to the airport directly," Steffent said. "That would fit his profile. He'd expect the doctore
to make his own way home and he might have been scheduled to do so
before the serit would leave. When he doesn't get an answer to his
check-in calls he'll head over there or at least send one of his people.
That will trigger the official notice. They'll need some time to tidy up the
extra conditioning tapes and so on so if only one man comes out he
might delay calling anyone but Gred. We have observers in place and
taps on the phone line in the house and the ones at the ranger station.
The two hides we used were reinforced and the third was repaired
enough not to be hazardous. I wonder who Gred will call first when he
sees the mess? Us or his father?"

"I'd bet he calls his father," Feneir said. "To alert him that they'll
need a new plan, or to revise this one. Again."

Chapter 11

Gred got out of the car at the estate and slammed the door. He was fuming. Timing was now tight and he'd been forced to drive all the way out here instead of sleeping in and relaxing for the morning. No one had answered when he called to confirm the flight time. He'd called five times, starting late yesterday. They had to be at the airport in a little over three hours and the drive itself was over an hour. There might be traffic once they reached the city. He did *not* want to stay here another week or have to take a crowded commercial flight. That would be a stressor on the conditioning. He opened the main door and recoiled. The guard behind him pulled him back and had his weapon in his hand before Gred could process what he'd seen in the foyer.

"Wait in the car, ser," he said, pulling his weapon. "Talsin, back the car out a hundred meters."

Gred didn't argue as the other guard escorted him back to the car and moved it away from the house, then remained poised to flee if there was further danger.

About fifteen minutes went by and Bergrant reappeared and jogged over to the car.

"The guards are all dead, ser," he said, "But worse, I can't find serit Jaren. He might have gotten away, but I would have to say it's more likely that he's been kidnapped."

"Any sign that the kidnappers saw the basement room?"

"I took a quick look down there. No sign that the serit had been there when they attacked. The door was closed. None of the tapes were removed. Falg Hantel was in the living room and I think he died when he fell against the fireplace. Everyone else was shot in the head, ser. We *have* to report in. We can't hope to cover any of this up. Not with us being expected back today."

Gred took a deep breath and his brain started working. "Is the phone line still up?" At the guard's nod, he reached for the car's door handle. "I think we should call in and I'll have to confess to the drug intervention to explain Hantel's body," he said. "Secure the premises but don't touch what you don't have to on the main floor. While I call in, you both have some work to do. Get the tapes into the trunk but leave the one labelled addiction treatment. Get Falg Hantel's neuronal whip and any other implements he had that don't fit with his cover persona. Check his room and both vehicles to be sure. Then do a sweep outside and see if you can spot where the kidnappers were watching from. Don't mess with those sites, just identify where they are. Whoever did this must have had the house under observation for a while."

He clenched his fists. They had been so close to success with this plan! But now, it might be better: no Jaren to complicate their inheritance meant that his father would inherit once Darit did them the favour of dying. And he would be recognized at the ultimate heir. So, this wasn't that bad a development. He wished he'd thought of it years ago. It was much simpler than what they were planning.

He let the panic he'd felt earlier colour his voice. The trouble number was a free call from any phone anywhere in the world and there was always someone on duty.

"Alanyo Holdings, how may I help you?" came a female voice.

"This is Gred Calyno. I came to pick Jaren Alanyo up from our vacation rental and everyone is dead. Jaren's missing." He made sure to speak quickly, as if he was out of breath.

"What is the nearest subsidiary or city?" she asked, still calm. He wasn't sure how.

"AR&D near Belgarath is about an hour away. We were supposed to catch a company plane from the city airport this afternoon. I'm not sure if there is somewhere closer."

"We have a team coming by helicopter and another two by car, ser Calyno. Arrival time for the helicopter team is half an hour. The cars should be approximately one and a half hours. Is there anything else you require?"

"I need to notify ser Alanyo."

"That is being done by one of our other operators, ser. Please remain near the phone if possible as more information will be required. Main security has been notified."

Gred hung up the phone and took a deep breath. He'd call his father once the incriminating tapes and other items were safely tucked into the trunk of the car. He headed up the stairs to check Jaren's room. Where had the little shit been when the attack happened?

"Dad?" he asked ten minutes later. "We have a problem. A big one. Jaren's missing, probably kidnapped and all the guards are dead. So's the doctor. I couldn't cover it all up so I called in. Nothing else was possible right now but getting the other conditioning tapes out of here and making sure nothing of Hantel's can be linked to anything out of the ordinary seemed a priority."

"What? Are you all right, son?"

"I'm fine. I just arrived and found everything a mess. Bergrant thinks it must have happened much earlier this week by the smell of the bodies. I have no idea, but I hadn't spoken to Hantel or anyone here since I called about Darit's command to contact him."

"Did you call security already?"

"First thing. We now have the other conditioning tapes stashed in my car along with my extra gear. The response teams will be here soon," he checked his watch, "Half hour by helicopter. I expect to get a call from Steffent any minute."

He heard his father drumming a pen against his desk. "Good so far, Gred. Any idea where Jaren was when they found him?"

"Not sure. But there were papers up in his room as if he were working on his AR&D report. They were on the desk, not in his case where they were when last I saw them. None of his stuff had been packed. Hantel was keeping the impostor operational to do some final testing when I last talked to him, so that's probably where Jaren was."

"Phone me back later if you can," Adnil said. "I'll let Kessem know what's happened. He may be able to find some information on who would dare kidnap a clan heir. This *could* be our opportunity if Jaren doesn't come home."

"I know. Talk to you soon, Dad," Gred replied.

The phone rang almost as soon as he hung up. "Hello?" he said, trying for an *oh, shit, I am in way over my head* tone.

"This is Chief Steffent," growled the voice. "Just got the word. No sign of serit Jaren?"

"None. The guards were all shot and the doctor died in the living room when his head hit the fireplace. My guards think this happened earlier this week, but we can't be sure. I last spoke with Jaren early this week in the morning to relay a message from ser Darit."

"Doctor? Why was a doctor there?"

Gred made himself take an audibly deep breath. "Jaren asked for my help to set this vacation up. Why we're out here instead of someplace with more to do."

"Why?" the growl repeated.

"He was popping," Gred rushed the words out. "And he wanted to stop using them. I knew some people who'd used a conditioner to make sure they never did whatever their problem was again. He's been here for a week or so."

"And before that? What was serit Jaren doing with his holiday time?"

"Withdrawal," Gred said in a small voice. "Cramps. Really bad ones sometimes. He tried to taper off while we were at AR&D but I had no idea he'd been using so much. He took the last one the day we left there. It was over a week before the cramps eased off. I didn't want to leave him with just the guards here but I had to get back to the facility or there would have been questions he didn't want anyone to ask."

"I will inform ser Alanyo," Steffent said. "We'll hold the plane until you and your men can board. Wait until the teams get there and answer any questions they have. Once they check in with me, head for the air-field and bring all of serit Jaren's things with you. Understand?"

"Yes, Chief." He still played meek and shaken.

The phone went dead and the dial tone returned. Gred smiled. All would be well. If the kidnappers could be contacted and paid off prop-erly, then Jaren would be dead. He regretted the waste of money this set up had cost, but having a wonderful explanation with no ties back to them for Jaren's death meant that first his father, then he *would* sit in Darit's office. The old man couldn't hope to engender another child at his age. He wrinkled his nose at the smell from one of the bodies as he went back up to his room to pack the rest of his weekend gear to put in the trunk of his car. And his neuronal whip. It wouldn't do to have the response teams see *that* implement.

Chapter 12

Jaren realized his left arm hurt. His head felt odd, as if he still slept. He lay on his right side and something stank nearby. Opening his eyes revealed a bare light grey room. He was partly covered by a scratchy blanket and when he reached up with his right hand, pain shot up his left and he groaned. Metal clinked. He'd been handcuffed. Why?

Panic had him sitting up far too quickly and the smell intensified. Another spike of pain. When he was able to looked down, he saw an open floor drain a few inches away and his pants were pushed halfway down his thighs.

Swallowing, he bit at his lip. What had happened? He'd been going downstairs, then there had been... men in dark clothing. Masks. Kidnappers. And something had hit his arm. Pain, lots of it. Then nothing. He shut out the world, squeezing his eyes shut to deny reality. Even as he did so, he knew it wouldn't work. He had to be strong. Like the father master would want. Assess the situation, that's what he had to do.

They hadn't taken his clothes or shoes, which Feneir had said sometimes happened. He wasn't just handcuffed: similar cuffs circled his ankles and a short chain linked them. A longer chain went from that one to an eye-bolt set into the floor. It took several minutes for him to get onto his knees to pull up his pants, zip the fly and fasten the belt. Every time his left arm moved the pain arched up his arm and he froze until the pain abated. Tears stained his cheeks but he couldn't risk more pain to brush them away. He sat back down and pulled the blanket back around his shoulders.

A screeching sound drew his attention. A wide metal door opened halfway and two men entered. Both were dressed in dark colours, with ski masks covering their faces and dark goggles. Both had pistols holstered on their right hip and neuronal whips on the other. One had a slim newspaper tucked under his arm, the other had an instant camera around his neck.

"Our little serit's finally awake," said the one with the newspaper. His accent was that of the lower classes. "It's 'mazing. Knew the toffs like to laze about but this took the record!"

"About time," the second said. A similar accent. "He can sit up for his picture today. Make a nice change for your daddy, kid."

"Today?" Jaren asked. He tried to be calm, to act as the man the father master would expect him to be. He wanted nothing more than to cry from the pain and panic he felt.

"And he can talk." said the second. "Legibly, too."

The first voice dropped a copy of *News Now!* onto his lap and the second voice stopped about two meters away.

"Hold the paper up and look at the camera," second voice said. The flash blinded him for a second and first voice grabbed the paper before he could see any of the headlines or determine the print date. It was thinner than he thought it should be: probably just the first section, with the main headlines. Proof he was alive today.

"Okay," said the second voice as he pulled the film cassette out of the camera and checked his watch. "Just make sure it came out, then we're done for now."

"Did your bodyguards ever go over kidnapping protocols, kid?"

"Yes, they did." Jaren replied.

"Good. Remember them. You knows the score. Don't give us trouble, especially don't try to see any of us and eventually you'll get home safe. Do anything we don't like and you get hurt. Understand?"

"Yes."

"This is what it feels like when we're not happy," second voice said. They jerked him to his feet. His abdomen exploded in pain before he could brace for the blow and he couldn't breathe. He fell as they released him and landed on his left elbow, sending another wave of pain up into his shoulder and chest.

"You think he gots the idea, boss?" asked first voice.

"Might need a reminder later on," said second voice. A ripping sound. "Picture's good. We'll see how he behaves tomorrow."

Jaren heard them walk past his head then the door screeched closed. He heard a few footsteps, then nothing.

Once his aches subsided, Jaren opened his eyes and looked around. There wasn't a lot of light in the room but there were a couple of windows high up the wall to one side. A bare light bulb hung from the ceiling near the door with a string to turn it on.

He had to remind himself that the father master would expect him to

get all the information possible so the guards could catch the kidnappers
once he was released. He paused. He didn't want to think of how much
trouble he'd be in if the father master had to pay a *big* ransom. He'd
never be able to pay back that debt, especially if the master father found
out about the poppers. If he could get away without costing the father
master much money it would go better for him in the long run. He took a
deep breath despite the pain in his stomach.

'*Assess conditions before taking action*' was one of the Suntz quotes he'd
thought was pretty obvious at school. Here it made a lot more sense.
There was a blanket, even if it was scratchy and not very thick. It was
cool in here on the concrete floor. There was just one door with its des-
perately-needing-oil hinges in the room. The walls looked like brick,
painted over and over until the brick shape had lost much of the defini-
tion. Up was a low ceiling, partly fallen down in one corner with lots of
water staining on the walls and floor beneath it.

The floor was concrete, stained with dirt and other things. The floor
drain was now about a metre away with a metal canteen near it.

So much for surroundings. How many days had it been since they
took him? He felt his chin and cheeks, trying not to move his left arm
any more than necessary. Several days, maybe a week? He'd seldom gone
more than a day without shaving once he went to university so he
couldn't be sure of how many days' growth this would be.

Other aches made their presence known as he became used to the
ache from his arm. Several other sources were on his back and he didn't
want to try to reach around to feel them and jar his arm again. Both
wrists had abrasions from the cuffs that were angry and red.

Jaren looked at his left arm again and pulled up the sleeve as far as he
could. The area around his elbow was swollen and bruised. The kidnappers had neuronal whips with them. One must have hit him in the arm.
That must be how they'd captured him. He tried making a fist but
couldn't get his fingers to move that well. Flexing his wrist or elbow just
sent jolts of pain up his arm up into his shoulder. This time he did grimace. The whip must have been on maximum. Feneir had told him about
neuronal whips when he'd gone over the kidnapping protocols. He never
imagined that he would ever need that information.

The fact he was here meant that all the guards at the estate were dead
or maybe they'd just been left to recover from whip strikes. No. They
wouldn't risk leaving any witnesses alive. Dr. Sumon was probably dead
as well. They wouldn't have bothered to keep anyone other than him
alive. An injured witness might alert the trouble line, or worse the police, and send the rescue teams in before the kidnappers could make
their getaway. There weren't many roads in the surrounding area. Even

if they'd taken out the phone at the house, there was a ranger station for the wilderness preserve not that far away. He'd hoped to do some riding there but the severity of the withdrawal cramps had scuttled that idea. Swimming, or rather floating in the shallow end of the pool, had been the best he'd been able to do most days of his so-called holiday.

What could he *do* now? He took a slightly deeper breath, his stomach still aching. Both kidnappers were taller and heavier than he was. Even at his best, Feneir always beat him at boxing or wrestling and these guys were stockier than Feneir and looked like they fought all the time. There must be several others he hadn't seen yet. Likely there were six or maybe even eight of them. One of him, already injured. They would have needed that many to take out all the guards at the estate. Direct action wasn't possible. Not now, and maybe he'd just have to sit here and wait for the father master to pay the ransom. Or not.

Jaren looked back at the canteen. He was thirsty. That he could do something about. Then he would review what he could remember about the kidnapping protocols. It was the only way he could push back the fear and dread that filled him.

*　*　*

The slave lurked in the back of the impostor's thoughts as he dozed with the blanket wrapped around him. This was terrible! The masters would be angry at *him* no matter what happened. How the slave could have stopped them, he didn't know, but the masters would expect him to do something. He tried to open the eyes but he had no control over the body while another personality was active. He certainly didn't want to be active and actually feel the pain the impostor was feeling right now. He knew how much neuronal whip strikes could hurt, even days later from a low setting. This one had been from a full strength hit. How many days had it been? He wasn't sure, but possibly four or maybe five days. All he could do was make sure the primary had the same memories as the impostor. The memories of the actual event wouldn't need any adjustment, but what happened now might. The imposter couldn't handle much stress, though concentrating on the protocols had helped.

Could he activate the primary on his own? He had been trained not to swap who was active unless he had specific orders. He imagined doing it and the sharp pain of the whip arched through him as a reminder that he only allowed to do what they ordered him to. At least this time the pain of the whip went away when he stopped trying to do what they forbade. That was a relief.

There was something he *hadn't* transferred before now that might be useful to the imposter in his effort to escape. The primary had played something called E&E with his bodyguards. A grown up version of hide and seek, he thought. It hadn't been on the tapes, so he hadn't looked closely at those memories and hadn't bothered to transfer them. There had been too many other memories that he had to alter and transfer that they *did* know about. He didn't want to be punished for not doing all they had ordered. Maybe something in those memories could help them get away. He would go through them now and hope they were useful.

* * *

The door wailed in protest as it opened. Jaren looked up from the floor, still stiff and chilled. A cool breeze had eeled its way through the hole in the roof some time ago. Two men appeared in the opening. They were different from yesterday's by their size and bulk and also wore ski masks and goggles. The one by the door had a pistol holstered at his side and a neuronal whip swinging in his other hand. Jaren clenched his right fist as hard as he could to keep from showing the fear that filled him. The first one had a canteen in one hand and an open can in the other. He also had a holstered pistol at his side.

"Grub. Best eat it, kid. It's all you get til tomorrow," said the guard in front. He set the canteen and can down and took the other canteen away. The door protested as it closed and he could hear their footfalls moving off to the left. Back to whatever place they were using as a barracks.

Jaren took a deep breath, then unwrapped the blanket and had to untangle it from the eye-bolt chain before he could go over to the food and water and bring them back to the blanket. He'd moved as far from the stinking drain as he could.

Consule's Chunky Beef Stew, the label said. He'd never seen an example of their wares before and had certainly never eaten anything they produced. He did know that the Consule clan had a major presence in the food industry. He let facts about them float to mind as a distraction while he started to eat. His stomach growled but he didn't bolt the stew. Or he'd vomit it back and that wouldn't help the stench in here, or give him enough energy to pay attention and maybe discover how to get away.

So. The clan Consule. They had chosen to use vertical integration, so they owned or otherwise controlled farms, ranches, processing plants, canning facilities and the transport to get their products to market. No other clan could interfere with their production and distribution channels. He'd known some of their extended cousins at university. Not bad company during a dance or to work on joint projects with, but none were particular friends of his.

The stew was pretty bland but maybe the masses who ate it didn't know how to make better. He alternated water and stew, using his fingers to get the chunks of vegetables out and sipping the gravy. He did encounter two pieces of what he was fairly sure was beef. He couldn't identify several other lumps and only the thought that he needed to keep his strength up made him chew and swallow them. As he tried to lift the canteen after setting the empty can down on top of the drain to block the smell, he realized he'd been drugged. But by which? The water or the gravy in the stew? He looked at the can, then tried to wrap the blanket around his shoulders and lay down before he passed out.

***

The slave tried to start the transfer of how to play E&E but couldn't stay awake either. Drugged sleep wasn't the same as natural sleep. It shut down *any* active personality. Tomorrow, he thought. Surely the imposter would nap during the day, from boredom if nothing else. Then he could find all of those memories and transfer them.

Chapter 13

Feneir watched with clenched teeth as two of the guards took Jaren from the trunk of the car into the dilapidated outbuilding they'd decided to use as the holding area. That Jaren was still unconscious didn't bother him. At least that's what he told himself.

It was the memory of using the whip at his side to disable Jaren's left arm. And the fact that the two Kendef guards were dragging Jaren by the wrists instead of carrying him, adding to the scrapes on his back. He let them do their work, arranging Jaren by the drain and locking a chain from the eye bolt to the ankle chain. He went outside to bring the camping gear from the other cars in to the semi-useful farmhouse.

He watched from the spyhole they'd established as the guards took the *'he's alive'* picture the next afternoon, then punched Jaren in the stomach. He followed them back toward the farmhouse, grinding his teeth. "Did you *have* to do that?" he asked when they were well clear of the outbuilding so there was no chance of Jaren hearing them.

"Hit him?" Markine said. "Yea, we did, Caldon. Real kidnappers would use physical intimidation at the outset so we have to. He's fine. Soft tissue hit so he might get a bruise. A little out of breath for a minute but not really hurt."

"I'm surprised that he was awake," Naren said. "I thought we'd just need to do another static shot."

Feneir took a deep breath as they entered the farmhouse. "I know. I hate all of this."

"Hate those really responsible. We know this isn't easy on you, Caldon," Markine said, putting a hand on Feneir's shoulder. "You've been close to him for years."

Semant came in and took off his coat. "Perimeter is good." He looked from Feneir to the other guards. "Everything okay here?"

"We punched him in the stomach after we took the picture," Naren said. "Window dressing."

"Was he different?" Semant asked. "Chief Steffent said the call from him on early last week was probably the impostor."

"Hard to tell since he didn't say much," Feneir admitted. "He needs the lock-picks from his belt and he'll have to climb out that hole in the ceiling to get to the roof. Once he's that far it's pretty easy to get away from here. If I was a real kidnapper this place is marginal to keep someone with the training we gave him. He always had a good eye for cover when we practised E&E."

"You never made his expertise known outside of your team and a few Alanyo guards to be your hunters?" Feneir nodded. "Smart of you." Naren replied. "His left arm's still pretty useless and it's hurting. He might need another day so he *can* climb out. He'd never bother with that door unless we gave him a can of penetrating oil and a week to use it."

Feneir used the crack in the wall to watch Jaren off and on during the day. As time went on, he was confused by the passive boy. He hadn't tried any of the techniques he *knew* that Jaren had learned to get a sense of the limits of his reach and to exercise his left arm. The more he tried to use that arm the faster it would be useful. He'd *told* Jaren that. He'd even thought about giving him a low level jolt so he'd know what it felt like and how to work through the pain and stiffness. The knowledge that ser Darit would not approve had kept that offer from being made. And even if ser Darit had been away visiting various subsidiaries, the other guards and servants would have known something was wrong and that would be almost as bad. Same for doing it while they were at university. The other students would spread rumours far and wide.

He stopped that train of thought with a muffled curse. *Jaren* knew what to do. This *wasn't* the Jaren that he had trained. The impostor must still be active. He slipped down from the box and hurried back to their quarters. They might have to change the scenario and fast.

"Chief Steffent," he said ten minutes later. One of the Kendef men had rigged a connection to the old phone line that allowed them to call out with a phone run off the car batteries. "Can you bring ser Alanyo into this call?"

"What's up, Caldon?" Steffent replied.

"I don't think the impostor has any knowledge of E&E. He doesn't know there are lock picks in his belt and that means he *can't* escape. And I'm pretty sure he is the one we have here. He's not the real Jaren."

"Damn. I'll get the ser."

Feneir waited impatiently, tapping his foot against the table leg, Semant beside him.

"I'm here, Caldon. On speaker. This Jaren doesn't remember what you taught him about evasion techniques?" Ser Darit sounded testy.

"I don't believe so, ser. His attitude this afternoon was too passive. He hasn't done a number of things I was sure he would do if he was given *all* of Jaren's memories. The plan for his escape depends on him having those memories. Can someone ask Doctor Hallent if he has any idea why the impostor doesn't have those memories?"

"Will do. Do you want to stage another raid?" Steffent asked. "It'll take us a day or three to get enough men to you that we can do it properly. I don't want to let the Bayside men that far into the secret. I trust them, but taking the serit away in triumph from the rest stop is one thing..."

"That would make it more likely that someone will make an incautious comment. I agree that a raid may be necessary," ser Darit said. "Give him another day or two and if nothing happens we'll rethink. Banak will let the Kendefs know about the progress, or lack thereof."

"Anything from the Calyno we need to know, ser?" Feneir asked.

"I enjoyed tearing a strip from Gred on the addiction cure," said ser Darit, the pleasure evident in his voice. "We've brought both of them into the compound, in case the kidnappers wanted to have a pair instead of just one hostage."

"And it means we have complete coverage of everything they say and do thanks to the covert microphones," Steffent said, also sounding very satisfied. "Their offices in the tower have also been bugged. Harder to get at their mansion, but they won't be home for the next week or so. Not as much of a problem. I'm sure we can get at least the telephones before they move back. Ser Adnil contacted Kessem from the office to see if he knows who's responsible for the kidnapping. They'd like to pay the kidnappers extra to arrange that Jaren not survive the experience. They may be hoping that ser Darit would have a heart attack, possibly with help, once he gets word of serit Jaren's body being found."

"*They* are not going to survive their plot," ser Alanyo said, all emotion gone from his voice. "Tell Caldon about the loan."

"They borrowed a half million from Rader Kessem to buy into an electronics company. It was one ser Adnil wanted the clan to invest in a few years ago but ser Alanyo refused. KRT Electronics. Now they're making payments on the loan, but the prototyping isn't going as well as they'd hoped. The company may never have a viable product."

"How much of the company did they buy?" Feneir asked.

"About twenty percent. And they're paying ten percent interest, compounding daily. We have their financials and they don't have any idea we know anything. The loan isn't under water yet but it'll be there in a little while if nothing changes. I think that's all our news for now. Check in at the regular time."

That evening Feneir watched Jaren eat the drugged stew. Then he lay down and wrapped himself in the blanket before the drug knocked him out completely. He walked out into the darkness and stared at the out-building for a long time. How could he keep Jaren safe when he had to do such things to him? Would he be able to admit it once this was over? And would Jaren ever be able to forgive him for the deception?

Chapter 14

Gred looked around the suite he'd been given in the main house in the compound. A separate room with a bed big enough for a threesome with room left over, a walk in closet, large bath and a comfortable sitting area with a phone and a vid unit. A man's suite, burgundy patterned wall paper and dark mahogany furnishings. Good paintings, mostly landscapes. Nothing frilly or dainty.

"The bar is fully stocked, ser," the footman said as he set down Gred's suitcases. "I or one of the other servants will restock it as needed. If there is a brand you prefer, just let us know. If the brand is not in our cellar, it will be brought in."

"Thank you. I'm sure everything will be suitable."

"One of the other servants will be here shortly to unpack your case. He will act as your valet during this visit. If your time here is extended, your own man will, of course, be brought in."

"I hope this visit won't be very long," Gred said with a slight grin. The footman bowed slightly and left. Having his own man here was preferable, but he could manage for a week. Maybe more. But he had to unpack the neuronal whip before anyone else opened the case.

Uncertain where he could hide it for now, he stared at the bed. He slid the whip between the two mattresses at the foot, pushing it far enough in that someone making the bed wouldn't disturb it.

He went over to the bar and his eyes widened at the selection. He fingered two bottles. He'd had each of them exactly once. Too expensive for daily sipping. Now he had unlimited access to them. Not that he would drink to excess: that would not be in character. Besides, it would be a crime to guzzle any of the superb whiskeys that bar already contained. He poured a small amount into a glass and sniffed the amber liquid. Rolled some on his tongue. Bliss.

He smiled: staying here also let them conserve their own resources to ensure they'd keep paying down on the principal. Too bad most of their wealth wasn't very liquid. Every spare credit helped just now.

He'd stayed here occasionally in the past, but never more than a couple of nights at a time. Now he and his father were living here, where they should be. When he'd been picked up at the airport, the car had come here rather than to their own house. He wasn't all that surprised when he thought about it but tried to seem nervous about the change in plans. Since it meant he'd also been in danger from the kidnappers.

"Ser Darit wishes to speak to you, ser," the same footman said after tapping on the door and opening it at his response. He hadn't realised how much time had passed. The footman led the way to Darit's office. What was the man's name? Hartner, that was it. He'd see what use he could make of the man in the next few days. Having a source inside the house would make countering Darit's plans much easier. Another plus to not having their own servants with them. Then again, their own guards were here, and socializing and living with the locals. He was sure they'd get caught up on any gossip. While they drove to the office would be a good time for learning if anything interesting was happening.

Hartner knocked on the office door and opened it. "Ser Gred." Gred followed him in and the door closed behind him. A deep breath, showing a little fear. He was surprised he didn't want to endure this lecture. Another reason to hate Darit. And Jaren.

"Sit," Darit ordered. Gred sat on the edge of the visitor's chair and leaned slightly forward. The posture of someone who knows he screwed up and expects to get reamed for it.

"Tell me everything you saw when you arrived at that estate."

Gred started to explain. In as much detail as he could remember. He eventually ran out of things to say without repeating the obvious.

Darit was still looking at him and he allowed himself to squirm and swallow nervously. He'd relaxed inside, though he still showed the uneasiness that was expected.

"What about these – poppers? When did Jaren start abusing them?"

"I honestly don't know when he started, ser. Probably at university but he never told me about that part. I think he was ashamed that he did use them. When you had him start to analyze those subsidiaries, he began using them more, to be sure his reports were the best they could be. To please you and show he was, worthy, I guess. Then he decided he had to quit. I guess he finally realized that his use was out of control."

"And why didn't you tell me the instant you knew about it?"

"He asked me not to?" Gred tried for an '*honestly, I was just trying to help'* look. "He realized he'd screwed up and wanted to make it right *be-fore* you found out. He didn't want any hint of it to get out into clan or public knowledge. I think Sarnd was getting the pills for him since he graduated, ser. From my own time at university, poppers are readily available, especially around end of term. That's also why he didn't take Caldon with him on our trip. Jaren didn't want him to know about his addiction either. I have no idea how Jaren managed to hide his use from him all this time."

"Humph."

"Lots of people do at least one really stupid thing in their lives, ser. Jaren started taking pills. I was trying to help him. We're family. We're supposed to help each other, aren't we?"

The floodgates of invective opened. His stomach coiled into knots.

When he was finally allowed to leave the office, he immediately saw his father coming along the main hallway. "Dad." A sigh of relief in case anyone was watching. Honestly, he never wanted to go through anything like that ever again. That should be the last from Darit. He was sure that Chief Steffent would have other queries. But those would be easier to manage. They couldn't yell at him.

"Survived your trip through the wringer?" Dad was concerned.

"Yes. You?" A faint smile to imply that he was all right.

"Not so much wringing in our talk. He accused me of having an idiot son, but that comment worked both ways, more on his side than mine. I want you to know that I am proud of you for trying to help Jaren. It's not your fault that someone else screwed with your plan. Come on up to my room. I'm just down the hall from you, I think." His father gave him a quick shoulder hug.

"I would like to hear about what happened this morning," his dad said once they were in his sitting room. The arrangement of the suite was identical to his but had light green wallpaper and medium dark accents instead of burgundy and mahogany. "Get a drink. You deserve it after all you've been through today. Seeing the bodies couldn't have been easy for you." Gred noticed the same excellent brands of whiskeys and poured one of the others that he'd always wanted to try. His stomach relaxed as the liquid teased his taste buds.

He went over the story again but with extra details.

"Any word from Kessem?" he asked quietly. That was one drawback to being here. Too many servants they didn't know or control. He'd have to be careful what he left in his room. He'd need to keep a suitcase to keep his whip in at the very least or maybe he should send it back to the house. That might be best. He wouldn't have any opportunity to use it until this fiasco was over and done and hiding it in the bed wasn't very secure. Then again, just holding it would let him remember what he'd done with it. Worth the risk to keep it, he decided. He'd keep the case locked while it was here and after the servant had put his things away. At least for a little while. He could always send it back later.

"He was surprised someone tried, let alone succeeded. There haven't been any rumours of anything like this in the works. He'll try some other contacts in the next few days. The last kidnapping of someone high up in the clans was nearly six years ago. They were caught at the payoff site and turned into mindless drones for their trouble. The whole organization was demolished and the clan kept all the assets that the gang had. They also turned all their dependents into indentured for the costs of the clan operation and for a couple million to the kidnapee for his pain and suffering, such as it was. They won't pay off in two generations, and it could take three or even four. That risk tends to limit who might want to try anything like that next."

"What about lower level executives?" He'd never paid much attention to that section of the news sheets. "Are many of them taken? I haven't heard of anyone we know vanishing."

"They've never been much of a target, but there are one or two a year. Lower ransom to split but a better success rate of getting away with it, I've heard. Last one from our clan was maybe twenty years back, I think. I wonder if they might have been after you and took Jaren by mistake or simply because he was there and you weren't."

Gred took another sip of his whiskey, savouring the taste. "The lease *was* in my name. But why would they attack on that night and not when they *knew* I was there on the weekend? That was really bad planning on their part if that were the case."

"If they missed seeing you leave, maybe they *were* trying for both of you. More risk with the extra guards on the weekend but having the only two potential heirs to the entire holding would have been quite a coup. Maybe that's why Darit is so peeved. A week's holiday there wouldn't be much of a security risk, but the longer time may have been what attracted the kidnappers' notice in the first place."

Bergrant rode in with him when they all went to the offices the next day. There had been five vehicles in the convoy and all the guards had rifles and neuronal whips in addition to their normal weapons. Gred waited until they arrived to speak to Bergrant as the others headed up the elevators.

"Did you destroy the tapes?" He asked in almost a normal tone so no one would be curious about the conversation.

"Yes, ser. Put them on the fire myself when I went back to the house with your extra luggage. That tape sure burns quickly. Almost lost an eyebrow. All that was left went into three different dump bins."

"You'll find a bonus in your pay this week. Same for your partner." Another car came in and more executives passed them. Gred raised his voice back to normal. "I'd like you to stop by the house and get me some more clothing. All I have is what I had taken with me to AR&D."

"Of course, ser. I'll phone and ask your valet to pick out what you'll need for a longer stay. Your things from the trip are being cleaned. Shall I bring all of your cases back later?"

"I'll keep one with me," Gred said. "The smaller one should do. Once I have a few more suits and things to wear I won't have to worry about getting my laundry done."

"I'll call as soon as you are settled in upstairs, ser," Bergrant replied.

Gred was surprised to get a summons to Darit's office after lunch.

"Come in, ser." Steffent said as he approached the door. Gred could see his father already seated by the coffee table in the corner of the room. "The kidnappers finally dropped off a ransom demand."

The sheet of paper was covered with words and letters cut from a newspaper. It looked like a child's collage. What it said was much more chilling. At least, he hoped that was what his expression conveyed. Inside, he smiled. This was everything they'd hoped for.

'So you finally noticed the heir was missing. Congratulations. It'll cost you a million to get him back. We'll send instructions for the transfer later. Try anything we don't like and he'll be missing a few parts when you see him next.'

There were four instant pictures of Jaren, one in the trunk of a car with a paper next to him. His wrists and ankles were cuffed and a short chain linked his feet together. He wouldn't be able to run, never mind walk with that kind of restraint in place. The other three pictures were close ups of Jaren's face and the relevant days' papers. Darkening of his jaw showed beard growth. A bruise on one cheek also changed, from reddish to purple and yellowing. A fifth picture showed Sarnd's body, lying in a bed, the same initial paper on his chest and a hole in his forehead. The pillow below his head was dark with fresh blood.

"They had to be watching the estate from a distance to know we'd just found out what happened. And they have someone here in the city to deliver this and likely others," Steffent said. "No picture from yesterday or today, so he's probably within two days' road travel, which is still a huge area. The envelope was dropped off down at reception by a kid who said a guy had paid him twenty to do so. I have someone tracking the kid down so we can hopefully get a description."

Gred looked at his father and tried not to smile. He hoped Kessem managed to find the kidnappers first.

"It seems that they were just after Jaren," his father said.

"Maybe," Steffent replied, not sounding convinced. "I'd rather not take chances based on that note just now, sers. Keeping you all safe is our priority. Next is getting the serit back. We've recalled Caldon and Semant from their holidays. Neither is thrilled, as you might guess. They're going directly out to check out the estate and work with our people, since they were both near there, rather than waste time coming back here and returning."

Shortly after a supper no one had really eaten, Hartner knocked softly on Gred's door and came in. "You wish something, ser?" he asked. Gred had sent for him a few minutes ago.

"I'm hoping you can help me," Gred said with his most innocent expression as he rose from the couch. "I'm really worried about my cousins. Ser Darit's not a young man and with Jaren in such danger, I'd feel better knowing a little ahead of time if something happens and I or my father aren't here."

"Are you asking me to provide information?" the man asked. A little wariness, but that was expected. Spies didn't survive long in any clan.

"I suppose, yes," Gred said. "Just to let his cousins know if there's anything we can help with, you understand? Nothing secret, of course. Just a warning. If there's something we can do to help."

"I suppose that would be all right," Hartner said slowly. "You are family, after all."

"Thank you," Gred handed the man a *100 note and a small sheet of paper with a phone number. "That's my valet's number. He'll relay anything you can send us if I'm not here."

"Of course, ser." The money disappeared into a pocket and he looked at the number. "I'd be happy to let you know anything I can."

Chapter 15

The slave found a wealth of material when he could finally immerse himself in the E&E game memories. It wasn't a simple game as he'd thought at first. It was serious training in how to get away from enemies, like the kidnappers. The impostor's drugged sleep finally changed to natural sleep and the slave woke while the impostor slept on. He started to work.

One of the best memories the slave found was from when Jaren was seventeen, in the early summer. His father had been away for business and Feneir had arranged a night exercise. The slave immersed himself into the memory, taking it into himself so he could transfer all the knowledge and experience to the impostor. He'd need it to get them away from here in one piece.

* * *

"The object tonight is to reach that big oak near the greenhouses," Feneir said as they walked to the little house on the grounds. Jaren didn't know why or when it had been built but it did serve as a convenient place to have their E&E lessons or do other things his father might not approve of. "For this exercise, it is next to the compound wall and some branches are large enough that you could use them to get over the wall. Touch the tree before the guards catch you and you win."

Jaren smiled. "And the challenge to slow me down?" There was always one now that he was getting better at sneaking.

"Starting from inside here, and you'll be handcuffed. To the stair railing this time." Feneir opened the front door and pulled the set of padded handcuffs from his pocket. He pointed at a hassock in the sitting area. "Grab that and come over to the stairs."

When he'd done so, Feneir looked at him, then at the stairs and moved the hassock halfway along the balustrade. "Get up there and raise your arms. Stick your hands through the uprights." He went up the stairs and Jaren stepped onto the footstool, then held his hands up high, then slid them past an upright.

"So, it looks like I'm going to be hanging around for a while," he said with a chuckle. Feneir smiled at him.

The first cuff snapped closed and Feneir glanced down past him. Then he smiled and grabbed his other hand, closing that cuff. He stood and went down the stairs and stood behind Jaren. "Comfy?" he asked.

"I'll do," Jaren replied. The hassock vanished beneath his feet and Jaren's knees thumped against the wall.

"You have an hour to get to the goal or you forfeit." Feneir took the hassock back to the sitting room. "See you soon."

"And I'll be at the tree when you do," Jaren called as he heard the door close. His first task was to get his weight off his wrists. The stairs had uprights every few inches but he easily wedged a foot up onto one of the outside stair treads. If Feneir had chained his ankles together, that might not have worked. Something to think about for his practices. The wedged foot gave him enough leverage to get one hand onto an upright.

He scrunched upward and was soon balanced on the outside of the stairs with his hands near his waist. He reached for the lock-picks in his belt. These handcuffs were padded, unlike real ones, but the locking mechanism was the same. Feneir had said he wasn't going to get them both in trouble by having Jaren's wrists bandaged when his father came home from his trip.

The cuff locks were simple, once you knew the secret. He put them into his pocket and the picks back into his belt. Soon he was at the back door, looking through the window from the side of the door. Something caught his eye. One of the guards was there, hiding behind a tree.

Someone would be near the front door, also well hidden. Jaren smiled. There *was* another way out of here. One of the larger trees was quite close to an upper bedroom window on the side of the house. He thought that if he could get onto that tree, then he'd be away without the watchers noticing. He went upstairs and eased that window open. It was difficult but he managed to grab a resilient branch and worked his way overhanded to a major limb. He also realised that he needed to do more arm strengthening exercises. He hated pull ups but they'd help develop those muscles. He was able to transfer to another tree before coming down to ground level to further confuse the watchers. He shook his hands to get more blood flowing into them. More pull-ups in his routine for sure.

He moved from tree to bush to another hiding place until he came to one of the gardens. There was no cover available but low bushes and flowers still in bud. He could crawl through, keeping lower than the bushes but that would take time. Going around would also take time and he knew that Feneir had at least four men after him and the timer was counting down. Sunset had been two hours ago but one moon shone at half phase through clouds. That was good and bad. He could see better but so would the men trying to catch him. He paused at edge of the garden, then spotted an empty barrow and smiled. A piece of luck. He stood up, unzipped his jacket, then slouched as best he could over to the barrow and trundled it toward the greenhouses, muttering as if he'd been told to fetch it when someone else had left it littering the garden.

Once he was clear of the garden and back in shadow, he tucked the barrow under a tree and started to move silently toward the big oak. Just as he was about to touch it, a bright light came from the garden behind him, flashing back and forth.

"Serit?" Feneir's voice carried through the darkness. He was still on the other side of the garden, Jaren thought with glee. "Toadstool. We have to cancel. All bets are off. Your father is on his way home. He'll be here in about twenty minutes. You'll need the time to clean up and be ready to greet him. Sorry, there's no time to finish this."

Jaren set a hand on the tree and took a deep breath. Feneir had used the 'this is real, not a trick' codeword. He'd fallen for the trick once. Feneir had pretending he'd been forced to call for him by the enemy. "I'm away, Feneir. And I'm already at the tree," he called. "All done and I win!"

"Drat," came a cheerful voice about five meters away. It was one of the house guards. "How'd you get past the garden area? I didn't see you at all on my side."

"Went straight through it." Jaren said. "With the barrow." The guard came up to him and smiled.

"Good use of camouflage. Let's get you back to the house," the guard said. "And we owe you fifty."

"That means I get to try the rifle again." Shooting was a possibly useless skill to acquire but he enjoyed the challenge.

* * *

The slave smiled. This would definitely help them get away. A little fear that the father master might not approve of his being out that late, and that the guards might be punished for teaching him how to use a weapon and the new memory would be complete. They might survive this and not have the masters or the father master angry at them.

* * *

Jaren felt the push of something against his leg and opened his eyes.

"Stand up." It was second voice from yesterday morning.

He had to roll onto his right side before getting to his feet to keep from being tangled in the eye-bolt chain. Every movement of his left arm still hurt but he thought it might be less than before.

"Good boy," said first voice. A newspaper was slapped against his chest. "Hold it like that and look at the camera." The flash didn't catch him as much by surprise this time.

"Just stand there, boy." First voice took the paper back from him and they retreated to near the door to wait until the instant picture finished the development cycle. They left without a word. Jaren sat back down and wrapped the blanket around his shoulders.

There was a slight noise beyond the door. Jaren stood up as quickly and quietly as he could. They hadn't *said* he could sit down. He was so stupid, he thought. He had to obey them completely or they'd hit him again. He didn't want that to happen, not now. That would make it harder to get away and he needed to get back to the father master before he became more angry and maybe paid the ransom. Jaren tossed the blanket near where he remembered it had been when they left. The door squealed open.

"Good boy." it was second voice this time. "I guess even a serit can learn how to behave." He tossed a bar at Jaren's feet. "You can sit down now. Enjoy your breakfast, boy." The door shut and the footfalls, louder now, trailed off, still to the left.

Jaren sat down and regarded the bar. He didn't recognize the brand name but that didn't surprise him. Meal replacement was in smaller print. His stomach growled and he managed to open the wrapper one handed. The bar wasn't bad if you liked chocolate flavoured chewy sawdust. He ate about half, needing water with every bite to get it down. He'd save the rest for later, in case this was all he had until darkness brought another can of drugged stew.

His left arm still hurt but he recalled Feneir saying that if you exercised the whip-affected area it sped recovery, not retarded it. It sounded insane but he trusted that Feneir would have told him the truth. He made sure the blanket hid his attempts. The father master would be happy when he escaped, but he couldn't do it unless his arm was better. The only way out of this place was the hole in the ceiling. The sound from breaking one of the windows would be almost as bad as trying to open the rusted door. He wasn't sure he'd be able to fit through the windows even if he could break one silently. If they had been lower to the ground it would be worthwhile to consider them.

After a while he couldn't stand any more pain from his arm and tucked it against his side and blinked tears away. He sipped from the water in the canteen and used the drain. It stank worse now that he was using it and there wasn't anything he could put over it to keep the smell away until he had another empty stew can.

He retreated as far as he could from the hole.

By the time the can of stew and a new canteen of water arrived that evening, Jaren was surprised at how much more mobile his arm was. He made a fist. Not the same strength as his right hand, but much better than yesterday or even this morning. Should he try to escape tonight? He managed to remove the lock-picks from his belt and practised unlocking the handcuffs while pretending to sleep during the afternoon.

His left hand ached more when he moved it so it was harder to get the right cuff off. The ankle ones were easiest, since his left hand only had to keep either cuff from moving. He might have to leave the right wrist cuff on if he tried to escape tonight. He tried to not look at the ceiling hole while studying how he might manage to get up to the rafters to pull himself up and out of here.

He didn't think the kidnappers could check him once it was dark, assuming that he was drugged into sleep. The light near the door couldn't be turned on from the outside and the door's screeching hinges gave ample warning of someone coming in. The only way they could see him without making any noise would be to look in through one of the windows. They were dirty enough that it would be hard to see in. Plus, there wouldn't be any light in here except for any moonlight that made it past the dirty film or down the hole in the ceiling. He decided to try. If his arm was up to it, he'd be away. If not, he'd put the cuffs back on, finish the gravy in the can, sleep and try again tomorrow night. And every night until he was out of here.

***

Feneir looked up from cleaning his pistol as Pagil came into the farmhouse kitchen with a smile. "I think Jaren is going to try escaping tonight," his partner said.

"How do you know?" one of the others asked, stirring a pot of stew on the camp stove. He tasted it, grimaced, put down the spoon and added some seasonings from a selection of bottles.

"He ate, then wrapped up in the blanket but he's still moving. Not much but he's definitely still awake. I think he's picking the cuffs and waiting for full night."

"It all depends on him getting out the ceiling," Feneir mused. "If he can, great, but if his arm's still not up to it, he tries again in a day or so."

"Smart." Markine said. "He was exercising the arm today while I watched. Tried to hide what he was doing but I saw his arm moving."

Feneir felt the smile leave his face. "How?"

"How what?" Pagil asked. He turned from pouring coffee.

"How does the imposter *know* to exercise his arm and how to find the lock picks? I'm sure he didn't have that information yesterday. He just sat or lay there and did nothing all afternoon. Get back to the spyhole and see what he's doing," Feneir told Pagil. "I'm going to call in and let them know what's going on. They'll alert the hitchhiker cars but they should tell them to stand by until we know he's leaving."

"How could he suddenly know how to escape?" ser Darit asked. "Or is he the real Jaren now?"

"I have no idea which version of Jaren he is right now, ser," Feneir responded. "All I know is that he was exercising his arm during the afternoon and Pagil saw him working on the restraints just now. We're on standby until he makes it out the ceiling. It might not be tonight, but we're prepared if he does get out."

"I'll have someone contact Doctor Hallent and see if he has any idea how it's possible for the imposter to learn new things so quickly. Let me know if he can make it out. I want him back here as soon as possible."

"Of course, ser."

Feneir moved down the corridor toward Jaren's prison. His shoes had soft soles and he rolled on the sides of his feet so he made no noise as he walked. He saw Pagil on the box they'd moved into place to reach the crack in the wall. A lens inside the crack allowed them to see what happened in the room with no chance that Jaren could detect them.

Pagil looked toward him and grimaced. He carefully stepped down from the box and allowed Feneir to take his place. There was a little light in the room from the moon shining in the windows.

Jaren was leaning against the back wall, holding his left arm against his body. He looked up at the hole in the ceiling, then back down at his arm and shook his head. He pushed off the wall and came back to where the can of stew and the restraints were. He untied the blanket from around his waist and put the canteen down next to the stew can, reattached the leg cuffs first, then the handcuffs. Once they were back in place, he took a long drink of water, then drank from the stew can, lying down almost immediately. Minutes later, his breathing slowed.

Feneir motioned Pagil to follow him. They didn't speak until they were back in the farmhouse.

"He almost made it a couple of times," Pagil said, shaking his head. "But he couldn't get his left hand to hold a grip on the rafter. Needs two hands to pull himself up. Didn't get any exercise in the past few weeks, so it's not surprising he's lost muscle tone. I think his arm is still hurting too much for him to use it properly."

"Smart kid, though," Markine said. "Shows he can plan. I'll bet he makes it out of here tomorrow night."

"I'll call in and let them know to stand down for tonight," Naren said. "Then we should get some shuteye."

The next day was a repeat of the previous one, but the guards didn't use any other intimidation techniques. Feneir hoped that Jaren's meekness was just an act, but was it? The escape attempt showed he wasn't truly cowed, but any time one of the guards went into the room, he behaved like a frightened boy. They hadn't really covered much on how to behave to make captors underestimate him when they'd done the original E&E training. Jaren had been more interested in the evasion part of the curriculum. Typical teenager.

Once night fell, he made his way to the outbuilding. Naren had slipped in to report that Jaren was getting ready to make another attempt. Pagil was still watching. This time, Feneir didn't call in immediately. He'd wait until Jaren made it out of the room before he alerted the others and raised their hopes.

Feneir got his eye to the lens in time to see Jaren's shoes disappear into the ceiling. The two men froze, hearing sounds from the roof and then a thump. Outside the building. They stayed in place for several minutes, then took deep breaths and smiled.

"Took the canteen and the blanket," Pagil said quietly. "Same as last night. Ate the solid bits of stew, scraped off the gravy. Must have figured that the sleeping pill was dissolved in it. He needed a couple of tries to leap up to catch the rafter, but he kept at it. I'll check in here once he's far enough away not to hear this damned door open."

"I'll go spread the good news, then we need to get ourselves packed up. Get the lens out of the crack and this box out into the trash heap once you think it's safe to go inside. I want to give Jaren a couple of hours to get to the rest stop. We'll keep checking in with Chief Steffent so we don't leave here until Jaren's had a chance to phone in."

"He's away this time," Feneir said on the phone, this time to Chief Steffent. "Any idea on how he knows E&E now?"

"Just ended a call with Doctor Hallent. He's still not sure but he's going to call back as soon as he comes up with a theory. Apparently that shouldn't be possible for what's currently known about conditioning. What is your team doing now?"

"We're packing up. Quietly. I think the serit's beyond our perimeter now, but the outer guards are still patrolling. We're trying to keep everything quiet so we don't spook him. Or trip over him. We'd need an assault team to rescue him if that happened. We'd have to punish him and that means he wouldn't be able to try another escape for a week or more. That's not how we want this to play out."

"Good enough. I'll let everyone know that he's on the move. The cars will be in position in ten minutes or so. If they don't spot him, they'll circle back for another try."

Markine went out to check on their perimeter guards and discover if they'd noticed any sign of Jaren's passing. He came back a half hour later with a grin.

"Harl said the serit passed him about ten minutes after he made his escape. Good sneaking skills and he almost missed seeing the serit. He's heading for the rest stop, if he keeps going the same direction." He glanced at his watch. "About two and a half, maybe three hours, to the intersection, depending how fast he can travel once he's out of hearing range. Do you want to show any sign that we noticed he's gone?"

"Not really," Feneir replied. "Maybe we can go to the rest stop once he reaches there and calls in. Show that we've left here and he'll be safe to wait for the Bayside guards. All his training was good, but I don't want to panic him into moving too fast and getting hurt."

Chapter 16

Jaren leapt again for the rafter and his fingers were finally on the top of it. He managed to raise his left arm and got a decent grip on the old wood, unlike last night. Once he had that, he used his feet against the walls to gain a few more inches upward. That allowed a new grip and before he knew it, he was above the ceiling and could use his arms to push down on the rafter rather than pulling himself up through them.

He took several deep breaths and listened. Some moonlight shone through the roof hole and he saw some planks and roofing lying on the rafters. He tightened the blanket around his waist and pushed the canteen to sit in the small of his back.

He skulked a little way from the building and paused under a bush. There weren't many tall trees around here. It had been a ranch, he thought. Not abandoned long enough to allow the trees to get too big but long enough to let the shrubbery provide decent cover for him to get away. He noticed some brighter lights on the horizon. Something made a loud noise far away. It took another repetition of the noise for him to recognize it as a speeding vehicle. That meant roads. Roads meant people. He grinned briefly then reality hit him. He needed to find a *phone*, not just a ride. If anyone outside the clan knew that he'd been kidnapped, the father master would not be happy at the loss of prestige. It would be up to the father master if *any* of this was revealed. He could only trust the holding's guards, not some random traveller late at night. If they recognised him, he might only trade one set of captors for another. He took slow breaths to calm himself for his next movements.

He saw a perimeter guard, walking slowly, holding a pistol ready for use. There was a rifle on his back. He looked to either side, occasionally stopped and turned, slowly checking his back trail. He'd look up if there was anything above him, Jaren realized. He stayed absolutely still until the guard was well past him, then crouched and moved as silently as he could, toes first so he wouldn't make any betraying noise by stepping on a branch and cracking it.

He started to relax after nearly an hour of travel through dried grasses and other plants. He found an animal track that more or less headed toward the brighter lights. There had been dilapidated wire fences that he crossed with care for the rusty barbs, so this had been a ranch at some time. He turned to look back again. He could barely make out the buildings, but no flash of lights or noise from the door signalled pursuit. He watched and listened for a few minutes and there was no change. A deep sigh of relief.

Unless they discovered his escape in the next little while, he should be safe. But he couldn't let his guard down, not until he really *was* safe. To fail now would anger the father master. And the kidnappers would beat him until he couldn't move. Too many strikes from a neuronal whip could result in permanent damage and that would enrage the father master for his stupidity in trying to escape in the first place.

The lights in front of him marked a major intersection, he thought. He saw a wider, dimmer glow off to the right. That would be a town or hopefully a city, depending on how far away it was. The clan had subsidiaries in many cities. He just hoped this was one of them.

His luck ran out when he stepped into a shadowed hole on the side of the faint trail he was following. He went down hard and the pain from his left ankle dwarfed that from his already injured left arm. He lay still until he could see through the tears and felt down his leg. He didn't think his ankle was broken, but he wouldn't be able to move quickly any more. Slower meant they could find him. If they were looking for him.

He took a deep drink from the canteen while he listened for any sounds of pursuit. There wasn't anything he could hear, but staying hidden here in the woods was not an option. He had to reach the intersection and other people. He tucked his left hand into the front of his pants to limit its motion. Crawling toward another fence line, he found a thinner pole from a wire gate to use as a crutch. It did allow him to move better but it was still much slower than before. He couldn't use his left arm for much except stabilizing the pole. He managed to keep moving by counting a hundred steps and resting until his breathing returned to normal. Then another hundred. And another.

The intersection was all he needed, he realised, sighing in relief. He stopped well short of it to study the area and determine if it was safe to approach. It was also a rest stop, with a small set of restrooms, a large map attached to the side of the building with a light above it, a couple of picnic tables and a telephone with a small light above it. He waited but there was no sign of anyone. The kidnappers hadn't slipped around him and weren't lying in wait. At least he thought that there was no signs of them. He took a deep breath and approached slowly. He couldn't run if they *were* here, so he stopped every few steps to listen with his eyes closed. Nothing but normal night sounds or a vehicle on the highway.

The map said he was near the town that Bayside Chemicals was in. They'd only taken him an hour or so from the estate. His spirits rose. Now if only the phone worked. He went over to it, lifted the receiver and let out a breath he hadn't realized he was holding when he heard the ready tone. He tucked the handset between his head and shoulder. He dialled quickly and took a deep breath.

"Alanyo Holdings, how may I help you?" The voice was male and calm.

"This is Jaren Alanyo." he said. He had to keep the need and panic out of his voice. That he as strong as the father master demanded that he be.

"Serit, where are you?" came a quick response. "Are you all right?"

"I'm nearest Bayside Chemicals. There's a rest stop at the junction of highways seventy-four and nine. I'm slightly bunged up but okay."

"Are you pursued at this time?"

"No. I don't think they're after me right now. I haven't heard them or their cars on my back trail. I don't think they check on me at night. Sleeping pills in the last food of the day. Does everyone know what happened?" Had the father master put *all* the holding departments on alert for him? He would be in lots of trouble.

"Only our department and the heads of various security forces," the voice said. "We're alerting security at Bayside Chemicals. Guards should be at your location in an hour, possibly less. Is there somewhere safe for you to wait for them to arrive? Not visible from the rest stop is best."

"There's a small grove of trees a little way down highway nine toward the city. I'll be in there."

Car sounds made him turn toward the highway. Whoever they were, they were slowing down. Maybe stopping. Were they his kidnappers? There hadn't been any noise from the site. Maybe.

"There's a car coming. Should I try to get a ride instead?"

There was a slight pause. "Not at this time, serit. I will inform ser Alanyo that you have escaped."

Jaren hung up and limped as quickly as he could around to the back of the restrooms. He couldn't reach a better hiding place before the car and its betraying headlights arrived. He hoped it wasn't the kidnappers. They'd search the entire area and find him. He leaned against the wall and took a better grip on the pole. It made a terrible weapon but it was all he had.

The vehicle stopped and he heard three male voices going into the rest rooms. They sounded young, but Jaren couldn't make out what they were saying. He let out a quiet breath in relief. He knew that accents and slang varied among the worker groups but these comments were completely unintelligible. For them to find a somewhat helpless scion of their bosses might mean bad things for him. It might not, but Jaren wasn't prepared to find out, not when guards he knew and could trust were on their way to bring him home.

The car left after a few minutes with gravel spinning away as they accelerated. Jaren took a deep breath before moving. He still couldn't put much weight onto his ankle and his left arm ached with the effort of using the clumsy pole to walk. He'd head for that stand of trees soon. First, he would fill the canteen in the restroom, then move out. He still moved slowly, though. He couldn't move much faster. Not right now.

The bright light of the rest rooms made it hard to see. He didn't look at himself in the bank of mirrors, just pissed, then drank some water and refilled the canteen. Outside, everything was dark. His night vision was gone. Another stupid mistake. Sounds of another vehicle on the highway sent him back behind the building but they didn't stop. He took a deep breath and started toward his chosen hiding place.

Halfway to the stand of trees he tripped and fell as his right foot slipped off a loose, unstable rock. His left arm and side took the brunt of it. Again. Rocks pushed into his legs and arm. His left knee twinged. He had to close his eyes and fight back the tears. When he could pay attention to his surroundings he decided not to continue to those trees. It was just too far for him to walk right now. All of his muscles were leaden and aching. No muscle tone after the withdrawal, then however long they'd kept him unconscious. He should have asked the call operator what day it was, but he wasn't going back there. He'd find out soon enough.

He should have done many other things, starting with saying no to the damned poppers in the first place when Vanis had offered him some during a joint project that they'd waited too long to finish off. Two all night work binges had resulted in a good grade but he'd kept using the dammed pills. A crutch that kept weakening him until he couldn't function without them.

Several vehicles streaked past but he was far enough into the ditch not to be noticed. He looked away from the highway, then struggled up onto a small rise covered with chest-high bushes. He glanced back toward the ranch and he held his breath so he could hear better. He had to wait until his heart rate went down far enough so he could hear the night noises over the pounding in his head.

He caught the faint sound of engines from that direction. He undid the blanket, drawing it around his shoulders to break up his silhouette and hide his light coloured shirt. Moving behind a bush that still had some leaves would give him cover. He lay down carefully, propped up by his right arm.

The engine noises revved louder, then dropped. A few minutes later he saw them. Three sets of lights. They seemed to be heading away from the buildings but he waited and tried not to shake in fear. One of them appeared several minutes later on the highway he overlooked and he heard the crunch of gravel. They must be at the rest stop.

He was glad he hadn't stayed near there. A shot rang out, then he heard them moving through the grasses near the parking area. He ducked lower, still keeping the rest area in sight as best he could. Two other vehicles came into the parking lot and six men stood in the light of the restroom sign, arguing quietly. There wasn't enough light to see any of them clearly.

After a few minutes, they all returned to the vehicles and sped off, going down the road away from him. He couldn't believe they'd given up so quickly.

His mind slipped into wondering what might have happened if they'd stayed to search here or around the buildings. Or worse, headed overland toward the lights of the rest stop. He couldn't help himself. If the kidnappers hadn't known *when* he escaped, they might guess he'd called for help or gotten a ride.

They might have been searching around the buildings for some time. If he hadn't twisted his ankle, his travel time would have been a lot less. Best to leave before they were caught. Very angry that they hadn't gotten the ransom after all their effort.

Jaren knew he had been very, very lucky. Maybe he should have waited another day to escape, but a host of scenarios had forced themselves into his brain, each one a worse outcome than the others.

He kept the blanket on. A breeze came up and it was cool on his bare neck so he pulled a corner of the blanket over his head. He moved to the fence line to find a post he could lean against and keep an eye on the road and rest stop. He knew if he stayed lying down now he'd be asleep in minutes. Several big transports passed but none stopped. His eyes closed during a lull in the traffic. He jerked awake as his left arm fell to his side and protested. The larger moon was still close to setting so he hadn't slept that long, he thought with relief.

A convoy of three unmarked sedans pulled into the rest stop. At least four guards from each vehicle, all armed and armoured, boiled out and started securing the area.

"Ser Jaren," called one as he trotted along the ditch toward the stand of trees. "It's Darthan. The lark of evening."

He remembered Darthan. He'd been Jaren's driver when he'd been here for that dratted paper. His presence meant Jaren was safe. Now all he had to do was get over to them. He levered himself up using the fence post, aching all over. He couldn't put any weight on his left leg any more and his left elbow was also swollen and hard to flex.

"Gets eaten by a fox." What a stupid sign and counter. But it would be hard to guess the right response. "Over here," he called, waving his right arm while leaning on the fence post to stay upright. "Good to see you, Darthan."

Several of the guards headed toward him.

"Are you injured, ser?" Darthan asked.

"I twisted my ankle back that way," he said, pointing back toward the ranch. "Couldn't get to the trees that I was trying for. Too tired and I fell again on my way here from the rest stop."

"Is that the direction to their lair?"

"Was. An abandoned ranch. I think they left a while ago. Half an hour or so after I called in. They went to the rest stop and headed that way afterwards." He pointed toward the highway heading away from them. "I heard a shot before they left."

"Rest your arms on our shoulders, ser," another guard said as two of them came up on either side of him. They handed off their rifles to their companions and their shoulders slid under his arms, lifting them slightly higher. He tightened what grip he could, trying not to use his left arm or hand at all.

"Just sit down, ser," the guard said. "This is the fastest way to get you to the car." Jaren let his weight settle onto their arms under his rear end and they stood up and carried him carefully down the slope.

One of the guards got into the middle car and drove it onto the highway, so his carriers only had to move him about five or six meters. They let him down just outside the opened door so all he had to do was sit down again. One even made sure he didn't bump his head. He blinked in the now bright light from the dome. He couldn't start to cry now. He had to show strength, not weakness. The father master would expect strength and courtesy to his guards, not the tears of a weakling.

"Our orders are to take you to President Cahtharan's house, ser," Darthan said. "Bath and bed await. We haven't heard about other travel plans. Tomorrow is more likely than right now."

"Sounds good to me, especially the bath," Jaren said. "And a snack would be good after that. Thanks for the lift." He gave them a quick smile. The father master expected graciousness to any underlings.

"All in a day's work, ser," Darthan said. "Any other aches or pains?"

"Just my left arm. I was hit by a neuronal whip when they caught me. I landed on my elbow when I fell and it's now swollen and hard to move." Hisses of anger greeted his comment.

"You should have said something before we lifted you, ser. Wouldn't want to make it worse."

One of the guards pulled out a med kit from the trunk. Ice packs were soon wrapped around his ankle, knee and elbow. A simple sling for his left arm kept it from shifting. He scooted further into the seat to keep his ankle and knee elevated.

"The phone was shot out," said another of the guards he recognized from his previous visit as their vehicles came up to join his. "No signal. We'll send an anonymous message to the road department in the morning."

"How very rude of them," Jaren said. "Not very civic minded at all. What if someone had a real emergency here?" He heard snorts of not quite laughter and smiled in response.

* * *

Sanil woke with her mom's hand on her shoulder. "Jaren freed himself this evening," she said. "He'll be picked up by the guards soon and will be in Bayside's compound within an hour or two. Perhaps returning here tomorrow or possibly the day after. Caldon and the men are on their way back here."

She let loose a sigh of relief, then looked at her mom. "What's the problem? Is Jaren okay?"

"Get dressed and come into your dad's office. We need to discuss the recent events."

She was still adjusting to the brightness of the room as she looked at her bedside clock. It was three am. She was never at her best at this hour. She pulled a shirt and slacks from her closet and dressed quickly.

"Jaren's okay, isn't he?" she asked as soon as she closed the door to Dad's office.

"A twisted ankle and some scrapes and such, otherwise he's fine," Dad replied. "This is something different. The doctor is fairly sure that Jaren's impostor personality was active when he woke up, as we guessed might be the case. That personality didn't know what Jaren did about E&E. His man Caldon was positive as the imposter did nothing to work through the stiffness the first day. *Overnight*, he had that information. No one knows how. Doctor Hallent is baffled. It's supposed to be impossible to transfer information to a constructed personality without it being input the way he did with the kidnapping material or as a result of life experiences once the construct is active. It can't just *appear*. He's baffled and so are we."

"But Jaren's okay now," Sanil sighed in relief. "We can find out what's happened and get these other things out of his head."

"There is another problem," Julin said. "The doctor found something else in the tapes. A suicide imperative. Both the controller and the impostor constructs have it, and it may have been transferred to the real Jaren as well. It makes sense for this type of scenario, that a construct would suicide before admitting that someone had implemented changes. Nothing relating to the conditioning can be admitted. We can't just ask him or try on our own to activate the other personalities to find out what was done or how to undo it. It's a great fail safe and points to the sera's thought of a murder-suicide scenario. There is too much we don't know about what was done to the serit to risk any questioning him at all on these matters."

"Then what about the popper conditioning? Is it booby-trapped too?"

"That is what they *want* him to admit to if needed," Dad said. "If their plan had gone as they wanted, Jaren would have returned home with no sign that the impostor or the controller existed or that he'd been addicted to poppers and was now cured. No one but Gred, Jaren and the guards they brought home would have known about the poppers. He would have believed the withdrawal effects as an explanation for his longer-than-planned stay at the estate. His father remains unaware of his failure. He would be grateful to Gred that he helped Jaren cover up a serious error in judgement. Gred gains influence over him and there is the probability of continued close contact so he could monitor Jaren until they do whatever has been programmed into the impostor."

"What about me?" Sanil said. "How was he going to explain the addiction to me? I'd disagree with him if we hadn't found out about this. I know he's not an addict!"

"Sit down, dear," Mom said. Sanil reached behind her to make sure a chair was there, then bit at her lip as she sank into it. "The impostor may not know about you at all. Certainly no one else did. It all depends on how much the controller transferred about Jaren's private life and what they had on the tapes. Neither Gred nor Adnil have mentioned anything about you in their conversations so we are not sure if they knew or know about you. Hantel may have also kept the information from Gred as part of his own plans. There was no indication from his notes either way. We simply don't know. You're what is referred to as a wild card in many card games. The one unknown thing that could change the board in ways no one expects or has plans for."

"And that's why you're going back to university later today," Dad said in a *'there will be no further discussion'* voice. "The Jaren that's coming back may not know you exist and any direct communication from you before the real one comes back might activate that suicide imperative."

Tears ran down her cheeks. "How long do I have to stay away from him, Papa?"

"I assume that Gred will quickly find a way to shut down the impostor and bring your Jaren back. They wouldn't try to activate the impostor's conditioning to do whatever they're planning on top of this excitement. Caldon's notion was a very good one. My guess is a month and likely several more at a minimum before any attempt is made to do anything related to their plan. You'll be back to communicating via Caldon and Casteron's good will fairly quickly." Dad looked at her sternly. "We still don't want any secret meetings between you two."

"I did promise," Sanil said. "But letters will have to do for now. He might even let me know how to respond about the poppers."

Breakfast was tense. Two of her brothers were home and awake early and they hadn't been brought into the secret yet. There was so much she still wanted to talk to Mom about. In the bustle to go back to Sacarnil, she didn't have a chance.

It wasn't until she was on her way back to university that the answer came to her as she dozed in the car. She hadn't been able to get back to sleep earlier after everything that had happened.

"Julin, I know how the impostor found out about escaping!"

Casteron turned from his forward seat. "It came to you in a dream?"

"No, well yes, but listen." The driver glanced in the mirror. "How could the impostor find out everything that happens to Jaren while he wasn't active?"

"It depends on what their plan is, seris," the driver said. "If it was something quick, a lack of knowledge on a recent topic wouldn't matter. The sera's thought of ser Darit's murder, then the serit's suicide is an example of that kind of plan. I do wonder what sort of excuse they'd make for a lack of a suicide note."

"Or the imposter would be programmed to write one before carrying out his instructions. A long term plan is not as likely," Julin said. "They seek gain and ultimately control of the holding. How does a delay in their control give them the reward they desire?"

"By ensuring that no one associates what just happened with anything else." Sanil saw both men start to process the ideas. Slowly.

"It wouldn't have to be very long delay, a half year at most." the driver said. "Without the kidnapping, the popper conditioning would have blown over within a couple of weeks, two months tops. That is, if anyone else had any idea the conditioning had been done. If their plan had gone as they anticipated, no one would know anything was wrong."

"This has nothing to do with how the impostor found out how to access Jaren's E&E expertise." Julin turned in his seat to look at her.

"If it is a longer term plan and not Mom's theory, how would the impostor know what had happened between now and when it is activated to do whatever it's supposed to do?" *Men.* Sometimes you had to repeat things before they clued in. Multiple times.

"Someone would have to tell it what had been happening," Julin said slowly. "And do so without Jaren vanishing and being conditioned, as the kidnapping scenario was added. That took two days, not just one. His records show that it took Hantel over two weeks to put the impostor and the controller in, along with the popper conditioning. We have no idea how long it took him to put those tapes together. A month or maybe more? I'll have someone find out. If something happened to ser Darit, Jaren couldn't be missing for long before someone became suspicious about where he was. They couldn't risk anyone raising questions."

"The *controller* has to be the key," Sanil said. "It was used to transfer Jaren's memories during the conditioning process, that's what Doctor Hallent thought that its purpose is. Was. It slanted Jaren's memories to whatever they wanted for the imposter. What if it stays active now, keeping the impostor up to date on a regular basis? Maybe once a week or so. It may be eavesdropping when either personality is active or it came on line once the imposter woke up and realised he'd been kidnapped. Then it could look through Jaren's memories when it realized that the impostor didn't have critical information for the escape. Then it just moved those memories, probably slanting them to fit the imposter's beliefs. Overnight."

"That...would explain a lot about their plan," the driver said slowly.

"I'll phone it in once we get to the dorm and get you settled in," Julin promised.

Chapter 17

Jaren dozed in the car but Darthan woke him as they neared President Cahtharan's house. "We let them know you're not very mobile, ser," Darthan said. "A suite on the main floor's been prepared. A wheelchair was brought in so we don't have to carry you around."

"That's a good idea," Jaren replied. "Any word on the lair?"

"The men we left haven't seen anyone in the area. They hid their car nearby and have kept the site under observation since we left. Two other teams were heading there but they're still a half hour out. They'll search the place, see if they can get some clue who these guys were. They'll be looking for fingerprints we can use to identify them."

"There were six of them at the rest stop in three cars. I did see four different ones up close but they always wore ski masks and gloves, but that's not enough to keep watch with a prisoner to worry about. There was at least one walking a perimeter with a rifle when I left. Competent. Kept looking all around, back and up. The trees near the buildings aren't very tall, but he still checked them. I was hiding behind a bush a couple of meters away and managed not to attract his attention. Waited until he was well past me before I moved any further."

"They'd have to be competent to take out your guards," Darthan said.

Jaren tightened his right fist. He couldn't let the tears come now. He had to stay strong.

"Here's the house," Darthan said. The bulk of the house was dark but Jaren saw several guards in the front garden. The side entrance had more guards and three men in civilian clothes. And the wheelchair. He recognized Ser Cahtharan and took a deep breath. Strength and confidence. Inside he just wanted to curl up in a bed under the covers and cry.

"Serit Alanyo," Cahtharan waited until he'd been unloaded from the car to come forward. "I hadn't realized you were badly injured. We'll get a proper doctor in at once."

"I only twisted my ankle," Jaren said. He did *not* want a doctor anywhere near him until he'd had more sleep. He might say something the father master wouldn't like. "And I'm not sure what I did to my elbow but it'll be fine until I get a bath, some food and sleep."

"Then it shall be so," he said. He turned to Darthan "The serit might need a hand. The blue room in the family wing is prepared. It is on the main floor for ease of movement."

"Thank you, Ser," Jaren said with a small smile. "Let my father know I'll call him in the morning. Well, once it really *is* morning, not just evening that been around too long."

Ser Cahtharan snorted, hiding his mouth behind a hand and several of the guards had sudden coughing fits.

The hot bath almost sent him to sleep and did a lot toward making his legs feel less like limp noodles. Darthan had to help him wash his hair since he couldn't get his left arm to bend more than ten degrees. Getting the pyjama top on had been tricky given his swollen elbow and the residual pain from the whip. Bandaging his ankle with a tensor had been simple but it was swollen and aching. Darthan shook his head at the various scrapes and bruises. He insisted on bandaging them all, including his wrists and ankles.

"The ointment will help the scrapes heal quicker." he said. "I think you need a real doctor to look at all of these. And we should put your arm in a sling at least overnight and keep it from moving, ser. Take these." He held out three pills, all different colours.

"What are they?" Jaren was nervous but didn't know why. They didn't look like any pills he'd ever seen before.

Darthan pointed to each in turn. "Painkiller, muscle relaxer, and for inflammation our medic said. The kitchen should have your snack ready and then, it's bed time. Sleep as long as you like. Or noon."

"All right." He took the pills and let Darthan help him into the wheelchair and push him to a table.

A knock sounded at the door and Jaren realized there were a pair of guards in the hallway flanking a footman with a trolley. "There's two men outside the window and eight more men through the house and grounds." Darthan said. "We're not taking any chances on the kidnappers coming to try to find you."

"I know," Jaren replied. The smell of hot chicken soup filled his nostrils. He'd mourn the dead later. Once he was really alone.

The morning brought stiffness and pain and he couldn't get out of the bed at first. Thankfully Darthan had more pills. And water.

"Did you get some sleep?" Jaren asked. Darthan looked too alert to have stayed up all night.

"A bit. Do you want to get dressed or just layer a dressing gown on?"

"Dressing gown for now. I need to call my father first thing. I may not be going anywhere today. Have you heard anything about transport?"

"Not yet. Ser Cahtharan's home office is on the other side of the house. He said you should use it as your own. He's gone in to the plant at his usual time in case the kidnappers were watching the house in hopes of learning if you were here. We scrounged up some clothes that should fit if you need to travel today. If not, we'll get something better in for tomorrow. Chief Steffent let my boss know your sizes."

The dressing gown fit over the sling with some tugging while Jaren balanced against the bathroom door. "It'll do," Jaren said as he slumped into the wheelchair.

"Let's go then." Darthan opened the door and the two guards flanked him down the corridor.

Ser Cahtharan's office was much like any other he'd seen, large desk, separate sitting area for chatting with guests, tasteful art on the walls and a plush carpet underfoot.

Darthan parked him near the phone. "I'll be right outside, ser."

Jaren couldn't let it pass any longer. Last night he could use the excuse that the guards were too focused on his retrieval to worry about proper address, but this was morning and all was calm. "I'm only twenty-one, Darthan. Not a ser. Serit. Until next spring."

"It used to mean any adult, responsible for your actions, before it turned into a clan thing. I've met some men that use it and have never reached what it means and they were older than your father. Others get there earlier than you did. I don't know if any of your friends from university would have managed to escape a kidnapping. The rest of the men agreed with me. Ser."

Jaren knew he'd gone beet red. He didn't deserve the honour but couldn't explain why. "Thank you," he said softly. "I- I should phone."

"I'll let the kitchen know you'll be needing some breakfast soon, ser."

Jaren waited until Darthan closed the door and took a deep breath. Now if the father master would also approve of what he'd done.

He dialled the father master's direct line at the office. It rang twice, then Chief Steffent came on the line. He clenched the phone. The same as the call on that last day of freedom: the father master didn't want to hear his excuses of failure.

"Serit, it is good to hear your voice," Steffent said. "I've just seen the updated reports. How is your arm?"

"Still swollen and aching," Jaren admitted. "I fell on it a couple of times on my way to the road. My ankle's feeling better, so I should be able to walk in a few days. Same with my knee. I think it twisted when my ankle did. There was a hole in the side of the trail I didn't see. There's also some minor scrapes and such."

"Good. We don't have any planes we can reroute to pick you up without a lot of notice. We've arranged for you and two guards to take a two pm commercial flight to Hantil airport. Seats in executive class, of course. The tickets will be at the gate. I'll let Bayside Security know the flight number and gate assignment. We may have you stop in at a doctor once you get here about your arm. I have someone setting that up and will have the confirmation shortly."

Jaren looked at the clock: nine-thirty. "I should get to the airport by one, do you think? It takes a lot longer to get anywhere with the wheel-chair. Getting in and out of a car takes more time than just standing up."

"That will be good. Caldon will meet you at the airport here. We dragged him back from his holiday when this happened. He's very peeved that Sarnd didn't take better care of you."

"I don't think it would have mattered who was there, Chief," Jaren said. "The attack was very well planned and executed. I had no idea any-thing was wrong until I went downstairs and walked into them. Actually, I'm not sure who was more surprised, me or them."

"Neuronal whips are nasty, filthy things," Steffent said. "I'm glad that you recovered enough to escape. We'll do a complete debrief of everything once you're back here and feeling better."

"What cover are we using?"

"We're not entirely sure yet. Did you shave last night?"

"No. Getting clean, fed and bandaged were higher priorities. Should I do so? I haven't gotten dressed yet."

"Maybe just neaten it up if it's scruffy. Gives us options."

"All right. Is - my father there?" Jaren hated sounding needy but wondered why he wasn't there. What had he thought more important?

"He was called out to deal with one of his politicians. End of the world, you'd think by the carrying on. He'll be home this evening and I'll pass on an update as soon as he's free. By the way, the sers Calyno are staying at the compound. We weren't sure that ser Gred wasn't also a target given your location."

"Thank you. I'd better get something to eat," Jaren said. "See you later." He hung up the phone and stared at it. Politicians were always calling about their problems. The father master seldom let their whinging distract him from important matters. That he was dealing with the politician told Jaren exactly where he stood. He was in serious trouble. The father master must have found out about the poppers. The more he thought about it, the more he was *sure* that the father master knew. The teams would have found the room in the basement even if the kidnappers hadn't. And a tape labelled addiction cure meant that all of them knew. Soon Darthan and his team would know and that would be the last ser he'd get from them.

A knock at the door made him blink back the tears. "Ready for some brunch?" Darthan asked.

"Yes, then we'll need to get me dressed and trim this growth on my face. Airport at one for a two pm flight." Steffent hadn't mentioned anyone being assigned as his escorts. "How would you like to come with me? And you can bring a friend."

"Sure thing. Haven't seen Hantil in ages. I'll check with my lieutenant and see who'd like to come with."

* * *

Darit glared at the conditioner. "Are you saying that I have to pretend that my son is an impostor? One that *I* created?"

"Yes, ser. Right now we can't challenge any of his belief systems in case something triggers that suicide imperative. I've been listening to those tapes since I was given them. This morning I realized I'd missed a critical point. It's in the early years tape," Doctor Hallent said.

"I skimmed through that section when serit Jaren first arrived at the clinic. The tape describes the early life of a ten year old orphan. He was there from early infancy, it seems. No idea who his parents had been. He'd been abandoned at a hospital with nothing to identify him later. It included some general details of his life in the orphanage, realizing that he had to repay all the costs of his schooling, bed and board before he could hope to do whatever he wanted. To be free. Tested quite high in intelligence, by the way. They may have used serit Jaren's actual test scores if they were able to access them."

"And I would have insisted on an intelligent one, wouldn't I? The rest seems like a typical child indentured," Darit said. "At least he wasn't sold into it because of idiot parents who just wanted money to pay off debts. Most do very well, before and after they've paid out. We have many in the holding's factories and other tasks. All treated well."

"And conditioned to be grateful, good, productive workers until they do manage to pay out," the doctor said. "And after as well."

"Well, of course," Darit said. "So that is what I supposedly did? Took a smart orphan who looked like Jaren and used him to replace my allegedly dead son? To what end?"

"So that your line would not die out."

"Hmph. By your reckoning, it did, rather would have."

"But if no one *knew* or would admit the original Jaren had died in the crash, the legacy continues. Father to son in direct inheritance for eight generations. Nine when Jaren inherits. No other clan can claim that distinction. Your pride in that legacy is well known, ser. For their grand plan, it would make sense to outsiders. Especially to your enemies."

"True," Darit said slowly. "It *was* one of the reasons I married again, even though Adnil and then Gred were my acknowledged heirs after the bombing. A last chance to keep the name going. Only Jaren lived. She tried, but after the fourth miscarriage tore her up, we had to stop trying for another child. Then she died. I couldn't bear to try again. All my hopes were on Jaren, but I couldn't make time for him even before the accident. Now he's become someone that I barely know. We seldom talked and it hasn't changed much, and that's mostly in the car going or coming from the office. And those conversations are mostly about business. Nothing personal at all. Never had a hint that he'd found someone that he wanted to marry."

"And that is the basis of the impostor, ser." Hallent's voice broke into his grief and memory. Darit took a deep breath to push his pain away.

"Hmph. So the Jaren heading home believes that I am an ogre he has to keep pleasing. What was the story the tape said the impostor believed? That if he fails me he'll be sent off to the mine at Stilthen without being conditioned to accept it. To remember the life of luxury he had and the harsh reality of gem mining by hand. Never seeing the sun and never being able to pay off the massive debt he owes me. Nearly a slave in name, but one in fact. You want me to reinforce those fears. Threaten him and make him fear me even more."

"Yes and no, ser. Don't mention the mines right now. The suicide imperative would make him keep that secret from everyone and there could be a listener. For the near future, concentrate on the pills and his stupidity in getting addicted in the first place. That will be enough. Some veiled threat about his future would be expected. You'll need these as evidence when you confront him." The doctor handed him a clear pill bottle with no label. It was half full of oblong pale pink pills.

"We found these in Sarnd's bags. They're poppers, in case you hadn't seen them before. I would assume that Jaren believes Sarnd had become his supplier once he joined the detail. Part of the window dressing for the reality portion of the conditioning. They did some role playing while Jaren was drugged to mimic the pain of withdrawal according to the notes we found. It helped solidify the implanted memories."

"You want me to challenge him on the addiction?" He shook a pill out of the bottle and stared at it.

"You have to, ser. The impostor will expect it. If your Jaren became a popper addict and tried something like this to hide it you would be furious. Channel that anger. I'm sure that Gred will shut the impostor down as quickly as he can. They don't *want* him active when an incautious word could reveal his existence. We just need a day or so for him to act. Having them at the compound will give Gred plenty of opportunities to be alone with Jaren for a short time. And with the transmitters all over the estate, we can overhear any instructions."

Darit put the pill back into the bottle and put it on the desk.

"If need be, we can also use Jaren's injuries to give him some sedatives to keep things from escalating. He should get a sleeping pill tonight, just in case. A guard outside his door and one for his balcony will keep him from wandering around in case the pill isn't enough."

"You still don't know *how* they planned to use the impostor against me or the holding," Darit said.

"Not yet, ser. I'm going though the impostor tape again. A kilometre or so left, I think. The workmanship on these tapes is amazing. Heinous, but I don't know of anyone else who has done anything as elaborate. We need to search Hantel's residence and offices to see if there are any other examples of his work. My guess is that it took over a month of dedicated work to put those tapes together."

"Hmph," Darit said. "I just hope it cost them a lot to hire the slime. And it will cost them everything else once Jaren is finally safe from what they've done to him."

Darit returned to his office after his usual lunch. "Any news?" he asked Steffent as his secretary took his coat.

"Caldon and Semant arrived early this morning and are asleep downstairs. They'll meet the plane once it arrives and add to the security. Serit Jaren is at the airport ready for boarding, using his own name," Steffent said. "Two guards from Bayside are with him. His cover is that he was injured in a riding accident at the wilderness preserve and is headed home. He's been told not to talk to anyone. We need a little more time to get all the evidence in place. I don't want to chance any reporters calling the site before we've finished the set dressing and rehearsing the story with the witnesses. The rangers are upset that we want to kill a bear. I am as well, but we needed a valid reason that Sarnd is dead. Defending the serit should read well for public consumption."

"Hmph. A riding accident does fit his injuries, I suppose. I wish we had been able to use one of our planes to pick him up, but that would expose too much, I think. And a long car ride with those injuries wasn't a good idea either. Any word on the clinic? Can they fit him in?"

"Ser Kendef sent word to them that they *would* fit serit Jaren in this afternoon. He'll go there directly from the airport. If there is any serious damage to his elbow, this doctor is the best bone surgeon on the continent. Being injured will also limit whatever they have planned to do."

"Good. Arrange that Adnil and Gred be at supper with us. The doctor wants me to be an ogre and I'd rather not stress Jaren much this evening. I'll gird myself to drop a load of wrath on him tomorrow morning. That will also give them a chance to arrange to shut this impostor down and give me my son back." Darit glowered in Steffent's direction, then sat down and shook his head.

"Arrange for guards on Jeran at all times. The doctor isn't sure what the impostor is supposed to do and doesn't want to give him a chance to do anything or go anywhere unobserved. The cover is that we're worried the kidnappers might try for him again, even in the compound. Higher security all around."

"By the way, ser, I was just sent word that one of the footmen, Hartner, is now working for Gred," Steffent said as he paused at the door. "He went directly to the compound commander to report the bribe, as the staff has been ordered. He'll give copies of any messages to and from Gred to us."

"Good. Make sure we're paying him triple what Gred is. If he tries to double cross us, kill him. The roses have been looking sickly."

Chapter 18

Jaren had only been on a commercial flight twice before this. All the other times he'd flown it had been in the holding's fleet of private aircraft. It seemed strange not to know any of the staff or the other passengers. He almost smiled at a steward, then remembered that Darthan had relayed a message from Steffent before they'd left Ser Cahtharan's mansion for the airport.

The riding accident cover isn't set in stone yet. Don't talk to anyone but your guards. You injuries are the result of a fall and the pills aren't quite enough to mask the pain. Surly wouldn't be a bad description of your attitude.

He took a copy of a newspaper from the steward at the plane's door and thought he'd use it to keep the other stewards and passengers away from him. Besides, he was out of touch with what had been going on in the world. He glanced down at his right wrist. The shirt he wore had long sleeves and they hid the healing marks from the handcuffs. Bandages would have been too bulky to hide, Darthan had decided. The left wrist was safely hidden in the folds of the sling for now.

Several passengers gave him a quick glance, trying to place him, Jaren thought. Because of the sling, he guessed. Most took briefcases from assistants and started working immediately. One man kept glancing at him as the staff went through the usual drills and warnings. What had the father master thought, sending him home in such an open setting? Had he thought that this would make Jaren feel worse about getting kidnapped? Or was it the poppers? Whatever the reason, he was in deep trouble once he was back at the compound. The plane took off and he watched the world fall away beneath them before it vanished as they entered the clouds. To bad that he couldn't escape all his other problems the same way.

"Do I know you, ser?" The man who'd kept glancing at him was standing near his seat.

"No." Jaren turned back to the window.

"I'm sure I do, ser. How were you injured?"

Jaren glanced back at his guards. Darthan released his seat belt and came to stand at Jaren's shoulder.

"The ser does not wish company at this time, ser. Please return to your seat and cease annoying him."

"Or?" The man smiled a *'you wouldn't dare do anything to me'* smile.

"I will offer your clan an apology for your death." Darthan said calmly. The man's smile vanished as he took in the pistol now visible under Darthan's coat and the knife handle up his sleeve. After several seconds with his mouth hanging open, he went back to his seat. Quietly.

"Thank you," Jaren said quietly.

"Not a problem, ser." Darthan smiled and glanced in the direction of the now nervous passenger.

The rest of the flight was quiet in their corner of the compartment. Jaren gave up on the paper: it was impossible to manage the pages with one hand and he worried that the sleeve could slip down and reveal his other injuries. The father master would not be happy if he ruined whatever plan they had come up with. The clouds and landscape beneath him lulled him into a doze.

Pagil met them at the gate with a wheelchair. Jaren grimaced as he sat down in it and lifted his feet into the supports. It would soon be time for more pills. Feneir waited at the car that picked them up.

"I'm glad to see you both," Jaren said after they slid him into the car and stowed the wheelchair in the trunk. A shiver as a cold breeze swirled around them. He'd almost forgotten it was winter up here. "Are we heading to the compound or a hospital?"

"A stop at a bone clinic first," Pagil said. "Getting your arm, knee and ankle checked out."

"It is a Kendef subsidiary," Feneir said. Jaren stared at him, eyes wide.

"Kendef? Father hates them. Why have me go there?"

"Their head surgeon is the best on this continent." Feneir said. "I wasn't privy to any – communications that may have expedited this visit. I understand they are always booked months ahead."

The brusque doctor who came into the exam room didn't seem pleased at their disruption of his schedule but he did handle Jaren's arm carefully and said nothing about the abrasions around his wrists. He pulled and pushed against the joint testing the range of motion. Jaren gritted his teeth against the pain. The bruising was colourfully shading into yellow and green and now extended half way up and down his arm from the elbow. Another yellowing group of bruises affected his shoulder from his various falls.

"Bone scans first," he said to an assistant. "Two angles of the elbow, one above and below, one of the shoulder and get the ankle and knee as well, top and side, to be sure any damage is just soft tissue."

"Of course, doctor. I'll alert the technicians." The woman left.

"How many times did you fall on that elbow?"

"Twice, no, three times, I think," Jaren replied. "Once on concrete, the others on hard ground with rocks. Is it broken?"

"I don't think it is a bad break if there is one. A fracture is certainly possible beneath the tissue damage. The scans will tell me for sure. What have you been taking for the pain?"

Jaren waved at Darthan. "He has the pills."

Darthan handed over a list. "I can't pronounce the names, doctor."

"Hmm. They'll do, but double up on the anti-inflammatory for the next three days. If you need more, let my assistant know and we'll courier them to the holding tower. We'll use a better sling than that one to immobilize your arm for the time being. The swelling from the bruises is interfering with my diagnosis."

The door opened and the assistant returned, followed by two men in scrub suits. "They'll take the serit to the scan room. Only one guard may accompany the serit. The rest of you can wait in the lobby."

Feneir nodded toward Darthan, indicating that he accompany Jaren. Jaren realized that Feneir and Pagil were also really mad at him. And for much the same reasons as the father master. Why had he been so stupid about the poppers?

* * *

Gred hadn't been at a more uncomfortable dinner in his life. The food was excellent as usual, but Darit scowled, Jaren was silent except for murmured thank you's to the staff and he and his father didn't want to say anything to set the old man off.

Jaren looked tired and the strapped on sling holding his arm immobilized didn't seem at all comfortable. Someone in the kitchen had provided him with pre-cut chicken so he could manage one handed.

Gred noticed that Jaren didn't have wine as the rest of them did. Juice of some kind filled the only glass at his place. He didn't even *have* a wine glass. Was that why he'd been so happy that first night at the estate? Being treated his age, not as a child? Maybe Hantel had been right. Jaren did have serious daddy issues.

Gred managed to get into the elevator with Jaren and dismiss the footman, not his man, who'd been pushing him, leaving them alone once the door closed.

"Is your elbow broken, Jaren?"

"No idea," Jaren replied. "The doctor wanted time to study the scans, but if it is, no big pieces are sticking out so it can't be that bad. Lots of bruising, though. Can't really use it at all with the swelling. I suppose he'll report to Father once he figures it out."

"I should have phoned during the week," Gred said. "We'd have known sooner."

"I don't think it would have changed much, Gred. I could barely use my arm when they did let me wake up. Does – Father find out about the poppers?" Jaren asked.

"Yeah." The elevator door opened and Gred pushed him out and along the corridor toward his suite. "Sorry, but they found the conditioning set up and the doctor's body along with all the guards. There was no way to cover it up. If the doctor had left when I did on Sunday or early on Monday morning, his stuff wouldn't have been there. I couldn't explain away his body *and* the equipment. I only had two men with me and we couldn't have cleaned everything up before the first team arrived. They'd have known something was wrong if there was a missing body but extra bloodstains."

"I thought Father knew. I'm sorry I got you into so much trouble. It should have been so easy. And that no one would ever know."

"I survived." Jaren's suite door opened and Caldon stepped out.

"See you tomorrow, Jaren. Sleep well." Gred said, surrendering the wheelchair to the bodyguard.

"Yeah. Thanks, Gred."

Chapter 19

Gred went further along the corridor to his father's suite and slipped inside. His father was just pouring some whiskey and held up the bottle in silent question. He nodded and went over to the bar.

"Was that the impostor or the original we just had dinner with?" His father poured a second glass and handed it to Gred.

"I have *no* idea. He didn't say much in the elevator. Apologized for getting me into trouble." Both smiled and clinked glasses. "Asked about the poppers, so either way, that part of the conditioning is intact. He trusts me and is sorry that I'm now in trouble with the old man."

"I suppose that's good, since it was the whole point to the exercise," his father said as he sat down on the leather couch. "If he *is* the impostor, how soon can we swap him back to the original?"

"I'll have to get to him soon and find out from the controller which one he is," Gred sat opposite his father. "I *think* this is the impostor. If Hantel left the impostor active after I called to do his testing and have him start to write up the playpen report, he was probably still active when the kidnappers showed up that night. And with no one to reset him, the impostor stays active. The controller doesn't have the ability to do more than keep the memories in sync unless he's been ordered to swap who is active and when."

"That means we may have the unstable Jaren on our hands. He could crack at any time. Although, he did seem to be in control during dinner." His father sipped at his whiskey. "We hadn't counted on this amount of stress so early in the plan."

"I figure he's going to be drugged into sleep tonight. That's no good for what we need. Caldon was waiting in his room when I pushed him up just now. I'll see Jaren tomorrow during the day. Just pop into his room to chat, all concerned cousin. All I need is a few minutes alone with him to give the controller his instructions." After he finished his drink he headed on to his own suite to relax. And perhaps sample another of the excellent whiskies there.

"Ser, luncheon will be served in ten minutes." Hartner looked around at the hallway after opening the door.

"Has something else happened?" Gred asked. "Is my cousin all right?"

"I helped serit Jaren up to his room about two hours ago. He was with ser Darit in his office before that. He looked shaken and spent the rest of the morning alone in his suite."

"Any idea why he looked so upset?"

"None, ser. But I thought you should know."

Gred slipped him a *twenty. "Thank you. Dinner last night was very tense. I'm worried how Darit might treat Jaren now. He needs time to re-cover and get over what those animals did to him."

"I will let you know what else I can discover," Hartner said. Then he left, closing the door softly.

Gred wondered how much information he might get from the man over a longer term. Just the concern of a cousin, nothing truly heinous like spying for a rival clan. But when they did take over, he'd have a fatal accident since he'd already proven he wasn't trustworthy.

Getting into Jaren's room that afternoon was easier than he envisioned. Jaren appeared, pushed into the dining room by one of the foot-men. His footman, Hartner, in fact. When Jaren wasn't looking, he gave the man a smile and received a nod in return.

"Was it your turn on the hot seat this morning?" Gred asked as he finished his coffee. His father had eaten quickly and gone into the city of-fices to deal with an emergency, he said. He had to pretend he didn't know what had happened this morning.

"Yes," Jaren replied to his question with a wry smile. "About what I'd figured. And I'm late with the report on AR&D. He wants it tomorrow morning. Right after breakfast."

Gred shook his head. "Harsh."

"I did have most of it done," Jaren said. "Not really that much to do in between – other things. And it wasn't a full analysis anyway. I should be able to get it finished today. The major points are fairly simple."

"Do you want a push upstairs?" Gred asked when they'd finished.

"Sure. I did have a question on those engine patents. Maybe you know some of those details."

"If I don't, I'll call the team and find out for you," Gred said as he stood and moved around the table.

Once the door to Jaren's room closed and Gred was sure no one else was there, he pronounced the code phrase. Jaren's eyes immediately unfocused and he sat unmoving. Another phrase and the slave blinked.

"Stay in the chair," Gred growled as the slave started to fall to the floor as he'd been trained. "You'll damage him further and that is not allowed at this time."

"Yes, master," the slave responded, head lowered and torso bent forward. Gred stood over him. "Your slave understands."

"Have you been transferring memories?"

"Yes, master. All but this morning. The body must be asleep to allow the transfer." The slave bowed his head.

"What happened at the estate? How did they get in?"

"The impostor was active for testing, master. The other master was observing him, treating him as the primary. He was writing the report for the father master all day and after they ate in the evening. He was going downstairs for a snack when the kidnappers struck. They used the whip to subdue him. There was no sign that anything was amiss. That is all your slave knows until the imposter woke at the ranch. Drugged sleep affects all."

"And then?"

"He escaped after three days and called the trouble line from a rest stop on the highway."

"How did his elbow get damaged? And the ankle?"

"The whip hit him in the arm near his elbow, master. The kidnappers punched him in the stomach after he woke to show their strength and his weakness. He could not breathe, then fell and hit the same elbow on the floor. After he escaped, he fell several times while running away. That is when he hurt the ankle, knee and his elbow again."

Gred raised his hand and the slave cringed. He'd been watching Gred to gauge his reactions to the bad news. Gred smiled.

"How *did* he escape?"

"The primary had learned to pick locks, master. Caldon taught him Escape and Evasion techniques before he went to university. The knowledge was passed to the impostor by your slave, as the other master ordered."

"He didn't mention that to me. Who else knew Jaren could do anything like that?" Gred took a deep breath.

"Only his guards, master. No one else. Sarnd had not been informed so could not relay the information to you and the other master."

"Very well. Activate the primary tonight. Continue to update the impostor's memories with the primary's and do whatever is necessary to keep them synched. I may need to move quickly. Do you understand?"

"Yes, master," the slave responded. "Your slave understands."

"Do it." Another jaw-cracking phrase. Random syllables strung together as words to make them easier to pronounce. At least no one would ever accidentally use any of the phrases. A safety feature, Hantel had pointed out after Gred complained. After the explanation, he practised them diligently. Jaren went glassy eyed again then blinked.

"So, what did you want to know about the engine patents?" Gred went over to Jaren's desk, now covered with papers.

Once he finished answering Jaren's questions, he went to his suite and called the office. "Dad?" he asked as his father answered.

"Yes, Gred. All is well?"

"It will be," Gred responded. "Tonight."

"Excellent. I should be back there in an hour or so. Not as big an emergency as I'd been told."

"See you soon, then."

Chapter 20

Jaren didn't know if he was glad Gred and Adnil were there at dinner or not. The father master didn't look at him or even speak to him. Neither of the others said anything either but he saw them looking at him and each other. Were they afraid of the father master too?

Gred helped him up to his room, confirming that the father master knew about the poppers. Then Feneir had come out and Gred went on to his own suite.

Feneir helped him through the bathroom, into pyjamas and buckled the sling back around him, all in silence. Jaren sat down on the bed so Feneir could check the tensor on his ankle.

"Feneir, I'm sorry," Jaren said. "I was stupid. I never should have started taking those things."

Feneir looked at him, then put his discarded clothing onto a chair. "It *was* stupid," he said. "Why did you start using them?"

"I just wanted to do well, to make him proud of me. There were so many assignments at the end of that semester, it was the only way to stay alert and focused." Jaren looked down at his free hand, the wrist now bandaged along with the scrapes on his back. "I wanted to be worthy of him, of the clan." *And if I didn't do what he wanted, or failed at school, he'd send me away from everything.* But he couldn't tell Feneir that or the father master would have him killed. He couldn't do that to him. It was bad enough that Tossem had died protecting him.

"You did kick it, though," Feneir brought another chair over and faced him. "Ser Gred told us everything when he returned here. You had withdrawal cramps for over a week. And you didn't take any more pills even when the doctor you hired suggested taking some to wean yourself off it gradually." It would have cut down on the symptoms but extended his suffering. And the father master might have sent for him before the conditioning was done and he fully recovered.

"Then you were kidnapped and escaped. That's beyond rare, Jaren. Why did you take the risk? If they'd caught you again you could have been hurt badly. Your father was prepared to pay the entire ransom to get you back. I heard him say so." Feneir's voice was calm now, but Jaren still couldn't look at him.

"Shame. Having the other clan heads know that he couldn't keep me safe, that I could be taken by some group and all my guards killed. The money we'd lose to the criminals. The holding can't afford a big loss, not for anyone. He's proud of our name and I couldn't do anything that would tarnish his reputation or jeopardize the clan."

Feneir was silent. Jaren kept looking down, not wanting to see what expression Feneir had. Pity, maybe, or disgust: he didn't know and didn't want to.

"He is proud of you," Feneir said. "I know he is."

Jaren shook his head. The father master couldn't be proud of him, not after the mess he'd made of his life. Feneir rose silently and went into the bathroom. He heard water running.

"Take your pills," Feneir said, holding out a glass and putting several pills in a small cup on the bedside table. There were five instead of the usual three. Two were identical and one he hadn't seen before. Jaren glanced at him.

"You need to get a good night's sleep," Feneir said. "It will help."

Things didn't look much brighter to him in the morning. Breakfast appeared on a trolley. Darthan came in to help him get dressed once it had been taken away. He took a deep breath. He had to at least live up to Darthan's belief in him.

"We're just here til tomorrow evening, ser," Darthan said. "There's a shipment of unmentionables headed off to Bayside and we have this afternoon and tomorrow to sight see, visit friends or to catch up on our sleep."

"I'm glad you came with me," Jaren replied. "Did you get an update on the ranch investigation from Chief Steffent?"

"Nothing there gives us any idea who the men were. No sign of the cars you spotted and no one in the area saw anything unusual. No one's lived there for twenty years or so, the neighbours said. Those men were professionals, ser. The team did figure there were just the six of them, as you'd thought. Wore gloves all the time, by the smudges the forensic team found. There might have been more at the estate, but they couldn't be sure. Another was definitely in the city, I heard. Dropped the first ransom demand off at the reception desk via a kid. No real description from the kid once they managed to track him down. Tall, well dressed, dark glasses. Paid him *twenty to drop the envelope off."

Jaren fingered his incipient beard. The father master didn't like facial hair. He'd be facing the father master today, he was sure of it. "How about we find my razor and get this fur off me? I don't think I'll need to be in disguise in the next week or two."

Shortly after Darthan left him alone, Jaren tried to start organizing the papers on the AR&D report. He had to get it finished quickly and whoever had packed his things had just shoved it all in without putting the numbered pages in order. He knew the papers had been properly sorted when he'd left the room to go downstairs for a snack. Maybe the kidnappers had tossed his room looking for something, but he wasn't sure what, other than a few hundred he had in his wallet.

A soft knock at the door jolted him out of his musing.

"Come," he said. The door opened and Hartner, one of the footmen, came in.

"Ser Alanyo wishes to speak with you, serit." the man bowed slightly.

"Of course. If you would give me a push?"

The father master sat at his desk reading a report as Hartner wheeled Jaren in. The dark oak desk was as usual, dark green blotter with matching accessories, telephone and a neat pile of files to the left side of the expanse. After the footman left, closing the door softly, the father master looked up.

"Hmph."

"Ser, you wished to see me?"

"Stand up, boy." Jaren stood, balancing on his good leg, the left holding as little weight as he could manage. He was too far from the desk to use it as a support and the wheelchair's brake hadn't been set so he couldn't lean against it either.

"You did escape, which is something," the father master said. "Still, you wouldn't have been captured if you hadn't been stupid."

"Yes, ser," Jaren responded.

A pill bottle appeared on the desk. He recognized the poppers immediately. "These were found in Sarnd's room. Are they yours?"

"They were, ser."

"Were?" the father master looked down at the bottle, then back at Jaren. "Explain yourself."

"I can't use them any more, ser," he said. "The doctor guaranteed that I would never again voluntarily use them, or any other frivolous drugs. Ever again."

"A guarantee. Hmph. Did he test you?"

"Yes, ser."

"You'll prove it to me now." The father master opened the bottle and took out a pill. He set it down within Jaren's reach. "Pick it up."

"Ser," he started.

"Pick it up. Now." The father master cut off his protest.

Jaren hopped forward to the edge of the desk and leaned on it slightly, then reached forward with his right hand over the pen holder and letter opener. The nausea and cramping starting immediately. Sweat sprang onto his forehead. He swallowed. To get sick on the father master's desk or carpet would be punished. Not picking up the pill wasn't an option. His hand reached further.

"Pick. It. Up." He heard, as if the father master was going away.

Jaren blinked. He was on his side, lying on the carpet. He heard papers shuffling and realized he was still in the father master's office. He slowly rose to his knees and used the seat of the wheelchair to stand again. His head ached and he blinked to try to focus. It didn't quite work.

"The guarantee seems to work," the father master observed after a long moment. He didn't look up from the report.

"Yes, ser," Jaren said. He was still groggy. Doctor Sumon said it could take twenty minutes or more to recover from the effects of the conditioning if he pushed it too far.

"Since I cannot trust you to act independently as an adult, I will treat you as the irresponsible child you are. You will not travel outside the compound unless you have my direct permission or accompany me. Your accounts are frozen. Any expenditure needs my signature to implement. You will pay for the three airplane tickets and the salaries of the guards from Bayside who accompanied you here. From the day you left AR&D you will not be paid your salary or any vacation pay. Likewise, no sick pay. Until you formally return to work you will not be paid, nor will you receive an allowance. You will deliver the report on AR&D tomorrow morning at nine-thirty. Ser Ofelan will be here with me. Do you understand these conditions?"

"Yes, ser."

"If you fail again, there are more stringent measures that will be utilized. You're *supposed* to be intelligent. I have too much invested in you to allow the failure of my plans. Too many have met you. Do you understand me, boy?"

"Yes, ser." It wouldn't be the mines, Jaren realized. His next failure would cause a total personality wipe so that he'd always be the perfect son. He swallowed.

"Sit." The father master pushed the buzzer on his desk and Hartner entered a minute later.

"The serit needs to return to his suite. He has some work to complete for tomorrow morning."

"Of course, ser." The footman wheeled him out of the room.

Hartner appeared to take him downstairs for lunch but didn't say anything to him. The father master wasn't there, but Gred was. His father was there, but left quickly for a meeting. Jaren didn't say much and Gred didn't either.

Gred took him back upstairs and helped him with the report. Jaren hadn't known him well before this due to their age difference but he was glad Gred was family. Arranging the conditioner and the time away on his own would have been impossible.

* * *

Feneir pushed Jaren down the hall to ser Darit's office to meet with him and ser Ofelan. This morning, he was sure the original Jaren was back. He seemed stronger, less like the boy who'd almost lost control last night. He'd have to speak to the men listening to the bugs and look over their transcripts. Having one in Jaren's wheelchair meant that anything that was said around him would be picked up and monitored. Too bad they were still so bulky. And the batteries needed changing every other day. Developing a miniature version would make work like this much easier. Maybe Chief Steffent could suggest that as a project for AR&D.

A footman opened the door to the office for them, murmuring that ser Ofelan was already with ser Alanyo. Jaren nodded thanks and shifted the file on his lap.

Ser Ofelan rose to greet Jaren from the sitting area near the bay window. A chair had been moved to make room for the wheelchair, Feneir saw. He parked the chair so that Jaren would be able to reach the coffee table easily and locked the wheels.

"Thank you," Jaren said.

He left, hearing ser Ofelan ask after Jaren's injuries.

The security office wasn't in the main house, but in a two story, rather plain structure hidden from its view by a double row of conifers. He went down to the lower level, which was three times the size of the visible one. Another level existed below this one for very secure storage.

"Anything from the serit's room or the wheelchair when Gred was with him?" he asked the guard heading the surveillance operation.

"Just finished transcribing the serit's room information," he said, holding up a folder. "We could use a couple more sets of ears to cover all the devices we have in play now that the serit is home. We won't have to bother re-listening to all the feeds and can concentrate on the relevant material if we can get some events timestamped as they happen. The chair material is better quality but we wanted to double check some details. The controller was activated yesterday, Caldon. Chief Steffent will need to see the report before it goes to the ser. It's all the proof we need about the conditioning. "

Feneir all but tore the folder out of the guard's hands and went to an empty desk to read it. He couldn't decide what he felt: anger or horror at what Gred had done to Jaren as he read on.

"Come into my office and give me the summary," Steffent said to him twenty minutes later. He'd been staring at the closed folder for several minutes. "I'll see about editing it for the ser."

"And it *will* need editing for the seran," Feneir said, following him in and shutting the door behind him. "Doctor Hallent will be happy since the controller was activated. The code phrases are quite clear: the transcribers double checked the pronunciation and made a copy of that section of the tape for him. The controller had instructions to bring the original Jaren back this morning. I thought he seemed more like himself but I wasn't entirely sure. He was quieter than usual, but that could be the result of the popper conditioning. Or he might not be sleeping well, even with the pill."

"I'm just relieved we've got the right one active again," Steffent said, sitting behind his desk.

"The fact that Gred referred to the controller as *slave* isn't. And the controller referred to himself as *your slave* and called Gred *master*." Steffent bounded back to his feet and stared. Feneir handed him the opened transcript so he could read it for himself.

"Not that I want to tell them but they'll need to know," Steffent said once the document lay on his desk. "Maybe we should let Doctor Hallent tell them?" Neither man obviously wanted that task.

"Just tell me why we can't shoot Gred and his father now." Feneir growled. "I can make it look like someone else did it. No problem."

"We can't and that's that," Steffent said. "Ser Darit wants to add security to Jaren. It can't be obvious, though."

Feneir deliberately relaxed his jaw. He'd need new teeth if he didn't stop grinding them. "A servant would be best. A new footman?" He cocked his head. "And I do need to replace Sarnd in the detail. Any ideas for a replacement there?"

"I'll get some names for you," Steffent said. "There's a couple of men who've shown promise. Wasted in the regular guards."

"And I think all of our men on patrol need something to protect them from neuronal whips," Feneir added. "They were very effective on our raid. Too effective if you know what I mean. Scary. We need some sort of armour to keep the charge away from us. No idea how to make something like that work, but we need it."

Steffent nodded. "Point taken. Your team had no casualties and no one even broke a sweat, from what I heard. You had a 7:3 advantage though. The other three guards were asleep. With Gred's two men available the result might have been different."

"I killed one of the perimeter guards with my whip," Feneir said. "The thong went around his neck instead of his chest and the shock knocked him dead instantly and quietly. I shot him immediately so he looked like the others."

"Maybe we should ask the inmates at AR&D to look into it? And smaller listening devices would also be a good thing."

"Getting something useful from anywhere would be an advantage."

* * *

The conference call later that night was tense. Fortunately, seris Sanil had been left off the invitation list on his recommendation.

Doctor Hallent started off. "According to the transcripts, the original Jaren is now active. The controller was instructed to keep the impostor's memories synced to the primary's. Nothing else is scheduled to happen. This is where they planned to have the serit at the end of the holiday/drug conditioning. I understand that you tested that conditioning today, ser Alanyo."

"I told Jaren to pick up one of the pills the AR&D teams found at the estate. He passed out before he could touch it. Seemed to be having some cramps and was sweating beforehand and was groggy after. I have no idea how long it took before he was fully recovered."

"As I said before, Hantel did very good work," the doctor continued. "Serit Jaren can't voluntarily take *any* of the so-called recreational drugs. One of my assistants went through that tape very carefully. It describes the appearance of all currently available drugs and has the ability to add to the list when new ones are described in the popular media. I would want to go through it more stringently, but it seems to be a better anti-drug conditioning than any currently available."

"You'd use it?" sera Barith asked. "On someone else?"

"Yes," the doctor replied. "There were actually two addiction tapes, seran. The first provided a history of his addiction starting in his second year at university and his withdrawal at the estate. From Hantel's notes, he used a drug to mimic the withdrawal cramps while the serit was awake and aware. Gred was likely present for some of this as well as Sarnd. Having both men there, people whom Jeran knows and who could refer to those experiences after they were all back here, created real memories that reinforced the conditioned memories. The combination is very effective." The sound of someone forcefully setting a cup down was the only sound for several seconds.

"The second tape is designed as a stand-alone conditioning against using drugs. It may be a major part of Hantel, or rather Sumon's considerable public practice. My first testing would be on volunteers, of course. There are always those who want to stop their addictive behaviours but don't have the money to pay for it. A public service, as you will."

"Hmph." said ser Darit. "Check with Chief Steffent when you're ready to do your testing. I'm sure we can scare up a few dozen subjects from the holdings. What about Jaren? Will he be all right if he sees someone else taking one of these pills? He wouldn't collapse on them?"

"Not at all, seran. In less controlled conditions, I'm sure the serit would have stopped trying to pick up the pill long before he collapsed. Since it was *you* ordering him to do it, he was motivated to follow your instructions completely. In a social situation, he can easily walk away from whoever is offering it and tell them no."

"All right," he said heavily. "Had to keep telling him to pick it up. Hated to do it to the boy but you told me to push that I was thoroughly ticked off at him."

"What else happened at your interview?" sera Barith asked.

"Hmph. Told him if he couldn't act like an adult, he wasn't going to get treated as one. Froze his accounts, he's not going anywhere I don't know about, that sort of thing. Hinted that if he failed again *other unmentioned things* would happen."

"Reasonable, given the situation," Hallent said. "And since he's not able to get around on his own right now, the travel restrictions are meaningless except as a threat. Thank you. That should keep all the personalities safe for now."

"Did you hear from our medics?" Ser Kendef asked. "Did the clinic give you any trouble?"

"None, ser," Feneir responded. "The doctor reported in late yesterday. The bone scans show a hairline fracture of the ulna near the elbow joint. The bruising is likely due to a combination of the whip strike and the falls after he escaped. He fell in a rocky section of the highway ditch, among others. His ankle is not broken, merely sprained and the swelling is going down quickly. The knee likewise. No ligaments were damaged.

He'll be walking in a day or three, with a cane at first."

"The fracture in his arm. Did it happen when he fell in the holding area?" sera Barith again.

"Unknown, sera." Feneir said. "The serit was able to use his arm in his escape, which suggests the fracture happened afterwards. It's possible for that fall to have weakened the bone and the second or third fall caused the actual fracture."

"I have not yet heard a reason why my daughter should have been excluded from this call," sera Barith said. "What *haven't* you said yet?"

Feneir took a deep breath but the doctor spoke first. Thankfully.

"We have more information on the controller, seran. It, or rather he, is a *third* fairly complete personality, not a simple transfer mechanism as I had first thought. I believe seris Sanil's theory is correct. The controller must have active access to all the memories that the impostor and the primary have and can move those memories *as required* to update the inactive personality and protect the scenario. We still aren't sure what the end result the sers Calyno envision is, by the way. That ability of the controller to transfer memories independent of new orders is the only way the impostor could learn overnight how to pick locks and escape detection by the guards." A rustling sound came from the speaker.

"Ser Gred activated the controller yesterday afternoon with instructions to bring the primary back on waking this morning. He used a term I *didn't* want seris Sanil to hear without warning. I'm not sure I want any of you to hear it, but you need this knowledge to move forward."

"Stop nattering and just tell us." ser Kendef's voice was sharp.

"Ser Gred called the controller *slave*. The controller refers to himself in the third person and addresses Gred as *master*. There was no physical abuse yesterday but there was undoubtedly some and possibly a great deal during the conditioning process. The doctor and Gred both had neuronal whips. One was found in the room used for the conditioning, the other in Gred's bedroom. Neither was in place after Gred left the estate. Caldon reported to me that there are several scars on Jaren's back that weren't there before his trip." Silence.

"Sanil will *not* learn of this," sera Barith said. "Not until I can tell her personally. I can leave in a day with a good cover for a trip to a subsidiary near the university."

"Of course, sera," came various replies. Relief they didn't have to do it, Feneir thought. He didn't want to either.

"Ser Kendef," ser Alanyo's voice was angry. "How would you like to help me ruin them?"

"Delighted, ser Alanyo. Men like these *should* be put down as a public service. I have some nice explosives available and men trained to use them. When do you want them in tiny pieces?"

"I have some very good explosives as well," Darit replied. "And some, like Caldon, who are excellent shots at substantial distances."

"Please, sers. *Don't* blow them up or shoot them just now," Doctor Hallent said. "I would like to finish my analysis of the tapes first. If you kill them, they can't be questioned. Information they have might be vital in understanding what was done and how to the serit. I don't know how the impostor or the controller might react if they suddenly died. There might be no reaction, or one of them could activate the suicide imperative. Please. Plan all you want, and do anything covert but nothing obvious that might warn them you know anything."

"Hmph." "Grrr."

"Go after them economically for now," sera Barith suggested. "Blow them up when they're destitute and you can step on them like ants."

"That does have some merit," ser Alanyo said. "And we can watch them squirm in the meantime. That will be amusing. I know they have a large loan with Rader Kessem for a stock purchase."

"And *he* helped them with men and the introduction to Hantel," ser Kendef said. "Destroying him at the same time has some appeal and it will be easier now, before the traitors die. It is also a public service." He sounded smug.

"I'll send you our information on the company they invested in and what we know of Kessem's operations. We can coordinate our attacks." Ser Alanyo snorted and Feneir saw him smile. "We might as well use an existing channel to share that information. Caldon and Casteron are used to sending notes back and forth. We'll use the same sort of conduit for physical items."

"I'm sure Casteron will happily cooperate," Feneir said. "As will I, seran."

Chapter 21

Darit shut his eyes as his son collapsed. The pill lay untouched on the desk. He put it back into the vial and tucked it into a drawer for Banak to dispose of later. He rose and went around the side of the desk. Jaren lay on his left side, his injured arm trapped beneath him, his breathing slowing as the conditioned panic subsided.

"You'd better be right about this," he muttered, wishing the doctor had not wanted him to act the ogre. To be the loving, caring father he'd hoped to be when he had first held Jaren as an infant. Not someone feared by his son.

He wasn't sure how they'd grown so far apart. He hadn't had much free time when Jaren was young but he'd cherished every moment. Jaren had always run to greet him whenever he appeared to show what he'd been doing or what he'd learned in his classes. Darit had been too involved with the holdings, still trying to replace dead relatives with hopefully trustworthy employees and keeping other clans from moving into their subsidiaries. Then Farillie died and he'd nearly lost Jaren and the workload had only increased. But he could have, should have made more time to be with his son, especially once he'd returned from the hospital and had to grieve his mother's death alone. So many regrets. So little time left in his life to make everything right and protect his son.

He noticed the white bandage circling Jaren's wrist, some yellowish stain leaking through the gauze. Window dressing, Caldon had said, grinding his teeth as he'd admitted all that had been done, even to being the one who'd used a neuronal whip on his son.

He reached down and touched Jaren's hair, trying to think of the last time he'd done that. It had been far too many years, he realized. Far too long for many things. He thought they were building a new kind of relationship with work. Jaren had the option to go in by himself to and from the office, but generally chose to travel with him. He'd never said how much that meant to him and now it would have to wait until this sordid mess was cleaned up. He had to keep being the ogre that Jaren was used to and feared.

Jaren moved slightly as he began to recover. Time for the ogre to surface again. He went back to his chair and picked up the report. He'd have to read the whole blasted thing again once Jaren left and he calmed down: he had no idea what the report contained or why he should care about anything in it. That it was on his desk meant it was important. Possibly crucial to the clan's future. For Jaren's future as their leader. With or without a Kendef beside him and her father growling on the sidelines.

The restrictions he listed to the boy were unreasonable, mostly window dressing for the impostor, especially the bit about stringent measures. With any luck, Doctor Hallent would soon understand how to reverse the conditioning and Gred and Adnil would be punished for what they had done and planned to do.

They would go to the beach house and just be together and he'd explain about Adnil and Gred. They hadn't been there together since Jaren started university. He blinked in memory. Who *had* gone there with Jaren after his first analysis had been rewarded with a free weekend? Sanil was the most likely candidate. Right under his nose, the sneaky boy. Maybe he'd ask her the next time he saw her. She'd blush and that would also alert her parents on how they'd all been duped.

He watched as Jaren was pushed out of the room and sighed. Perhaps he'd go into the office in the city and work there today. He didn't want to face any of them just now. He wasn't sure he could be civil to Adnil or Gred. Not without some time to deal with his anger.

The conference call was a shock. At least Paknol would be aiding in Adnil and Gred's destruction. After the call was over, he turned to Banak. "Get copies of the reports on the electronics company, KRT, that Adnil put together back when we were looking at them, as well as whatever we have on the current situation with them and Rader Kessem. That's how we can attack them but not let them know what's happening. How easy will it be to insert someone to keep an eye on their progress?"

"As a technician, not very likely, ser. They probably only have a few and we'd have to eliminate one to get a man in. That could cause suspicions. Menial staff is more doable. I'll look at their staffing and see about creating a janitorial opening for the evening shift if we can manage it. An offer of higher pay somewhere else should do it to ensure an opening or two. We can always make room for someone at one of our nearby facilities. I doubt they're paying anything above minimum and without any real benefits. That sort doesn't usually care about their workers, just what profits they can make and how high they can force their share prices to get working capital."

"Hmph. Someone who goes everywhere and would be ignored by everyone. Good. Get the rest of the surveillance equipment installed at Adnil's as soon as possible but make sure no one there suspects anything."

"We can arrange a power outage with a drunk driver hitting a pole," Stefent said. "Knock out all their alarms and all the staff will be looking in the wrong direction. We can attach the units to existing power so we don't have to worry about changing batteries."

Jaren's presentation the next morning both shocked and amazed him. It was everything he'd hoped for and more. He glanced at Ofelan. His eyes were a bit wider than normal. Good. He'd let Ofelan lead the questions for now. The ogre had to keep up appearances. Jumping up and down for joy would confuse Jaren and his doctor would not be happy at that level of exertion. Not with his heart condition, which he had concealed from everyone but the doctor and Steffent. He was glad Adnil and Gred didn't know or they might have come up with a very different plan to eliminate him and Jaren.

"How did they get into such a sorry state?" Ofelan asked. "Why hasn't it shown up before? I was sure we'd gotten good reporting."

"Their overall profits were always going up," Jaren said with a shrug. "Even with the increased costs of salaries and toys for the inmates, if profits are up and patent generation seem to be holding steady there is less inclination to look beyond into the murky pond of statistics. Suntz says 'What is obvious is often the lie. Look below and find the layers'."

"That one's actually appropriate. What tipped you off?" Ofelan cocked his head to one side.

"There is a lot of tension between the inmates and the engineers and other staff. My guide, Ralth Calthor, was pissed off at the inmates when I first met him and I dismissed it at first thinking it was simply jealousy. They have great salaries and he didn't but too many things weren't right. The real scope of the problem hit me when I finally tracked down the numbers and types of patents for the last ten years." Jaren pulled a hand-drawn graph out of the folder.

"Profits are in green, the number of patents in red," he said, handing it across the table.

"The number of patents hasn't changed that much," Darit growled.

"That graph is from last year's annual report showing the ten year history. But if you look at only new ideas, rather than improvements on already patented ideas, you get this." He pulled out another graph. "This was *much* harder to find, sers. The descending line is novel idea patents. The other is the improvement ones."

"Only two novel patents last year?" Ofelan sat back in his chair. "And they dared ask for raises?" Ofelan looked at Darit. "I can feel the need to stomp coming on, ser."

"I agree. With very large boots."

"Another thing that I think has slowed down progress is the residual income the inmates get. I think some are coasting on past glory rather than working to get new inventions into production. They also try to sabotage experiments from other groups if they're more senior, possibly to impede the newer inmates. They order the engineers to put their work first. It can take several days to shut down one test set up and put everything in place to run another. Without a Chief Science Officer, there isn't much that can be done. The president certainly isn't doing much but damage control and that isn't working very well."

"We can't do much about the residual income," Ofelan said. "It's written into their contracts. And the CSO would keep the experiments in proper order. We will need to find someone quickly, even if all they do is keep that sort of sabotage from continuing." Darit nodded.

"I managed to find the template for their contracts in the computer records. It actually says they get a percentage of the *profits*, sers. Not the income. What if the accountants adjust those profits so they're zero for the next quarter or three?" Both men stared at him.

"There's always costs for any line item, even older ones. And the contracts' expiration dates should be checked to ensure they're all up to date. Putting a time limit on their future payouts or use a decreasing scale so they get nothing after a few years could encourage them to be more productive. I also think the bonus should extend to the entire team, including the engineers and the techs involved."

A slight grin made Darit clench his jaw so he wouldn't smile back. He guessed where Jaren was going with that statement.

"The inmates will share the bonus with them. Retroactively, of course. The idea is one thing, turning it into a product we can sell is very different and perhaps more important than the original idea was. That would also raise morale among all the junior scientists and the engineering teams. They may not be giving their best efforts because of how the senior researchers see and treat them."

Ofelan snorted. "Ingenious. That should spur them to new efforts."

"There's also a major problem with the computer log-in procedure. The top inmates and upper management have specific log-in names and passwords. Everyone else, engineers to the accountants, use Guest, with visitor as the password. That gives them very limited access to any of the data and other records about a project. The administrative password is root, with inmate as the password. That also needs to be changed. Soon." Jaren paused. "I did reveal the admin codes to one of the engineers. He may have passed them on. Otherwise, I think he was close to quitting. And with the knowledge he has of the stalled projects, that would not be a good idea."

Darit tried not to smirk. All were very good ideas. Deciding which one to implement first would be an enjoyable interlude. He waved a finger at Ofelan to ask another question.

"The science officer position is crucial. Who did you think to promote?" Ofelan picked up his coffee.

"None of the existing inmates, sers. I'd find someone completely outside their cliques and rivalries: outside the company completely if we have to. Someone older, with considerable scientific knowledge, who can also stomp as required. Some inmates might be too disruptive to keep on so the history of every one of them needs to be examined. It might be possible to intimidate some into behaving but other measures might be needed for others. I also recommend a new position: Chief Engineering Officer. They need someone with equal authority to the CSO to champion their efforts. They and their equipment can be reassigned when they are in the middle of a delicate experiment and they have to shut everything down and do it. It takes time to move everything for the other project and the same thing could happen to that one. The CSO might not be able to be effective in both positions." Jaren paused.

"The president has let the inmates get away with too much to leave him in place. Same with the other upper level managers. The way the patent data was presented in the annual report means they're aware of the problem and haven't done anything to fix it or they've tried and can't do anything. They've all colluded in hiding the truth. Find them somewhere where they won't have the same problems with the employees or retire them. I found projects that could make us millions that just need a little more work. I'm glad now that I took two years of the science and technology survey course at university. It helped a lot trying to understand what the new inventions were supposed to do."

"Give me an example of these hidden best-sellers you found." Darit sipped at his own coffee.

Jaren pulled a piece of paper with another piece of paper stuck to its centre out of his file folder. "This is a gummynote. It's a dumb name but that's what marketers are for." He lifted the smaller sheet off, then set it back down, ran his finger along the top and lifted the original sheet by the edge. The gummynote didn't fall off. He held it sideways and the paper didn't fall off. Then upside down. The bottom edge slumped down but it stayed attached. Both men glanced at each other.

"The basis for it is a truly terrible adhesive," Jaren said. "The team responsible was trying for something like epoxy but stronger, slightly flexible and more durable for situations where two parts will shift a little in use. This was way worse on strength, so the inmates ignored it as not filling their mandate. It *never* forms a permanent bond with anything, from what I understand. One of the engineers by the name of Marthon thought it had possibilities and worked on it in his spare time because he thought it would be useful. He has been in trouble several times for keeping the development of this and other projects active when he'd been told to ignore them."

Darit extended a hand and took the sheet as Jeran leaned forward. He lifted and replaced the gummynote several times, then looked at the back of it. A centimetre wide discolouration was the adhesive.

"So, no more adhesive tape?" he asked.

"That will still be in use for more permanent applications, but if you want to leave someone a quick note and don't want it buried on their desk, you can use a gummynote to leave it on the handset of their telephone, or on a wall, or anywhere. And because it's *such* a terrible adhesive, it won't damage the wall or even wall paper. You could leave yourself a note on your house or suite door so you don't forget to take something to work. Another use listed in the report I read was a smaller version in bright colours for marking places in a report where signatures were needed or something important was mentioned and using a permanent marker on the document was not desirable. I managed to find Marthon's report on them in their database. It listed forty different applications. A copy of that report is in here. I printed it out late at night so no one knew I had it." He lifted the file folder from his lap.

"I didn't speak to the engineer directly about the gummynotes so I wouldn't let anyone know what I was really looking for. We need copies of all the *failed* projects they've let languish, sers. There could be another fifty or more of these money-makers hidden away and we have no idea what they are. Someone else could come up with a similar adhesive today and we would lose any rights to patent it, or possibly to use this one in competition with theirs. We would have no legal recourse. If we had even a provisional patent in the queue, we would be covered."

"He's right," Ofelan said. "This could be a huge seller. In all markets, not just for business applications. My wife would want a longer sheet to use for a shopping list. And it could sit on the fridge until grocery day for everyone to add to it. A pad for phone messages for every receptionist and household: business and personal markets."

"We don't have a subsidiary that could manufacture it," Darit pointed out, the ogre dismissing Jaren's achievement. "Licensing production would limit our profits."

"We may, sers," Jaren said. "I asked my secretary to check the subsidiary listings yesterday morning. Bayside should be able to produce the adhesive if I read that part of the report correctly. Coron Cards makes speciality envelopes along with fancy holiday cards. They'd need new production lines to make the gummynotes but they also have space available to expand their plant. There are workers available in that area, so the construction and then staffing will stimulate the local economy. A paper mill that's being expanded and belongs to the Staris clan is two hours away. They may also expand if you wish to continue to use them for the paper supply. If these become as popular as I think, we'd have to set up one or more separate facility to keep up with demand and the different sizes and maybe shapes. The marketers should be involved early on to determine what product we produce first. Although, I think we'd need a lot of them ready to ship to restock immediately after the launch. Or have them in warehouses in all the major cities before the official day. Whichever might be faster to keep product on the shelves for people to buy. Large containers full all ready to reach the stores."

"Have you thought of a way to retrieve all the information on the other projects without alerting the inmates that their days are numbered?" Ser Ofelan was playing with the gummynote now. Darit looked at him, wanting to take it back. He wished Jaren had been able to sneak more samples away. Perhaps the guide Jeran had mentioned would be useful for more information and samples. He'd get the man's name later and have someone contact him. A promotion and raise would show that his efforts were valued. Of course, there might need to be some theatre to keep the inmates from discovering what was about to happen to their comfortable existence. He repressed a smile.

"Off-site storage of data," Jaren said promptly. "Things have the potential to go boom, there. Not as probable as at Bayside Deada facility but there is still the potential. Storing the data off site is done at many subsidiaries, generally at the president's residence. AR&D's president lives too close to the facility to guarantee their basement storage as truly safe. We order copies of the tapes be sent here by sending a memo from someone down the chain in Records, not anyone near the top. That will help give with the illusion that it's a routine precaution, not because we're eager to get them. That will be a slower process, but better than someone showing up with a case or ten of tape reels and demanding immediate access to their data room. That same person should send similar memos to all the subsidiaries, in fact. It's a good idea in general, I think. I'm sure there are people in ser Ofelan's department who can go over the other playpen files to determine how viable they are. I picked the gummynotes because I felt they were a product that was close to marketability. I could only get one in case someone noticed me going through the engineer's desk when I should have been somewhere else."

"Very good work," Darit said, forgetting to channel the ogre. "Ser Ofelan will take it from here. You concentrate on getting better. You'll have a lot more to do once we get those tapes." He was surprised to see a flush on Jaren's cheeks. Why was the real Jaren so astonished that his father would congratulate him on such an accomplishment? Once all this was over, he wanted to spend time rebuilding their relationship. If it was even possible after all this time.

Chapter 22

Jaren could barely contain his smile as Hartner pushed him back to his rooms. Father thought his information was valuable. This would go a long way to getting the blasted restrictions lifted, showing that he *was* adult enough to be trusted. Father wouldn't forget about the poppers for months but he would realize that Jaren could make valuable contributions to the running of the holding. He couldn't wait until he got back up to his room to start a letter to Sanil. He was sure Feneir would get it to her, but any thank you money would have to wait until his accounts were unlocked. He did remember to smile and thank the footman who'd pushed him up here. Once the door closed he rolled the wheelchair over to his desk and pulled out pen and paper.

'Dearest Sanil,' he started the letter. '*I have to confess to a really, really stupid thing...*'

Feneir gave him a little smile when he saw the envelope on Jaren's bedside table when he came to help him get to bed that night. He tucked it in his coat pocket and nodded. Jaren smiled back.

"Your ankle's a lot less swollen," Feneir said as he re-wrapped the tensor. "I'll call one of our medics tomorrow and have him take a look. Likewise your knee."

"It's doing okay. I think it was the shock of the later falls that made everything worse."

"Could be. There wasn't any damage in the scans. I know you really love the wheelchair but you need to get back on your feet."

"I know. I fell in the ditch because I just couldn't walk any more. Neither leg could support me, so I found some bushes to hide behind until the Bayside guards arrived." That thought led to another, darker one. "Is there any word on the kidnappers?"

"Not that I've heard," Feneir replied. "It does seem they kept you unconscious for several days from the pictures that were sent here. I'd consider that a bonus so you didn't hurt as much from the whip. They did one instant photo a day, you know. And because of the withdrawal cramps, you had more like three weeks of very limited mobility, not just a couple of days. It's no wonder that you were exhausted when you reached the highway. There's not much we can do exercise-wise until your ankle is better. And there won't be much stress we can put on your arm for a couple of weeks. Maybe we'll start some crunches tomorrow, and light weights with your right hand."

Thinking about the kidnappers just before trying to sleep hadn't been the best plan, Jaren realized. First, he'd had trouble getting to sleep, but he'd now woken up twice with nightmares.

He got out of bed and into the wheelchair and out into the sitting room to his desk, intending to read some of his other purloined playpen documents that hadn't quite fit into the report. He could send those observations in through his secretary up to Ser Ofelan. To show him how much he'd learned before the kidnapping.

A noise from the suite's main door startled him. Pagil's face in the opening reassured him.

"Everything all right, ser? Saw the light come on a few minutes ago. Thought you'd just needed the bathroom so I didn't want to bother you. It's been a half hour now."

"I had a nightmare. Asking Feneir about the kidnappers just before bed was a stupid idea. Thought I'd work a while to clear my head before trying to get to sleep again."

"I have a better cure than reading dull reports. Food. You need feeding up." Pagil came into the room and closed the door over. "Does that sound like a better plan?"

Jaren's stomach growled. He could use a snack. "Sure. Let's go."

The house seemed very quiet. There was a guard in full armour near the elevator and he nodded as they passed. There were several other guards in the corridors.

"Is having all these guards in the house usual? I can't remember ever seeing this many guards at night." Then again, he was hardly ever out of his suite at this hour so he couldn't be sure. He sort of turned in the chair to look at Pagil.

"We brought in a few more men to augment the current staff," Pagil replied. "Mostly we'd be outside, but Chief Steffent was upset when he found out the kidnappers had eliminated the pair of outside guards at the estate very easily and only one person was awake in the house except for that doctor and you. That guard was near the front door, as if he was just going to do a circuit or to check on the other two. They might have been waiting for him when he opened the door. Bad timing, we hope. No weapons of theirs were fired or even out of their holsters. At all. Complete and total surprise. So you understand he's very concerned. So are we, as you might guess. There have been more cameras installed on the perimeter and at various entrances. The men inside can also be seen by at least two others. We also get to check in at random times, but about twice an hour. Chief Steffent wants to be sure everyone here is safe."

"And I wasn't paying attention to much of anything that night, just went down the stairs and walked right into them. The whip hit my arm and that's all I remember until I woke up in that building."

They reached the two-way door to the kitchens and Pagil backed them through. The light panel was easy to spot with the single light shining in the middle of the room. Pagil flicked all the levers up. Light bloomed behind him. Then the chair swivelled around and he could see the kitchen. He'd never imagined it would be so large.

The perimeter of the kitchen was filled with counters, storage units and three six burner gas stoves with vent hoods. A myriad of pots hung from the ceiling and three gleaming work surfaces filled the middle of the room.

"I've never been in here before," he said, looking around. "How many people get fed from here? Everyone in the compound?" And how big was a kitchen in a worker's house or apartment? Those couldn't be this big! There'd be no room for anything else. Wait: The small house on the grounds had a kitchen that was perhaps one tenth the size of this one. That must be what most people had. Unless they had a huge family or ate in shifts.

"Not that many in general. Mostly you and the ser right now. Visitors. This is set up mostly for parties or large fancy dinners. Us guards and the servants have a cafeteria by the barracks. Didn't you ever wander downstairs for a snack when you were a teen? My mom always complained that me and my brothers never left any food in the fridge when we were growing. Growled all the time and grinned like anything when we were measured and were taller."

"I had a small fridge and cupboard in my room that a footman kept stocked back then so I didn't have to disturb anyone if my stomach started growling late at night. I didn't know you had siblings. Do you see them often?"

"Mostly we write. My mom always said a sandwich and cocoa were the best cure for nightmares," Pagil said. He parked Jaren next to a small table and moved into the kitchen area. A kettle was soon heating and he vanished into a cooler, then stuck his head back out. "Ham, cheese and mustard okay?"

"Yes," Jaren was bemused. "I've never seen anyone cook before."

Pagil snorted. "This isn't cooking, it's only snackage. Cooking is an art form when it's done properly."

Whatever it was, the sandwich was good. Pagil toasted the bread and the cheese melted into the thinly sliced ham. The cocoa had something different as well, but he couldn't identify it.

"What exactly were you dreaming, ser?" Pagil also had a mug of cocoa but only took a small sip before speaking.

"Not you too," Jaren said, taking a deep breath. "I tried to tell Darthan I'm not a ser yet before we got on the plane. He said that he didn't care that my birthday is in the spring. Next spring."

"And he told Caldon the same thing he told you when *Caldon* called him on it the day you returned. All of us on your detail thought about it and agreed. We won't use the term in front of your father or anyone else, mind, but you'll hear it from us from now on. So, *ser*, the dreams."

Jaren sipped a couple of times at the cocoa to give himself time to prepare what he would say. "I was lying on my back, couldn't move and hurt all over, not just my arm. Had some trouble breathing, because of the pain, I think. Somebody was standing near my head but I couldn't see them clearly. Barely out of my line of sight, I think. No one said or did anything." He shrugged.

"That dream is nothing that I actually remember happening when I was kidnapped. I suppose it might be echoing the withdrawal cramps but that pain was different. In the dream it was more all through my torso and back, not just my stomach. The anti-drug conditioning triggers nausea whenever I get near one of the listed drugs. The doctor stimulated it several times so I'd recognize the symptoms and leave where I was before it peaked. It was nothing like the dream either."

"Probably an overactive imagination," Pagil said. "You went through what we in the trade call a traumatic event, ser. Something *we're* supposed to protect you from. Do you ever remember seeing a vid show that had those elements? Could have been years ago."

Jaren thought while chewing another bite of the sandwich. "Not offhand, but yes, probably. Had a phase where I watched a lot of horror vids. Father did not approve of them and I stopped after a while. I did have some nightmares at the time, since about the only time I could watch anything without him knowing about it was late at night with a bath towel to block the vid light from showing under my door so the guards wouldn't know I was still awake. Could a book also trigger one?"

"Might. Vivid memories can give vivid dreams. Doesn't matter where your brain gets the idea. Movies and real life are the usual. Just so you know, having nightmares after what you went through *is* normal."

Jaren's eyebrows raised since his mouth was full.

"I know. Sounded really stupid when I first heard it too. Read some studies, talked to older guards, and they all said the same thing. The dreams are big part of coping with what happened to you. They do go away." Pagil sipped his cocoa.

"It wouldn't be soon enough for me," Jeran said after he swallowed. "How long will they keep bothering me?"

"Hard to tell. If you're still having a lot of them next week, it would be worthwhile talking to a professional. We have a good doc on tap for the guards now. She might be able to help if you need it."

"We'll give it a week, then. I also have to do a full debrief on the kidnapping and my escape for Chief Steffent. And Father." The sandwich was gone and the cocoa cup was drained. He did feel better, in spite of the knowledge that he'd have to talk to someone about everything that had happened. Maybe it would be Feneir. Or would someone he didn't know make it easier to admit how much he'd messed up and how afraid he'd been?

"Then let's get you back to bed. Morning isn't that far away. I'll leave word that you might need a nap later today."

An opened newspaper sat at his place for breakfast the next day. '*Mystery man threatened your reporter at ten thousand meters!*' It was the headline on the clan news/gossip page. Adnil and Gred weren't down yet, the footman who'd pushed him this morning had said quietly. Only his father was there, ready to go into the office. He glanced at the article below. There wasn't much content. '*A young, injured, bearded man had threatened the reporter with DEATH for asking a simple question about his identity! The stewards did NOTHING! All attempts to identify the man have failed. What are the clans coming to?*'

"Did you speak to him?" Father asked.

"I only said no to someone who said he thought he knew me," Jaren replied. "As I was ordered to. Surly was the word Chief Steffent used to describe how he wanted me to behave. He'd said the rest of the cover wasn't in place. I did not speak to anyone else, not even the stewards."

"How did he get a death threat out of that simple statement?"

"Darthan may have been a little out of line," Jaren said. "He did ask the man nicely to go away first. When the man didn't want to, Darthan said that he'd apologize later to his clan for killing him. I guess he's the reporter who wrote the article."

"Hmph." His father's lips twitched. At least Jaren had managed to amuse him.

Jaren moved the paper to one side and nodded thanks as Marin poured his coffee. He needed it with the few hours of sleep he'd gotten. Even when he got back into bed, it had taken an hour or so before the last time he remembered what time the clock showed.

"We need to get you obviously back here and spread that cover story around," his father said slowly. "Steffent should have had you tell everyone on the plane about the riding accident. That estate is remote enough no reporter could have done anything to discredit the story in the time available. Maybe we should arrange a leak of your identity. And an interview with that fellow to shut him up." A grimace at that. Father hated the press, many of whom didn't know when to stop investigating or writing when they were just starting out. Had very noble and stupid ideas of revealing all the Truth about some incident. Either they were smart and learned or they were stupid and vanished.

"I didn't know he was a reporter. I didn't recognize him at all," Jaren said. "I don't generally look at that section of the paper." He sipped at the coffee.

"Nor do I," his father admitted after a deep breath. "My secretary noticed the article and sent word to Marin."

Gred and Adnil came in together.

"Sorry I'm late," Adnil said. "Couldn't find the shirt I wanted to wear today and then realized it was still at home. Any news?"

"I'm expecting a report from Steffent this afternoon," Father said. "The kidnappers would be harder on anyone taken now, since Jaren managed to escape. I would guess another week might be safest, Adnil. I don't want to lose any other relatives. Not now."

"I know, Darit," Adnil said. Jaren could see the pain of loss in both older men. Gred just looked puzzled. Marin, bringing in the breakfast offerings, broke the mood.

"And how is your ankle today, Jaren?" Gred asked.

"Feneir's going to bring one of our medics in today to check on it. He thinks I should be mobile soon. Then he's going to get me back into shape." He did grimace. "Treadmills, my favourite." The others smiled openly, including his father. That was so strange.

The appearance of the bill from the flight home on his desk depressed him. His father had said it would be his responsibility but he hadn't realised how expensive one executive class ticket would be, let alone three. And their salaries for the trip and the time they'd been here. At double time as the assignment merited potential hazard pay. He found his most recent account statement in a drawer. Fortunately there was more than enough to cover the costs. A section of a blank authorization sheet had enough space for other disbursements. He stared at it for several minutes as thoughts raced through his head.

There were other obligations he had: the rescue teams and especially Darthan deserved a bonus. Tossem Sarnd's family and the families of the other dead guards also deserved a personal thank you for their sacrifice. And the doctor's family, if he had one. It was expected. He reached for a pen and added the names and information. Now he really *was* broke. If Father approved the total disbursement. If he didn't approve then he'd send letters and as soon as he had control of his own money again, he'd send double.

* * *

The slave watched from the background. He'd tried to update the impostor last night but the nightmares had kept waking the primary. He didn't have the luxury of sleep since the master had said to keep the other two in sync. That meant nightly updates. Constant monitoring of what went on in the primary's life now that he was the active one. He was glad that the primary had written to his love yesterday. That knowledge would not be transferred. The congratulations from the father master after the presentation yesterday would be tempered. The impostor would hear it differently: *it's about time you proved your worth*, not the sincere congratulations of a proud parent.

This morning's comment on bringing Jaren back officially, from the father master, would be tempered as well. He would have to think what would best advance the masters' plans. He paused. Master Gred said to keep the impostor updated and do *whatever* was necessary. That meant the imposter needed to be activated to process the memories and fully integrate them. Part of it could be done during sleep, but only when the personality was awake could it be done properly. Once the primary was alone in his room for an evening, the imposter could come out safely. Could he do it? The slave imagined activating the impostor and no pain resulted. He stopped and considered what might be possible now. Perhaps he could actually thwart the master's plans. So they all might live.

* * *

Jaren sighed as Harten pushed him down a secondary corridor in the house. Smaller offices and meeting rooms for the staff. Time for his debriefing, Feneir told him after breakfast.

A partly opened door was their destination. Harten stopped the chair, then knocked. An older woman came to the door and smiled at them. Light brown hair, carefully styled. She wore a subdued skirt set of the type that was common for middle management women. Not someone that you'd notice in a crowd, but her smile did seem sincere. He guessed she'd had a lot of practice in using it over the years.

"Serit Jaren. I'm Doctor Tessill Margrail. Please come in."

"Doctor." She moved away, opening the door fully, and Harten carefully pushed the wheelchair through the narrower than usual door.

Harten positioned the chair beside a small table, then left, shutting the door after him. Some papers, a recorder and a box of eye-wipes sat on it. The rest of the office was sparsely furnished. No art on the light blue walls, a full bookcase in one corner, a small desk and several file cabinets. A tiny cupboard held a covered water pitcher and small glasses.

"Do you have any questions before we begin, serit?" She sat on the other side of the table.

"Why am I talking to *you*, Doctor?" Came out before he could help it. He did notice a recorder on her desk but didn't think it was active. Yet.

"And not one of your bodyguards, or at the very least, someone from the security office?" She didn't seem offended by his question.

He nodded.

"As Pagil said he told you, I help various of the staff and guards deal with upsets in their lives, be it in the course of their duties or from personal issues. I've worked for the clan for the past twenty years, so I have seen and heard a great deal about missions that haven't gone as planned and a thousand bruised and broken hearts and minds. Chief Steffent suggested that I start to do all the debriefings about three years ago. It has worked out very well, since anyone who needs my other help is identified quickly."

"Oh. I didn't think the guards needed any help. I mean, they're trained to do missions. Aren't they?"

"They are, but there is still an emotional cost to what they do. Some need little help, others need more. Part of my job is to help new staff and especially new guards to learn some important coping skills before an event happens that can cause problems."

He shifted in the wheelchair. It wasn't very comfortable.

"Why not sit in the proper chair? It is much more comfortable than the wheelchair is."

He nodded. It was going to be hard to talk to her about all the things that had happened. He might as well be sitting on something comfortable while he squirmed. She helped him stand up and shift to the chair. She was right. It was better. And he might need someone stronger than she was to help him up once this was over since the seat was lower than he could rise from easily.

"So. Let's start at the beginning, shall we? I understand that Ser Gred

Calyno was the one who told you about Doctor Sumon, the conditioner, and arranged for him to meet you at the estate." He heard a small noise as the recorder started. She set a small microphone on the table.

Jaren nodded. "He set things up for me, and his guards and some others from AR&D were there with us. I managed to convince Caldon that he needed a holiday too, so I only had Sarnd with me. Sarnd was the only one of my people who knew about the poppers. He'd been getting them for me after university and was the one who made me realize I needed help because I was using them too much. Everything was going really well just before the attack. The withdrawal took over a week, Doctor Sumon said. I wasn't really coherent a lot of the time in the beginning because of the cramps. That delayed the conditioning since I couldn't relax even with the drugs until the cramps went away. He was a little pissed that he'd come out and had to hang around until I was better."

"Was Ser Calyno with you the entire time?"

"Not after the first week. Gred had to go back to playpen, AR&D, after his holiday time was up, but he came back on the weekends to keep me company. I wasn't able to do much, but I was glad he came. There weren't any signs we were being watched. None of the guards said anything and they would have taken us all to somewhere safe or called for more guards if they'd had any hints of danger."

"Two hiding places were found by the first teams on site," the therapist said. "One on either side of the house where they had quite a good view of everyone and could see how the guards patrolled."

"How long did they watch the house? Any idea?" Had those guards been *that* incompetent? Or had they sold the information and been paid with a quick death instead of a pile of cash?

"Just a few days, I'm told. Three at most. One of them might have followed ser Gred there from AR&D and that's how they learned of your location. And that you were alone there during the week."

Jaren took a breath to bring his mind back to his recitation of the facts. "Anyway, I was working on the report on playpen for my father and my stomach started growling. It was late, full dark. I'm not sure of the exact time. I hadn't eaten much while the cramps were hitting me so I'd lost weight. The doctor suggested I eat whenever I felt hungry and I'd started doing some exercises to regain my lost muscle tone. We didn't want anyone suspicious of my sudden weight loss when I came back. Feneir would have known something was different immediately.

"That night, I went down to the main level to raid the kitchen as I had the past couple of nights. The bedrooms are all upstairs. I walked right into one of the kidnappers. Then everything went dark. When... when I woke up, it was at the ranch they were using to keep me. My left arm really hurt. I guessed it was from a neuronal whip. Caldon described the pain to me a few years ago. Back when we went over the kidnapping protocols. I think he downplayed how much it would hurt, even several days later. I guess he didn't want to scare me."

"All the guards were taken down with neuronal whips, then shot," the doctor said. "That's the general belief, at any rate. Doctor Sumon wasn't shot, but he died when his head hit the fireplace surround after he was stunned by a neuronal whip. We don't know if the kidnappers knew exactly who he was. Possibly they thought he was helping you with some analysis. He is also under investigation to ensure he wasn't the one to give away your location. That is still ongoing, but at first glance, he wasn't involved. They might have brought him with you if he'd lived, in case he was someone important. They wouldn't want to stay long in case Ser Calyno returned without notice."

"But Sumon died." Jaren looked at his right wrist, the bandage peeking out. "I was handcuffed when I woke up, with another set on my ankles. There was a lock and a chain from the ankle chain that led to a bolt set into the concrete of the floor. I had a canteen and a blanket. That was it. I couldn't reach a wall, and the door hinges hadn't been oiled in years so if I undid the cuffs and was loose I couldn't go out that way or they might hear the door opening."

"Was your mind affected when you woke?"

"The first day I was awake it was like I was in a fog, doctor. Couldn't really concentrate. All I did was sit there like a lump. Obeyed them when they wanted a picture to send to Father to prove I was still alive."

"We'll talk more about that later, Jaren." Her voice changed. Softer but still authority in it. "But with the drugs they would likely used to transport you and keep you unconscious, in addition to the neuronal damage, it is not surprising that you were less than coherent at first. That passed by the next day, didn't it?"

"Yes. When I woke up the next morning it was better. Caldon had told me about how to work through the pain from a whip, and I started doing all the exercise I could stand. And I had my lock-picking tools in my belt. Caldon taught me about how to use them a few years ago."

"A very good thing he did, Jaren. How many men did you see there?"

"Four different ones came into the outbuilding where they kept me, but I knew there had to be more. They all wore dark clothing and ski masks. They didn't talk much but it was lower class speech. Workers. But there wasn't a lot of slang, as I might have expected. Only a few words I didn't understand. I saw six of them, in three cars, at the rest stop after I arrived there and called in. One of them shot out the phone before they left and headed away from the city."

The rest was soon told. Facts only. When Jaren reached the part where the Bayside guards reached him, the doctor nodded and shut off the recorder. Put the microphone beside it on the desk.

"That's it?" He hoped. Wanted to get back to his room and crawl under the covers. All the things he hadn't said. How worthless he'd felt. All the training he'd done and he'd just stood there while the kidnapper had taken him down.

"How do you feel?" she asked. Gently now.

"I hurt all over, doctor. My pain meds are wearing off, so the aches are getting worse. Another week or two before everything heals up, I was told. I hope it doesn't take that long."

"I didn't mean physically, Jaren. Emotionally. How do you feel?"

"I'm fine," he replied after a moment. "Can you call someone to push me back to my room?"

"What will you do there?" Still a gentle voice.

"Rest." A polite response. "I can't do much else until everything heals, according to the medics."

"Do you know what just about every male person has ever said in regard to the question on how they are feeling after a traumatic event?"

"I don't know." Why wouldn't she want him to leave?

"They say they feel fine. But they are not fine. The same way you aren't fine, Jaren. If I let you return to your room right now, you will crawl into your bed and cry until you sleep. Then you will put on that brave face you show the world, leave that room and pretend that nothing is wrong. Every time you leave the safety of your room, this is what happens. Will continue to happen."

He didn't respond or look up at her.

"And if you keep on like this, and if nothing changes, Jaren, one day you will die. Likely by your own hand. And none of your friends or your father will understand why. They won't know the amount of pain you're carrying around and it will consume you. Completely. I can help you to deal with that pain. So that you can heal emotionally and have many years of life ahead of you."

"You don't know what I feel," Jaren said. "Or anything about me. I'm leaving now."

He managed to lever himself out of the chair and opened the door. Pushed the chair out and used it to support his bad leg and left. He was *not* weak. He had Sanil to keep him from doing anything stupid.

* * *

Feneir listened to the live feed from Doctor Margrail's office in a small room buried in the security bunker. When the doctor said that Jaren *would*, not just *might*, kill himself someday shocked him. Jaren wouldn't... He had to remember that this was the first real trauma Jaren had endured since his mother died. He paused. And maybe Jaren hadn't fully recovered from *that* loss. His teeth ground. Why hadn't he seen that the boy was in such pain? Maybe he needed to actually go to this doctor and talk to her himself.

"You don't know what I feel," Jaren's voice had changed. Harder than he'd ever heard it. Almost sounding like an angry ser Darit. "Or anything about me. I'm leaving now." Sounds that were harder to interpret. Then the sound of a door opening and closing with more than reasonable force.

A heavy sigh. Movement sounds. A drawer opening and closing. He cut the feed and stopped the tape. The Chief would get Doctor Margrail's official report later today. There wasn't anything Jaren said that needed to be adjusted for that report.

Feneir had to decide what to tell Ser Darit of Jaren's own precarious mental state. He *had* to get Jaren back into that room. Voluntarily. Or all of their efforts would be wasted. He'd talk to Pagil first. See if he had any ideas. Then with the doctor. Dealing with his charge's emotional problems had never been on his official list of responsibilities. Maybe it should be a part of bodyguard training in the future.

Chapter 23

Sanil regarded her mother's appearance with suspicion. "What's going on, Mom?" she asked. "You've never come visit me at school before. Is everything okay?"

"It is," her mom said as she sank into Sanil's favourite lounging chair. "I happen to have an errand to one of our subsidiaries in the vicinity, with the welcome bonus of seeing my favourite daughter."

"Lucky for me I'm the only one," Sanil pointed out with a fake smile.

"I do have something for Casteron as well," Mom said. "Since we were coming here, I thought it polite to bring it along with me." Her personal guard pulled an envelope out of his pocket and handed it to Julin who nodded thanks and opened it. Another envelope and a folded piece of paper came out.

"This one seems to be for you, seris," Julin didn't smile outwardly but the skin around his eyes crinkled. She knew.

"From Jaren! He's himself now?" She turned to her mother and hugged her.

"He is himself, dear. But there are things that you do need to know before you answer that letter."

Julin made a noise, then lowered his own note and tucked it into his pocket. From Caldon, she guessed. She couldn't decode this expression. That sobered her quickly. Jaren was still in danger, or was hurt worse than she'd already been told.

"We'll be out in the common area, sera. I'll have some tea ready when you're ready." The other guard left with him, his face also solemn.

"This is getting ominous, Mom," she said. "What's going on?"

"Several things, dear. Not all of them are bad. Sit down and I'll tell you." Sanil grabbed her desk chair and sat next to her mother.

"Jaren is recovering well from the injuries he sustained escaping. His forearm has a hairline fracture near the elbow so it will be a little while before he can start to use it, mostly to allow the considerable swelling to go down. His ankle is also getting better quickly and he should be walking with a cane by the end of the week. What caused my visit is something the surveillance recordings picked up. Your theory that the controller is much more active and aware than we suspected is quite true. He must have moved the memories of the E&E techniques from Jeran's memories to the impostor. Overnight, as you guessed."

"This is interesting and I'm relieved Jaren's getting better, but not very visit-worthy, Mom." She bit at her lip. What *didn't* Mom want to tell her about him? It had to be *very* bad if it was taking her this long to say what it was.

"The controller's status is." Her mother paused. "Doctor Hallent did not want to tell us and your father and I debated telling you. Strenuously. I am very happy that we invested in extra sound proofing for the office last year. It unsettles the staff when he gets that excited. Eventually we decided that if you and Jaren are truly serious about each other, you need to know what he's going through so that you can help him move forward with his life once this nightmare is over."

"And? You can't stop there, Mom. Not now." Sanil sat on the edge of her chair, the envelope crumpled and forgotten in her hands.

"Gred is a sadist. If you've never heard the term, it means a person who enjoys causing pain to someone else. Doctor Sumon, Falg Hantel, was one as well, from new evidence. As part of the conditioning process, they turned the controller into their slave. He is not allowed to refer to himself in the first person and calls Gred his master. He did whatever they ordered him to do or he was punished with a neuronal whip. Likely on a very low setting since there is little obvious nerve damage to Jaren. That would have revealed the conditioning. One of the neuronal whips found on site had a wider range of settings than normal. We believe it is the one Gred currently has in his luggage at the compound."

Sanil couldn't think. "That's illegal!" She couldn't think of anything else to say. Her mind was *not* working.

"I was appalled, as were your father and ser Darit. That sort of behaviour is illegal, but such sadism and domination *is* more prevalent than one thinks it should be. As parents, we have tried to keep the majority of the more sordid details of life from you and your brothers, at least until you were old enough to understand the depths of depravity found in some people. We would not normally have this conversation for at least two or possibly three years. I do not cherish being the one to explain this to you, but your father is beyond incensed. Everyone on the floor here would know that something was seriously wrong if he had come with me.

We can not allow any rumours to start regarding these events." She took a deep breath to continue.

"For instance, entertainment businesses like Rader Kessem's often have indentured people who have been conditioned and taught to believe that they are owned completely and totally. They can *never* pay off a debt they are told is ten or twenty times what it actually is. They must pay for food, lodging and medical care so only a little is ever paid on the principal of that debt. There is *nothing* done to them that they do not accept completely as their duty. They cannot say no, to use another metaphor you may recognize. One of the more common examples of this level of subjugation are high-class brothels that cater to the sadists in our midst."

"Why would someone want that? Hurting people is fun for them?" It made no sense to her and her horrified expression obviously showed it.

"I am very relieved that you do not understand their mentality, my dear." Mom took a deep breath. "I pray that you never do."

"So, let me think in small bits, because that's all I can do right now. Gred's beating on the controller, who has to let him do it. Eewww." Sanil said. "Wait. Does my Jaren know what's going on with the controller? Or could the imposter know anything?"

"Your Jaren does not know about any of his alternates. I think that the imposter has no idea of the others either. Only the controller knows that there are any others. There are some scars on Jaren's back that no one has mentioned to him. The guard from Bayside had only been his driver when he visited that facility for a class project, so did not know what might have been new or old injuries when he acted as valet to the imposter on his arrival at the Bayside president's residence. The marks are faint, but Caldon is very sure they were not there before this trip. Once the scrapes and so on from the kidnappers heal they will blend in. There also seems to be some leakage of information from the controller or the imposter. Jaren had severe nightmares two nights ago. He was disturbed enough to get up. Semant was on duty and Jaren went to the kitchen with him as a distraction. He described the dreams to Semant and he relayed the information to Caldon and thus to ser Darit, your father and me the next morning."

"He dreamt of being hurt? How?"

"Yes. Immobilized and in severe pain. A figure that he couldn't identify standing over him." Mom took another deep breath before she continued. "He thinks that the kidnappers may have done something else to him, but since his arm was the only area that had been damaged by a whip when he woke, he's confused about the source of the dreams. Semant led him to think that his mind had conflated a scene from a vid program or a horror novel with reality to help him process the emotional trauma of the kidnapping."

"What level would let Gred or Hantel hurt him but let him stay conscious? I thought one hit and you were out. That's what happened to the evil guards when Julin rescued him, wasn't it, Mom?"

"During the attack our men used the highest setting possible to drop the guards as quickly as they could. I don't know the answer to your question. Casteron or my guard will know if it is important. It would have to be a very low setting, as I said. Semant told Jaren he'd heard of people having similar nightmares after getting kidnapped or other traumatic events. He said that talking to a therapist might do him some good if the nightmares don't go away. He also pointed out that it was only a few days, really, since he'd woken up with the kidnappers. Once his injuries are healed, that can also help his mental state, distancing him from the trauma. We hope."

"What can I do to help him?"

"Read your letter, dear. Doctor Hallett would like to know what he wrote, but if you wish to keep it private, I understand and will protect that privacy, even from your father." Mom turned to the door and raised her voice slightly. "Tea would be welcome shortly."

Sanil looked down at the letter. She'd crushed it in her hands. She took a deep breath and slowly smoothed it, then opened the envelope.

'Dearest Sanil,' it started. 'I have to confess to a really, really stupid thing. I started using poppers during university and it got way out of control in the fall after you'd headed back. I was so stressed about the analyses I was doing for Father. I'd hoped to get off them and still be able to come up and see you at winter break as we'd planned, but it took a long time to get the withdrawal symptoms under control.'

She looked up, tears running down her face.

"He does remember me and is sorry he didn't get here for break because of the poppers."

"What else does it say?" Sanil nodded, smoothed the paper and began to read out loud.

'I can't ever take the recreational drugs again. Not voluntarily. At least that part worked well. That was the only good thing to come out of these past weeks. I have to ask you not to share the rest of my news with anyone, not even Casteron.

I was kidnapped over a week ago and all my guards were killed in the attack. And the doctor I'd hired to get rid of the addiction. Fortunately Gred wasn't there. Or I don't know what we would have done. He discovered the evidence of the attack. Guards we both knew for years, all dead.

I'm just glad Feneir wasn't with me then. I don't know what I'd do without him, especially now.

I managed to get loose and escape a couple of days ago. I'm not very mobile right now and won't be for a few weeks. I twisted my ankle in a rodent hole and cracked a bone in my arm during my shuffling escape. Both are healing okay. I'll be very happy to get out of this wheelchair. The dammed sling I have to wear won't let me move my arm or shoulder at all and my balance is terrible. It will take time to rebuild all my muscles. They're all like well-cooked noodles at the moment.

Father wasn't pleased about the poppers, as you'd imagine. He's piled a lot of restrictions on me, including freezing my accounts. I won't be able to see you until things calm down. No one is sure who the kidnappers were or if they'll try to grab me or my cousins again. Security is very high, even in the compound.

Please write me back. Soon. Feneir and Casteron can get the letters back and forth without letting anyone know about our love.

Again, I'm sorry I didn't tell you about the poppers sooner.

I love you and miss you.

Jaren'

Sanil handed the letter to her mom. "There's nothing else there that needs to be kept secret," she said. Mom read the letter quickly, then folded it and handed it back. "I'll make a copy of it and a copy of what I write to him when I send my reply."

A soft knock at the door heralded the guards with a tray of tea and nibbles. She wasn't sure she could eat anything after hearing all this. Mom forced a cup into her hands and they trembled. After a moment, she realised why. She wasn't afraid. She wanted revenge on Jaren's cousins and whoever they'd hired to do this to him. She looked up at her mother. Who was smiling at her expression.

"It seems that you've inherited your father's temper after all dear. Use it wisely."

* * *

Pagil pushed the wheelchair down to the basement workout room. There wasn't much Jaren could do physically, but Feneir insisted that he start working out. He wanted to start walking too. Anything to fill the empty hours he had while everyone else was at work with only time to think about what happened to him. Too much time to just sit and stare at the walls. Nothing on the vid even tempted him.

"Just a short time on the treadmill," Pagil said. "And leaning on the sides so your balance won't be off as badly."

Jaren managed to stand without help this time. "How slow can you set it to go? I might be up to a slow shuffle."

"We're using an older model for now. It's been in storage for a couple of years but it works fine. The user sets the speed by how fast they walk or run but that's a couple of weeks in the future. I tested it this morning while you were at breakfast. There's also a button that locks the mechanism for getting on and off safely."

Soon he was standing near the front of the machine. By leaning on the stand he could shuffle along, moving one foot at a time so the tread under his feet didn't move any faster than he could.

Fifteen minutes later, Pagil smiled. "That's it for now. How do your legs feel?"

"My ankle's not too bad," Jaren said. "My balance is terrible, though. I hope I can get rid of this sling soon."

"Another few days, from what I heard," Pagil replied. "Some light weights next, then a shower."

"I'll really need one," Jaren said. Pagil handed him a small towel so he could dry off his face.

They were waiting for the elevator when Pagil came around to the front of the chair so Jaren could see him. "How did your debrief go?"

"Okay. Didn't you see the transcript?"

"The official one. Nothing after she shut down the recorder. What did Doctor Margrail say about the nightmares?"

"That they were normal," he lied. "She said she'd helped a lot of the guards get over things that happened while they were on missions."

"And you haven't gone back to talk to her," Pagil said. "I asked her when I went to chat with her. She didn't say what you'd talked about once the recorder shut down. Just mentioned that she hoped you'd go back and talk with her. Soon."

"You went to her?" Jaren paused and ignored the rest of what Pagil had said. "Why?"

"Because Feneir and I failed you. We thought of ourselves, not you. And because we were away having fun, you were kidnapped."

"But I didn't *want* either of you with me, Pagil. I never wanted either of you to know about the dammed poppers. How addicted I was. I knew you and Feneir wouldn't approve of why I kept using them."

The elevator door opened and Pagil pushed the chair in. "We know that in our heads, Jaren. It's our hearts that still blame ourselves for everything that happened. Talking helps let that hurt out. Feneir told me he's made an appointment." A huff of breath. "And he's never gone to see *anyone* before. I told him a couple of visits to her office would be a lot cheaper than what he's going to spend at the dentist if he keeps grinding his teeth together. Our dental coverage is good, but not for complete replacement, and that's what he's heading for."

"I don't understand," Jaren said as the doors opened on the upper floor. "He doesn't seem that upset."

"When he's around you, he's on his guard," Pagil said as they went toward his suite. "It's when he's not that he shows how upset he is. We have to replace one of the fighting bags in our gym. He broke it two days ago. Stuffing everywhere. You've used them before. You know how tough they are. How hard you have to hit them to make them move."

"Oh." His door was open and Feneir came out.

"How'd you do?" He asked.

"Shuffled for fifteen minutes and then some weights with my right arm," Jaren said. "Shower time."

Feneir wrinkled his nose. "It's well past time for that. I think that sling needs cleaning too. Pagil, can you pop over to medical and see if they have something Jaren can use in the meantime?"

"Sure thing. Be back up in a few minutes."

Jaren didn't say anything while Feneir helped him out of the sling and his clothing in the bathroom. "I think I can manage," he said. He rotated his shoulder. "That's going to take a while to get back to full strength."

"How are the muscles? Tight? We can bring a masseuse in."

"Not really. Noodles." Jaren let his arm fall down to his side and tried to move it forward and back. It didn't move far. "Noodles all around."

"Immobility does that," Feneir said. "Go get wet."

His hair was the hardest to wash, but he managed with one hand. The warm water helped other muscles relax. Was what Pagil told him really how Feneir felt about the kidnapping? How could he ask without revealing that Pagil had told him?

Pagil was in his bedroom when he opened the door, with a robe mostly on. Feneir wasn't.

"Feneir's gone to kill another fighting bag," Pagil said. "I'd suggest he take a vacation but that is not going to happen anytime soon."

"He really thinks he's to blame for my kidnapping?"

"Yes. And maybe the poppers too. He's not talking much. Hope the doc can get him talking to her." Pagil helped him to a chair, then went into the bedroom to bring some clothing out.

"Doctor Margrail said some people kill themselves from the things that happen to them. Is... Feneir going to... to die?" The last word caught in his throat.

"I don't think so," Pagil said. "If he can work through his guilt and realize that he's not at fault, and gets to thump the stuffing out of someone who was responsible in the near future, he'll be fine."

Jaren let Pagil help him dress and put the tensor back on his ankle and a much more comfortable sling on his arm.

"I see what Doctor Margrail meant now," Jaren said. "But she doesn't know about Sanil. She'll keep me safe. I'm not as alone as she must think that I am."

"But you can only exchange letters for now," Pagil said. "That may not be good enough, Jaren. What happens when you keep waking up in the middle of the night with memories of what happened? We'll do all we can, but it may not be enough. Ham and cheese isn't a cure for that level of sadness or anger at yourself."

Jaren nodded and looked down at his hand. "I felt so useless, Pagil. Especially when I woke up at the ranch. I was so foggy that first day. And even after, I had to follow their orders. So they wouldn't beat me up or use the neuronal whip on me again. I wanted to escape, but, I feared what they'd do if they caught me." He stared at something on the floor, unwilling to see what Pagil thought of him. Weak, useless, not a ser. Never would be worthy of his father's title as leader of their clan.

"Then I'll let Doctor Margrail know you want to talk. Tomorrow, mid-morning. I'll take you down myself. All right?" Pagil's voice was gentle. "We know sort of what you're going through. It'll be okay."

Jaren nodded. Unsure if he believed it. He wished he could talk to Sanil. But he couldn't tell her all the really bad things either. Maybe the doctor was right. He might have to kill himself to escape the pain.

Chapter 24

Gred looked around the foyer of their own mansion with satisfaction. He'd missed the freedom they had living here. The compound was great, but there would have to be changes when they moved there for good. That many guards would make it difficult for some of his excursions or discrete visitors to his suite.

Then again, maybe they were just there because of the possible threat from the kidnappers. Personally, any incursion at the compound was a very stupid idea for even the most radical of kidnappers. Far too many people lived there. He'd asked his footman, Hartner, to keep an eye on his cousins. Just because he was concerned, of course. His cousins' safety was very important to him. And the extra *hundred hadn't hurt. A good investment that would pay excellent dividends for their future plans.

"It is good to see you back home, sers," their butler said. "All of your personal luggage was brought back this morning. Is there anything you need at this time?"

"A dinner without interruption," Adnil said with a smile. "It is good to be back home. Thank you." The footman took his overcoat.

"Dinner is in preparation, sers. It will be served in twenty minutes."

"Go get changed," Adnil told him when they were alone. "You'll need to go out tonight and meet with Kessem. I have the latest payment in my case. I'll fetch it once we've eaten."

"Of course, Dad," Gred replied. "And I'll take a couple of extra men with me, in case Darit's worry about kidnappers is real."

"Kessem may also have more information on them by now."

Rader Kessem leaned back in his office chair, his feet up on his desk. The bright red curtains and rug clashed with the darker maroon of a sofa and green of the pool table. Gred didn't let his distaste show. The man had no sense of decor or style.

"That was a real cock-up," he said. "All the guards dead and Falg Hantel as well. That man will be missed. Some men went through his home and the public office late one night. No one touched the other one, so we may be able to continue using the tapes and such he had there for our entertainers. They don't need anything personalized. I've also started a search for someone to replace him. That's going to be hard. The men he has working in his regular practice don't have enough smarts to do the special work that he did."

"The guards you sent all died without a struggle," Gred said with scorn in his voice. "You said they were good. And I lost men as well."

"Your dead men are your problem, but my dead men are also your problem. Did you add them to the holding database as I told you?"

"Yes," Gred said sourly. "No one is looking at them. Hantel could be a problem if they ask the right people. So far, everyone thinks his name is Sumon. The people who searched his offices were probably sent by Steffent to check up on him. To check if he was working with the kidnappers. We know he wasn't, but they're being very paranoid about the possibility. The number of guards at the main estate was higher than usual."

"And you can be appalled and say that you had no idea who Sumon really was if they do discover his real identity. All his papers and the vehicles were in his cover name. He might serve to have been the one to alert the kidnappers, if they find out who he really was. They killed him accidentally in the heat of the attack, or to prevent him from ratting them out. Either way works." Kessem shrugged.

"Any word from your associates on *who* the kidnappers might be?"

"Nobody that I know thinks that going after a direct heir to any of the clans, no matter how small they are, is a bright move. Alanyo is one of the smaller clans, but no one is talking about any attempts or even planning an attempt. I didn't mention names of course, just put out some feelers if there was someone interested." His feet came off the desk and he stood. "To business. Did you bring the loan payment with you?"

Gred lifted his briefcase. "All here." He opened the case and handed over the cash filled envelope. Falg Hantel's neuronal whip fit in here much better than the other one had. Using the lowered settings would extend the time and increase the pleasure he craved.

Kessem opened it and swiftly counted the money. "Paying just the interest again, I see," he said as he slipped the envelope in a desk drawer.

"I had to pay the expenses for the operation, including all the salaries," Gred said. "My cousin will be reimbursing me soon so next month's payment should include some on the principal. Now, if you don't mind, I'll go downstairs and release a little tension." Gred shut the case and turned toward the door.

"Nope." Gred spun back around to stare at Kessem.

"What?" His grip on the case tightened.

"You're going on a cash up front plan downstairs," Kessem said. "Your investment isn't doing well and I don't believe in throwing good money after bad. You can't add your fun to the loan any more. Unless you have *three hundred in your pocket right now, go home and you and your dad start to figure out how to start pay down on the principal without the little serit's money."

"We have an arrangement," Gred said, his jaw clenching.

"So we do. If you read the fine print on the contract you and your dad signed, you'll see that I have the right to call the loan if the value of your shares in the company reaches a hundred-twenty percent of the loan. I might just ask for enough to bring it back to the minimum, or I can call the entire loan. It's up to me, not you. Any court will back me up if you want to go that route. Doesn't matter how many judges your family has in your pocket. According to the figures you've provided, it's at a hundred-thirty percent right now. I'd start paying some principal if I were you." Kessem's jacket slid further open, showing a holstered weapon.

Gred steamed but then nodded and left. He had *five hundred in his pocket, but realistically they might need it if they were that close to the margin limit. Now he had to go home and tell his father of Rader Kessem's treachery. Taking out Kessem was not a viable option at this time. And it would not clear the loan, which would have to be paid off.

* * *

Hartner appeared in the doorway of the Security Office and went over to the reception desk. The woman behind it intimidated him. He'd seen her in the gym and weight room over the past few years. She could tear him apart and not exert herself.

"Is the Chief available? I need to report a bribe."

"From and to?"

"From Ser Gred. And to me. He also wants updates." Two other men came closer. The staff had all been told to report anything relating to the Sers Calyno. He was not disloyal to the Alanyo. He was doing his job.

He hoped he'd survive anyway.

The woman nodded at him. "Sit there." She went into the Chief's office. The other guards were between him and any exit. Both were armed with neuronal whips.

"He'll see you," she said, holding the office door open. A tiny movement of her head and the guards eased away.

Hartner managed to stand up and walk mostly normally to the office door. It was shut behind him as soon as he cleared the threshold and nearly hit him on the back since he wasn't hurrying.

"Come and sit down," Chief Steffent said, pointing at a chair facing his desk. "Ser Gred wants some information. What sort? And the payments?"

Hartner took a bit of solace from his tone of voice. At least he wouldn't die in the next few minutes. "He said that he was worried about the Ser and serit Jaren. That things might happen that they'd like to know about. To help, he said. I was wary, but eventually agreed. He gave me a number to reach his valet once they leave. And gave me *two hundred twenty over the time of their stay." He put the bills onto the desk, along with the contact information.

"Put those bills back in your pocket. They're going home today, as you may know. In a couple of days, I'll let you know what to send for your first message. Any other contact with them without my sanction won't be dealt with gently."

"I know, Chief."

"Get back to work. Don't tell anyone else about this arrangement."

Harten managed to stand again as the chief did. "I won't, Chief." He turned and left the room. Walked past the reception desk and back out into the fresh air.

That's when the shakes started. At least he wasn't actually on duty for another hour. Right now, he didn't think he could pour himself a drink without spilling it.

Chapter 25

Jaren walked slowly across the suite, his un-tensored ankle slightly twinging with every cautious step. A cane lay on his desk on the other side of the sitting room. There was a soft knock on the door and Feneir slipped in. He saw that the cane was not in Jaren's hand, shook his head and gave him a Look.

"The medic did say five days with the cane," Feneir said. "Not three. At least, that's what I remember him saying. No doubt I've started imagining things in my old age."

"My ankle *is* better," Jaren said, stopping and sinking into an over-stuffed chair. "Any word on when I can stop using this sling or at least go with something with fewer straps and such? It's still throwing me off balance. And once it *is* off, I'll still be off balance because I'll still be trying to compensate for it for another week or more." He sighed loudly.

"Two more days with it, minimum. No weights until you demonstrate full, and I do mean full, range of motion. It will take some time to get basic strength back since it's been immobilized for so long."

Jaren sighed again. "Any idea from the medics how long after that until I can go back to work?"

"I didn't think you'd be that eager," Feneir said, picking up the cane and bringing it to him with a Look that said 'you *will* use this until the medic clears you' or else.

"I'm bored," Jaren admitted. "*Really* bored. I tried reading but nothing quite holds my attention and I can't *do* much. There's only so many letters I can write to Sanil. I don't really have anything I can say, since I'm not able to do anything. Hobbies generally need both hands. Maybe I can get Father to send my next project here, with Talfer to do the typing and so on. Set up a temporary office downstairs. At least I'd be doing something instead of staring at the walls in between exercising."

"The ser will be home in twenty minutes," Feneir said, coming to stand next to him. "Why don't you ask him at dinner?"

"I will." Jaren looked up. "You didn't come in just to let me know Father will be home on time."

An envelope appeared in Feneir's hand. "Speaking of Sanil, you have mail." He dropped the envelope and Jaren grabbed it out of the air. "I'll send one of the footmen to remind you when it's time for dinner. And use the cane *and* the elevator."

Jaren barely heard him leave. All of his attention was on ripping open the envelope.

'Dearest love.' He read. Tension he hadn't realized he had released in his chest and shoulders.

'I thought something was bothering you during the summer, but I didn't want to press. Next time I think you're hiding something, be prepared to get nagged. Incessantly. I've been taking lessons from my mom since I was little. You will tell me if there is a next time. There had better not be.

How are your ankle and arm? Can you walk yet? One of my brothers twisted his ankle last year and it took two weeks for him to walk properly.

No one's heard anything about a kidnapping and I won't tell a soul. Any word on who was responsible? I'm so glad that you were able to get away. Maybe I should get Julin to teach me some E&E if I can come up with a good excuse.

There was a strange article in the clan news last week: was that you who threatened the reporter on your way home? They're such parasites. At least he didn't manage to identify you. What cover story are you using to explain how you were hurt?

I've been at school except for a quick trip home during winter break. I'm trying to get all my course work finished off so I can leave here early, since all of my courses are project based with no exams. I should be home in five weeks or so. It may take some time for us to see each other, but at least we'll be in the same city from then on.

Your dad's restrictions are so unfair. He's insufferable.

I just want to hug you. Then thump you for hiding things from me. Then kiss you. A lot.

Love, Sanil'

He was still staring at it when Hartner summoned him to dinner. He tucked the letter into his jacket pocket and limped to the elevator, using the cane as ordered. He needed the time the walk took to refocus on getting back to work. What argument would work best with his father? He opted for the truth once the meal was served.

"Is it possible to set up an office for me here at the house?"

"Work from here?" Father stared at him over the laden table. "Why?"

"Mostly because I'm very bored, Father," Jaren admitted. "I can't do a full day at the office right now. Feneir has me doing exercises off and on. Ten repetitions of a weight routine, but done spaced thru the day rather than all at once is what the medic suggested. Walking up and down the corridor with the cane every hour. That sort of thing. I can't do any real site visits when I can't walk. I *can* sit and read. And think."

"I agree your exercise regimen would not be appropriate at the office." Father ate for a few minutes and Jaren copied him. "The first of the data tapes from AR&D came in yesterday and the projects are being printed off. Ofelan said there were ten promising ones that his people have identified so far. So there might be a hundred or more by the time all the tapes have been examined. No idea how viable any of them will be, of course. Even ten percent would make a significant addition to the holding's wealth. The gummynotes alone could increase our total profits by three or five percent once the market realizes how useful they are."

"I hadn't realized there were that many projects," Jaren said. "I couldn't access the system for long at night and get enough sleep to keep up with all the demonstrations and evening entertainments they put on. I guess President Tilner meant it when he said they liked visits from head office. I don't know how Gred gets any work done. Maybe he's been there enough times that they've gotten used to him, or they just wanted to razzle and dazzle me because of who I am. The time and effort wasted on entertainments also meant they have someone to blame for any decreased productivity if they need an excuse. Added to the mix was that almost all the senior inmates and a few junior ones were politicking for the science officer position. That became tedious very quickly at the parties, since I'd just manage to get away from one of them and other would appear. I had to be there for nearly the whole time or they kept asking me if I was all right. If I'd caught a cold, or if I was bored."

Marin came in to clear their plates and bring in dessert and coffee. Neither spoke until he had left.

"What did you tell the eager aspirants?"

"The truth: I had absolutely no input on the decision. I was just there to observe the management style. They didn't seem to believe me. They also wanted substantial raises and new, very expensive equipment that I'm not entirely sure had any purpose in their research. They may have expected me to whip out a chequebook on the spot. I know some of them looked very disappointed when I didn't hand out stacks of toys and bonus cheques every day."

"Hmph. How *did* you find out about the gummynotes? You never did say during our meeting."

"I saw some the engineer had on his file cabinet during the first tour.

Calthor, my guide, introduced me to him about another project which was stalled because of the lead scientist's attitude to suggestions from the engineering staff. They both were very disgusted about that project and the computer log-in idiocy. I did a specific search for adhesives in the computer that night. Had to sneak into the engineer's cubicle during breakfast one morning and grab the one that I brought back off a small stack of them. The managers all thought I had overslept. The harder part was getting away from Sarnd. He really didn't want to let me out of his sight. Caldon's orders, I think. I did a few trips late at night and none of the local guards spotted me, which did surprise me."

"Hmph. That was part of that E&E training Caldon put you through? Useful in several ways, it turns out."

"Yes. I'm just glad I remembered how to unlock handcuffs." Jaren looked off out the window, remembering. He took a deep breath and held it for a count of four, then let it out slowly. One of Doctor Margrail's ways to deal with memories of that dark time.

"Bayside will be able to produce the adhesive, such as it is." Father's comment broke into his thoughts. "Ofelan and some of his people are putting together a nice bit of theatre to keep the inmates from understanding what we're planning. Your engineer is being transferred to Bayside to supervise production. Your guide has been quite helpful and sent Ofelan some samples of the final product. He'll go with the engineer as his secretary. Double his current salary, so he's quite happy. AR&D only knows the engineer has been demoted for wasting resources pursuing inactive programs and the guide dismissed because of his attitude. They're going to ensure everyone knows he was fired. At least for now, that is."

Jaren smiled. "And the stomping? When is that scheduled?"

"Awaiting completion of the new management team. The major administrative officers have been selected but not yet briefed. Ofelan is having a hard time finding someone within the clan with the requisite science knowledge for the CSO position. He's expanding the search parameters. We have a number of good people with very specific knowledge bases outside of the denizens there. That's the problem: their knowledge is too limited to give them the ability to manage all the inmates. We need someone who already knows about a large variety of areas, not just one tiny sliver."

"One of the professors at university was able to teach the entire overview of science and technology course. And her information was all up to date." Jaren said. "I have no idea what kind of business sense she has. Or if she'd even be interested in giving it a try."

"We have people with business sense all through the clan holdings. We were looking for an engineering officer with the same criteria but managed to find someone quickly. He's studying up on what's already in the pipeline and he'll be getting a precis of each stalled project as they're sorted. The Science Officer position has been impossible so far. Either they don't have the breadth of knowledge or they're terrible at communication. Let Ofelan know about your professor tomorrow. She'll be free of classes for the summer in a few months. Perhaps a trial, and we'll keep searching. Then again, she may know of someone else who would be suitable and interested."

The butler refilled their coffee cups and left them alone again.

"A half day of work means half pay." his father looked over his cup.

"I know."

"Your account balance is very low."

"I had obligations other than the plane tickets."

"I agreed. Sarnd had no family, so that donation went to the general guard retirement plan."

"As it should."

"Hmph. Tomorrow afternoon your secretary will be here with a set of files. The smaller meeting room should be adequate until you are more mobile."

"Thank you, Father."

"A number of messages and letters have been received for you. Marin has them, I believe. Spread the story of your riding accident but check with Banak on the details first. A few public appearances would be in order once you are more mobile."

* * *

Darit pushed himself away from the desk. It was past the time he should head home to eat a solitary meal. Jaren would be home already, changing to attend a party one of his university friends was holding at their compound a short drive from theirs. His first truly public appearance since his injuries.

Everyone now knew about the riding accident and Publicity had arranged an interview with the threatened reporter in apology. Jaren had blamed his rude behaviour on the pain (from his elbow, ankle, knee and numerous bruises) and the inadequate level of drugs needed to limit same. The guard had been perhaps a little overzealous in his duties, but he wasn't used to dealing with people, just guarding things. Jaren's personal guard had died in the same accident, saving his charge's life. It made for a touching article. There was considerable sympathy and a deluge of invitations. The problem was sorting those invitations, since several were for the same night.

Banak appeared in the open door.

"Any news from the listening devices at the Calyno estate?" Darit asked.

"Lots of talking, but nothing of any substance from either of them. Three weeks with nary a peep about their plans to use the imposter to kill you. Or whatever their ultimate plan is." Steffent sat down at his wave. "How long do you want to stretch this out, ser?"

"I don't think we can act directly at this point. So keep that going. On the other hand, our man monitoring the electronic firm's listening devices says they have the third digit problem licked in the prototype. A big demonstration is being planned in a week or so." Darit smiled. "Paknol slipped one of his brighter techs in as a janitor and he found the plans the second night. The idiots hadn't even locked them up when they weren't in use! The tech has a duplicate of the prototype ready to swap in and it will fail miserably on the day of the demonstration. Something about a bad connection or three that will fail intermittently. He also built one that does work, so we're sure that the technology is as good as they've hyped. He's building another so Paknol and I each have one."

"I bet the Calynos will be counting on that bump in value to get their loan under control." Steffent said. "Based on the payments we've been able to trace, they have dropped the principal about five percent in the last two weeks. Sold a couple of personal paintings from their collection to do it. Said they didn't fit with the decor when someone asked why they were selling. What happens if they bail out of the company to clear the debt entirely? Especially when the prototype fails?"

"They won't do that," Darit said confidently. "Especially when the prototype worked at the lower number of digits. They're looking for profits later rather than sooner, unlike many investors. Once that calculator goes into production and they get a few other devices into the pipeline, that single company will rival most of the clans in total income. They could set up their own clan based on those profits. Some more nervous investors, on the other hand, *will* sell on the bad news and Paknol and I are waiting for them. We've set up four dummy investors with deep pockets and glazed eyes at the possibilities. They'll get a percentage of the company as a bonus, so they're quite willing to act for us and vote their shares as we direct in the future.

"We should control the company completely within another month or two. Then we announce the real working prototype, convene a special session of the board, fire those greedy managers and move the idea idiot and all his equipment to AR&D to let him concentrate on making it work. With some competent engineers and technicians to actually build the prototypes, of course. Kendef has a radio manufacturer that we'll use to build the first runs of the calculator. They haven't been totally informed but are preparing for new assembly stations in one of their plants."

"The joys of product development," Steffent said with a smile.

"How can we stir things up for them personally?" Darit mused. "We have them on the run economically, but it's obviously not enough for them to change their game plan. Not yet. Doctor Hallent still doesn't know what their end game is. The impostor is borderline crazy, from what he has learned from the tapes. He'll have a nervous breakdown at some point because he thinks he's not worthy of being my son, but no one is sure what the timing or the final stressor could be. I'm beginning to think the actual orders would come directly from Gred and weren't part of the conditioning at all. Things might change significantly from now to when they activate him and they would have to modify the plan to ensure their success. The time needed to adjust the conditioning would be very hard to arrange during a crisis."

Steffent nodded his head several times, thinking. "I think," he started, "that Jaren should get engaged, or least be seen to be looking for a bride. It would be much harder for Adnil to take your place if we add to the number of heirs in their way. That should accelerate their timetable so we can end this before much longer."

"Jaren's too young..." Darit said, then paused. "He'll be of age in two months now. Hmph. Given my age, it would make sense that I want to see him married as soon as possible. Maybe a grandchild or three by the time I die. Knowing the legacy is being carried on."

"We should also encourage Gred to marry," Banak added with a grin. "*That* ought to help confuse them. Let them think you're all for getting the core clan numbers back up. In fact, you could berate Gred for *not* getting married. He's twenty-eight, isn't he? Well past time, you could say. There could be two or even four children already if he'd done his duty properly." Darit smiled back.

"Turned twenty-nine last fall. I am surprised that Adnil hasn't pushed Gred to marry. Or even remarried himself years ago. He was in his mid thirties at the time, I think. Never any hint that he was even thinking about it. I wonder why neither of them married." He smiled and a twinkle touched his eyes. "Let's invite them out this weekend for a clan meeting. We can discuss the lack of future heirs. We won't mention any names, just suggest that the young men need to find partners. Soon. Or their dear fathers will have to do it for them." The two men smiled at each other. "I know who I'll suggest for Jaren if he doesn't finally admit to me that he's in love with Sanil." Both smiles turned to smirks.

"We do need to do something about the kidnappers as well," Darit said, his smirk fading. "There's no evidence for their continued existence and I'm tired of pretending I'm expecting another attack. I'd rather use my energy for more important things."

"We could track them down and blow them up." Banak suggested. "Or they could attack a dummy convoy and get shot or blown up by valiant and courageous guards, who'd been trolling for them, trying to attract such an attack."

"But who are they? Who could they be?" Darit asked. "Besides Caldon and company, that is. We don't have any outright enemies and few independents would dare to kidnap a clan heir. Some clans would jump at the chance to snatch up our subsidiaries if we had money problems, but they wouldn't dare start a war. Everyone else would be on their backs in an instant. That's one reason why the clans forced the Unification."

"We could go back to an earlier enemy, ser," Banak said after a long silence. "The bastards that attacked the clan picnic years ago. The internal story could be that they had kids we didn't find at the time. Now those kids have grown up and are trying to finish the job. They had no intention of releasing Jaren, they wanted the ransom money and then they planned on killing him and sending him back in pieces. They probably missed Gred's departure and thought they were getting both heirs at once."

Darit shuddered. That time had been full of horrors. But... "It should hold together." he paused. "Talk it over with your top men. See what we'd need, and a source of the bodies if we need physical proof. How many would make a reasonable gang?"

"At least eight or ten. Fanatics all with slightly varied ages. I'd include several women since all male offspring would be a stretch. It will take some time to set up," Steffent warned. "We couldn't get that many bodies from just this city's morgue, not all at one time."

"Timing on bodies doesn't matter just now. I would like you to have a rough outline by the weekend. Hints and theories will do. It'll give Adnil a fright. He was so much younger when it happened that he'll believe what we're saying. I don't know how much Jaren knows about the attack, and he deserves to know the whole story, so be sure to lay it all out."

"I am sure that Gred will try to arrange to activate the controller to check on him," Steffent said. "How do you want to handle that?"

"He can't do anything physical this time. Have your teams install those small surveillance units everywhere you think they might go to be completely alone. Think like a young couple looking for privacy. That's where he'll take Jaren."

Chapter 26

Jaren leaned back in the car. It felt very good to be relatively healthy again. And Doctor Margrail's ideas were helping. He hadn't realized how just talking about Father's inattention over the years could help them build a new relationship. She still didn't know about Sanil. He hoped they'd be able to see each other soon. Even at a minor party like this one now that Father actually let him go out for fun by himself. Well, with extra guards of course.

The elbow fracture had finally healed enough for Feneir to allow him to accelerate the exercise program, starting to bring that arm and shoulder back up to strength. He still had a sling, but it was now an option rather than a requirement. A band of black silk for occasional support, not that steel and webbing torture device. The silk was currently tucked into his jacket pocket.

"You should use the sling, ser." Feneir said from his forward seat. "Especially when you enter the hall."

"I'd already thought of that," Jaren replied. "Poor wounded Jaren. He might break. Don't touch. Yuck. I'd rather keep it for later when I know my arm will get tired."

"He's going to be mobbed," Pagil commented from behind the wheel. "Girls all over him from now on, mark my words."

"You could tuck your hand in your pants or jacket pocket to start with. That'll give you some support during the evening without sending the wrong message, ser." Mathin always had practical suggestions. It made a nice change. And Father had allowed him to choose between the final three candidates. That still confused him.

Jaren didn't reply right away. Mathin wasn't in on the secret of Sanil yet. That would have to change soon. "I promise I'll throw all the girls who drape themselves over me back in the pond," he said. "I doubt there will be that many unattached ones tonight."

The few cars visible in the parking area reassured him. The gate guards smiled and waved them through with a minimal check of identity. Not good if someone wanted to sneak a strike team in, but maybe he was just being paranoid.

"One of us will be close at all times," Feneir said. "Don't leave the main hall unless one of us knows about it."

"Yes, Feneir," Jaren said with a slight roll of his eyes. Pagil bit his lip. "I'll be a good boy."

Dayil met them at the door. "Jaren, great to see you! Come on in." Their butler, looking faintly disapproving, stood nearby to take coats and hand them off to the pair of footmen.

"Are many people coming tonight?" Jaren asked. Dayil shook his head and grinned.

"You're about the last. Funny, you live closest and arrive nearly last. I also invited your cousin, you know. I think he's here already. Everyone's in the conservatory: you know the way. I'll stick here for a few more minutes, then I *need* to hear about your accident."

Jeran knew he'd be repeating that story all night. He sighed. If only it had been that simple. Feneir appeared beside him and raised an eyebrow in question.

"The thought of endless repetitions about an accident that never happened is daunting," Jaren said quietly as they walked down the corridor toward the conservatory. He heard music playing, but it was background music, not dance music. At least not now.

The attendance was mostly male, the scattering of girls already engaged or almost at that state. He realised that he knew most, if not all of them. That would make this evening easier.

Gred was there, chatting with one of the Consule cousins he'd been to university with. Too bad Jaren couldn't ask him if he'd *ever* actually eaten their stew and what were those unidentifiable solid chunks?

Jaren took a glass of orange juice from Feneir in his right hand and put the left in his pants pocket. The drink was alcohol free and if he put it down he would *not* pick it up again. Spiking untended drinks was one of Dayil's annoying habits. Getting drunk two months before his birthday was not in his plan to convince his father to lift the restrictions he chafed under. He could count the number of drinks he'd had on, well, now two hands, since he was up to six. He'd almost forgotten the wine he'd had with Gred at the estate before the withdrawal cramps had made *any* eating or drinking problematic.

"Hi, Jaren," the Consule cousin said as he approached them. "You're looking better. No sling?"

"Not the torture device that I had to wear originally. My arm still gets tired easily though. I have a small sling in my pocket just in case. Hi, Gred," Jaren said with a smile. "It's been hours."

Gred snorted. "All of, what five or so since the staff meeting?" A girl, Jaren wasn't quite sure who she was, swooped on the Consule and dragged him away, leaving Gred and him alone.

"I did want to chat with you, Jaren," Gred said, looking around the room. "It's impossible to be really private at the office. Can we meet up later this week, maybe?"

"What's up?" Jaren asked.

"I'd rather not say too much in company. But. Come over here by the wall. At least we'll be out of eavesdropping range." Jaren followed, fending off two other acquaintances with a promise to return shortly. At least Gred wasn't suggesting they go outside. He didn't want to push Feneir's paranoia about going anywhere alone onto Gred.

"I hate asking," Gred said quietly after checking around them. "But I need some money, Jaren. You had promised to pay part of the vacation costs and the doctor's fees. I paid it *all*. I've had some expenses I didn't plan on and I was counting on getting the money from you before this."

"I'm sorry, Gred. What with everything that happened, I completely forgot." He bit at his lip. "Father froze my accounts and made me pay for the plane ride back here after I managed to escape. Just about cleaned me out. I'm at least back on the payroll now. He has to personally approve all my withdrawals because of the dratted poppers. Do you have a list of the expenses? I'll tell him I owe you. Even if he has to give me an advance on my salary, I'll get you the money as soon as I can."

"Thanks, Jaren. I knew I could count on you." Gred clapped him on his good shoulder and nodded.

Dayil came up to them with a drink in each hand. "Everyone's here so let's party!"

Jaren caught a scent in the air and looked around. He wasn't sure at first, then he saw an idiot with a pipe. He felt the first stirrings of the nausea and decided to skip the rest of the story and go straight to the ending. "... and I ended up with bruises all down my side, the cracked bone in my arm and an almost dislocated ankle when I fell off. The damned horses ran away. Completely unhurt." He tried to smile. This was the fifth repetition. Or maybe the sixth.

"Did someone get the bear?" The Consule's girlfriend asked.

"That's how my bodyguard was killed. He just had a hand weapon and put all seven bullets into its head. But it was huge, 200 kilos at least, and objects in motion tend to run over you." There were faint smiles at the comment. "I'm going to get a refill." He waved his mostly empty glass as evidence and headed for the main door, away from the smoke.

Jaren left the room and drew a deep breath as the nausea subsided. Pagil was beside him as soon as he cleared the door. "Is there a problem, ser?"

"I found something else that was in the no drug list. One of the idiots is smoking canaba in there. Just smelling it triggered the '*don't take the pills, dummy*' nausea. That's why I came out."

"And you'll get sick and pass out if you stay in the room. Do you want to leave entirely?"

Jaren glanced at his watch. Past eleven. "Probably. I'm more tired than I thought I'd be."

Dayil came out of the bathroom, wavering slightly thanks to the drinks he'd been tossing back all evening. "Jaren, are you heading out so soon? It's still early!"

"I think so," Jaren replied. "Not enough stamina to keep up with you guys any more. And I have an early morning meeting in the city."

"Too bad. Maybe we can get together on the weekend or an evening sometime soon. Just us. I miss having all our friends around, like at university."

"Don't take this the wrong way, but why are you still living here, Dayil? You're of age, and I don't see any computers here. You said you wanted to get into programming once you graduated."

"My father doesn't believe in computers," Dayil said, shaking his head. "And I suck at analysis, you know that. I just want to tinker with things. I have a little workshop in one of the outbuildings, but it's not going as well as I hoped. Dad was all bent about the programming courses I did take. He'll flip entirely if he knew that's all I want to do."

"Maybe search though your holdings and see if one of them has a project you'd like to be involved in. It would be better if it's far away. We're using more computer based inventory systems and it saves a lot on costs. Also makes it harder for people to steal from any shipments. See if that could work for your dad. Saving money usually gets positive parental or managerial attention."

Dayil muttered something, then headed back to the party with his shoulders hunched. Jaren watched him go. Why wasn't he fighting for what he loved?

Father's announcement at breakfast about a clan meeting on the weekend surprised him. Then, lots of little things Father was doing lately surprised him. He took a bite of the omelet Marin placed in front of him.

"What's going on, Father?" he asked. "Why do we need a meeting?"

"There are some things the four of us need to discuss. How was the gathering last night?"

"Thanks for letting me attend, Father. They'll spread the accident story further, so it was probably worthwhile." He paused. "It felt... strange. Most of them haven't done anything since they got out of university, or they're in jobs they don't seem to like and work at as little as possible. Dayil's actually a great programmer but since his father doesn't trust computers, they don't have a subsidiary that he can work in that utilizes his strengths. He's not very good at management or analysis. He's the fifth child and has nothing to make him excited to go to work."

He wondered if Father would approve of hiring him. Or if Dayil's father would object. Jaren wasn't sure about that sort of clan interaction. But there wasn't really an overlap in what they produced. And allies were always a good thing.

"It is a problem in some clans," Father said. "If decent positions are limited for family members, they stay children and cause trouble. Some-thing we all need to take notice of."

"Gred was there. Not sure why Dayil invited him but I was glad to see him outside the office." Might as well let Father know that the bill would be along soon. Possibly today, if Gred was that hard up for some cash.

"What needed saying outside of the office?" Father's tone was sud-denly cool, almost chilly.

"I need to repay Gred for the costs of the drug conditioning vacation. He said that we'd split some things, like the rental costs, but the doctor's fees were mine. He's short of cash, he said."

"And how much is this cost?" Father was pissed, he knew now. But because Jaren hadn't yet paid his share or that the conditioning had been necessary in the first place, he wasn't sure. Possibly both.

"I'm not sure. He's going to bring a list of the expenses in today. Maybe I can give a draft to him while they're here this weekend."

"Hmph."

* * *

"We think we know who the kidnappers could be," Chief Steffent said. The four of them were sitting in a row of four comfortable chairs behind a laden coffee table that hadn't been touched. The older men sat in the middle, each with a son on the outside of the group.

"Ser Gred knows some of this. Serit Jeran, some of this may be new material to you but I assume you know about the clan picnic that was bombed twenty-five years ago?"

Jaren nodded. "Not much beyond that it happened. Mom showed me some family pictures when I asked why we didn't have a lot of relatives. I didn't really understand at the time."

"Thirty family and twenty guards died immediately. Fifteen others, family and guards, thankfully still unconscious due to the extent of their injuries, died within the week. Men, women and children. No one who'd been there lived." Steffent handed several photographs to Jaren and Gred. He glanced at them but couldn't look at the pictures for long. They weren't whole people any more.

"Those claiming responsibility were a worker group who decided they were owed more than they were prepared to labour for. They stole a vehicle and some explosives from a demolition project and ran the car through the perimeter and detonated it when it reached the picnic tables." Jaren stole a look at his father. He was looking at the table, not up at Steffent.

"We tracked the group down with police assistance and all were killed during the arrests or conditioned and sent to our mines. Other clans also provided information that aided the effort. None of them wanted this group free to try again. And every clan wanted to send the message that while a similar group might seem to succeed, they and their families would all pay a very high price for their actions. No other group has tried anything like this since, so the response had its desired effect."

Jaren took a deep breath. "You think that they didn't get everyone."

"True. Sers Darit and Andil were heading to the event from the office. There had been an emergency that had delayed them long enough to save their lives. Ser Gred was about four years old and had been left home with his nanny because he had a bad cold and his mother had not wanted all the other children to catch it."

Jaren looked back at his father. He was sitting there, obviously remembering. Jaren knew that he'd had half-siblings that had died. Their mother died with them. Three years later, Father married his mom. Then she'd died when he was ten. Doctor Margrail's breathing exercise helped calm him.

"The reason I brought these workers up is that Jaren's kidnappers might be the children of that original group come back to finish the job." Everyone except his father stared at Steffent.

"How do you *know*?" Adnil asked. "Is there any real proof?"

"Nothing that I can be absolutely certain of," Steffent said. He didn't seem comfortable with the admission. "Hearsay and some trace evidence that was deemed irrelevant at the time. But there are no others claiming responsibility or on anyone's short list of suspects. However, since it has been twenty-five years, the possibility of an anniversary event has to be considered. It was not originally considered since everyone we knew of had been captured." A heavy sigh.

"A short recess?" Jaren heard himself say. "Half hour?"

"Of course, sers," Steffent bowed slightly and left the room.

"I – hadn't realized," Gred said. His eyes were shiny. Jaren knew his were as well.

"I'm going outside for a minute, Father," he said. "Do you need anything?" He needed a little space and time alone to let his brain catch up with his emotions. Something else that Doctor Margrail had told him.

"Some whiskey would help," Father said quietly. "Adnil?"

"Yes, thank you." Adnil's head came up to look at his son, then sank back down to stare at his hands.

Jaren poured both drinks with a generous hand and slipped out the side door. He went to the family cemetery, tucked behind the greenhouses. Benches were scattered on the pathways and in summer flowers bloomed at every marker. The older stones were at the front of the area. Four generations were buried here, he knew. The earlier ones were still at the seaside mining town the clan had started from and still owned.

The taller monument of a clan head that marked his father's future place was flanked by two smaller stones. One had three smaller others beside it. His half-siblings and their mother. On the other side, his own mother. He remembered days of crying there, once they finally let him come home from the hospital and rehab centre. He'd been unconscious and in surgery at the time of her funeral. He sat on the bench nearest her grave. Stared at it.

A few minutes later, Gred joined him. Gred said something but Jaren didn't understand it.

* * *

The slave did. He leaned forward, putting his head much lower than the master's. Out in the open like this, the master would not want any to know that he spoke to the slave. Here, it would look like the loss and grief of the primary, not the submission of a slave to his master.

"Don't kneel – yet," the master said. "Are you moving memories, keeping the impostor in sync? We may need him on short notice."

"Yes, master," the slave replied. "Every night. This knowledge will be powerful for the impostor. He will remember and know how unworthy he is. He replaces not only the original primary, but those lost to the father master and that sorrow. He can never take their places no matter what he does."

"Good. In a couple of days, the primary is going to attend a party with me. We're going to have much more time to talk about what you're doing. I'll want some other information as well. Find out what's happening with AR&D. My contact there is reporting rumours of a shakeup but doesn't have any solid information. If the primary doesn't know, make him curious to find out. Do you understand?"

"Yes, master. Your slave understands."

* * *

Jaren turned his head to look at the graves again. So much loss over the years. And people wondered why he got depressed.

"I'd been told about it before," Gred said. "But I never really understood it. Didn't realise anything beyond it was quieter at the house."

"Me either," Jaren answered, sitting up and looking past his mother's grave. "I knew Father had been married before, and he had kids. But I never looked at them." His gaze shifted to look further down the rows. The same date of death. "All those relatives we never knew."

After a quiet lunch Jaren was stunned again but for a very different reason. "You want both of us to get married? Right now?" Father would froth and rage at the knowledge that he and Sanil wanted to wed. He needed her. Wanted her.

"Not immediately," Father said with a wave of his hand. At least he'd come out of that dark mood of this morning's news. "For one thing, you're not of age yet. Later this summer will do. But Gred, surely you know some suitable female?"

"I know several of them," Gred replied. "But can we ask a woman, or rather two, to marry us just so we can repopulate the clan? And maybe have them get kidnapped or killed by these insane workers?"

"It's their duty." Adnil said. He'd been shocked but now had a smile. "And yours. I'm sure we can find a nice pair of women." He turned to Father. "I didn't push Gred to marry because, well, I didn't know how you'd take it. My line having more heirs while you had to wait for Jaren to grow up."

"I'm sorry too," Father said. "I should have said something to you years ago about this. There could have been two or three grandchildren for you by now. Even other children of your own. I'd welcome all of them, Adnil. You know I would."

Gred turned to him. "I don't think we're getting a vote on this insanity, do you?"

Jaren shook his head. "Not even a tenth of a vote."

Chapter 27

Sanil could hardly believe that she was done with university. Two months early. Her friends were astonished that she'd managed an Honours designation. They didn't know she was preparing to be joint-heir-apparent at Alanyo Holdings. Jaren knew she wanted to join him at work, but no one else, unless Mom had figured it out, knew her ultimate goal. '*Hide your goals from the unworthy,*' was one of the Sunz quotes Jaren had used on her to convince her that they shouldn't tell their parents until she was of age. One more year to go.

Now, life was looking up. Back at last in Hantil, she expected to see Jaren at this party. His last letter had been full of congratulations on her early escape into reality. He *should* be here, she thought. She'd spotted his father a few minutes ago, dancing sedately with the niece of one of his top executives, Ofelan, she thought the name had been. He'd mentioned her to Jaren, he'd said in the last letter. A nice girl, his father thought. Jaren thought they'd have to come clean on their relationship soon or he'd find himself engaged to some tart by default. He hadn't used the word tart, but that's how she thought about the girl. Ser Darit was sneaky. At least Mom had explained ser Darit's reasoning on pushing Jaren and Gred to marry *before* she'd gotten that letter.

She spotted Jaren near several of his friends, halfway across the ballroom. They seemed to be joking about something.

"You got loose!" Carille said as she hugged Sanil. "That's excellent! Why'd you bother, though? It was just two more months."

"I was really tired of that place," Sanil replied. "The parties kept getting louder and most of the people on my floor weren't doing any work to speak of. It was either finish off or get a hotel room. So I thought I'd get everything out of the way and come back home. It was easier because all of my courses were project based, not sit in class with my eyes open and write exams. I was so tired of those wastes of time. I'm looking through our subsidiaries to find a place to get started. I'd rather stay in the city but it all depends on what I find. In a couple of months I might move out of the house."

"But I can't see your dad letting you have an apartment or house if you stay in town. And you'd have to have a place for your detail to live. And a cook and so on. Much easier to just stay at home. Or find a subsidiary with on site apartments for the staff. Still..." She paused. "Or are you interested in someone that you couldn't bring home?"

"Not yet," Sanil lied. "But you must admit that my dad is a good way to keep the discards from coming around looking hopeful about a second chance." Both of them grinned. Out on the dance floor the music faded.

"Good luck with your search," Carille replied. "And be prepared that nothing you spent four years learning will be anything close to what you need in the real world."

"A friend wrote to congratulate me and said sort of the same thing," she admitted. "But..." someone came up from behind her and stood next to her, just out of her range of vision.

"See you later," Carille said with a smile. "Have fun!"

Sanil turned slightly to see Jaren next to her. "Why are you here?" she said softly.

"Being a very dutiful son. I am obeying my father's orders to chat up suitable females." His eyes gleamed and he could barely keep his smirk under control.

"I'm not sure he would consider me suitable," she replied. '*But he had better accept me once we get this mess sorted out.*'

"I do have an ulterior motive," he said with a wistful smile. "To dance with you. I've missed you so much and this is the only way we can be together until the kidnappers get caught. Feneir flatly refused to arrange anything with Casteron. Said it would be completely irresponsible of us."

The beginning notes of her favourite music made her sigh. It was the same music as their first dance. The one they usually tried to dance to whenever they could. "Well then, let's be together." He smiled and bowed over her hand, and drew her out to the dance floor.

"Any progress on finding the kidnappers?" she asked as he took her into his arms.

"I'd rather not talk about them," he said. "Let's just dance. Be together now the way we will be soon."

He didn't want to let go of her once the music ended and to be fair, she didn't want to let him loose either but they couldn't risk two dances in a row. Not yet. Vanis came up to them and asked her for a dance and Jaren let her go with a bow and lingering pressure on her hand. There *would* be another dance later this evening. She wished that Caldon would relent on a meeting. Even a short one, like the picnics. To give Jaren some time just to hold her. Work up the courage to talk to her about all the things he was thinking and feeling. She'd talk to one of his other guards about that possibility. Have Julin send one of them a letter.

An hour later Mom sat next to her at their table. Sanil had told the last two hopeful suitors that she was going to sit out the next few dances. Her feet were starting to ache. She'd spent entirely too much time at her desk and not enough in the gym or on the dance floor in the past few months. Getting her projects done and returning to Jaren had been her top priority.

"You danced with him," Mom said, not looking directly at her.

"We've done it before," she said, not looking back. "Plenty of times. No one really notices. Or they think we're rebelling against our fathers and their unreasonable enmity. Didn't you ever do something because you knew it would make your parents growl at you?"

"I did. Marrying your father was the greatest of them. They and your father's parents did change their minds after a year or so. When I revealed that I was pregnant with your oldest brother. A month after the wedding." Sanil blinked at that news. Would Mom mind that they'd spent two nights together? And not tell Dad? Maybe that would be pushing her mother's acceptance of their love. For now, anyway.

Mom paused while a knot of young people wandered by the table close enough to hear what they said. "Did you know that he just won at least *two thousand betting that you *would* dance with him?"

"That sneak," she said, scanning the crowd and seeing him with a tart in his arms. "Why would he do that?"

"His accounts are still frozen by Ser Darit," Mom pointed out. "And your brother overheard him tell his cousin about the bet, so that he could get in on a sure thing. He's trying to repay his cousin for all his help in curing his addiction. Dad had a word with your brother not to do anything rash, like challenge Jaren to a fight. We should let him into the secret soon, Dad thinks. He also seems to have inherited your father's temper and we cannot risk any incautious actions at this stage."

"Shit!"

"Those are my sentiments as well but not a word I hope to hear from you again, dear." Mom glanced at her with a frown. "Unless you are in the process of having a baby. There are no language restrictions on that activity. You'll find that out in good time." Sanil glared in Jaren's direction but he wasn't looking at her.

"The bet *was* very reasonable from his point of view. You would not refuse to dance with him, especially to that music, so there was no chance of loss. He could use some extra money, since he had to take an advance on his salary to repay Gred for his share of the vacation rental expenses and ser Darit is charging him interest under the 'what would a pissed off ogre do' scenario. He was quite resistant to the idea but Chief Steffent managed to convince him it was and is necessary. He can always give Jaren the money back once this is over. The expenses for the vacation were greatly overstated, I might add. I saw the list and did my own calculations. He has great loyalty and still admires his cousin. I suppose they are using the money to pay the principal on their loan."

"I know, but I can't wait until this is over. I hate that Jaren's money will just go to Kessem." She glanced at Mom. "I will make Jaren pay for what he did, though. Tomorrow's letter will just be the beginning."

"That's my girl." Mom rose as Dad appeared from the crowd to take her onto the dance floor. "Make him work at keeping you happy. It will help distract him from his own troubles."

Chapter 28

Gred clenched his fists. How could the prototype have failed? He'd *seen* it work. He'd even done some math with it. Random numbers to prove to himself nothing was pre-programmed. It had worked! It did three digit, four function math. At the semi-public demonstration it had barely managed to add five and seven and come up with the right answer twice in a row. Seventeen had come up the first time. It managed twelve, then fourteen. Everyone started yelling at that point.

"We may have a spy in our company," the president said that evening. The board had been summoned to a special session in the wake of the disaster. His father was on Grathil inspecting one of the subsidiaries he oversaw and wouldn't be back for another week. He'd have to call with an update once this travesty ended.

The board room had a view of the city but all one could see at this hour was dim lights from the real towers of industry in the city centre. The large table with overstuffed leather chairs, the original paintings on the wall, all of it said *we are great!* The cluster of the top officials' offices just down the hall said the same thing. The other offices, the production and research areas were another matter.

"This *is* the same unit as we saw last week?" one of the other investor board members said as he raised his hand. "No chance someone stole the original and replaced it?"

"No. We've had it guarded at all times. All the components match what we have purchased. It *is* the same unit. Karthgat is taking it apart right now to try to isolate the fault. There could have been an intermittent circuit failure due to heat stress or a weld that cracked. We just don't know the scope of the damage right now. All of you have seen that the calculator works. Don't let this destroy your faith in Karthgat and this company. Don't you all want to be rich beyond your fondest dreams?

We are going to change the world with this invention!"

They had absolutely no idea what had happened, Gred realized. Blaming their failure on spies, or heat stress or anything else the president and the other officers could think of rather than accept that they needed a real engineering team. Not Karthgat's best friend who barely made it out of university and a couple of technicians who couldn't get a job at any clan subsidiary. This wasn't what he and his father had been expecting when they'd invested. They were too near success to sell out. He refused to contemplate that Darit had been correct in his initial assessment: management would kill the entire endeavour.

Maybe they could get other investors interested in a vote of non confidence to get the current management out of the picture. They could find some real techs who'd actually understand how to build something that would last. There was no use in bringing something to market that failed within the month.

"When the autopsy's complete, let us know what the real cause is," another new investor said. Gred didn't know much about him, but he'd bought enough shares in the past month to gain a seat at this table.

"I agree," Gred said. "And be sure to find someone who understands electronics to figure out why it failed."

He'd get a listing of all the investors. With enough shares, they could get the project back on track to success. He repressed the thought of what might happen if Kessem called their loan. The share price had dropped significantly. He might have to really lean on Jaren to pay off his share of the expenses. Dropping the principal instead of using the cash to have some fun. He wanted to grind his teeth but settled for muttering. Everyone would think he was upset at the failed demonstration.

* * *

Two of the newer investors shared a cab at the end of the meeting. Identical sighs of relief once they pulled away from the knot of people on the sidewalk. "They're a bunch of idiots," one said. Dark hair and eyes. A man few people would recognise unless they really knew him. "Should have sold out to Ser Alanyo in the beginning. But no, they wanted all the money for themselves. Unlike us." He shook his head.

"That's been our thought, sers," said the driver. One of Ser Alanyo's men. Their conduit to both clans. "What did they think of the fake calculator's failure? Any idea why it's wrong?"

"They don't think it *is* a fake," the other investor said. A chuckle. "Blamed the failure on cracked welds and heat stress. The stocks should drop again tomorrow, once word spreads. We should have a chance to buy up more of the small investors shares in the next couple of days. I think they'll have to bring the older one back out for a demonstration to stabilise the share price. We'll buy before that happens. But getting any other shares was a priority, we were told at the start."

"Just let your other contact know how much money you need," the driver said. "The sers will split the shares once they take control. Sounds like it won't be much longer, from what I've heard."

"Our shares will keep us in comfort once we do retire," the first said as he checked his watch. The cab pulled into a crowded theatre parking lot. "Good. Last curtain should be soon. Glad that we have decent under-studies so we could make that meeting."

* * *

Gred choked back a comment as Steffent revealed that same group of killers who had almost wiped out the clan when he was a young child might be those responsible for Jaren's kidnapping. He suppressed his questions when Jaren went outside alone. He needed to check in on the slave and this might be his best opportunity since there was no plan for them to stay overnight. He followed Jaren cautiously, then smiled as he headed for the cemetery. The slave reported all was well. That was a re-lief. He'd have a longer time to question the slave later in the week. At least he had the draft in his pocket when they left the compound.

"Are you going to the Marchard party?" Gred asked as they waited for the elevator together two days later after a joint meeting.

"Hadn't really planned to," Jaren said. "That crowd's not really one I know and I don't think I was invited. Heard about it from someone else. Is Marchand a good friend of yours?"

"He is and I also know some of his relatives. If you come with me there's no issue with a formal invitation. Or we could show up for a half hour and go on to some other places. Have some fun. You're not getting out much these days."

"Feneir would have a stroke," Jaren replied, shaking his head. "His paranoia is at epic levels with this threat. He seems to think if he'd been at the estate the kidnappers wouldn't have taken me. He won't let me out of sight of a guard, preferably him, when we're outside the compound or here and I keep tripping over them at home. I thought the extra guards would be gone by now but they're still in place. I don't dare leave my suite at night without calling out to warn them I'm coming out. They're all armed with fingers on the triggers."

"What about the dance the other night? I didn't see any of your men in the room. Where were they?"

"He and Mathin were in the upper balconies along with one of Father's men. All three had sniper rifles and they hit whatever they're aiming at. I saw them on the range last weekend. Three hundred meters away from the target and three bullets were in an area less than the size of my palm. If someone even looked like they were trying to abduct me, Father, you or your dad, there would have been bloodstains all over. I've no idea how they convinced the Korolian to allow it, but they did."

"Wow. I hadn't thought we were in that much danger."

"The kidnappers killed seven men to get me, Gred. I'm sure that I don't want them to get their hands on me again or anybody else I like. So, no trips for me outside of the screen. You and your dad should take more precautions if you aren't already. We really don't know if it was just me they were after. If it is that worker group, they might not just try for kidnapping anyone the next time. Feneir wants me to wear a protective vest whenever we're out of the compound. But I've managed to convince him that it isn't necessary, at least for now. If Chief Steffent finds any credible information, I know that I'll be wearing one whether I want to or not."

Gred raised one hand in surrender. "We do take precautions, but they aren't *that* excessive. By the way, thanks on that tip at the dance. I wasn't sure at first, but I won fifteen hundred from some other doubters. How did you manage it?"

Jaren smiled. "That song is her favourite of all times and she loves to dance to it."

"You knew when they'd be playing it? How?"

"Of course I knew it was coming up. I requested it and at that specific time so I would know when to be next to her to ask her. '*Hidden plans make your enemies fail*' you know."

Gred snorted. "A Kendef. What did your dad say about her?"

"Nothing. If he asked, I can honestly say that I've danced with her before and I know she likes that music."

"And he didn't clue in to the bet?"

"Not that he's mentioned. I was a little surprised when he didn't say anything about it, but very relieved. I have some pocket money for a change." The door opened and they entered. No one else was with them. For now. He couldn't count on this trip staying private. Gred pushed both floor buttons and Jaren smiled in thanks.

"Maybe you could just come over to our place one night and I'll invite just a couple of people over. Do you think that would that keep Caldon and Chief Steffent happy?"

"It might. I'll have him chat with Bergrant and see what they can set up." He sighed. "And I'll have to clear it with Father."

Gred raised an eyebrow. "Why?"

"Part of his *'I'm pissed at you about the poppers'* restrictions. I need his approval to leave the compound or I have to travel with him. That's why I always come in and go home with him now that I'm back at work full time. It's simpler this way. I'm hoping he gets over being pissed soon. Maybe he'll treat me like an adult when my birthday rolls around. Another month to go. But I'm not sure that's actually going to happen."

"Being heir number three sounds like I'm having a lot more fun."

The door opened onto Gred's floor and Jaren gave him a wave as he exited the elevator. The door closed silently

"Crap," he said as he stalked to his office. He wouldn't be able to spend as much time with the slave as he wanted if Jaren came to their house. Just an hour or maybe two late at night. But...

The overnight visit was eventually approved, three days later. Jaren would go home with him and Adnil and come in with them in the morning. Caldon and another guard would be quartered in the house and would patrol with their house guards.

"This will be your room," Gred said, opening the door of the special guest suite. "Smaller than the ones at the compound, but I like the colour scheme myself. I'm just down the hall, by the way." Dark blue curtains and patterned wallpaper was brightened by light oak furnishings. The room had a seating area with a coffee table between a couch and three chairs, a desk and a modestly sized bed. Doors indicated a bathroom on the outer wall and a walk in closet on the inner one.

"It looks great, Gred. The first year I was in my suite I had to keep the door to the bedroom closed at night. It was way too big."

"How old were you?" *Small talk to be the trustworthy cousin. Blah.*

"I'd just returned to the compound from the rehab centre, so maybe eleven. Those rooms there were a quarter the size of this one, so the whole suite was overwhelming for the first couple of months. I wasn't allowed to stay in the nursery wing any more, Father decided. I was old enough for a real suite, he said. A couple of nights early on I stayed in the closet. Every noise out in the halls or outside scared me." A faint blush.

"Makes sense for what you went through," Gred answered. They heard a muffled bell from the main floor. "Dinner's in a half hour. Go more casual if you like. Sounds like the others are starting to arrive. I'm going to change to something slightly more casual and we'll meet up in the sitting room near the front door."

"All right."

Gred hadn't picked his guests for late nights, competition drinking or racy talk. All had solid positions in the clan and all had slipped Gred a 'thank you' envelope to ensure their invitation to meet the Alanyo heir. It would be a profitable evening in many ways. They needed the cash to keep ahead of that dammed hundred-twenty percent ceiling. Several other investors had panicked and sold out, but they didn't have enough spare cash to buy up those shares. There hadn't been any real reason the dammed prototype had failed. The earlier versions still worked, so they'd been brought out for another demonstration that had bolstered the stock price. For now. They were still trying to pay down the principal as much as they could. Three more paintings had sold this week, the art dealer reported.

Once the house had settled for the night, Gred opened the hidden door to the narrow corridor that led directly from his to Jaren's room. No one realised it existed outside of himself and his father. It went along the inside wall next to the corridor, its presence hidden by the walk-in closets that weren't as wide as they seemed to be from the rooms. He took a small flashlight from his desk drawer and turned it on, then went down the narrow corridor.

It was a little over two meters to the exit panel and Gred smiled as he listened once the panel was ajar. Jaren was sleeping, breathing heavily and lying on his back. Not quite a snore. Gred walked quietly over to him and set the light down on the bedside table. Jaren's mouth was soon covered by his hand and he whispered the code as soon as Jaren's eyes opened. The slave stopped moving immediately. "No talking until I give you permission," he said softly. The slave bowed his head in submission.

The slave followed him through the corridor and fell to his knees as soon as they entered into Gred's suite. He closed the panel then went to sit in his favourite chair.

"Kneel before me, slave. And get rid of that top." The slave didn't fully rise before coming over and kneeling again, within easy reach of Gred's neuronal whip. The pyjama top went next.

"Talk to me, slave. What is happening at playpen? Speak quietly. The guards may wander down the corridor and no one can know that you are in here with me."

"Master, your slave has found that they are searching outside the clan for a new chief science officer for the facility. A new position of chief engineering officer is also planned. They have the engineer and wait on the science officer before sending both to take charge." The slave glanced up to see how Gred took that news. He nodded. It made sense.

"The primary found many projects that have great potential for profit had been abandoned due to tension between the inventors and the engineers. He seeks to bring them into production to please his father and show his worth. He found one: called gummynotes while you and he were at the facility in the winter. They can be lifted and replaced on other surfaces many times. The adhesive is now being produced now at Bayside Chemicals. The items will be produced at Coron Cards once the new production lines are in place. More facilities are planned and much profit could be made."

"So that's what happened to that snotty engineer," Gred mused. "I'd wondered about him. Everyone thought he'd been demoted, not given a new product line to manage. I didn't think that project would ever go anywhere." He slid the neuronal whip free from its hiding place in the chair and twirled it in his fingers. The slave's head lowered further.

"Do any suspect that you or the impostor exist?"

"No, master. The evil ones from before are still the main thrust of the guards' investigations. No one is suspicious of your slave."

"Good." He flicked his wrist and the thong of the whip now lay across the slave's back. Too bad he didn't know that Gred *couldn't* use it tonight. Having Jaren visibly ill or in pain after being here would not do their plans any good. Even the lightest setting, the effect of a strike would be noticeable tomorrow morning.

"Once a week, starting next week at midnight, you will activate and phone me here unless we are both at a party. You'll let me know what is going on at AR&D and with the primary. Do you understand?"

"Yes, master. Your slave understands."

"How is the impostor reacting to the news about the kidnappers and the wedding plans?"

"Both frighten him, master. The kidnappers because he fears that he will disgrace himself and the clan if he has to face them again. He was barely able to think of escape but his fears of the father master's reaction were more than his fear of the kidnappers. The plans for marriage terrify him because he knows he is not worthy of the place the father master seeks for him. He is more unstable than before, master."

"And he was such a pillar of strength then," Gred muttered.

"He was not, master." The slave's quiet comment broke into his thoughts.

"What do you mean, slave?" He'd meant the question to be rhetorical, but if the slave had information about the impostor and if he might crack now, Gred and his father did need to know.

"From the outside, he might seem normal, master. Inside, your slave can hear his thoughts. They all speak of the need to please the father master and not cause dishonour to the clan. He forces himself to do what will be seen and approved of. That is why he dared escape. He believed that the father master would have been very angry with him if a ransom needed to be paid." Another quick glance up at him.

"In his mind, any ransom would be added to his debt. When the father master spoke to him of the kidnapping and the drug use, he believed that his next error would cause the father master to send him to a conditioner to completely rewrite his personality. He would never do anything the father master did not like."

To kill him, in deed rather than fact. A potent threat. Gred drew the thong across the slave's back and smiled as the slave shuddered in memory of the other times he'd knelt before Gred. Not as satisfying as turning on the whip would be, but it would also not cause any damage to be explained away. He flicked the thong to lie along the slave's spine again and drew it slowly toward him. Life was good.

Jaren did look pretty tired the next morning but Gred had given orders to brew up the highest caffeine containing coffee they had for breakfast. That would keep him going until they were well back at the office. The phone calls would be less fun, but much easier to get the information they needed to keep things under control. For just a little while longer.

Chapter 29

Feneir hated the idea of Jaren going to Gred's house, even overnight. He made a conscious effort to keep his teeth from grinding.

"It is likely that the controller will be activated," Steffent said.

"I'd describe those odds as certain." Feneir drummed his fingers on Steffent's desk. "Probably why he came up with the idea in the first place. The only good news is that Gred can't do anything that has a physical effect. Even on that damned whip's lowest setting, there would be pain that can't be hidden the next day. He can't afford to make anyone suspicious if Jaren suddenly can't use his arm, for instance."

Steffent pulled a set of blueprints onto the desk and flipped to the third sheet. "This is the second floor, where the family bedroom suites are. Gred is here with his father across the hall. This one is likely where Jaren will stay. It's adjacent to Gred's but there are no connecting doors or balconies. If he wants Jaren to go to him or goes into the room, he'll have to use the corridor. One of you will need to focus on that and not get distracted by any pattern Bergrant comes up with to allow his boss access to Jaren."

"I'll let Mathin take the inside. I'll wander outside for a while then pretend to get some sleep. I'll put a surveillance device into Jaren's room while they're downstairs so I'll be able to hear anything that happens."

"About the best we can do," Steffent said. "I think it will be enough to keep the serit safe. They can't do much if they want to keep up the appearance of being loyal to the clan and ser Darit."

Feneir nodded. He hoped so.

Now Feneir lay in the darkness, listening to the faint noises of Jaren sleeping upstairs on the monitor. It was hard to just lay there in the dark without falling asleep himself, so he sat on the edge of the bed. He was fully dressed except for his jacket and all of his weapons were ready.

A slight creaking sound woke him completely. Jaren's breathing changed, then it sounded like the bed covers were moving. A voice said something that he couldn't make out. More sounds like someone walked from the bed. Another creak. Then silence again. Damn. There *must* be some other way out of the suite. He vowed to check the room tomorrow morning as soon as Jaren was out the door for breakfast.

He let out a deep breath. It was nearly an hour by his watch until the slight creaking of a door marked Jaren's return. The noises became louder, and he heard a soft groan as the bed shifted. Then silence for a time, finally followed by a return of the sleeping noises.

Jaren looked tired the next morning but Feneir couldn't tell if there was any other damage. Jaren didn't say anything until they were in his office and Talfer had been in with a large cup of coffee and left.

"Had another nightmare last night," Jaren sighed, rubbing his eyes. "So I didn't get a lot of sleep. I'd hoped they were gone for good."

"Same as before?" Feneir asked.

"Mostly. Couldn't move, everything hurt, someone standing over me. Felt menacing."

"What was different from the others?"

"Seemed to be a different place and I was kneeling instead of lying face up. Might have been because of sleeping in a different room than I'm used to. Doctor Margrail said the dreams might come back if something changed in my life. Yuck." Jaren took a sip of the coffee and shook himself. "Did you and Mathin have a good evening?"

"Quiet, as we thought," Feneir responded. "A bodyguard's best day. Lots of prep, training and planning but nothing actually happens. I'll be in the security office here for the rest of the morning. Maybe have a quick nap. Chief Steffent wanted to update me on the various investigations. I'll check the mail on my way back up for lunch. There might be something for you in my slot."

"I hope so. It's been a week. Have fun." Jaren smiled at the thought of hearing from Sanil, then turned to the papers on his desk. Another subsidiary to be gone over and eventually meet with. Feneir would take extra security with them in case of the kidnappers. Jaren might complain a bit, but he'd been good about the extra security. So far. Feneir hadn't really pushed on Jaren to wear a protective vest, on Pagil's advice. Jaren wanted to protect *him*. Which was very backward, but not having to worry about him sneaking off was a good thing. If he did, then the imposter was active and they'd need to follow him. Nothing was going to happen to Jaren again. Ever.

"There has to be a secret passage," Feneir said when he reached Steffent's office. "Gred did something to him, I've no idea what. Jaren just told me he had a nightmare last night and he hasn't had one for several weeks. It was slightly different from the others he's had."

Steffent pulled the floor plans from a pile and spread them out on a work table. "Shit. Any idea on the length of the passageway?"

Feneir looked at the plans, then ran a finger along the inner wall. "The closets and bathrooms of these two suites back onto one another. I think the closet isn't as wide as these plans show. I didn't get a chance to check it out because Gred's valet packed up Jaren's things and brought them down before I could get up there. I barely had time to retrieve the transmitter before we had to leave. There isn't anywhere else it could be. That sort of construction would be easy to do and might have been done years ago or even when the house was built. It's nearly eighty years old so any builders or craftsmen are long dead."

"How long was the serit out of the room?"

"About an hour. I was debating trying to get to Gred's balcony via Jaren's to see what I could learn when I heard him return."

There was a conference call the next week. Jaren turned in early saying he was tired from the dance he'd attended, so there was no need to worry about him wandering into his father's office. Still, Mathin was on duty on the upper floor.

"Between Paknol and myself we now control thirty five percent of KRT Electronics through our agents. The drop in share prices after the failed demo worked in our favour. With Gred and Adnil's twenty percent, we have a clear majority," ser Darit said with satisfaction. "We can vote out the current management as soon as we finish this. However, the agents were approached by Adnil to help them with a coup. They're cautiously in favour but there hasn't been a timeline mentioned."

"And we also have two copies of the prototype that do everything they claimed," Paknol said. "How's the wedding stressor working?"

"Still not quite enough," ser Darit replied. "That boy needs some incentive to declare himself. Why hasn't he told me about you, Sanil? I know about your dances. Three of them tonight, weren't there? There hasn't been anything in the gossip pages, but people are beginning to notice that you two dance at every event you're both at."

"Because he's still not sure you'll go along with it," Sanil said with some heat. "All that 'Kendef are the enemy' rhetoric you've been spouting for years is still uppermost in his mind. We originally planned to tell all of you once I reached twenty-two. No one could stop us."

"Well then, how do you propose that I tell him your engagement is acceptable?" ser Darit leaned back in his chair. "Or that I know *anything* about your attachment to each other?"

"You can blame me," Feneir said into the silence. "Tell him I let it slip when I found out he'd been kidnapped because it might have been ser Kendef that grabbed him when he found out about their association. If the only thing I was told was that Jaren was missing, it would be a reasonable assumption that ser Kendef could be upset about their relationship and wanted to let Jaren know how he felt in no uncertain terms. You've started negotiations on the engagement, thought you'd have another couple of months to sort things out. Sanil has forced your hands by finishing university early and they're being more obvious. The gossip reporters are watching them now, so you don't have a lot of options. It's either go ahead or shut them down. And you would normally be worried about Jaren's coping skills in regard to the kidnapping without her."

He heard a giggle from Sanil, and other expressions of agreement from the others.

"Hmph," from ser Darit, seated across the table from himself and Steffent. "It may have merit. And just having them see each other openly might be enough to kick start the final operation."

"*If* we agree to the marriage," ser Paknol growled. "That's still under discussion."

"It does allow for more of a chance to finish this quickly," sera Barith said. Feneir could imagine her hand on her husband's arm, deflecting his attention and anger.

"And we are going to be married," Sanil's voice cut into his reverie. "If we have to wait until I'm of age so we can just do it, then so be it."

"Never let your opponent know your final position at the start of negotiations, dear," sera Barith said calmly. "Especially men. They do fuss and bluster when you back them into a corner. I thought that I'd taught you better than that."

The three men looked at each other and shrugged. Feneir wondered what shade of red ser Paknol's face was.

"Very well," ser Darit said with a smile that bordered on a smirk. "I'll surprise Jaren on the weekend with the news that we've been discussing an alliance. It will have been a secret from you as well, Sanil. So you both can rail about your fathers running around behind your backs while you were running around behind ours."

His growl was cut off as the connection ended.

Chapter 30

Jaren sighed at the summons to his father's office. He'd hoped to go out to the gun range this morning. Feneir had reluctantly agreed that he should keep up his handgun skills in case the kidnappers made another try at him. He hadn't seemed happy about it, though. Frustration at the lack of progress on hunting the evildoers down, no doubt. It did feel good to shoot at something. Likewise, he kept imagining the kidnappers as he worked on the punching bag. He knew he'd never beat them in an actual fight, but maybe if they were caught, he'd have a chance to help show them the error of their ways. Before they died.

He smiled at Hartner, who brought the message up to him, and headed downstairs. His father sat in the conference area, not behind his desk, a neutral expression on his face. Coffee and pastries sat on the table. It couldn't be too bad, or he'd be behind the desk, scowling, and there wouldn't be coffee.

"You wanted to see me, Father?" Jaren asked.

"I did. Sit, have some coffee." Father already had a steaming cup on the table in front of him.

Jaren poured and added sugar. "Is there some news?" A good general opening line. There were many possibilities that could require an update on a weekend. Business, the kidnappers, just about...

"I just wanted to let you know I've been in some negotiations."

"About what?" Jaren raised the cup to his lips and sipped.

"Your marriage to Sanil Kendef." Jaren choked as the hot coffee went up his nose and he set the cup down quickly to pick up a napkin. Coffee slopped out of the cup and onto the saucer. Another napkin.

"Sorry," Father said but Jaren saw the smirk through his tears. That coffee had been hot! Father wasn't sorry. He'd waited until exactly the right second to speak.

"How did... you find out?" he managed to get out in between coughs and streaming eyes.

"Actually, it was Caldon who let it slip when we first learned that you'd been kidnapped," his father said with a wave of his hand. "He didn't know about the dead guards when he was first informed you were missing and said something about ser Kendef possibly being upset with you about something. Steffent was side tracked that morning trying to find out where the seris was and if you were with her. Just in case the Kendefs were very irate about your meetings. They were, by the way. Ser Kendef still is, so you should be prepared for that meeting. Her mother is the calmer one to deal with. By far."

"Did Sanil know that her parents knew about us?"

"Not in the least. She's learning about our involvement this morning as well," Father said. "We've been discussing things, her parents and I, over the past few months. None of us is particularly happy about it, given our past differences, but Caldon and Casteron have been forthcoming about the strength of your attachment. Sera Kendef is cautiously in favour, so you have her on your side."

"I see," Jaren said, putting down the napkin. Did he dare try the coffee again? Maybe he'd wait. "What changed your minds?"

"Kendef and I decided that keeping you apart might be fostering the attachment rather than decreasing your fervour. So, last night we decided that since absence wasn't working, especially since she finished her course work early, we'd try letting you officially see each other. We do want you to continue to pretend in public that you didn't know each other well. If you both continue to feel the same way in a few months, we'll move to phase two."

"She finished university early so she could come home. She wanted things to be easier for us to see each other," Jaren pointed out. "We'd planned to have some meetings when I went out to site visits, but then the kidnappers..."

"And you have seen her since you started going out without me, within the constraints of my instructions. Those dances were inspired. Meeting in public with no one the wiser of your intentions. Bravo."

"And mostly because of Feneir's paranoia about the kidnappers," Jaren added, wanting to deflect any further comment on dances in general and the monetary component of one in particular. "And I managed to convince him I didn't need a protective vest whenever I left the estate or the office. That's one reason I went over to Gred's two weeks ago instead of the party he wanted to take me to. He didn't intend to stay there long and wanted to find some fun, I think he put it, once we left there. I have no idea where else he planned to take me, but didn't want to strain Feneir's paranoia. I think he'd stuff me into the trunk himself to keep me from doing anything stupid like that."

"Did he," Father said, not happy at all about that revelation. "Well, you were sensible."

"There is a party where Sanil and I hoped to meet at next week," Jaren said. "I should get in touch with her. It will be strange to do it myself. All our communications have gone through Caldon and her guard Casteron so no one would suspect we were meeting."

Father glanced at his watch. "The letters, yes. Hmph. Give ser Paknol another half hour or so to wind up his tirade. He said he'd be inspired when we arranged our timing for these little chats."

It did seem strange to be dialling Sanil's personal extension. He waited for three rings, then she came on.

"Hello?" came her cautious voice.

"It's me, Sanil," Jaren said. "How did your talk go?"

"I'm still fuming," she said shortly. "Have you told Caldon he's at the top of my hit list?"

"And mine. I think he's hiding from me right now," Jaren said. "It also sort of explains why he's been so paranoid since the kidnapping. Maybe. I'm going to track him down after we talk."

"Dad said he wants us to pretend that we're just getting acquainted. They have some secret plans he wasn't willing to tell me about. I tried to entice him into telling me but he didn't say anything. Did your father mention that as well?"

"Yes. I think that it might have something to do with the kidnappers. Keeping you safe rather than making you a major target."

"At least having them agreeing on us seeing each other does solve the problem of him pushing you to see other potential partners," Sanil said. Her voice relaxed. "And that also gives us more chances to be together."

"Like next week. We can have more than a couple of dances." He smiled, even though he couldn't see her. To have time to chat...

"We'll be meeting sooner than that, love. Mom says she's coming over with me tomorrow afternoon for tea. Three pm, she said."

"She's... you're...?" Jaren managed to stammer.

"That was pretty much my reaction," Sanil said. "You'll let your people know?"

"I will. I just..."

"Shock, love. Don't worry. Mom promised to be on her best behaviour. She likes creme pastries, so you know. And Dad isn't coming, so you won't face his temper for another week or three."

"All right. I'm still going to hunt Feneir down, once I get done with Marin and tell Father about the visit. See you tomorrow."

***

Darit grinned as Jaren left his office after the revelation. He hadn't had so much fun in years. Doubtless Caldon was going to get an earful when Jaren caught up to him, but he was hiding out in the security office sub-basement for the next hour or so. Unlikely that anyone would tell Jaren where Caldon was. He glanced at his watch again, then went to his desk, picked up the phone and dialled.

"Hello, Paknol. Jaren just left my office."

"How did he take it?"

"Got him to snort his coffee." Paknol laughed with him. "Otherwise, he bought the story completely. Is Sanil ready with her part? I told him to wait a bit, as you might be inspired that they were seeing each other and hiding it from you."

Paknol snorted another laugh. "She's ready. I did remind her earlier this morning how I felt about the whole hiding a relationship issue. And Barith had a great idea. She and Sanil will visit you for tea tomorrow."

"Sanil will let him know?"

"Of course. He can tell you and the staff."

"I'll act surprised. Hartner, the footman who Gred thinks is on his payroll, will send a message after the event to Gred afterwards so he's informed." Darit sighed. "This should get them on track to do something instead of sitting around whinging about how much of a tyrant I am."

The afternoon tea the next day went well. There was definitely a change in the servants, he realized. Shock for many, amazement that the world hadn't ended for others and the chef had been beside herself in anticipation of parties and dinners showcasing the engaged couple and the chance to show off her talents and skills.

The servants and footmen cleaned the already immaculate parlour and the rest of the main floor, just in case, after Jaren's announcement. The terrace was scrubbed to be ready if the weather cooperated and they would have their tea there. Given the chill wind at noon, the small parlour had been settled upon.

When the call came that the Kendef cars were at the gate, Jaren sprang to his feet. They were in his office. Darit was at his desk, trying to read a report. Jaren had been sitting, but nervously, on the edge of the chair half the time and pacing the other half. Both wore formal suits and Jaren kept pulling at his collar. It hadn't been tight before but it did show how nervous the boy was about this.

"Calm down," Darit said. "We have plenty of time to get to the front door. Have you ever formally met sera Kendef?"

"Only in passing," Jaren admitted after a deep breath. "Not truly formally. I never attended any parties at their house or ones they sponsored at a hotel. Sanil thought that might be stretching our luck."

"So she never attended any of ours in return."

Jaren opened the door for him, startling the footman on the other side. "No. We went to the parties of mutual friends when we were both here and the library when we were at university. Last summer we had some picnics by ourselves."

Darit noted he still hadn't admitted to the beach house weekend. What had the two of them gotten up to? Sanil had only spoken in generalities without a blush and the staff hadn't seen anything that could cause comment once Steffent enquired. Other than the fact she'd been the only guest that weekend. Both beds had needed making up in the morning and none of the house guards had seen anyone sneaking along the corridor between the two rooms, but no one had been in the upstairs hallway every instant. And there were no cameras on that hallway. Jaren had experience from that evasion training from Caldon. He wondered if he should ask. No, not now, he decided. Maybe once all this was over.

Sera Barith was cool in her greeting. Darit didn't know how he hadn't laughed out loud at Jaren's expression. The realization that the only reason they had to go through this farce was Gred and Adnil's idiot plans sobered him.

At least half the pastries had creme of one sort or another. Good thing that boy listened when you told him something, even when he'd been blindsided. After a cup of tea, which neither of them finished, the couple was dismissed to walk in the gardens. They vanished almost instantly, followed by Caldon and Casteron, with a few others not as close.

"I thought you were going to spoil everything earlier," Barith said when they were alone. She accepted another cup of tea and selected a crème brulee. "Laughter was not an appropriate response to our arrival."

"It was close, Barith," Darit replied. "In other circumstances, it would be hilarious, you must admit. But there is a question that has no answer, at least not one any of us can discover." She looked at him with a slight frown. "*Why* will this be a surprise to Gred and Adnil? We haven't heard anything on the surveillance tapes that disproves our belief that they have no idea there wasn't already a long term relationship. The controller would have told them if he knew. And he has to know, Barith. Sanil is too important to Jaren. The controller *is* another Jaren, for all intents, Hallent said. He has access to all of Jaren's memories as well as those from the imposter's life. She's a large part of his stability and focus. He's been talking to our staff therapist about the kidnapping and some other issues. Steffent won't tell me exactly why or what they've discussed but

Jaren seems happier now. More relaxed and we're talking more about the little things, not just work related items. We'd drifted apart, mostly because I've been so busy with the company, he was at university and I hadn't made time for him when he was home."

"I hadn't thought of that aspect of the missing information," she admitted. "For the impostor to function as Jaren, he must know all that Jaren does. The E&E training I can accept as a detail that made no difference at the time of the initial transfers, given the time constraints they were working under. The knowledge of their relationship would have been of prime importance. Perhaps Gred is pretending for Jaren? A double cross, of sorts?"

"The question came to me this morning but I haven't had a chance to let the doctor know. I'll have Banak give him a call later. We must try to find out. That answer may change our entire strategy."

Chapter 31

Gred sat in shock. His footman at the compound, Hartner, he recalled the name after several moments, had phoned in a message though his valet and he'd just finished reading it aloud to his father. Sanil Kendef and her mother had been at the compound that afternoon and had tea with Jaren and his father. There had been lots of cleaning and preparation starting early the previous afternoon. He hadn't sent the message then, not wanting to risk a false report.

Jaren had an interview with ser Darit that morning and shortly after, the announcement had been made. The young people had gone for a walk yesterday, unsupervised except for their normal guards, all of whom were smiling. Nothing had been formally announced. Yet. No one in the compound knew if the couple had been more than acquaintances before this. If they did, no one was saying more than platitudes.

"A *Kendef*? Is Darit mad?" Dad said. "They've been our enemies for years! Why them and more importantly, why start talking to them now?"

"The big question is if they had a relationship no one knew about?" Gred said. "Remember those cash expenditures we turned into drug purchases for the scenario? Paying off guards to arrange their trysts would be a possible explanation. But the controller would know." He took a deep breath to calm himself enough to think. "In fact, that *means* they haven't been together before this. The controller knows better than to leave such vital information out of the transfers."

"I agree, but double check on your next call. We must rethink our strategy, Gred," Dad said after taking a deep drink of his whiskey. "We never anticipated that the impostor would have any real support except for Caldon and some senior management like Ofelan. Having *Kendef* on his side changes everything. He wouldn't really care if Jaren was an impostor if his daughter becomes Jaren's wife. He could control the whole clan and add it to his own if she whelps before the imposter Jaren cracks. He'd do anything to get total control of our clan and then *we'd* be in danger from him! We have to do something, and soon."

Gred took a large sip of his whiskey. "We'll have to break them up. Or kill one or both of them. With the kidnappers still out there, we can blame anything bad on them. Keep ourselves in the clear."

"That sounds like it might be our best choice. Leave the Kendef out of it completely. The kidnappers will still be blamed and it will keep the Kendef and his people out of our hair once Jaren is dead."

"I'll find out Wednesday night what shape the impostor is in, Dad. If he's unstable enough, we could use him to panic and crack now. That would stop any wedding plans."

Dad took a deep breath. "That might work as well. I don't want to do anything in haste just now. We need to calm down and think this through. Come up with a couple of different scenarios based on probabilities. I'm glad you started to get the updates by phone. Makes it easier to get the information and you don't have to worry about Caldon hovering over every conversation you have with him. We can't let anyone know that we know anything about this, not until we're told officially," Adnil continued. "That will likely be tomorrow morning at the office. Be surprised and happy if Jaren says anything to you."

Gred nodded. He wished he had some extra cash. He needed to hit something and make it scream with pain. A lot.

The party that night would generate several column inches in the gossip pages, Gred thought. He did his best to smile, as he had when Jaren told him early at work that his father had been arranging his marriage. Gred had been goggle eyed, but Jaren hadn't been paying much attention to him. He was still obviously in denial.

"I was shocked that morning when he told me," he said. "I mean, Sanil and I have known each other for a couple of years, but I never thought Father would go to *them* and arrange everything behind my back! I've thought for years that they were enemies. And now..."

"But you're not against marrying her," Gred replied. "Are you? Is there someone else you've been seeing?"

"No. Not really. I go to the parties, but I haven't seen any of the girls as someone I wanted to share my life with. As for Sanil, well, she *is* nice, that's why I kept sneaking those dances with her. She liked the idea of us thumbing our noses at our parents." His voice started to rise. "But I still don't know why Father decided this was a good idea!"

They hadn't arrived together but four dances and chatting through several others had been Noticed. No one, Gred thought, would ask directly. Just in case.

The old man had not been present at the start of the party but had come in late, about ten minutes after the Kendefs, thought Gred. Just enough time to imply random arrival times staged after an earlier meeting. There had been a dance after the parental arrivals, with all three watching with satisfied expressions. The fix was definitely in. They had to come up with a new plan to eliminate Jaren. And his father. Soon.

The Wednesday night call was twenty minutes late. The slave spoke and apologized quietly.

"Your slave could not call earlier, master. The father master wished the primary to accompany him to a meeting concerning AR&D. They just arrived home."

"Tell me about the girl first. Sanil."

"The primary was very surprised, master. He had not known of the negotiations. Neither had the girl from what she told him."

"Did they know each other before?"

"They did, but only as acquaintances. They did like to dance together to cause irritation to their fathers. They had no thought to carry it further as both believed their fathers would object most strenuously."

"There was no serious relationship?"

"No, master. They spoke on the phone after the announcement and were surprised that their parents were considering their marriage. It was a shock to both of them."

"What about the impostor? How's he dealing with this?"

"He is *very* confused, master. Since the Kendef have been enemies of the clan for so long, he is unsure of the father master's plan. He does not know what to think. What should he come to believe?"

"He'll think that he's being sold to the Kendef," Gred said. "In return for Kendef supervision and support. He'll know the father master doesn't trust him to stay strong enough to keep the lineage going on his own. He doesn't trust any of his current allies in the other clans to have the strength to do the same. So, the marriage is arranged."

"Your slave will make it so, master."

Gred took a deep breath. "What's happening with the inmates?"

"The chief science officer has been chosen and is reviewing the projects that are in the production track. She and the new engineering officer will go there within the month, with the new managers. All the senior managers are being fired, retired or reassigned. Ser Darit will send ser Ofelan to introduce the newcomers to the current employees.

All senior scientists must prove their worth and loyalty to keep their jobs or be demoted to lesser positions."

"Who is the science officer?"

"A professor from the university. Ragellin. The primary had thought she might be a good choice since she has a broad range of knowledge and expertise. She will stay for a year, and help them find a replacement. She wishes to return to the university rather than make a career change and will take the year off as a sabbatical."

"I remember her lectures. She does know a lot of different subjects." He wasn't sure how this would change his own plans for playpen. It might be much more profitable than before, which was always good for increased dividend income. "And the production of gummynotes?"

"The production lines are still under construction but more prototyping is being done at Bayside now that they have produced sufficient quantities of the adhesive. All pages are currently hand stacked in preparation for a product reveal in about one month. The marketing people are very busy with name choice and design of the first offerings. The primary is kept apprised of their progress."

Rader Kessem raised an eyebrow. "Explosives? That's a very different way of dealing with your problems than you've considered in the past."

"Yes," Gred almost snarled. "We found out that the old man has been negotiating with clan Kendef. They're going to marry Jaren to the daughter, by the end of summer if the rumours I've heard are true. She'll still be underage but with parental consent it's not a problem. Jaren will be of age in about a month."

"That *would* be a setback for your plan," Kessem said. "So we come to plan B, or is this C?" He waved a hand. "No matter. When do you want the bomb and what needs to blow up?"

"Within two weeks, if possible. It has to fit into this case." He set a briefcase, identical to Jaren's own, on the table. "We want a radio activation, just in case the situation changes. I'll have someone get it into their car. We plan to use it when we're all going to the compound together."

"That's on the small side to ensure complete destruction," Kessem said, looking at the briefcase. "If it gets placed near a full gas tank, it might do to take out several cars. I'll have my expert take a look and do the math. We've sourced a quantity of the new explosives the army's been developing. It might work if we use that. Smaller size for the same effect of boom. That should make up for the smaller case."

"Fine. I'll call tomorrow night to make sure it's in progress."

"This is extra," Kessem said, a warning note in his voice. "Cash only, no adding to the loan."

"Fine." Gred growled as he left the office. He wished he had enough cash in his pockets to go downstairs and let out his tension and anger.

* * *

Doctor Hallent called Darit at the office a week later concerning his question of why Adnil and Gred had no knowledge of Jaren and Sanil's love affair. The controller obviously hadn't told them.

"We really need to think about this," he began. "I've been going over the tapes again. The controller must have extraordinary abilities to keep the both sets of memories straight and change the focus of events depending on who is active. Have you ever noticed Jaren behaving as he did that first night he was back? Or when he first woke at the kidanpping site? Fearful and hesitant?"

"No, I haven't."

"I'll check with Caldon later," Steffent added. "And check the surveillance tapes we've stockpiled. Why and what should we be looking for? If anything. A hint would be helpful rather than telling the guards to look for something *off*. They don't know Jaren that well so might not catch something minor. And Caldon and Semant do need to sleep sometimes."

"It occurred to me that the impostor must be activated on a regular basis to process the information that he's being given. If they wait until the formal activation point, he'd have too much suddenly appearing in his mind to be able to cope with whatever event they're planning without time to process the events. Jaren's reaction to the news of your negotiations over seris Sanil is a good example of how he would behave but at a tiny percentage of the confusion of several months or years of data that he had to suddenly integrate."

"And that means?" Darit asked.

"To activate the impostor for the update processing, the controller has to be able to swap the personalities on and off without outside instructions. A rigid schedule could ruin everything by having the wrong one active at the wrong time. There hasn't been any indication Gred has ordered anything during the phone calls, but there's an outside chance he's given the orders while they're at the office. Alone in the elevator or in a washroom would give enough privacy, but I don't think that is how it's being done. The controller has to decide when and who should be active by himself. No controlling construct I've ever heard of can do that. This is an incredible advance in programming. Researchers are going to want to experiment with the technique. Since we have the tapes, it may be possible to replicate the conditioning."

"It's also in my son's head," Darit barked. "And I want it out."

"I know, I know, ser. This is very good news. It means that the controller is our ally, not another enemy we need to worry about. He's been protecting Sanil from the start. And Jaren. I wonder what else is he capable of doing? Does he know that we know? How can he help us and how can we help him?"

"How can we tell it... him... whatever... what we're planning or rather, what Adnil and Gred are planning?" Steffent asked. "And without the real Jaren finding out, or activating that suicide imperative?"

"I'm not sure. The controller now phones Gred once a week and you have it all on tape, plus all the other conversations you've recorded. The controller is the *only* one of the three personalities that Gred can talk to about the plan. If anyone but Gred asks the impostor directly, it could trigger his suicide. Same with the real Jaren." Silence. "*We* could call the controller and tell him what he should know about Gred's final solution once you figure it out." More silence.

"Pretend that *we're* Gred?" Darit sat back in his chair, thinking this was getting more complex by the day. The decision to terminate a threat like this was much simpler when the enemy wasn't family.

"We could use your tapes of Gred's voice to construct a new message. It'll be tough to word so that the controller doesn't panic on the suicide front, but lets him know what we think Gred's plan is. With that knowledge, we hope that *he* can change other parts of the programming. Or transfer the information to one or both of the other personalities."

"Like deleting the damned suicide imperative," Banak rubbed at his jaw. "Or modifying it so that Jaren will survive with his mind intact. Get me some wording and I'll get the tape ready, doctor."

Two days later they knew the next variation in the plan. A bomb, likely destined for their car. Steffent didn't stop swearing for ten minutes. Darit stared at his hands. Why were they so intent of destroying him and Jaren? And what else had they planned? Those had been failures. Or had they?

Chapter 32

Jaren answered the phone without thinking or lifting his eyes from the report. "Hello?"

The slave blinked. The master had never done this before, activating him during a work day and by the phone. "Master?" he asked tentatively, putting the pages down. His gaze automatically lowered in response to the master's voice.

"We're changing the plan. There will be a bomb in the old man's car soon. I'll let you know when to activate the impostor. Do you understand me, slave?"

"Yes, master, your slave understands."

Jaren looked at the phone, hearing only the dial tone. "That was weird. Must have realized they'd dialled the wrong extension." he said, then went back to the report.

The slave was confused. The master had never mentioned any of his plans before. Given orders, but never spoke of how the slave's part fit into the larger plan. Maybe, the father master had figured out what had happened. But how? He suppressed the suicide imperative. He didn't *know* that they knew. This call *had* been from master Gred. It was his voice. He paused, thinking. What could he do to protect all of them?

The days seemed to fly by. Trying to get the reports on the latest subsidiary done, keeping up with the exercise program Feneir insisted on, seeing Sanil at least two nights of the week and at least one day on the weekend. Jaren didn't have much time for thinking and was often tired in the mornings even though he'd gone to bed early. At least there hadn't been any more nightmares lately.

Feneir had apologized profusely for exposing their secret but Jaren couldn't really blame him for the slip. It was one of the things he and

Sanil had talked about at university: her father's anger and how to deflect it. For Feneir to hear only that he was missing from a vacation house, ser Kendef was a very logical reason why.

"Ser Darit asked that you be reminded about the clan meeting on the weekend," his secretary said. "The sers Calyno will be staying at the compound and will convoy out with you that night."

"Is it time for another? Seems like we just had one."

"It has been a busy month for you," Talfer replied.

"I guess we'll be talking about the betrothal/birthday plans." Jaren said. "I'm not sure what kind of timing is needed."

"Or the wedding plans." Jaren's eyes went wide and Talfer left with a grin. He'd seen a lot more of those since news of his (still potential, according to ser Paknol) engagement had spread through the building. The clan news/gossip page still held back on a definitive statement, but there were rumours floating through every party they attended together. His true friends were glad for him and the others just wanted details to sell to the news sheets.

"One more day at the office," Jaren muttered as he headed for the bathroom. Despite everything, he was groggy and kept yawning, even in the shower. He turned the water to cold and that helped. For a while. Staying up all night hadn't been fun, but necessary.

"Are you sure you want to go in?" Father asked at the breakfast table. "You don't look well. Did you drink anything odd at the party last night? Something that might have triggered the drug avoidance symptoms?"

"No. Just my usual juice and soda. I feel like I didn't sleep at all last night. Some coffee will set me up until I get to the office. We're still assembling the data on Crogets Confections."

"Very well. Is Sanil coming out for brunch tomorrow?"

"That's the plan. Both parents may be with her, or possibly one of her brothers, she wasn't sure. Using the main dining room might make more sense than our little parlour if there's more than five. I'll call her later today and check on numbers."

Coffee didn't really help his drowsiness until the third cup that morning. When he left the office for lunch, he left his case on the side table. When they returned, it was on the floor by his desk. He shrugged. What would be couldn't be helped.

The afternoon was hectic with searching for copies of reports for his next analysis project, Crogets, a minor confectionery supplier the clan had owned for ten years now. At least it gave him something to do rather than staring at the walls. The files had many missing pieces, ones that did not bode well for his recommendations for replacing the entire management team. Cash flow details were crucial, not a maybe nice to have. He yawned again. "Could you get me some coffee, please."

"You won't be able to sleep tonight if you drink much more, serit," Talfer said. "I don't think we're going to get all the documents by this evening. I've called them twice to get copies sent out but it will be after the weekend at the very least before we see them. The ink might not be dry otherwise. They're going to have a busy few days. It might have been better to descend upon them in person before they have a chance to re-arrange the accounts."

"It won't matter in the long run." Jaren said. "The management isn't going to survive this review, based on what we already have. And I doubt I'll have much of a chance to get any work done this weekend anyway. Sanil's family are coming over for brunch tomorrow and we have the clan meeting tonight. I'll try to get to bed early. I don't think the meeting is going to go very late."

***

Gred carefully lifted the briefcase from the desk. It didn't feel heavier than his own, fully loaded with papers. "Looks good."

Kessem sat at his desk counting the money. He nodded and tucked the cash into the drawer.

"Best place to put it is near the gas tank," Rader Kessem said. "Other-wise the explosion might not get both cars. My guy said he couldn't put more explosive in otherwise the weight would be noticeable if you have the imposter carry it to the car."

"And the detonator?" Gred said.

Kessem took a larger case from under his desk. "It's in here. I'd leave it in your car on the day so that no one gets suspicious of you having two briefcases. It should fit under a seat, or tuck it in the trunk until you're ready to leave the building."

"Why is it so large?" Gred frowned. "It will be harder for us to hide."

"That battery has to be big enough to get the radio signal out and transmitters are bigger than receivers. The antenna is around the out-side walls of the case. As it is, the effective range is only two hundred meters. The moment you transmit the signal, your driver should hit his brakes if you're behind their car. Hard. If you're in front, stomp on the gas. A better method would be to have someone sitting at the point you want to blow up the car and have *him* push the button. A gas explosion can be a lot bigger than you think it could be."

"We've been planning and attempting to eliminate them for years," Gred said shaking his head. "My father wants to push the button himself to make sure nothing goes wrong this time."

Kessem shrugged. "It's your hit. This is how you operate it." He opened the larger case to reveal three thumbnail sized buttons, one green, one black and one red in among a complex of wires and components and a battery taking up half the case. "Green connects the power, black establishes the radio connection to the bomb case receiver and red makes it blow up. Let about a minute go by between pushing green and black. The transmitter needs a little time to warm up. Start setting it up about ten minutes before you want it to go boom. That battery's good for an hour or so."

"What about the bomb case? How big is that battery?"

Kessem took the other briefcase, set it on his desk and opened it. Three greyish bundles of explosives were fixed to the bottom and a smaller battery and receiver filled the rest of the case.

"When your man is ready to put it into the car, he needs to flip this switch." He indicated a toggle to the left of the battery. "That completes the circuit so the receiver starts to listen. That battery lasts about eight hours, so don't put it in the car earlier than noon. There aren't any anti-tampering devices in here since it could get bumped or thumped as you drive. Some roads on your usual route to the compound need a lot of work. You do not want something like this going off unexpectedly." He handed two sets of keys to Gred.

"Good. I'll let you know how it works out."

"I'm sure I'll hear all about it in the papers."

Gred waited impatiently to hear from the slave on their usual night. Finally, they'd be in their rightful places. At the top as they should be, not minor peons buried deep in the holding bureaucracy. When the phone rang, he was startled out of his reverie.

"Master?" the slave's voice was tentative. Now for a few last orders and he'd get some sleep. The next few days would be hectic ones and they couldn't afford any missteps.

"In two days, activate the impostor in the morning. I want to see how he's doing in person at work and this weekend. You can reactivate the primary in time for work next week. Understand?"

"Yes, master, your slave will obey."

"What other news do you have for me?"

"AR&D is now purged of all the top management, master. The father master decided that they had failed to control the inventors and are to blame for the loss of potential income. They will inform you of this on the weekend. Many projects were found that will boost profits."

"Damn." At least the place would generate more income for them in the future. And they would be seen as innocent of the upsets. With all the confusion coming up, no one would blame them for not swapping things back to the older system right away. After a while, they might have to purge anyone that kept objecting. Gred hoped that Kessem would be able to find another conditioner like Hantel within the year. That would ensure all the scientists kept producing.

"Does the primary know if I am being blamed for their failure?"

"No, master. The father master said you had followed your mandate on the engine design and he would have been angry if you had interfered with the management."

"Good. Same time next week." There wouldn't be a next week for his cousin, but it was what he usually said at the end of a call.

"Your slave obeys." there was a click, then the dial tone resumed.

Early that last morning Gred took the cases from their places in the hidden passageway and placed them on the coffee table in his suite. Bergrant and Lasteren, his father's lead guard, looked at them with interest.

"The bigger one is the transmitter," Gred said. "The smaller one is the bomb. These are the keys to the cases. Bergrant, you'll have to get the bomb into the trunk of their main car sometime after lunch so the battery doesn't run down. If you can't, let me know before we leave the building. We might be able to have Jaren take it with him if you can't get access. That's why I chose the same model as he has."

"Should be an easy job, sers. I'll go into the parking area looking for a missing document from your car and we usually park next to theirs. The cars are usually unlocked and I can open the trunk from the driver's seat. How do I activate it?" Gred unlocked the case to show him the switch.

All day he found it hard to focus on the work on his desk. Knowing that the weeks to come would find him in Darit's office, helping his father cope with the myriad of details involved in transferring control of the clan holdings to them. Bergrant came into his office slightly after lunch with a smile. Gred had eaten with Jaren under the guise of checking on how the impostor was integrated. If he hadn't known this was the imposter, he would not have guessed from his demeanour. Calm and self-assured. Just like the original these days. He even talked about the upcoming betrothal without showing any obvious signs of panic.

"That package you wanted to be delivered is on its way, ser," Bergrant said with a smile.

"Excellent. Soon the waiting will finally be over."

Jaren was late coming down and Gred smiled at his father. As a bonus, it looked like Chief Steffent was also in their vehicle. One of their men, probably Lasteren, would have that title soon and be able to deflect any internal or external investigations. There would have to be a reorganization of the guards, in any case. Such was the price of their failure to protect their charges.

"Soon," he said to his father with a smile. The drive out to the compound seemed longer than usual. When they left the occasionally slow traffic of the city, Adnil took the large case from Bergrant and set it on his lap. Gred handed him the keys to unlock it.

The place they'd picked had good cover on either side of the roadway and more importantly, few other vehicles at this hour. Killing the innocent had never been part of their plans, but a few workers wouldn't be missed much if necessary.

Adnil opened the case and pushed the green button, then the black a few minutes later. A faint hum came from the transmitter. A lone transport passed them heading toward the city. No one else was in sight. The two men smiled at each other and Adnil got ready to push the red button. Their driver was ready to brake on his order to avoid the fireball that would remove all of their problems. Gred and his father exchanged smiles. They were so ready for this.

"Five, four, three, two, one. Now!"

Chapter 33

Jaren picked up his case when Caldon appeared and they headed down to the garage. His father was already there, just getting into their car. Gred and Adnil were already waiting in theirs.

"Sorry I held up the parade," he said to his father as he handed the case to Feneir to hold up front. "We were trying to get all the documents for the confectionery today. I know they're in trouble and are trying to hide it. The cash flow statements weren't in with the first batch of files."

"Oh?" Father asked. The ensuing discussion actually helped keep him awake. It felt good to be just chatting about work.

Soon they were out of the city, going between acres of newly plowed fields. An explosion ripped the air behind them and dust blew past them. Things hit the car with clunks and dings. Jaren was pushed back in his seat as the driver accelerated.

"Which car?" he asked, then looked over at his father shaking his head sadly, unsurprised. How? He looked back but only saw a chase car behind them. Dust still obscured the wreckage further back.

"The Calyno," Feneir said from up front. He'd turned to face them almost as soon as the explosion had happened. "Totally destroyed. The middle chase is right behind us. The back chase will contain the scene until the police arrive."

"Why aren't..." Jaren the imposter took a deep breath.

The slave was in shock as well. They couldn't stop in case there was someone else waiting. Maybe with a sniper rifle or another bomb. Had the kidnappers detonated their bomb before the masters had been able to detonate theirs? Had Feneir moved the bomb in Jaren's briefcase to the other car? He couldn't warn Feneir that he might have a bomb next to his feet if he wasn't sure. That would reveal what he had to keep hidden. He would have take control of the body and open the case once they were alone to see what was actually in there. Without anyone else to control him, maybe he could make everything all right now.

The imposter spoke again. "Do you think it was the kidnappers?"

"Likely," the father master said, swaying as the car took a corner at much faster speed than the posted limit.

The imposter looked behind them a last time, seeing the column of smoke rising high. What would happen to them now?

* * *

Feneir saw Bergrant casually reach into the Alanyo main car and release the trunk latch. A briefcase, looking identical to Jaren's, went into the trunk and the lid closed. Moments later, Bergrant was at the Calyno main car, taking a large envelope out of a door pocket, then he left the parking area. He heard the elevator ding its arrival a minute later.

Semant and Chief Steffent came out of the shadows as soon as the elevator door closed. "I can't believe they'd really go through with it," Steffent said. "Damn."

"Let's get the damned thing out of the trunk before anyone comes down." Pagil said. "Is the bomb guy here yet?"

"He's waiting in my office," Steffent said. "He said there was a very good chance there aren't any motion sensors or anti-tampering devices in it since it's not attached to anything solid."

Pagil went to the car and popped the trunk. He picked the case up carefully, then shut the trunk. He gradually rotated the case until it was vertical. Then he took a deep breath and joined them at the elevator. No one paid much attention to them on the way to the security office.

The bomb expert was impressed by the device. First, he examined the case, then pulled a small set of tools and opened it as fast as a key would have. "Good attachment of the components to the base of the case," he said. "Elegant and simple design. Only one switch to activate so it's less likely to fail. No anti-tampering devices, as I suspected. Leaving it loose in the trunk of a car isn't the most stable platform for this kind of thing. A good, professional build." He flipped the switch, then detached a wire on one side of it and bent it well away from the switch. "It's disarmed now. Can't go boom any more."

"What about the explosives?" Feneir asked. "That stuff doesn't look like any regular dynamite I've seen."

The expert nodded. "This looks like the new tri-nitro plastics the army's been developing. They *will* be interested to know how it migrated into civilian hands. I can take some for testing if you like. We have a secure contact. The exact formula will give them a better idea where it came from and when. If someone is liberating their stocks, they'll thank us for the information." At Steffent's nod, he took out a knife and cut a chunk of it from one of the masses of the clay-looking stuff.

"This will be enough for them. The explosion will be a little smaller, but not enough to be a problem if it is near the gas tank as I understand they'd planned on." Feneir looked at the chief. So much for secrecy. The firm had a very good reputation and it shouldn't be a problem.

"It *will* go boom if you put that wire back, flip the switch and someone sends the authorization code," he said. Steffent nodded. "I'd put it in the trunk as they did for the best effect if you want to destroy a different vehicle. If there's nothing else?" He looked around quickly. No one responded. Admitting they intended to blow someone up was a stupid thing to do. "Then I'm off. My office will send the bill in the next few days. Have a nice weekend."

"Thank you," Feneir said.

Once the bomb expert left the office, Semant turned to them. "*Now* what do we do with it?"

"We ask ser Darit how he wants to handle this."

"Well," ser Darit said after they reported on the bomb. "We could just let them blow it up."

"And themselves." Feneir shrugged. "It is tidy."

"And justice." Steffent added. "We can blame it on the last of those who attacked the clan picnic, but there was only one left and he managed to access the Calyno car somehow. Maybe at one of those not nice parties or establishments that Gred frequents when he goes slumming. He was in a risky area two nights back according to the team I have watching them. The bomber figured that it would take out at least two cars, not just the one. There is no visible breach of our security and our problems are gone."

Ser Darit sat back in his chair, looking old and tired.

"We can't trust that they won't come up with something else, ser," Steffent said quietly. "Likewise keeping them around, even conditioned. People would ask questions about the changes in them and keeping them sequestered would also raise interest. Those would bring up information we don't want to release. The bigger clans might think to force a real investigation. We'd all be in trouble then. Serit Jaren should be clear, but I don't know what the imposter and controller might do. Assuming they and he survives tonight's revelations."

"True," ser Darit replied. "Put the bomb in their car. They'll get one last chance to change their minds about doing this. I will call Paknol in a few minutes to warn them. At least we have them as outside witnesses as

to what's been going on with our family." And they would also be implic-
ated in any real investigation. Including Sanil.

Feneir allowed Semant to arm and slide the bomb into the Calyno
vehicle. He watched from the elevator anteroom, in case someone decided to go home early or Bergrant came back down to check on his
handiwork.

Steffent called his contact at the morgue. After a short personal update, he brought up the real reason for the call. "We need a body. Male,
anywhere from fifty to sixty or so, heritage isn't an issue, had a tough
life." Feneir listened in on a second phone.

"No one to miss him?" the orderly asked.

"Of course. Do you have anyone suitable?" A pause. The sounds of
pages turning.

"Might. Do you mind if he was lightly toasted in a fire already?"

"Better from our side. Where's he from?"

"A fire in an apartment house two, three nights ago. Worker, mid
fifties, we think. No family listed and no one had a good word to say
about him from the paperwork. Died of smoke inhalation and he was
very drunk at the time of the fire. Cremation's scheduled for tonight,
along with three others. I'm on duty, so that won't be a problem."

"I'll send transport in two hours. Get him into used work clothes if he
isn't already. Any documentation on his past so we can work it into the
scenario we'll announce later. You know the drill."

"I'll have it all set. Usual fee?"

"Of course. The pick up team will have it with them." Feneir set his
phone back on the hook carefully. Steffent finished getting the details
for the pickup as well as the corpse's name. In the outer office, Semant
had a tech showing him a suitcase. It had two flashlight batteries the size
of his fist and a radio unit in it.

"What's that?" he asked.

"A fake transmitter," the tech said. "It does work, but not on the same
frequency as the actual bomb. There won't be enough of that one left for
anyone to tell what it was set to. Window dressing and it'll look good in
the aftermath of the explosion. There won't be much if anything left of
the receiver, of course."

"You good for setting up the hide?" Feneir asked Semant.

"Sure thing. We have a can of gas and a grenade we can toss into the
wreck if we need to place things after the actual explosion. Did the Chief
find a body yet?"

"He did. Pickup in a few hours or so. That good timing for you?"

"Should be. We'll set it up in the most likely place and the body
should be close enough to be caught in the blevy. If not, we'll move it

after the blast and torch everything."

"Amateurs miscalculate the extent of a blevy all the time," the technician said with a grin. "Generally with fatal results."

Feneir went back into Steffent's office. "I want to keep them well away from the Alanyo main car," he said. "How about using the Calyno chase car as the middle one today? Our chase one, then Alanyo, the Calyno chase, Calyno and our back chase."

Steffent thought about it, then nodded. "Sounds like a good plan, Feneir. And reasonable. Our back chase can help contain the scene and with any changes to the staging if needed. We can hold the Calyno chase guards and isolate them once we get to the compound. Keep them there until we can figure out if they're involved in any of this."

"If they were, oh well," Feneir said. "The mines always need a few more workers. We'll have to go through all of their guards and servants, you know. Hantel might have done other work for them besides what he did to Jaren. We found one of his offices but all those leads were legitimate, documented work with two associates. He must have had another office with all of his illegal files. Could be at one of Kessem's holdings but we can't search those without tipping them off. That's not possible yet."

Steffent sighed. "Yeah. And then we'll have to trace any Calyno connections through the subsidiaries. All the time posing that we're trying to find anyone with a grudge against them if it wasn't the last of the bombers. It's going to be a busy couple of weeks for all of us."

"But I'll sleep a lot better at night knowing the real threats to Jaren and his father are gone."

Steffent got in with the sers while he took his usual seat behind the driver. Jaren was full of the possible problems in the latest subsidiary he was looking at. Their conversation did make the ride feel less tense, but only ser Darit was really paying attention.

The open fields made an excellent place for the bomb to go off and it seemed that Adnil and Gred agreed with that assessment. The bomb went off almost exactly where Feneir had thought it would and where Semant had set up their bomber during the afternoon.

Jaren hadn't panicked. He was shocked, yes, but that was expected. The imposter had changed from that first time they'd met, just after the kidnapping. He was more like the original Jaren. What had the controller managed to do and how had he done it? They were all silent after the driver had reported the attack to the compound and that the sers Alanyo were safe and inbound.

One last hurdle, Feneir thought as they passed through the gate and pulled up to the front of the house.

"My office for now," ser Darit said to Jaren. "We need to talk."

* * *

Feneir and Steffent followed the sers into the office and took positions around the seating area. Steffent sat next to ser Darit.

"Sit," ser Darit waved Jaren into one of the chairs near his desk.

"What do we need to discuss, Father?" Jaren asked. "What story the police will be told?" The father master nodded.

"Do we go public with my kidnapping and who you think is responsible? That might be the best."

"It was the kidnappers, with a few changes. There was never a kidnapping, of course. No need to get that complex and reveal to the public that we withheld that amount of information. One man set a bomb in sers Adnil and Gred's car and blew it up." Steffent said.

"Wait, it just happened and you've already decided who did it?"

"We knew it would happen, Jaren," ser Darit said. "There is a lot we need to cover, and it won't all be this evening." He sat up straighter. "We know about the conditioning, all of it. The impostor and the controller. You were never addicted to poppers. It just made a great excuse for them to create the alternate personalities. Gred and Adnil were behind the whole thing, seeking to change you. We still aren't sure what their original plan was. We've been trying to force their timetable for some time now. Their latest plan was our deaths in a car bombing. The actual bomb was already in their car, not in the briefcase you brought down with you. Your secretary put your papers for the weekend in it while you were out of the office for lunch."

"What?" Jaren said, his eyes going wide. "The... Who?"

"The impostor. I'm assuming that you're him." ser Darit raised his chin. "Based on the orders Gred gave the controller earlier this week. We've known all along. The Jaren who is really my son is somewhere in your brain, inactive. You were constructed by Falg Hantel, or Sumon as you might have known him during your holiday late last fall."

"You can't know what happened," Jaren said, shaking his head. He was in shock, hurting, confused but somehow focused at the same time. Feneir saw him set himself on the edge of the chair. "Now I have to..." Jaren leaped from the chair, but not toward Feneir and his gun as he was sure Jaren would have done.

He dashed to the desk, grabbed up the letter opener that sat on the blotter and raised it to his neck.

"I'm sorry, Father," the impostor said and closed his eyes as the letter opener pushed into the side of his throat.

Chapter 34

Jaren hurt. All over, but especially his back. It was a familiar pain, but that made no sense to him. He couldn't remember ever getting hurt like this.

"I think he's coming round," an unfamiliar voice said. Hands on his head opened an eye and Jaren jerked his head away, pressing it into a chair back. The face in front of him smiled and nodded. "Does your back hurt?"

"Yes," Jaren managed. "Who?" Even breathing hurt.

"I'm Doctor Hallent," the man said. "You've been under my care for some time now, even if you didn't know about it." He turned and Jaren looked in that direction. Mathin stood beside the door, visibly armed with a pistol in a shoulder harness and no jacket to conceal it. A neuronal whip was on his hip.

Jaren turned his head further, recognizing the room. His office at home. He tried to rise but the pain spiked and he had to shut his eyes and clench his teeth against it.

"Let ser Darit know he's awake," the doctor said to Mathin. "I'll finish the cognitive assessment." Mathin nodded and left.

"I'll bring you some painkillers and an anti-inflammatory very soon," the doctor continued in a soothing tone. "What is your last memory?"

"I remember going to bed so it's sometime after that." He looked toward the window. "By the amount of light, it had to be early evening. So maybe the next night?"

Jaren tried to raise his right hand to brush his hair out of his eyes but couldn't move his arm. He looked down, discovering he was sitting in his office chair, his wrists tied to the arms by cloth bandages from a med kit and his chest and upper arms wrapped in a wide tensor that went around the chair back. He tried moving his legs and couldn't move them either.

Probably more cloth bandages but he couldn't see that far down his legs.

His jacket had been removed but from the style of his shirt and trousers, he'd been at the office before this. Spots of what looked like dried blood dripped down the right side of the shirt front.

"Why am I tied up?" he asked. "And who are you?" He didn't remember ever seeing this man before.

"It's just a precaution. I hope," the doctor said. He pulled a chair from the seating area and moved it within a meter of Jaren's chair. Within comfortable speaking distance but too far for Jaren to reach even if his arms weren't tied to the chair arms. "I'm a doctor, as I said earlier. We haven't met, at least officially. I've been taking care of you since your kidnapping. Do you remember getting up this morning?"

"No. What difference does that make?"

"Excellent." The doctor uttered a series of nonsense words. Jaren stared at him, now even more confused. Who needed to be tied up, him or this doctor? A repetition of the same nonsense words, then another set of words, after looking up something in a notebook. He sighed. "A pity. I wish we'd been able to preserve them for study, but it seems the controller did manage to shut both of them down. Such a waste."

"Who? What are you talking about? You're the crazy one here, not me." Jaren twisted one hand. No way to untie it, especially with someone right here.

"Your father insists on explaining everything to you himself, but he's busy right now with the police investigators, giving them a statement. We weren't sure when you would wake up. It's been three hours, by the way. I arrived just before everything happened. Your father thought I would be needed and he was right."

"The police are here?" Jaren couldn't imagine his father taking time no matter what had happened *talking* to the police. Giving them orders, yes, but giving them information? "Is Sanil all right?"

"Perfectly fine. She's safe at home with her parents. All of her family are uninjured. We'll be phoning them shortly to let them know that you're also all right. Brunch tomorrow is still on, by the way. Or it might be moved to the day after, depending on how you feel."

"What happened? Was there some kind of accident?"

The doctor paused, obviously debating what to say. "Not as such. It was deliberate."

"If Father's all right, what about Adnil and Gred?"

"That's what ser Darit wants to talk to you about."

"They're dead, aren't they?"

"Well, yes. But... I'll get you the painkillers." The doctor rose and left, leaving him alone in the room, tied into his own chair.

How to get loose? Leaning forward was hard to do as the pain in his back increased the further he tried to bend down. Between them, the pain and the tensor conspired to keep him from getting his teeth anywhere near the bandages tying his wrists. He finally remembered where he'd felt pain like this before. It had been in his arm after the kidnapping. A neuronal whip had been responsible that time. There was something else that he couldn't quite recall, but it had been a similar pain.

The door opened and the doctor, his father and Feneir entered.

"Father," Jaren said. "Sorry, but I can't stand thanks to the doctor's restraints."

"Take the pills, Jaren. Please. It will be easier to concentrate without the pain distracting you."

"Who hit me with the whip?"

Feneir took a deep breath. "It was Chief Steffent. Level one. He was trying to stop you."

"From doing what?"

"Sticking my letter opener into your neck." Father said testily. "His whip hit you just as the point went in. You were supposed to go for Caldon's gun, which wouldn't fire. We didn't think there were other weapons available to him." Father glared at Feneir for some reason.

Jaren swallowed, realizing there was a bandage on his neck. And the blood on his shirt must be his. He'd tried to kill himself? *Why?*

"Why don't we all sit down," Doctor Hallent said with forced cheer. He had a glass of water in one hand and a small paper cup in the other.

"Untie him," Father said as Feneir pulled a chair over for him.

"Well," the doctor started, obviously still reluctant to let him loose. "I'm fairly sure he's fine, but I would like to wait a little longer. Just to be sure. Besides, the tensor is about the only thing holding him up in the chair, based on the whip level the guard used."

"His right arm, then." Father scowled at the doctor. Feneir came forward and untied the bandage and folded it before handing it to the doctor. Jaren reached up and felt the bandage on his neck. Whatever pain that wound was giving him was lost in the greater pain from his back.

"So." Jaren said, looking at his father after taking the now familiar pills. "What happened?"

"It started when you went on that holiday with Gred after your trip to AR&D." Father began.

He didn't believe them at first, but eventually had to. There were too many questions he remembered that they had the explanations for.

"So Sanil was in on it from the beginning," he said into the silence at the end of his father's recital. "All of you have lied to me. Constantly.

Since late fall. Nearly five months now."

"Yes. To protect you until we could understand what was going on."

"And the kidnappers? They weren't the bomber's children, were they?" He looked at Feneir, who was intently studying the carpet. That told him all he needed to know about that episode.

"Yes, it was our people," his father said, also looking at Feneir. "Semant and Casteron were there, as well as several Kendef guards who were the ones you did see at the ranch. As I said, Sanil was the one who started our investigation when you didn't meet her at university after your week's holiday with Gred. A feisty girl you have your heart set on."

Father had gotten more relaxed the further into the explanations they went. That was one of the things that made him believe their outrageous story. "I hope you're prepared to deal with her for a long time."

Jaren took a deep breath. The painkillers had kicked in sometime in the discussion enough that he felt human again. "Untie me," he said. "Now." He almost said please, but clamped his jaw shut. They didn't deserve any politeness. Not now.

"Of course." Father nodded at Feneir, who came over and undid his feet first, then his other hand and finally the chest tensor.

He stretched a little, knowing that any movement now would help lessen the pain in the future. A dull ache responded. "I need to think about everything you've just told me," he said. "And not here."

"Where? I would like you to stay nearby and safe."

"The beach house."

"Caldon, arrange it."

Jaren shook his head. "Mathin in charge and no men who knew anything about this to be with me."

"Reasonable." Father nodded agreement. "Prudent, even."

"Tonight. No brunch tomorrow. Maybe not the day after."

His father nodded again. Feneir looked hurt and ashamed at his exclusion. Jaren didn't care right now. He'd try to forgive Feneir later, but couldn't right now. He needed to think and understand what had been done to him.

"While they're setting up your travel, there are a few other things you need to be apprised of." Feneir left, shutting the door quietly.

Mathin was confused at first by the travel orders and his sudden promotion but within the hour they were on the road, reaching the beach house two hours later. Jaren lay down on the back seat and tried to concentrate on slow stretches and deep breaths. The guards had to wake him when they arrived. Father said he'd been tired all day but they didn't know why.

The imposter hadn't given them any clues for what he might have been doing at night. Nothing had been picked up on the monitors and no one knew he'd been awake. All they knew what that Gred had ordered the controller to activate him this morning. But the controller was able to do something that left him, the original, alive, when the others didn't exist any more. But *was* he the original? There was so much he didn't understand about any of this.

The house staff were happy to see him and he was soon ensconced in his usual room and the cook promised to have a light meal sent up within a few minutes. Jaren sat in the window seat, looking out at the dark sea, smelling the low tide aromas. Trying to make sense of what he'd been told.

Before and After. That's how he had to think of things now. What else had that programmer changed in him? The poppers were false, Feneir and the doctor had convinced him that was the truth. But that conditioning meant he never had to worry about becoming addicted to any of the drugs on the list. A small advantage.

What else was true? Sanil. They had been here before the changes, and Gred and Adnil had never known the truth of their love. The controller had hidden the knowledge of their attachment from the beginning. No one knew why or how the controller had diverted so completely from what Gred and Adnil had planned. They never knew their plans had been hijacked and their every word monitored. And their investment ruined. He smiled wryly. There was so much new information to get used to.

A knock on the door heralded a supper tray. And more pills. Eventually he moved over to the bed and slept again.

The next morning after pills, gentle stretches and a hot bath, he went up to the lookout high on the roof, pulled cushions out of the storage locker and settled into a lounger. He always liked it up here. You could see ships heading in to the harbour at Port Harron and the wind and the gulls didn't care who you were or what you thought.

He and Sanil had spent several bliss-filled hours up here on their weekend. It was only a sudden rain squall that had sent them to their lonely beds the second night. At least until the guards had stopped checking their hallway every three minutes. He had gone to her room again. To lay beside her, skin to skin. To touch each other, exploring the mystery of another person's body. Release for each of them, but no chance they could start a child. Being with each other *with* parental approval had seemed so far in the future that weekend, if not impossible.

Watching a storm from up here was always a reminder of true power and the indifference of the great for the lives of others. He'd always thought of himself as one of the little ones. Those at the mercy of others forever. His father, then Adnil and Gred had all been like a storm, tossing him around for their own purposes. Letting him fall or rise with no thought for his own desires. Maybe it was time for him to join the winds, controlling his own life. That raised another question he didn't have an answer for. Yet. What did *he* want his future to look like? Maybe now he could tell Doctor Margrail the truth about him and Sanil. She'd helped him before. And now he really needed someone outside of all this to help him make sense of it.

The suicide attempt still bothered him. Why had Feneir assumed that he would try for the pistol? He knew he never had a chance to take any of the guards' weapons from them. Countless workouts had proved that. Or was that something else the programmer had changed? Maybe he should start a list. Time passed as he watched the clouds and sea birds and tried to imagine what his life would be. What it could be.

A sound on the stair caught his attention. The trapdoor rose and Sanil came up, clutching something in her hand.

"I know you said you wanted to be alone, but you'll be alone with me the rest of your life, so you should start getting used to it," she said in a rush. "I know I helped deceive you, but we were all so worried about that suicide thing they'd built into the other personalities. We..."

He stood, carefully. Almost time for more pills. "I suppose I'll have to get used to it. I'm still not sure what's real and what they put into my mind, but I don't want to be without you," he said. That felt right on so many levels. No matter what else, he wanted her in his new life. "Come here." She hugged him gently then raised her face to him. She'd been crying, he realized. For him, and maybe for the others.

"We found something in the mail room," she said later. They were cuddled together on all the cushions from the locker in a corner of the lookout. "It was in Caldon's mail slot in the barracks yesterday morning, but he never checked for anything before leaving for the office because he was too busy making sure you and your father would be safe." She held up a small journal. "One of the other guards brought it to him late last night. Do you remember this?"

"Sort of. I used it briefly for Doctor Margrail's journal writing exercises, but I ripped those pages out and burned them a short time later. Writing down the things I feared. They were nothing like what Father told me was the truth."

"Where did you get it?"

"From someone for a birthday a couple of years ago. It was in a drawer in my suite. I think. What's in it now?" She held it out to him.

"The impostor wrote it for you," she said. "It tells you everything,

Jaren, from *their* point of view. He had to rush on Friday to finish it, that's why you, he, whoever was so tired yesterday and for the past week or so. We think he snuck it downstairs to the butler's pantry so it would go into the internal mail." She handed it to him, open to a page about halfway through the book. The handwriting spooked him. It was his but he knew he hadn't written this.

'I know that today, probably this evening, I'm going to die. Don't worry, I've had some time to get used to the idea and I can't think of any other way for everything to come out the way it should. I know that you'll blame yourself when you read this, but there was no other option that would give you the life you deserve. There was never another good way. There never was. We're sorry we couldn't do better.

Thank you for sharing your life with me, even though you didn't know it. I'm sure that our brother also wanted to say goodbye but he was hurt too much by your cousin to ever come forward this way, though he's the only reason that I was able to write this explanation for you. I hope this helps you understand and forgive us.'

There was no signature on the document.

He flipped to the beginning. Sanil cuddled close to him and they started to read it together.

* * *

Sanil looked at the small office, now containing two desks. One looked like it had always been here but the other was more of a small conference table. At least the chair looked comfortable. Jaren stood as she came in and that reassured her. Julin was settled in the outer office for now. He'd get a tour after lunch, he'd said.

"Sorry about the cramped quarters, love. Father says Adnil's office is nearly clear. We'll be moving into it next week. It'll be nice to have enough room for two real desks."

"You didn't say what I'd be doing. Or what you're doing." Both desks had piles of file folders.

"I'm still dealing with my last analysis project. The confectionery. A nightmare of incompetence and evasion. We're sacking the entire management team. I might have to go stomp on them in a week or so."

"That sounds trying. And on the other desk?" *Hers.*

"Files from Gred's desk. Most of it will be irrelevant, but there's a chance there's something linking him to Rader Kessem or Hantel. Once you're sure they're clear, they'll go to another analyst for regular over-sight. A boring job but one that needs someone who already knows about that connection."

"All right. Boring but finite. Is that your last analysis?"

"It is. But Father said he wants to send us on a tour of the subsidiaries together. Including the playpen, which is now mostly functioning again after that management team got sacked. "It will be about two months, two weeks at a time."

"That sounds easier. A couple of stops per trip and we'll have a chance of remembering who we met."

A tap on the door heralded Mathin. "Ser [dayil] is here, seran. Coffee and such is in the small conference room down the hall." Sanil realised that they had no room for extra chairs in here. Or even a coffee table.

"Excellent." Jaren turned to her. "I asked Father about poaching people from other clans that we need. He said to go ahead on this one."

"Dayil still doesn't have a job? He's so good with programming."

"And if he agrees, he'll be doing that for us. And possibly for the cal-culator project." He pulled one out of a drawer. "Father lent me his. Want to come help recruit him before you start on those files?"

She smiled. This was the future she wanted. They wanted. "Of course. It should be pretty simple."

Chapter 35

Darit looked at the lawyer standing in front of his desk, the last appointment of an already long day. "You are audacious," he said. "Bringing this up, especially since your employer provided the bomb that killed them two weeks ago."

"That was not my employer," the lawyer said. His '*my client is innocent*' face was quite good. "It was that nasty worker fanatic, it said so in all the papers and that's also what the police think. Do you wish to inform them they are wrong, or perhaps slightly mistaken?"

"Hmph. As it happens, I have a counter offer for you." The lawyer's eyebrows rose.

"I await your suggestion, ser."

"Ten percent of KRT Electronics. I have the assignment papers here." He slid the top pages out of the folder on his desk.

"It does seem to be in order," the lawyer responded after a quick scrutiny. "But a company that is one hair away from complete dissolution is scarcely equal to the remaining balance of the loan your cousins took from my principal."

"I thought I would make the offer," Darit said, leaning back in his chair. "Or you may have a cheque for the entire amount in your statement. Your choice." he pulled the cheque out and set it on the top of the file, facing the lawyer.

"The cheque, please." The lawyer smiled. "Not a flight of fancy."

"They may yet pull a miracle out of the ruin," Darit responded. "It sometimes happens."

"But not likely, from what we heard of their recent demonstration. Five plus seven should never equal seventeen. The cheque. Please."

Darit handed it over the table. The lawyer looked at it, then signed a paper from his briefcase and laid it on the desk.

"Our business is concluded. Thank you for your time and attention, ser Alanyo."

The lawyer left and Ofelan came in, shutting the door behind him.

"Did he take the cheque?"

Darit smiled. "Yes. Kessem will be quite upset at losing a fortune in addition to his other woes. In a month or so, we'll announce the calculator as a joint product with the Kendefs. Once that final board meeting is over, that is. Our people are truly up to four digits now. Be sure to have all the investors invited, especially the ones who sold all their shares to Kendef and me. I want to rub it in."

"So who gets the Calyno shares? I imagine neither of them left a will. And their twenty percent is needed by you and ser Kendef to maintain control of the company. That needs to be settled before you take control of the company. Stock proxies being what they are."

"Adnil had one leaving everything to Gred. Now, as their closest living relative, it will all come to me. The lawyers are already preparing the paperwork. Those shares will be split between Jaren and Sanil and the clan before the share price skyrockets. The ones bought with Ser Kendef are already clan property."

"Do they know about their good fortune yet?" Ofelan smiled.

"I'm planning to call it a wedding present. It's quite appropriate, I think. Seeing what they both went through over the past year."

"What about the presents you have for Kessem?"

"Caldon and a few others are delivering them tonight, now we have the proof the loan was paid off."

* * *

Feneir shifted position slightly on the factory roof. It wasn't comfortable up here with all the ventilation fans going full tilt and the acrid fumes from the factory below, but it had the best vantage point for the message he was going to deliver. It was a simple message, but those were sometimes the best.

Mathin was spotting for him and had his binoculars fixed on the window Feneir would deliver the message through. He'd just finished a sweep of the entire building, making sure that no one would be watching in their direction. It was so much easier to eliminate an unprepared target. And there was no chance that an innocent would be harmed.

The sniper rifle snugged against his shoulder, Feneir peered through the scope toward Kessem's den of iniquity and in particular at his office window. Their roof was almost one story higher, so he could easily see into the entire office. Kessem was there, playing a game of pool with one of his henchmen. Who was not really an innocent, but would become a good, conditioned worker after the trials. He would finally be of use to society in general. The entertainment workers would be sent to a proper facility after Doctor Hallent and his people undid whatever Falg Hantel had done to them. And the police would search all of Kessem's properties for Hantel's illegal conditioning office.

Feneir waited until he had the perfect shot. As Kessem prepared to sink his last ball, the bullet tore through his spine, halfway down his back. It wouldn't be fatal unless his luck was incredibly bad, but it *would* put him in a wheelchair for the rest of his miserable existence, which would be in prison. One of the many things he'd regret until his mind vanished.

The lights of police cars shone as they rounded the corner. Feneir grimaced. He'd waited almost too long. A tip had been phoned in earlier: there were indentured who were being mistreated within the club area. There were strict laws protecting the indentured, especially those in the entertainment industry. As a final measure, the cheque paying the balance of the Calyno loan would be missing when the lawyer went to deposit it tomorrow. Too bad they had lost it. A replacement? It's not our problem. The money would remain in escrow until the check became invalid: six months.

Do not mess with a clan head or his heir no matter how small that clan is at this point in time. You cannot win.

A simple message.

A good night's work, he thought. Now to get back to the compound and see what trouble Jaren was getting into with Sanil's help. He smiled as peace, at least for now, entered his soul.

About the Author

Lee F. Patrick is a resident of Calgary, AB and lives with her wonderful hubby Gary and cats who help her write, usually by sitting on her arms or the keyboard. She enjoys going to other worlds, since this one has too many rules. She writes thrilling science fiction, fantasy and hybrids that cross several genres, except for romance. The only one of those she tried turned out to be a 'horse and his boy' story. Her alter ego has training and interest in various financial matters, but not mind control or bomb-making. Sigh.

www.ingramcontent.com/pod-product-compliance
Lightning Source LLC
Chambersburg PA
CBHW020116030726
47498CB00006B/2136